A gift to the many k the people of Edson.

Ashes of Destruction
Book 2

Legacy of Betrayal

Susan Grace

Copyright © 2015 Susan Grace
All rights reserved.

ISBN: 1517142415
ISBN 13: 9781517142414
Library of Congress Control Number: 2015907210
CreateSpace Independent Publishing Platform
North Charleston, South Carolina

For Ed Senyk

Forever remembered

Presently the maiden stirred,
And something very strange occurred.
Into the room thru solid door
And silently across the floor
Her lost lover in spirit came,
And very softly called her name.

Joseph F. R. Shearn
(A poet from Edson, Canada)

(Author's note: I had the privilege of knowing Joseph Shearn, and I helped get his poems published in the mid-1980, shortly before his death. Little did I know that decades later, these lines from one of his poems would so closely mirror events in my own life and be so relevant to my novel. I think that would have amused Joseph.)

Ashes of Destruction— Legacy of Betrayal

Legacy of Betrayal, in three parts, is both the prequel and the sequel to *Ashes of Destruction.*

Part One—The Past—unravels the initial interaction between Zack Mackenzie with his family in Alberta in the 1940s, when he returns from Europe after World War II with Cassie, his English wife (leading to the background for the first book in the series, *Ashes of Destruction*). It also follows the lives of Jay, Stacey, Sally, and Ted before their fateful meeting.

Part Two—Moving On—takes up where *Ashes of Destruction* ended and follows Stacey through the next two decades as she tries to rebuild her life, after she flees back to Britain and her own family. In effect she is following in predestined footsteps, and mirroring many of the experiences that Cassie encountered four decades earlier.

Part Three—The Pilgrimage—brings Stacey full circle when Ted's spirit leads her to finally make the pilgrimage back to her heart's home, but this time to visit his grave. Therein she makes her final discoveries regarding the treachery and betrayal by Sally and her mother, and she finds closure.

Prologue

Grief

I believe that each of us carries within us a reservoir of grief that accumulates through life. This internal depositary is where we bury our most sorrowful experiences: events that are too painful to think about, to discuss, but which we can never forget. That reservoir maintains its level of grief as more losses, disappointments, and rejections supplement it over the years, staying within its sealed walls inside us.

We may not recognize that we hold so much inside until that moment when one final event pushes that reservoir to its limits and incites a deluge of grief and sorrow. A final trickle of suppressed tears tries to bury itself within its walls, but cannot be contained, and the reservoir spills over, like a dam collapsing, allowing a torrent of feelings and misery to spew forth, releasing all the previous heartaches, sorrows, and pain from their confines.

I experienced such a moment on the day I learned that Ted had died. The walls I had built around my own reservoir of grief finally blew apart, almost destroying every wish to continue living as unchecked sorrow surrounded me.

I had overcome so much, coming back from the depths of despair after losing one final baby plus everything else that I loved and cared for, all in the space of one year. From those shattered depths, I had rebuilt my life from zero, working my way through fear and sadness, until finally I was able to reclaim my daughter. In the course of that struggle, starting over once again, I eventually won respect from the people in the town who I had once thought were so hostile to me, gaining lifelong friends.

At that point, pushed by events, after I had relocated once more, leaving those new, kind friends behind me, yet again starting from scratch that I mistakenly believed all unhappiness was finally behind me.

It was not.

In the end, enduring rejection after rejection, with one disappointment following another, I eventually saw each one of my small personal victories diminished, and ultimately despair and loneliness took their place.

Ted's death, and the appearance of his spirit in my home, brought me the realization that I would not experience happiness, love, or closeness to another human being ever again. My soul mate, the link I never really lost, was gone forever; love was gone forever with no hope for the future, and I was left where I did not want to be.

It was then that the shattering effect of those events returned, still vivid in my memory, and I had to face the stark reality of all that had been wrought on my own soul by a legacy of betrayal that ruined a marriage, destroyed the unborn, caused another early death, and left an eternal battle with depression and loneliness for two survivors.

STACEY:

> *When two souls meet, when they connect, they will meet again no matter how great the distance between them or how long the separation, for that connection once made is never broken. Real love, once given, does not die, cannot be killed; it stays within you forever.*
>
> *For those soul mates unable to stay together throughout their lives, the longing remains, even though they may have to wait for death to reunite them.*
>
> –Anonymous

I read those words once and thought that they could have been written for Ted and me. The truth of that sentiment lay at the heart of our relationship. Despite all the denials, the lies, the drama, and the tragedy, we both knew the real truth. I accepted it openly, and he would never deny it.

Later I realized that his past demons had prevented him from overtly acknowledging how he felt, fearing all the changes it would bring to his life and his stability. So, for nearly a decade, he tormented me, not quite able to let me go or ignore me, watching me without realizing that I had seen him, leaving a lingering hope in my heart and eventually causing untold heartache for us both.

During that lost space in time, I tried to move on. Through sheer bloody-mindedness, I managed to return from the poverty his actions had brought about, but I never escaped the pain until finally I fled. There was no other way to be free of him, especially after his final, reluctant but tacit acknowledgment of the truth of what lay between us. So I walked away and cut all ties, vowing to put him in the past forever, to move on.

Twenty-five years later, his ghost materialized in my home, proving what I had always known deep down: the link that lay between us had stayed inside both our hearts no matter how far apart we were. We were and are soul mates, in life and in death, and that link has connected us even now.

At that time, when we were thrown together by circumstance, Ted was an unhappy husband but a dedicated father to his two daughters, which lay at the heart of his dilemma. His devotion to them lost him a chance to experience the fulfilling relationship he wanted, and unbeknownst to him, it cost him his unborn child.

Out of his depth, this experienced philanderer, scared by the depth of passion he felt, made terrible choices as he fought to handle a situation beyond his control. His decisions affected me in ways he could never imagine, leaving me stranded and alone, in a strange country, all the promised supports dissipating at the first sign of trouble. It condemned me to a solitude and inner loneliness from which I have never been able to escape no matter how hard I tried.

Back then, within that first year, everything I had trusted in, all that my husband had trusted in, was gone. Jay and I had lost it all, our marriage obliterated, our comfortable home and our savings. It had all gone, and our daughter Amy, the innocent victim of circumstances she had no hand in, was facing a life never intended for her. By the end there was no way to retrieve what had been our former happy life. It was lost forever—annihilated by betrayal, lies, and secrecy, all rooted in the shadows of the past.

Any chance of the happy future that we envisaged in this new country we were tempted to settle in vanished for evermore. Jay was lured into this purgatory by his father's kinfolk, who professed their love for him, filling his head with promises of a "New Eden", but they were in effect using him as a pawn to wreak revenge on his mother.

The assurances of assistance, so blithely proffered a year earlier, never came to fruition. Jay had rushed heedlessly into his new future at their behest, which even in the first week after he landed was doomed. Unsuspectingly, he walked into a family situation that had redirected his cousin's promised focus away from him. In her panic and determination to salvage her deteriorating marriage, Jay was cast aside. Sally shared nothing of her dilemma until way too late, and she had cloaked the actions of her husband in secrecy to avoid embarrassment in front of her family.

Jay had no hint from Sally that her circumstances had changed. She never explained that Ted's willingness to help her newly discovered cousin had dissipated, preventing her from providing the supports she and her mother had pledged barely a year earlier. In the end, both of them completely reneged on promises, oblivious to the destruction they caused, accepting no responsibility.

Their actions led him to bolster his failing ego by hurling himself into a bachelor lifestyle, disconnecting himself from our relationship, thus destroying the foundations of our marriage.

There was never an apology, or even an acknowledgment from the Zienkos or Logans of their culpability. Why would there be? Buried in loneliness and fear, I had provided them with the perfect scapegoat, an easy target to weave the strands of their lies around, and to abrogate all responsibility for any of the ensuing mayhem. A legacy of betrayal, that laid upon me the basis for a lifetime of misplaced guilt. They continued on in their insular life, sublimely uncaring about the family they had destroyed, accepting no responsibility for their contribution to the loss of our happiness or for the small child their actions harmed irreparably.

During the ensuing two decades, I had writhed in pain, assigning every bad thing that happened to me to the price I paid for being the perpetrator who had wrought all the havoc. My self-esteem was so low that I had no energy to rebel at the drudgery of the existence that followed. I accepted the message drilled into me for so long in the beginning. Everything was my fault, and mine alone, and it was my punishment to pay and keep on paying. It was not until Ted's ghost walked me through past events that I understood how blind I had been, as Karma finally took a hand to bring justice.

Our biggest mistake was in traveling separately, not remaining together to face this new life. By the time that I followed Jay to Canada months later, our house had been sold, putting money in our pockets. I expected a home to be waiting for me, instead Jay's disillusionment was well under way. The secretive nature of his father's family had rubbed off on him, so he shared nothing of his initial experiences with me, ever. It was left to me to unpick the threads all those long years afterwards, on my journey into the past.

His distant mien and cool attitude, which I thought was aimed at me, was in truth masking his disappointment with his new reality. Jay never understood that his demeanor catapulted me into an alien situation. I was left vulnerable, unhappy, and unusually unsure of myself, mired in misery.

This made me an easy prey for a sexual predator: a serial philander with his own agenda, who ironically found himself hoist with his own petard, caught in a trap of his own making. Naïvely I had trusted Ted's masquerade as my friend, and was inevitably dragged down a path from which there was no return for either of us. (As I wrote of this, I got a strong sense that his lingering spirit, overseeing my scribbling, was not comfortable with this part of my journey through the past, that he did not like this view of himself.)

No matter, Fate had determined that our two souls were destined to link up, and once that spark ignited, we become entangled by a bond that neither of us had expected. Our connection proved to be so strong that neither of us could break it, then or now, no matter how many miles or years apart we were, or which dimension we are now in. That link was still there when he died, and will be still with me when I die.

Silence, secrecy, self-interest, and betrayal fanned the flames of destruction, leaving a legacy of tragedy and the ashes of broken lives. It was a betrayal with its roots in one generation that re-emerged in the next. An unspoken but vicious vendetta trailing devastating consequences through the decades, from which there was no escape for Jay, Amy, or me. And eventually there was no escape for Ted or Sally either when Karma decided their time had come, just as it should.

REFLECTIONS

Examining the past and that treasured, momentous interlude with Ted stirred my soul again as I recalled that cataclysmic spark that set off such an irrevocable chain of events.

How different our lives could have been if he had not lacked so much faith in himself. If he only he could have understood that his daughters loved him well enough that they would not have forsaken him for falling in love with me. But, being nearly a decade older, he didn't trust that my emotions for him would stand the test of time. By the time he had worked it out years later, he had hurt me so badly, I couldn't trust him, and I had feared what might happen if I accepted his final invitation to go into his home again.

Could we have been happy together? I would have been; I would have made him a comfortable home, would have loved him, and showed my love for him. Once the link between us was forged, he was all I ever wanted. But would he have been able to make the change? At the time I thought so, but with hindsight, perhaps not.

If I had gone into Sally's house again that day, his marriage for sure would have been over. How would he have coped with leaving his home of twenty-five years? He would have become isolated from his family, for a while at least. And how would he have felt cramped into my little house, two doors down from his friend? Would his friend have remained so in the tight little portion of that community in which he lived? Wouldn't the possibility of isolation gave been the culmination of his life-long fear? Could he have coped with it?

In the end, he never did leave his home, stolidly staying put until his death, living with whatever demands Sally made upon him, using his energies to restake his claim, renovating every aspect of the house that he could: new bedroom, extended living room, new basement, and new roof. Was he seeking to drive out the memories of the cuckoo who had despoiled his nest? His post death appearance makes one wonder.

I have no doubt that Ted, like me, pushed everything deep down inside him. Perhaps as he had to face death, he finally admitted to himself the truth of his own heart.

It seems the only explanation for those early months after his departure from life when his spirit descended on my home, and seemed to exhibit such anger and such anguish. My cousin, a confirmed believer in the spirit world, remarked that the constant blowing of lights, stopping of clocks, misbehavior by electronics, and other things indicated a spirit in turmoil. Well, stupid Stacey had actually worked that part out for herself! Duh!

Perhaps it was my agony and recognizing his mistake that drove his soul to seek mine. I know with certainty that when Ted died, he had been thinking of me. What other explanation could there be for the emanation of his ghost arriving so swiftly after his earthly demise and for his spirit remaining in my house for so many months?

The arrival of that spirit brought back the passion I had not felt for over two decades. It seemed that same electricity which had sparked whenever we were near one another, overtook me again as his aura crackled through my home.

Ted's spirit was seeking solace then recognized he still had work to do. After absorbing the depths of my grief, he seemed to seek to provide answers, invading my thoughts, prompting my writing. At times it seemed almost as if he had penned phrases. On one occasion he erased a whole paragraph I had written, apparently in anger, but all the time pushing me to unravel the past and make sense of it. Seeming to want me to understand that when he had spoken to me of being so hurt, about me hurting him so badly, I would finally realize what at the time he couldn't and wouldn't admit.

His spirit's anguish clearly showed when I wrote of our lost child. His reaction had displayed in a myriad of kinetic actions that demonstrated intense agony. He would have loved our child.

When I finished writing, and came to the publication of the final manuscript, even then it seemed to be steered by a hand other than my own. My initial goal of publication in the first month of the year was delayed by so many stumbling blocks that the subsequent launch of the book in Alberta uncannily coincided with the first anniversary of Ted's death. Once again he seemed to be trying to make a point, one apparently not unnoticed by his own family, I discovered later.

I ached that I had never been able to return, to see him once more. The length of the journey was partly what had defeated returning in the past. To fly would be too expensive, and the time for the drive never seemed to fit in with other's timetables. But after his death, even though I knew it would be a long drive on my own, I decided to travel from my home in America's Great Lakes area out to almost the furthest reaches of Canada, deep in the heart of the oil-and-gas patch.

Strangely, once I made that decision, something calming settled inside me. And during my journey, I could sense that I was in safe hands, the spirit still regretful, and still watchful.

Overture to the Pilgrimage

Stacey, 2013

It had been twenty-five years almost to the day since I left Edmunston when I set out on my journey back. It wasn't that I hadn't wanted to go back, but life had always just gotten in the way. Either family illness, lack of money, or lack of time had prevented me from returning sooner. Or was that all it had been?

For two decades I had stumbled through life with a constant feeling that part of me was missing, try as I might to move forward, find new companionship, or love again.

If I was honest with myself, deep down the truth was that I was afraid of Ted and his power to hurt me still. I was afraid of Sally and the Mountain Reaches conclave who spread lies and gossip about me. I just was not brave enough to face it or risk the return of all those feelings I thought I had so successfully buried.

If I had ever gone back, would it have been possible to just see my friends without seeing him? Could I have approached him? Or, with the past so distant, would he have found it possible to speak to me, to discuss the past, answer some of my questions?

The bottom line is that decades later, I still feared the Logans and Zienkos and their cruelty and manipulation. But now, in 2013, that would not be an issue, two out of the three of my nemeses were dead; all I had to confront now was a headstone in a graveyard. I would not seek out an ailing widow. I would let her die in peace if she could.

Over the past few months, my uncertainties about the veracity of what had happened to us crystallized into a book, as Ted's aura guided me towards what I had not known and could not see at the time.

In the end, he had hurt me one more time, devastating me and catching me completely unaware. His death shocked me beyond belief, and I was bewildered by my own reaction. It stunned all my friends, leaving them wondering whose demise had turned fearless, skeptical, and practical (now immensely plump and even plainer) Stacey into a gibbering wreck saying a ghost haunted her house.

I found it impossible to speak about the past to them, to talk about him without dissolving into tears. I could not think about him when I was alone without great heaving sobs tearing me apart, and I think maybe it was my abject sorrow that kept his spirit near to me those first few months. At his death, I had died inside, it seemed. All love for anyone else frozen inside me, except for my unbreakable bond with Amy. But then Ted's aura appeared, staying for many months, always close, and in an odd way comforting me.

His death had regurgitated in stark detail all that had transpired decades before. Just as harsh and deep in the now. All the drama, hurt, and destruction, revived in my mind once more; the tragedy that resulted in the loss of our unborn child back to haunt my heart again. And then, Ted's spirit guided me to an understanding of the annihilation of our lives that started way before our actual move to Alberta and before Jay had landed, or had even been born.

He showed me that my part in the whole debacle was merely an afterthought masking the realities, because much of the end game would have been the same regardless of my interlude with Ted. In retrospect there had been no real commitment by Jay's paternal family to welcome him back into the fold, or any depth of sincerity in the promises made to help us. Instead their thoughtless, selfish intervention had ruined our happy little family and destroyed the future we might have had together in England.

As I drove down the highway, returning my heart and my body to where they have longed to be for twenty-five years, the last conversation with Ted on the telephone played through my head again. I had been thrust into flight mode by his sudden appearance in front of me; and I never questioned why he would have come out of his own house at that time, or be so insistent that I come in.

At the time, I didn't see that for him to take such a gigantic step toward me, given our past history and its dramatic aftermath, must have signified that something vital had changed for him. It didn't occur to me that his bitter and cruel comments later that evening were engendered by intense disappointment that I had refused his invitation to enter his home again. I just did not realize that he was risking everything by taking that momentous step toward me regardless of any drama that might ensue afterward. Poor Ted. He thought his gesture had been thrown back in his face.

A shattering mistake on my part, was borne out of fear that my hard-won reputation, for being honest and straightforward, was being threatened by his thoughtlessness. The horror of enduring that loneliness and despair once more, or losing my few good friends, had swept over me.

I knew I no longer possessed the strength to start over again in Edmunston; endure the pointing and whispering, the terror of being alone and I had run from him. For such a deep thinker, Ted ought to have understood that, but for all his depth of thought, communication about his deepest feelings was something he never mastered.

That last encounter and Amy's disintegrating health had been the impetus I needed, and so I had fled back to Britain, back to my family who loved me. They did, didn't they, or maybe not as much as I thought. Had I realized the truth, I might have made a different choice. My body might have fled, but my heart knew that Ted and I should have been together. Our souls had entwined. From the day I left Edmunston, I always knew that a part of me was missing.

Now, as I finally made my way west, in my head I made tentative farewells to my family, such as was left, not sure if I would return, or if I even wanted to. Ted's message more recently seemed to have been "join me, be with me, come to me."

At that point, I was tempted. I had given my life to my family for more than two decades while my soul withered inside me:

caring for them and working to become the breadwinner for all, as one disappointment after another ate away at what was left of my soul. Each time I had a foolish hope that there was finally something good within my grasp to cherish, each time those hopes were dashed away. Almost every anticipated pleasure was marred, returning me to that place of hopelessness and inner sorrow.

My reasoning to myself for accepting this was that Fate was still punishing me for my "sins"; until with Ted's guidance, I learned that it was the betrayal by others that had led to the unavoidable situation that destroyed my future and almost destroyed Amy's too.

Ironically, as I look around me today, I see many people who have restarted their lives with a new person. Who have had the courage to take that chance when their soul mates inconveniently appeared later in their life. But Ted lacked that courage to start his life over again, and at the time all those culpable had pointed the finger at me, destroying my self-confidence, ingraining in me that I was the instigator of all that had occurred, grinding me down. It was so far from the truth, but I, poor fool, too beaten down to refute them, carried that guilt around inside me for nearly three decades.

It wasn't that I hadn't tried to move on, I had. But it was not easy to start over alone with an ailing child, and a broken spirit, as I approached middle age. By shear stubbornness and fake bravado though, I had survived, as had Amy, although always fragile, often depressed, and with a self-esteem even lower than my own.

But I was determined to repair my life and provide a comfortable home for Amy once more. Eventually, I tried to start over with a new husband. The pity of it was that I failed to recognize that he carried more emotional baggage than did I. Despite all his bravado as he spoke about what he was going to do, in reality he was another lame duck. His previous wife put it best: "I was gonna" would be an apt epitaph for him.

One more man, who was incapable of voicing his real thoughts, making him emotionally unable to successfully maintain a warm, loving relationship. Even worse, physical love embarrassed him, if the truth were told. Sensuous, passionate Stacey died not long after that.

When we finally moved to America, it was like repeating my move to Canada in slow motion. Like Jay, Damon was a fish out of water and he, too, struggled to find work; he was always looking for "the big win," "something for free." He wanted the easy way to earn a living. It was just as well that I had experienced lessons in survival during the previous decade. In the end I had to step into the breach to keep the wolf from the door. So, back to square one, I was again the caregiver. It seemed to be my life's role.

As a child, "Take care of your brother, he is not as strong as you," was dinned in my ears. "Don't let him be bullied." my mother would say. Thereafter, I seemed to gather friends over and over who needed someone to prop them up, provide a sympathetic ear, run to their aid, and so it went on.

I gained a reputation for being the good listener, the softhearted one, the easy touch. Aided by the fact that I was tall and big-boned, making me a head taller than my peers, no one ever took the time to see the scared little girl hiding inside me. It has been this way all my life making me a lonely adult. Ironically it was the husband of one of my oldest friends in Edmunston was the only person I ever met who was perceptive enough to perceive that loneliness.

I led an active social life: going on trips and to parties from an early age. I felt I was having a great time, that I had good friends, belonged. Then, one day, I realized many of the invitations were just because I was useful, and for a while I was the only one with a car!

It revived a memory from when I was a ten-year-old. I was invited to the party of a younger child who had just broken her arm, only to be chastised by the mother as I tried to join in the fun. "I only asked you to come so that you could help."

Did that harsh comment start off the idea, which conditioned me at such an early age to believe that I was only acceptable if I was useful and helpful? Childhood impressions are deep and can shape your view of life: Ted's loss of his mother at the age of six, had left him with a fear of losing family, of being alone. We do such cruel things to our children.

Whatever the cause, I grew into the friend who could be relied upon at a party to stay and clear dishes, or help set things up. As the parties got a little wilder, I was the one walking the drunk girl around the block, to sober her up, or making sure someone else got home safely, while other girls snapped up the nice boys. Everyone always assumed that capable, useful Stacey would be there to fill the breach, and could manage just fine on her own and was a boon to lame ducks.

It was no wonder that I ended up being married to Jay once I heard about his troubled childhood. He was a candidate for me trying to make his life and his family a little happier. It was not surprising that my mother had immediately tagged him as "another lame duck" and rolled her eyes. (Muttering under her breath that for once couldn't I find someone with an 'ology'!)

Once I was included in Jay's family, I set about putting them all on a more contented path. I had invited his mother, a bitter, unhappy woman, to come and share in the birth of her first grandchild. Her response was to create havoc and snap off the proffered olive branch in my face. I hadn't changed her. Ultimately, didn't change Jay, who I recognized many years later was entirely cast in her image, despite bearing an uncanny physical likeness to his late father in his youth.

And then there was Ted. Should I also include him in the lame duck category? Would I have felt that pull toward him on that first fateful night if he hadn't mentioned his mother's death and how it had affected him? Immediately I had felt pity that he had been so young. He had looked so bleak at the memory of her. It tugged at my heartstrings. Would he have been so open to what transpired between us if he had not just recalled his early childhood vulnerability to mind and needed comfort? Or was it the mind-set he had reached after enduring Sally's wrath and a year of coldness and recriminations for his lapse in judgment the previous summer with Mariska?

Who knew? What did it matter? What does any of it matter now? He is dead, gone for more than two years now, taking what was left of my heart with him, and leaving that magnet inside me bereft, longing to join its mate, but connecting with nothing.

All love died within me the day I heard of his death, and I understood the dangers when the reservoir of grief we all carry inside overflows. As it drains whatever feelings remain inside, leave a vast void; a vacuum where nothing flourishes, except perhaps for a mother's love.

Ted's cruel abandonment of me, Sally's secrecy, and Aunt Penny's vengeful attitude combined to make my world an empty place. Their actions stole from me any chance of ever again experiencing that closeness, that link with another person that I shared with Ted. Never again would I lie beside someone; never again would I experience the sweeter things of life. I was left with just the memories of how it felt to lay naked beside a warm, laughing, passionate lover who wanted to please me as I pleased him. Then to cuddle and giggle over stupid things, as sleep overtakes....

It matters not. Nothing matters, as Ted is gone, and my soul, my heart, have withered.

PART ONE
THE PAST
LOGANS AND ZIENKOS

Fate and Vengeance: A Narration

Two generations of women in the Logan family left a legacy of betrayal in their wake. Their actions, peppered by jealously, secrecy, and spite, destroyed the lives of two generations of Mackenzie men. The culmination of their endeavors ruined the lives and families of both father and son.

In one generation two children endured an unhappy and deprived life as they grew up dragged back into the world from which their mother had originally sought to escape. It was far from what their father had envisaged for their future.

Decades later, ostensibly seeking to make reparation to that generation, the Logan women brought about the final annihilation of the life of one of those same children as their continued need for vengeance wrought havoc in yet another generation. In the process once more they all but destroyed an innocent child, subjecting her to her own horrors and impacting her life well into adulthood.

Two generations of Mackenzie husbands took their wives home to Alberta intent on settling with the rest of the Mackenzie clan, full of hope and high expectations that never came to fruition. In both cases, tragedy ensued, taking first the father and then the son to an early demise.

History repeated itself within an ironic circling twist of Fate. Both father and son died sad, lonely, disillusioned men, their promising futures coming to nothing, estranged from their closest family, bringing in their early ends an uncannily similar tragic circumstance.

The Mackenzie sisters, Penny and her sister Agatha, mercilessly drove out Cassie, their brother Zack's new English wife, who had returned with him from Europe after his brave exploits on the beaches of Italy during World War II. He had brought her with him to Canada, seeking to return to a normal life, hoping for a peace with his new bride, which would never materialize.

His two siblings, jealous of Cassie's beauty and her attraction for the men in their lives, exhibited an intense hostility toward her, which sent their new sister-in-law scurrying back to England with her toddler daughter and newborn son. Torn between his love for his home and his love for his wife and children, a bemused Zack trailed unwillingly in her wake. Cassie's repatriation did nothing to improve her attitude, and their new situation became ruinous to their marriage as they struggled with the poor economy in postwar Britain. Endlessly they tried to re-establish themselves, but their relationship disintegrated over the following years while their children, Jay and Isabella, sadly watched the wrangling and bitterness expand into the failure of their unhappy parents' partnership.

Cassie's bitterness and antipathy toward anything Canadian meant that they never spoke of their life in Alberta, thereby denying her children any knowledge about their father's early life. Zack, homesick beyond belief, was barred from discussing his family, or his love for his homeland. As they grew up, his children did not even give his past a thought, and were unaware of the family history that had separated him forever from the homeland that he loved and the family he missed.

After Zack's death, Jay and Isabella discovered treasured memorabilia demonstrating how much their father had missed his mountain home and the family they knew nothing about.

On a quest to find out more, Jay innocently made contact with his paternal family, starting a fatal journey toward the land of his birth and his own tragic destiny.

He found his father's family open and relaxed, in sharp contrast to the cool rigidity of his mother's relatives. Delighted by the warm welcome he received from his newly discovered family, Jay easily fell under the spell of his aunt Penny. Abetted by her daughter Sally and son-in-law Ted, Penny convinced Jay to move to Canada, where she told him he really belonged, with assurances that they would help him resettle. Full of expectations and excited about new plans for their future, Jay and Stacey returned home from their vacation to prepare for their move to Canada, unaware that an event on the eve of their departure changed everything between Sally and Ted and would ultimately destroy their own future together.

Sally, mortified by her situation, concealed the problems between herself and Ted, to save face, staying silent and doing nothing to forewarn her cousin that the promised support might now not be forthcoming.

Penny, unaware of her daughter's dilemma, and hearing that jobs were becoming scarce in the area, panicked her nephew into heading straight back to Canada, leaving Stacey alone to pack up their belongings and sell their house.

Soon after his arrival, Jay began to understand that Ted would do little to help him secure a job; neither did the family seem interested in his search for a new home. In an irony reflecting his father Zack's difficulties in post-war London, for weeks Jay looked for work amongst people who did not recognize his skills. To his chagrin, Jay finally found himself reduced from his previous managerial status to the level of a restaurant dishwasher as the promised family assistance dissipated.

Jay's relationship with Ted didn't prosper either, once he realized he had little in common with the raunchy, hard-drinking gas plant mechanic. He was unaware that Ted, despite his earlier assurances to assist, now had an ulterior motive for not wanting Jay and his family living nearby, making him deliberately unhelpful.

Jay's relationship with his aunt did not fare any better either. As she got to spend more time with her nephew, and without Stacey there as a buffer, Penny realized that he was not the reincarnation of her brother that she had wished for. Jay's resemblance to his father ended with his looks. More to the point, Penny found that his true personality was much more like the despised Cassie, and she began to lose interest in him. Sally, still wrapped up in her own troubles, followed Penny's lead, while wishing her mother had felt this way before Jay had arrived and salvaged her nerves.

Hurt and demoralized by the evaporation of the close relationship Jay thought had been built with his father's family, he was faced with having to give new credence to his mother's warnings about trusting the Logans. But he was unwilling to lose face and admit the truth to either Cassie or Stacey. So instead of halting the plans to move to Alberta, Jay took a job two hundred miles away from Edmunston. He revealed nothing about the duplicity of Zack's family, allowing everyone in Britain to believe that the Mackenzie clan was doing everything possible to help him.

Stacey finally arrived to reunite with the family she had come to love the year before, expecting to find at least a partial new home waiting for her in their hometown. Instead, she was disappointed to find Jay working many miles away, enjoying a bachelor lifestyle. Too ashamed to tell Stacey the real story or to seek her support, Jay coolly deposited Stacey with his aunt, leaving his wife hurt and confused.

Ted, his sights firmly focused on Stacey, fostered by his feelings from the year before, found an opportunity to take advantage of the situation as inevitably he and Stacey were thrown together. Partly by Jay's lassitude and after Sally cast an unsuspecting Stacey into the role of watchdog over her faithless husband before departing with her daughters for their summer camp.

Increasingly lonely and bewildered, Stacey became an easy target for serial philanderer Ted, who was now determined to make her another notch on his belt. Later, when the impact of their relationship developed into too much for him to deal with, Ted cruelly cut off contact with her.

The situation was destined to end in tragedy, with its aftermath enduring for three decades before Stacey uncovered the whole truth, from its beginnings in the 1940s all the way through to the present, with the assistance of Ted's intermittent ghostly presence revealing the legacy of betrayal as it finally played itself out.

Chapter One

Mountain Reaches, 1947

Cassie

Shaken her to her soul, the day after her brother-in-law Hal had tried to take liberties with her, and the ensuing violent reaction by her husband Zack, Cassie felt the need to escape. She asked her sister-in-law Penny if she would watch baby Izzie for a while. Untypically, Cassie had said, "I need some fresh air, to walk a little, be alone," and had escaped as quickly as she could.

Penny merely thought Cassie was homesick. She knew nothing yet of the previous evening's events, or the real reason that Cassie needed to get as far away from everyone as she could. In fact, Penny thought it was a good idea for Cassie to get out in the fresh air, and have some time to herself, as she looked very pale. Perhaps Cassie might start to like her surroundings and her new family more if she got used to them, so Penny was happy to take care of Izzie for a little while. Anyway, she liked babies.

She watched as her sister-in-law headed toward the path that wound up the hill into the trees. She was a little perplexed but then she shrugged. Cassie would be fine, and soon her sister Agatha would be over. They would have a coffee together and have a gossip about their unsuitable sister-in-law. Really, what had Zack been thinking?

Cassie followed the track that she had seen her other brother-in-law Chuck use when he took his girls for a walk, or trailed his camera over his shoulder. She had even been partway with them once. But as she had never been much for walking in the country, now she began to wonder what she thought she was doing. Apart from her initial shock about how isolated this place was, after the bedlam and bombs she had endured over the previous five years, the quiet and peace seemed like it might be beneficial to her overset nerves.

Then she found that quiet and peace was not what happened there. The trains were noisy, the colliery was noisy, and people constantly felt the need to pop in whether they were invited or not. So there was no peace in her home either. Her sisters-in-law did not turn out to be the kindly individuals she had been expecting. They judged her harshly, sniffed at her inability to do basic household chores and be a homemaker. Overall they made her feel entirely inadequate instead of helping her become accustomed to so many new devices.

But the main thing that bothered her was that her home was not secure, as she had found out last night. Given how many people seemed to feel free to walk in at any time, the door to her home might just as well not be in place, as it kept no one out! The lock also seemed superfluous, because even if it were turned, people still hammered to come in. She was not used to that kind of socializing; all she wanted was a quiet private life, and it just hadn't happened.

Now, after last night's events, she *had* to get away, but aside from walking up into the hills, there was no place to go. And this morning she really needed to be alone. Cassie trudged on; she wanted to go home to her mother and even her horrid little brother, but she wondered how she could ever go back. How could her life have turned out so horrible? It had been wonderful while her father was alive. She lived the life of a princess, but it seemed like since he died, the world was punishing her for being alive. Why should she have to live through all of this?

She shuddered. Those were bad thoughts, and she was not sure what to do next as she stumbled into a little clearing overlooking the valley below. It was fairly open, with a tree stump set in the middle of it. She moved toward the stump, brushed it off, and sat down wearily. Her shoulders drooped as she finally gave way to the flood of tears she had been holding back all night, weeping as though her heart would break.

She could not believe the aftermath of that tussle with Haley. When Zack had returned, she was still trembling with rage. She had torn into Zack for bringing her to, as she saw it, the end of the world, filled with rough, uncouth men and unattractive, unfriendly, jealous women.

"All I am here is a target for people like Haley, who've never seen a sophisticated woman before, who wolf whistle at me when I walk down the street, and think they can take the kind of liberties that Haley tried to take. You are never around to take care of me, your sisters despise me because I am not a good cook, I can't sew or knit, and I don't know how anything works. I *hate* it here!"

Zack heard only the first part of her screaming tirade and her words about the discomfort of her encounter with Haley's roaming hands. Haley! *Haley* had been mauling his wife, had taken liberties with his wife! A red rage whirled inside his head, focusing on that phrase. What had Cassie done to provoke that? How had she let him kiss her before slapping him?

Shaking with anger, he moved toward her, grabbed her by the shoulders, and said in the fiercest voice she had ever heard from him, "*You* let *Haley* touch you? You let him *kiss* you! *No! You* are *mine!* You belong to *me!* Don't you ever let anyone else touch you again! You want kisses, you need love, you want to be touched— you come to *me* for it!"

With that he pulled her close, kissed her hard, then roughly pushed her back into their bedroom, pulling at her clothes as he went, his fury getting the better of him. Zack took Cassie more in anger than in love, and set up yet another barrier between them. His furious passion was just one step short of rape. It was entirely the wrong reaction, the wrong way to behave in any circumstances. And he had traumatized the gently bred Cassie to her core.

Horrified by Zack's reaction, she lay awake next to him all night, numb, as silent tears made tracks down her face. She couldn't look at him next morning, or wait for him to leave for work. Once he was gone, she got ready, swiftly making her escape after she had left Izzie with Penny. And now what?

Huddled on the tree stump, her whole body shook with her sobs, so much so that she did not hear Chuck come up behind her. He was off shift and earlier had taken the opportunity to grab his camera to try and get some shots of the early spring sunshine.

For an instant, when he saw Cassie, he was going to turn and walk away. But he was a kind man, and he had a soft spot for his new sister-in-law. He was aware of how beset she was by the trials of trying to fit into a lifestyle clearly not made for her, and he remembered his own struggles when he had first left England to move to this country. Giving a sigh of exasperation, he made his way over to her, put his camera down, and laid a hand on her shoulder.

"Hey," he said gently, "Hey hinny, what's wrong?" his north-country accent, which he had never quite lost, coming to the fore.

Cassie barely heard him, and when she did, she pulled away from him, looking like a terrified rabbit that had just seen a hound coming after her, fearful of another male onslaught on her. Chuck saw the fear in her face and was shocked.

"Nay, lass," said he said gently, "I won't hurt you." And he put his arm around her shoulders and let her sob against his chest until she finally quietened down. Cassie sat there still, utterly spent. Then she realized that Chuck still had his arm around her, and she pulled away, staring at him apprehensively.

Chuck sat down on the ground beside her, saying quietly, "What has happened?"

Cassie shook her head, at first unable to put into words what had happened to her.

Chuck looked at her, his face full of sympathy, and tried to draw her out, asking, "The girls just being spiteful? Or one of the men here trying to take liberties with you?"

When Cassie took in a sharp breath and looked sharply at him, he knew he had hit the mark.

"Haley?" he said questioningly.

Surprised that he was so perceptive, haltingly and embarrassed, Cassie explained about her run-in with Haley the previous evening. She told Chuck about the violent response from Zack, who blamed her for the incident, and what had followed. How stunned she had been by his anger at her, when in effect she had been seeking his protection.

Chuck clicked his teeth. "Poor Zack," he said. "He's never been able to really express himself, or understand women, and he handled that all wrong. He should have kept that temper of his in check."

Cassie looked into his eyes, puzzled. "What do you mean?" she asked.

Chuck shrugged, smiling slightly. "Well, he did do all the right things, just not in the right order. He should have cuddled you, made sure you were OK, and then reassured you that he wouldn't let anyone try that with you again. He should have *told* you how much he loves you first and *then* made love to you, not taken out his rage with Haley on you. You didn't do anything wrong, and Zack, like all of us, knows Haley's reputation."

Cassie started to reply, blushed, then stopped. Again she was surprised by his thoughtful analysis, but what was she to do? Her shoulders sagged.

Watching her reactions, Chuck said, "Look, Cassie, that was not a nice thing to happen to you, but don't let it wear you down, and don't dwell on it. I know you are unhappy, but give it time. Eventually everyone will settle down with you and get over their prejudice. Don't let their jealousy rattle you. In the meantime,

I'll take Haley to one side and explain what he needs to do, or not do, in order to save himself a beating in the future, not only from Zack, but from me too. You might want to make sure that you keep your door locked now, too, when Zack isn't home."

Cassie looked at him, taken aback and deeply touched. He was offering to protect her, which Zack hadn't done, and that made her feel better. They stood up, Chuck pulling Cassie up with him, and then stopped as their eyes met. Cassie's mouth formed a shocked, "Oh," and Chuck took her face gently in his hands and kissed her.

Immediately he stepped away. "Cassie…no…that was wrong of me. Sorry, that's just what you didn't need, and it was a bad thing to do, but you really are the prettiest girl, and you looked so sad…and…" He stopped, as he knew he had no excuse, and he was a little shaken by his own reaction to her. Pretty or not, it wouldn't do!

Cassie just looked at him, tears starting in her eyes and all sorts of confused thoughts running through her head. She did not want to be the target of all this attention, but that kiss from Chuck hadn't fazed her the way that Haley's attack on her or Zack's attentions last night had. She did not know how to deal with this, and she held out her hands to him in a pleading gesture. Unexpectedly, when Chuck had held her, had… had… For that one brief moment she had felt safer than she had since her ship had docked so many months ago. It was stupid.

Chuck stepped back toward her, took her hands, and said softly, "Yes, I felt it too, but I'm not Haley, and I love Penny, so this can't be. I can't get involved with you. If I strayed, Penny would leave me and take my girls with her, and I won't break up my family. *But* I will be your friend and watch out for you. I will head off any further unwanted attentions that look like they might come your way. You will be safe; people don't cross me."

Cassie nodded. She understood, and she would not want to lose this one friend she finally felt she had found. To change the subject, which was becoming uncomfortable, she looked down at his camera. "Where were you going?" she asked.

"I was going further up the hill to take some shots across the valley, You can come with me if you like." Chuck said, smiling at her. "I think the exercise would do you good… blow the cobwebs away and give you a chance to calm down. If you like, later, or at the weekend, I'll take some photos of you and Izzie. Would you like that? You can send them home to your Mom."

Cassie nodded, she thought it would be nice to do that, and she spent a pleasant hour with him as he explained how he was trying to build a pictorial record of the town and the area, along with the rest of his life. He had first started when he came to Canada nearly three decades earlier, his camera capturing the wonder of the wide, open spaces he found. Cassie found it interesting, and it took her mind off her problems for a while. But as they were walking down the trail and were almost back into town, Chuck noticed tension building in her again. He put his arm around her shoulders, gave her a squeeze, and said, "Chin up, Cassie. You can cope." Then he added, "If things get that bad again, let me know, and I can meet you up at the tree stump so you can talk it out. You might want to get a camera, take your own pictures; it will give you another interest. You have a friend now. But, Cassie, that is all it is, and all there can be."

She nodded, smiling weakly, and said, "I know, I made the commitment when I married Zack, and we have Izzie. Anything else is not an option for me, either. But thank you for being so kind. You were right: the walk did do me good, and I feel better now. I'll have to find a way to deal with all of this."

With that, they went their separate ways, both realizing it would not be good to be seen walking back into town together. Neither would have been so complacent if they had realized that Penny had seen them. She started to get concerned about the length of time that Cassie had been gone so, leaving Izzie and her girls with Agatha she started to walk toward the trail when she spotted first Cassie, then Chuck.

Her blood boiled! Now here was *her* husband with his arm around Cassie's shoulders! Were all the men after her? Following fresh on the heels of the conversation she had with Agatha about what she had seen Haley and Cassie doing the night before, Penny also leapt to the wrong conclusion and was enraged. This English hussy that her brother had brought home with him was a hellish nightmare! What had he been thinking?

Well, Chuck had better not get any ideas about her. When they had seen an incident with Haley and another woman last year (which she had never told Agatha about), she had reminded him of her antecedents.

"Remember," she had said, laughing, but with a serious undertone, "I come from Indian stock, and we're all handy with knives. It won't be your scalp I am after, either!" On a more serious note, she also told him in no uncertain terms that if he ever tried anything like that, she would leave him and take his daughters with her. And he'd never find them, ever.

Chuck had grinned back, hugged her, and kissed her. "No need to worry about that," he had told her. "You are more than enough woman for me, and no other woman could or would ever replace you. I love you and my girls." Since then he had put her comments out of his mind. His only thought had been, I've lost one family and I will not lose another, no matter what the temptation. But his wife and his daughters knew nothing of his first family. They never would.

Chuck and Penny had been unaware that their youngest daughter, Sally, had overheard the conversation, and it resonated deeply, her mother's harsh words sticking in her mind. She buried it away in her brain until, as a grown woman, faced with a similar situation in her own life, she would remember that children could be used as a weapon and employ the tactic on her own husband.

Such seeds sown in the young will surface and bear fruit in the adult.

Although it was not exactly the following weekend, true to his word, once the weather improved and the women were outside in their summer wear, Chuck spent an afternoon taking pictures of Cassie and her baby daughter. For the first time he saw a side of her that people rarely saw, a mother's love. Cassie was glowing in the early stages of her next pregnancy, but her joy in her toddler daughter was evident as she tossed the little girl in the air and played with her. Chuck got some wonderful shots of her, and he once again realized that if he could ever be tempted away from his marriage, Cassie would be the cause.

Penny seethed when she saw the photos. Knowing Chuck's style, she could see his fascination with her highly photogenic sister-in-law. It set Penny wondering, and once again she reminded Chuck that in his own best interests, he should never consider whatever he might have in mind in regards to Cassie. Chuck just laughed at her, tweaked her dark curls, and kissed her, reiterating that she was all he needed, and that his interest had more to do with his photography and the light than the subject.

Cassie was highly delighted with her pictures. She was thrilled that she had photographed so well, but wondered if the photographer made the difference. Chuck had been encouraging and sweet with her and Izzie, and that had made her relax. Zack was ecstatic with the pictures and couldn't wait to boast to his chums about what a beautiful wife and daughter he had.

However, it sounded the death knoll for any kind of peace to reign between his wife and his sisters, both now determined to oust her from their lives. By the time autumn came, it was clear that Zack and Cassie needed to leave Mountain Reaches before his family was torn apart completely.

CHAPTER TWO

LONDON, 1948

ZACK

Zack was back in London with Cassie, baby Jay, and Izzie, and they were trying, not very successfully, to settle in. It wasn't comfortable. They were crammed in with Cassie's mother and her sulky younger brother Sydney, in their tiny semi-detached house in a once genteel part of the city, which was now more down-at-heel.

He was miserable, it was more difficult than he expected to find work in Britain. It wasn't helped by the fact that he didn't like living in this city any more than Cassie had liked living in his mountain mining village. The challenges to re-establish themselves here were not easily overcome, especially as Cassie got meaner by the day, and colder by the night. Ironically, his mother-in-law, Maria was kindest to him, but that was not enough to take away his dislike of this country, and he longed for his mountain home. He now knew he should have stayed in Edmonton, at least understanding by then that Mountain

Reaches had not been an option. He should have insisted that Cassie stay and give life in Canada another chance, and give him the opportunity to visit the mountains from time to time. Instead they had tramped back to England to start all over again. Here, in London, he was a fish out of water, and inwardly he raged at the circumstances that had brought him to this, angry that his own family had been so cold and hostile toward his wife.

Zack was still seething with anger with regard to his sisters and their husbands. They hadn't given him and Cassie a chance; they hadn't even tried to understand what Cassie had endured in London during the war, or what he had seen on the beaches of Italy! They had not realized how much he needed the tranquility of the mountains after those horrors to restore his soul; he needed to hear the call of the birds to drown out the cries of the dying and injured reverberating around in his head. He was haunted by the sounds of bombardment all around him, and the killing he had to do in order to survive. They hadn't seemed to care how much Cassie needed some serenity too; they had not even tried to understand that Zack wanted the chance to get back to a normal life after the traumas they had both endured in Europe.

Besotted by his beautiful and delicate wife, Zack had swaggered a little when he saw the way the men in the village eyed Cassie. But he had failed to understand the impact a sophisticated, city-bred girl would have on a small and isolated rural Canadian community. He also had not anticipated how his wife's beauty would draw his sisters' wrath down upon his head with such a vengeance as their husbands too noted Cassie's attractions. He relived the uncomfortable conversations he had with them about his wife, indignant because, as he saw it, the problem lay not with Cassie but with the roving eyes of his brothers-in-law and their wives' inability to keep them content in their own beds. Men happy in their own beds don't stray into another's, he thought.

So much for a happy homecoming!

It had not been the return of the prodigal son he had anticipated—the hero's welcome, with recognition of his battlefield bravery or admiration for his medals. Instead, his family were openly disappointed that he had married an English girl rather than returning home to wed his former sweetheart Gwenny, and they had shown their disapproval pretty much from the get-go. Zack had been bitterly disillusioned and so deeply hurt by their reaction. His sisters showed no interest in his experiences in the army, giving him no opportunity to tell them of his commendations, or explain how they had been won. Instead, they focused on the unsuitability of his bride, and they gave little support. If they had understood the horrors that both he and Cassie had endured, perhaps they might have been more sympathetic.

Instead, his sisters, particularly Agatha, did little to hide that his new wife was not to their liking. She was a "fast" city girl in their eyes, a view reinforced by the ogling eyes of the town's menfolk. Once they had taken against Cassie, they did very little to make her feel welcome, leading to some very unhappy months during their first year.

Cassie didn't fit in, they muttered. She was too sophisticated, smoked, wore makeup. She had few domestic skills, and to them it seemed she looked down on their rural way of life. This was aided and abetted by Cassie's complete lack of tact at times, which upset everyone.

Then came the run-in with Haley, followed by, according to Penny, Chuck's apparent interest in her, although Zack had not seen any sign of it himself. As a result, his family had practically chased him back to Edmonton, where Cassie and he stayed long enough for Jay's birth.

Zack had found work in Edmonton with the railroad almost immediately, but Cassie was unable, or maybe now unwilling, to make friends. Her disdain had its roots in her treatment by her hostile sisters-in-law and then Zack's aunts with whom they stayed for a while. It was all the excuse she needed to plead homesickness, and she beat a trail back to London at the first opportunity, taking her children with her, as Zack followed reluctantly behind.

Sitting in his mother-in-law's living room, Zack's thoughts wandered back to his confrontation with Agatha after Haley had made that pass at Cassie. It was still raw in his memory, and he cringed inside because he had never, ever before in his life had a fight that bad with either of his sisters.

"*Why* did you have to bring *her* here? *Why* didn't you stick to Gwenny and come back and marry her, like everyone expected?" hissed Agatha after Zack had threatened Haley with annihilation if he ever laid a finger on Cassie again. Agatha, a simple, undereducated woman, had sprung to her husband's defense, reiterating the criticism of Cassie's clothes, makeup, smoking, saying that Cassie was a troublemaker, not one of them at all, and she had caused the incident.

"She's a floozy, a harlot! She is no better than she should be, and she bewitched you in London!" she had screamed at him.

"Bewitched me? Don't be so stupid!" Zack had finally flung back, enraged, "I married Cassie to suit *myself*, not to please you, or Penny. I love her! That should be enough for you or anyone else in the family. Everything here is new to her, but you girls haven't given her a chance from day one! You don't know what she's had to live through in London, what all those poor people in Europe all have had to live through these past years! Instead of being spiteful and critical of her, you could have helped her. Where is your pity?"

His dander up, he roared at her, "It's *your* husband you should be concerned about! Give him what he needs at home so he doesn't have to go looking elsewhere, wrecking other people's happiness!" It had been a miserable and bitter conversation.

Cutting into his heart like a knife, it was exacerbated some time later when his younger and favorite sister Penny had taken him to one side. Firmly she had warned him make sure that Cassie stayed away from Chuck, too, adding that she didn't think it in their best interests to stay in the mountain village, as Cassie would never be a part of the family. She had been very clear about what she thought. "That wife of yours is going to ruin all our relationships, Zack. Take her back to Edmonton where she might fit in. I don't know what you were thinking bringing her here. I've already warned Chuck what will happen if he even contemplates canoodling with her."

Zack had been shocked. "Chuck? I haven't seen any sign of anything between them. I know he teases her, but then he teases all the women, young and old. Anyway, Cassie now seems to be doing her best to stay away from everyone, since she feels so unwelcome here! Thanks for that!" he had retorted.

But Penny would not be placated; although she did not mention seeing Chuck and Cassie come back from the woods together one day. She had also bristled over Chuck taking time to photograph Cassie and Izzie, but she did not want to add fuel to the flames. In any case, Zack had been thrilled with the pictures. He thought it had been good to have some nice shots of his wife and daughter, something Cassie could send home to her mom. Penny could have said that Chuck was walking in the woods with Cassie, but in truth, that was all it was. The rest was down to her imagination.

Zack sighed, thinking back to those conversations, which were still raw in his mind. He, his mom and sisters, and their stepfather had all been so close until the war came along and changed everything.

His mom had died while he was away in Europe, under fire in Italy, which had really hurt. Maybe if she had still been alive, she would have helped his new wife, been kind to her, taken her under her wing. Why couldn't his sisters have helped Cassie like that instead of harassing her? Why couldn't his brothers-in-law have been a bit better behaved around her? And how was it that she had never learned in the past how to deal with men?

Deep in thought, Zack's reflections about the past were interrupted as Maria, his mother-in-law, came into the room carrying some letters that the postman had just delivered. She handed two envelopes toward him, "Here, Zack, a couple of letters from home for you. They might cheer you up."

It was entirely the wrong moment to do that. Incensed with the negative thoughts about his family, miserable because he couldn't find work, and homesick for his mountain home, Zack snatched the letters. He furiously tore them into bits and threw them into the wastebasket, saying tersely, "I don't need these. I don't want to hear from them, and have nothing to say in reply to them." With that he stormed out of the room.

Maria was taken aback by his words, shocked by his reaction. She had not seen him this angry before, even when Cassie nagged at him. He hardly raised his voice when they had words; although Maria knew from a comment Cassie had made that Zack could lose his temper, with terrifying results, on occasion. She had just never seen it.

Zack only knew that he truly did not have very much he wanted to tell his sisters. His writing skills were poor, anyway, as he had quit school after eighth grade. So he tended to get Cassie to write his letters for him. This lack of basic literacy was proving to be another barrier to gaining employment here. What if he did try to respond to Penny or Agatha? What would he tell them?

"Hey, girls, can't find a job! My wife is a turning into a nag! My English brother-in-law hates us, just like you and your husbands do! You were right: I should have stuck with Gwenny. At least you wouldn't have chased *her* out of Mountain Reaches, and I could have stayed in the home that I love."

Venting his rage on his sisters' letters by ripping them up calmed Zack, and his anger subsided, giving way to melancholy. No, he thought sadly, this war had ruined everything. True, he had won medals for bravery, but what good were medals? Employers didn't care about medals. His own family didn't care about his medals.

What had he fought for on the beaches of Italy?

Why had he lived though all that horror?

His own world was not one bit the better for it, and his future had been stolen from him. He had been transplanted to a country he never, ever, would have visited, and torn away from his family and friends and way of life…for what? To live in a land that didn't want him, with a woman he was beginning to think didn't want him either.

His future had never seemed so bleak. Even though he loved his children and was still in love with Cassie, now he didn't like her so well, and she had clearly cooled toward him, if she had ever loved him at all. He had few skills that were of value in this country. When he followed Cassie back here, he had hoped for a better future for them. Now those dreams had been dashed as he struggled to find a reasonable job that he liked. How could he explain all that to his sisters?

No, it was too late now. It was all better left unsaid. He felt it was better to consign all of them and that life to the past. He had nothing at all in common with them now, so Zack never wrote to them again. Later that day he quietly said to Maria, "Sorry about losing my temper, but I don't know what I would write to them. I have nothing much to say that they would want to hear. Better just to leave it."

Maria took that as a signal that he didn't want to hear from his family again. Thereafter, whenever those letters arrived from Canada, not wanting see him so sad, Maria returned them, writing, "Moved away" on the envelope. She liked her handsome son-in-law, with his dark good looks, and he was very helpful with repairs and such to her house. She didn't want him leaving and going back to Canada. She didn't want him taking her beloved Cassie away again, or her grandchildren now, either.

Eventually letters stopped coming, and Zack never mentioned returning to his homeland again. He had no one to go back to now.

Chapter Three
London, 1964

Zack

Zack stared at his wife; his stomach dropped. Cassie had found his hiding place and was moving toward him, brandishing the gun in her hand. Her face, still beautiful, although now marked with bitter lines around her mouth, was a mask of fury, and he was glad the weapon wasn't loaded.

"Careful," he said. "You don't know what you are doing with that."

Cassie gasped. "Why? Don't tell me it's *loaded!*" She looked in horror at the gun but continued to wave it about.

Zack shook his head. "No, it's not loaded, but it's never good to wave a gun about. Put it *down*," he said sternly.

Vehemently, Cassie shook her head. "The only place I'm putting this is into the hands of a policeman! What did you think you were doing? You *know* it is *illegal* for it to be here. You don't have any kind of license for it! Worse, you have it hidden here, and one of the children or one of their friends could have found it!"

Zack shook his head. "I had it well hidden out of their way," he responded testily.

"Well," Cassie said scathingly. "It wasn't that well hidden under the floorboards. I found it! I knew you were up to something when you shut yourself away late at night."

"You only found it because you were snooping and spying on me!" Zack barked back.

Cassie just looked at him, disgust written all over her face, as she pursed her lips. "What did you think you were playing at? Do you *want* to go to jail? Do you **want** to bring shame on me and your children?"

Zack stared at her, and he felt his temper begin to effervesce inside him. Usually he tried to keep it in check; in the past when it got out of control it had led to ugly scenes. He had struggled a lot to overcome it when he was younger. He thought he had conquered it at one time, had it under control, but then the stress of living in this country, which had been so unkind to him, Cassie's persistent nagging, and her occasional unfaithfulness in thoughts if not action, had started pushing those buttons again.

Now the fuse was really smoldering, and as he gazed at his wife, the unfairness of it all hit him. His eyes narrowed, and he finally exploded.

"*Why?*" he yelled at her. "*Why?* I'll tell you why: because of your incessant demands for us to become a part of the elite. Buy me this! Buy me that! Join the Masons, join this club, go to that one. It all costs *money* that we don't have! I *had* to find a way to make more money to live up to *your* expectations, and doing private work at home has been helping." His face was flushed now. "Want to go to jail? You know, *yes*, it would almost be preferable to living with you and the hell you and your spiteful attitude put us all through!" By now his voice had risen to a roar, and he started moving toward her, his hands clenched.

Cassie looked alarmed and took a step back. "Don't you *dare* lay a hand on me," she hissed.

The very fear in her eyes stopped Zack in his tracks. He knew that if he stayed in the room with her, he might well lose control and smack her. He didn't want to go down that road. It would diminish him too much as a man, and lower him in the eyes of his children. He made a choking sound in his throat, turned on his heel, grabbed his jacket, and stormed out.

Fearful for the consequences of the police tracking an illegal gun to her home, and a little afraid that Zack might still turn around and hurt her, Cassie picked up the box, put the gun and ammunition back into it, and slid it into a shopping bag. She ran to get her coat, tied her scarf over her head, and scurried out of the door.

Her feet flew down the pavement, and within five minutes, she was at the local police station. Somewhat out of breath, for a moment she dithered under the blue lamp overhead, but she knew she could not stop now. Determinedly she walked up the steps and through the large oaken doors. Hesitantly, she moved toward the desk sergeant, a big burly man with a moustache who didn't look too friendly.

He was taking down details about a lost dog from an elderly gentleman who seemed very upset about his missing pet. Finally the sergeant completed his business with the old man, and then it was her turn. He looked up at her and asked what she wanted. Cassie took a deep breath, lifted her bag onto the desk, and took a step back.

A little alarmed by her demeanor, the policeman carefully opened the bag and eased the box gently out of it, afraid it might be some kind of unexploded bomb or grenade left over from the war. Frightened parents were constantly bringing them in after their children found them when they played on the old bombsites that still had not been cleared up or built over.

Gingerly he opened the lid, heaving a sigh of relief when he saw the gun. Then he looked somberly at Cassie.

"Where did you get this, Madam?" he asked sternly.

Cassie explained the circumstances, stuttering a little as the impact of what she was doing swept over her. The desk sergeant took down all the details and asked some searching questions about Cassie, her children, and Zack's employer. After that he gave her a receipt for the gun and said that someone would come round to see her in the next day, after they had spoken with Zack's employer. In the meantime, when Zack came home, the sergeant said she should tell her husband to come into the police station to give himself up.

It was nearly two hours later when Cassie finally arrived back at their little rented home. She found both Jay and Isabella sitting glumly in the kitchen. Isabella looked like she had been crying, and she gazed dolefully at her mother.

"What's going on?" Cassie asked them, almost knowing what they were going to say.

"Dad's gone!" Jay said.

"Gone, gone where?" cried Cassie.

"We don't know. He was looking for something, and then he smashed his fist into the wall and said you had ruined him. He told us that he would have to go to jail if he stayed, so he packed a bag and left. We don't know where he has gone," said Isabella, tearfully. "*How* could *you*, Mum?"

Cassie sat down with a thump, one half of her relieved that her shell of a marriage might finally be over, the other half in fear about what they would do now. Her tiny income was not going to stretch to keep all of them. What had she done?

Immediately on the defensive, brimming with righteous indignation, she stormed angrily at Isabella, "*Me?* Oh, no, *not* me! I'm not the one who has broken the law! It's your perfect father that has done that. I was protecting the rest of us from the results of his stupidity!"

Within hours, in total keeping with her view of her life, the whole scenario had become the fault of Fate. Once again it was robbing her of her position, leaving her with nothing. Then it was the fault of the man she married; he was so worthless, so useless. He had brought all this down on them, and now everything in the world was against her again. Poor Cassie.

Jay, in his mid-teens and still pretty much subservient to his mother's attitude, stayed quiet, but he wondered how he would be able to stay at school and go on to college now that his father had left. Isabella, who adored her father, would not be pacified, and she pouted with her mother for days.

Two weeks later, when the rent came due, with no means to pay it or feed her children, Cassie moved back in with her mother and brother, taking Jay with her, and intending to take his sister with her too.

But Isabella exerted her independence. She was eighteen and had just won a place at university in the autumn to start on her path to becoming a teacher. So she moved in with friends who owned a pub, and worked in their bar to earn money for her keep, while she hoped her father had not disappeared from her life forever.

In fact, it was over a year before Zack did get back in touch with his family. First he found Isabella, and then he contacted Jay, and finally, Cassie, but he never again lived with his family. The irony for Zack was that, no matter what, Cassie was still the flame, and he was still the moth. Even though she was no longer the charming English beauty he had married, nor was he the shining, handsome soldier of yore, who had swept her off her feet, like it or not, he still was in love with her. In any case, he really did not have any other place to go.

Life with her mother and Sydney proved to be too challenging, so eventually Jay and Cassie moved to a cavernous flat in an old vicarage in Notting Hill Gate. Eventually, Cassie took her ailing mother there too, some years later, when she became too frail to care for herself.

After his reappearance, Zack rented a one-roomed bedsit nearby, where he played out a lonely existence until his early demise from a lung disease contracted at the mining job he had back in the village that Cassie had so much despised.

In the interim, Zack was gradually invited back to visit with his family on high days and holidays. In his latter years, he found some peace with Cassie by making himself useful helping her take care of Maria, for whom he more affection now than for his wife. Nevertheless, despite accepting his help, Cassie always regarded him with barely concealed contempt, and his only real solace was his interaction with Isabella, Jay, his daughter-in-law Stacey, and eventually his beloved little granddaughter Amy. It was short-lived, and Zack's end came many years before it should have.

His funeral was a sad affair, the only mourners, his two children, their spouses, and the troubled and embittered Cassie, who in the aftermath of the following years suffered agonies of guilt over the way she had treated him.

Zack, like many other men of his generation, had survived the battlefields, shone with his gallantry, winning medals for his bravery, but when the war came to an end he found it had destroyed his rosy, settled future. Eventually it felled another victim in its wake, carrying a brave soldier to an early, sad, and lonely death, in a faraway land that he could never call home.

Chapter Four

Edmonton, 1965

Chuck and Penny

Chuck Logan put his arm around his wife's shoulders. "Well, Penny, I think it's time for me to make that trek back home. I haven't been back there for over forty years, and I'd like to see it again before I die. I need to go and see my relatives and visit the places where I grew up. Perhaps we will be able to find Zack too."

Penny looked at him, still a wiry, lively man. She still adored him. He had been such a good husband, and a good father, but now both girls were married, in their own homes, and it was time to do something for themselves.

Over the years they had tried unsuccessfully to track Zack down. Letters to his last known address in London were always returned with, "Not known at this address," or, "Moved away," written across them. They had even resorted to asking one of Chuck's cousins from Lancashire to try to find him on a trip to London. He had visited the house and said all he found was a surly young man, who looked a little weird and said he didn't know anyone by Zack's name.

Chuck's brother had even tried calling people named Mackenzie in the London telephone book. Even though Zack Mackenzie wasn't listed, he had hopes of tracking down one of the children. He had no success so finally they had given up.

Now Chuck presented Penny with an opportunity to maybe try again.

It ended up being a family trip, as Penny wanted to take Mattie with her for company while Chuck was renewing his acquaintanceship with his family. She had always been very close to her elder daughter, and she wasn't sure she wanted to be parted from her for so long. She also thought that Mattie would enjoy it too. Sally was too engrossed with her new husband, concentrating on producing a baby, a feat never achieved under her own steam by her elder sister, and reveling too much in the limelight to want to join them.

The journey was planned, and the rest of the Logan clan flew to England to be wrapped up in the arms of Chuck's family, who were excited to see him after his long absence, and meet his wife and daughter. He had kept in touch with them over the years: photos and letters had been exchanged. He was not a stranger to them, and the Canadian Logans were well received in the Lancashire hills.

Then came the trip to London, to seek out Zack. Not one to give up, Penny insisted on going back to the house that had been given as Zack and Cassie's first address in England nearly twenty years earlier. Chuck claimed tiredness, rare for him, and let them go on their quest without him, citing the amount of walking that would be required.

Eventually, Mattie and Penny found the street they were looking for: one of many similar roads with rows and rows of the same design of small, brick built houses. Most now looked a little run-down; they were older homes built with not a lot of style, but still presentable with neat front gardens. As they walked down the road, clearly unfamiliar with their surroundings, net curtains twitched all the way, silent witnesses viewing their progress.

Maria watched from her own net covered windows as she spotted the strangers walking toward her home. She pulled the nets back a smidgeon to see them more clearly, and then she felt shock as they got closer. The older woman was almost the living image of Zack, and she knew right then that Nemeses had arrived at her doorstep. She stood wringing her hands, alone in the house, as her mind ran through various scenarios.

Sydney was out, working at his job in the library of the British Museum, which suited his surly, antisocial personality. He loved to be among the old, dusty tomes and not having to interact with people, who mocked his odd quirks. Now Maria knew she would have to face these visitors alone. She couldn't avoid them, as she was sure they had seen her curtains move. She heard footsteps coming up the path, and then the doorbell rang. She trembled when she heard the knock, and her trepidation enhanced her appearance as a frail, shaky old lady as she pulled the door open to speak to the visitors.

In a familiar Canadian twang, the younger woman asked, "I wonder if you could help us? We are trying to find my uncle."

"Of course, my dear," Maria replied in a shaking voice. "How can I help?"

"We think he lived here in 1948 or 1949. His name is Zack Mackenzie," said Mattie, as Penny looked anxiously at Maria.

Maria feigned uncertainty, looked as if she was thinking, and then said, "I'm sorry, I don't know that name at all. It must have been before I lived here," she lied. "You know, a lot of people were put in temporary housing here after the war until they were able to rebuild the bombed areas. Maybe he was here then."

"Would anyone else on this street know, do you think?" Mattie countered.

"Oh, I shouldn't think so, dear. The neighbors on both sides have been here even less time than I have," replied Maria. Well, that was the truth, at least. She had lived on this street the longest of anyone.

Anxiously, Penny spoke up. "We've come a very long way. I lost touch with my brother, and we were so hoping to find him again." She was not entirely convinced by Maria.

"Oh, my dear, if I knew who he was and could help you, I would tell you," said Maria. "But I have no idea who he is or where you would find him."

At that point in time it was the absolute truth. Cassie had not heard from Zack since he ran off the year before, so her reply had the ring of sincerity, which convinced Penny.

"I am sorry I can't help you, and I hope you are able to find him. Good-bye." And with that, Maria shut the door on Zack's family and leaned against it for a moment with relief.

Maria never told Zack that she had met some of his family or that his sister had come to look for him. They were all too far in the past. And after all, hadn't he said quite clearly that he wanted nothing more to do with his family ever again? He had, hadn't he?

And she put the whole thing out of her mind, not even mentioning it to Sydney.

Chapter Five

Lancashire, 1965

Chuck Logan had encouraged his wife and daughter to make their trek to London seeking her brother, not only because he felt her mind would not be settled unless she did, but also to give him a day or so to himself for his own quest.

In all the years they had been married, Chuck had kept a secret from his wife and children, and his English family did not speak of it either, since only a few were aware of the circumstances.

Chuck had been married in the UK before he had left for Canada, his young wife and child falling victims to the flu epidemic that had swept across Europe in the aftermath of World War I. Although his wife had died, his young son had recovered but had been left weak and needing more care than Chuck could give. The coal-dust-filled air in his part of Lancashire had not been good for the boy either. With few choices left to him, Chuck had sent the baby to some Logan cousins who lived by the coast. With little money and no transportation, Chuck had been unable to visit his son, intending to try to make the trek in the summer, but a few months later, before he was able to leave, his cousins wrote to tell him that his son had died.

Devastated that he had lost all that he loved, Chuck escaped to Canada soon after with some other young men seeking to leave behind the horrors they had endured in the trenches of the fields of France and the losses from the flu epidemic. Like them, Chuck decided to search for his fortune in Canada, and so in May 1920, he embarked with others on the ship Megantic and sailed across the Atlantic, arriving a week later in Quebec.

From there he embarked on a trek across Canada, eventually discovering work in the coalmines of Alberta. Over a decade later, Chuck met and married Penny Mackenzie, giving him an opportunity for renewed happiness, and a positive future.

It had come as a shock to him many years later to learn from a relative back in England that his son had not died, as the cousins had told him. They had wanted to keep the boy. They were afraid that Chuck would take his son back with him after his summer visit, so they had told him a lie. But now they had both died, and another relative had told Chuck the truth; although they still had not told his son. Chuck found himself in a terrible position, but in the end decided to take no action. What could be gained by giving his son pain about the deception by the only people he had known as his parents all his life? Nevertheless, Chuck hoped he would be able to see the young man who bore his name maybe once before he died.

In part, that had prompted his wish to return home. He had not contacted his son, who had no idea that his real father was alive. He learned that his son was married and apparently doing well, but while Chuck did want to see him, he also did not want to go over old ground with Penny. It had nothing to do with his life with her or his daughters, and would disrupt his son's life. It was from another time, in another world.

Penny and Mattie trip to London gave Chuck the opportunity to try and see his son, Charles Logan. The boy had done well for himself and ran a small insurance agency in a nearby town, and Chuck drove over there in a borrowed car. On the pretext of needing cover for some items he was shipping back to Canada, Chuck walked into the agency, casting a look around.

As he entered, a man walked out of a small, enclosed office and greeted him with a smile. Chuck thought his heart would stop. It was like looking in a mirror and seeing his younger self. He was glad that over the years age had altered him facially, and he was now a little bent, but even so the younger man gave him a sharp glance. Chuck explained that he was visiting from Canada and what he wanted. That started a long conversation with the younger man, who noted that he thought he had some relatives in Canada, and he invited Chuck into his office.

Chuck spent an enjoyable half hour speaking with his son, using life comparisons to find out about Charles's life. He was married with a son and a daughter, who now had children of their own.

The younger man had briefly touched on his birth parents and how he had been adopted when they died. Gee, mused Chuck, I wonder what would happen if I told him that his father was not his father, and that I am his children's grandfather? In the end, though, he decided that his secret was best kept to himself. It would be too disruptive to both families to try to establish any kind of relationship.

Best not to destroy his image of himself, however wrong the original circumstances, thought Chuck. But he was satisfied. His Logan name would not die out, his son and his grandson would carry it on, and he left a happier man, without actually purchasing any insurance.

When Penny and Mattie returned, sharing their own lack of success, he was grateful that his quest had not faced a similar disappointment. If they had been successful, he might have shared his story with Penny, but now did not seem the time…maybe later. Anyway, he had Mattie and Sally. He had enjoyed raising them, loved them to pieces, and would not want to risk family upsets by adding in a brother they knew nothing about.

Soon he would have a Canadian grandchild, and another generation to carry on; even if they would not bear his last name, they carried his blood.

He was content.

Chapter Six

Edmunston, 1966

Ted

Ted thought she was the most perfect thing he had ever seen. The day-old Lauren smiled up at him, gurgling happily as she wrapped her tiny hand around his work-roughened finger, and he was lost.

How could *he* have made something so beautiful? How could he be responsible for producing this tiny, wonderful, angel? He knew her eyes could hardly see him, but she seemed to be gazing just at him, and a pure love that he never knew existed exploded inside of him. She was *his*, all his. His own child, *his*. She belonged to him. He was not alone any more, he would never be alone with her in his life.

In her perfect baby face, he could already tell that she had his mother's smile: the smile that he had missed so much after she died. Now gazing at his baby daughter, it was almost as if she had come back to him in Lauren, and he wished his father had survived long enough to see his granddaughter. Now at last he truly had a family, one that was his, that could not be taken away from him, as death had done so in the past.

As Lauren grew older, he was amazed every day at the depth of his love for her. She aroused such protective feelings inside him that he would never have believed possible. He so adored her that at times it scared him, particularly as she grew to womanhood and he had to be careful not to step over the boundaries of a loving parent.

It was not that she aroused any sexual feelings inside him, just that he wanted to be near her, to watch her grow and be loved by her. Later, after Corinne came along, he loved her too. Physically she more closely resembled her other grandmother, bearing that pioneer stance, with her stocky body, and a little native coloring that she had inherited too; nonetheless, she was very lovable and had the sweeter personality. At times he was afraid that she felt she had a secondary position in his life, even though he tried hard to treat her the same. But Lauren was his adored golden child. So beautiful, she was his love, his over-abiding reason for living, until Stacey arrived, bringing confusion within him, and conflict into his soul.

Too late he realized that Fate had been preparing him for the moment when Lauren would become an adult and go her own way, and was offering him the soul mate that he still sought. By the time he understood, he had done so much damage, created so much unhappiness, that he was left with nothing but the ashes of the destruction he had caused all around him and a deep crater inside his heart.

In the interim, his behavior had driven Lauren out into her future sooner than might otherwise have happened, as she sought to escape the unhappy place her childhood home had become. It had also changed her perception of him, and although over the years they got back to closeness again, especially after her children were born, Stacey's shadow fell across them, across their entire world, as reminders of her surfaced when they were least expected.

CHAPTER SEVEN

ECHOES, 1977

SALLY

It was just another day, how could she know that it would change her life forever? That morning Sally had been in town and picked up the mail and the papers, including the most recent *Edmonton Journal*. After making herself a quick lunch, Sally was sipping a cup of coffee at the kitchen table as she idly flipped through the newspapers. She'd take them across to her mom's house when she'd woken up from her afternoon nap.

As she scanned down the obituaries page, the name Mackenzie caught her eye. It was her mom's maiden name, and she wondered if the deceased was someone that they knew. She read the short obituary.

"Zack Mackenzie, born June 1914 in Edmonton, Alberta, died July 1977 in London, England. Zack leaves behind his widow, Cassie, daughter Isabella and her husband Anton, son Jay and his wife Stacey, one granddaughter Amy, and unknown relatives in Canada. Further

information can be obtained by writing to Jay Mackenzie at the following address..."

Sally stared at the notice, and then reached for the phone.

"Mattie?" she said into the handset. "Mattie, there's a notice in the *Journal* today, in the obituaries. Listen..." Sally read out the notice to her sister and then added, "Is this him?"

"Oh, my," Mattie said slowly. "Oh, my, this will kill Mom! All the details sound right. What should we do? You haven't told Mom yet?"

"No, she's still sleeping, and I don't really want to be the one to do that," replied Sally.

"OK, let's think about this. We need more information. Can you give me the address in the notice? I'll start a letter right now to...what was his name... Jay?" replied Mattie. "Call me from Mom's when you take the paper over to her, and we'll talk to her together. I'll tell her I'm already responding to find out more info."

And so it began: the echoes of the past whispering softly at their windows.

CHAPTER EIGHT

SCOTLAND, 1977

STACEY

Three-year-old Amy raced to the door as she heard the postman plop the mail through the letter box. She gathered them up and ran beaming into the kitchen, bringing them to me, her blond curls dancing, her dark-blue eyes sparkling.

"Letters!" she said triumphantly as they began fluttering to the floor.

I dried my hands quickly and bent down to scoop them up, "Careful, Amy." I laughed with her, and then my heart stopped. Among the bills and circulars was one letter with an unfamiliar stamp, a maple leaf prominent; it was from Canada.

"Can I speak to Jay, please?" I said into the phone minutes later.

"Och, yes, Stacey. Hold on. I'll find him," said his company's receptionist, Jeannie, who had become a good friend over the three years we had spent in Glasgow.

A few minutes later, Jay's voice came down the line. "Yea, Stacey, what's up?"

"Jay, there is a letter here from Canada. Do you want me to open it, or wait until you come home tonight?" I said, my voice shaking with anticipation.

Jay was silent, and just as I was wondering if he would answer, he said, his voice choked, "On this occasion, I think I'll come home for lunch. Thanks, Stacey, I'll leave here shortly."

A little after noon, his car pulled up outside, and he strode into the house, much to Amy's amazement. "Daddy!" she cried, her eyes alight with happiness. Jay scooped her up, gave her a quick peck on the cheek, and set her down again, his eyes on my face.

I stood in the doorway, holding the letter out to him. His hands trembled slightly as he slid his finger inside the flap and opened it. Inside was a handwritten letter, two pages long.

Dear Jay,

My name is Mattie, and I am writing on behalf of my mother, Penny Logan. We think that your late father was her brother and my uncle, but would appreciate confirmation of some details to be sure.

Her brother, Zack Mackenzie, was born in Edmonton, joined the Canadian forces, and fought in Europe during the war. He was based in England, and while he was there he met and married Cassie Connor. A year after the war ended, he and Cassie had a little girl, Izzie, who was named for my grandmother. In 1947, they came to Alberta, to the small town of Mountain Reaches, where my mother Penny and her husband Chuck, and my Aunt Agatha and her husband Haley lived.

They stayed for nearly a year before moving back to Edmonton where their son, Jay, was born in early 1948. Shortly after that, they moved back to England, but within a couple of years, Mom lost touch with him.

Mom and some other family members visited Britain in the mid-1960s, and they did try to find Uncle Zack, but had no success at all.

If you are the same Jay, and this story of our family matches yours, then you and I are first cousins, and my mother is your aunt. I also have a sister Sally, and we both remember our uncle and his wife from when we were quite young. I would have been about nine or so.

My mother loved and missed her brother very much, and for her sake we would appreciate if you could confirm the above and let us know how your father died, and also a bit more about you and your family.

Sincerely

Mattie Finkelbender

Jay leaned back against the sofa, shock registering in his face. "I have cousins and aunts," he commented, and a tear rolled out of the corner of his eye. I threw my arms around him, hugging him and crying too, "Oh, Jay, how sad for them. What a pity Zack never knew that they missed him. Poor Zack."

That evening, after calling Isabella and sharing the news with her, we wrote back to Jay's Canadian relatives, setting in motion the destruction of our way of life, our marriage, and our lives…

Chapter Nine

England, 1980

Stacey

The summer of 1980 is the last time I can ever remember feeling truly happy, content, and loved. I was secure in my life, sure of my future. How could I have known that within eighteen short months I would have lost everything: home, husband, two more babies, and be stranded almost penniless in a foreign country? I would have laughed at the idea, because apart from that first lost baby, my life was so close to ideal, who would have ever thought that would change?

It was a joyful summer. I loved my husband. I loved my daughter, my parents, and being part of a big, affectionate family. I loved sharing my life with all of them and they loved me too, didn't they? I never questioned that. They all loved me too, didn't they? We were a close-knit family, all friends, all raised to look for the best in people, to treat others politely, with respect, to be kind.

I adored being married and having someone to cuddle up to at night, to nestle with in bed on a Sunday morning as we drank our tea, nibbled on cookies, and canoodled before Amy's appearance turned it into family happy hour. Later most Sundays, while I cooked lunch, it was "Jay and Amy" time. They took our silver whippet, Candy, for walks in the nearby woods, building their happy relationship. Amy so idolized her father, but that adoration nearly ended up destroying her when Jay later betrayed her love by deciding that divorce applied to his relationship with his daughter as well as his ex-wife. Then he dispensed with his wife, in concert with his whole family, on both sides of the Atlantic, they had ostracized Amy too, their inbred cruelty surfacing, callous and uncaring, even toward an innocent child.

But at that time, I was content with the little house we had. We had put in a lot of work to make it cozy. It was a typical small British semi-detached house in a historic country town on the edge of the Cotswolds. The whole area was steeped in history. We even had our own, supposedly haunted, historic castle in the town, which once had housed Elizabeth the First. It was all so British, and as a lover of historical novels, I reveled in living there with Amy, our three cats, and our dog.

Jay and I had moved from Scotland three years before, and had accomplished a great deal with our home renovations. We had installed a new bathroom; updated the kitchen fixtures, and redecorated almost every room in the house. Jay put in the heavy work on the plumbing and such, with me doing everything else. My father had taught me to paint and wallpaper, and my mother had taught me to sew and knit. I loved to make sweaters and clothes for Jay and Amy, to sew curtains and cushions for our home, to fix and renovate old furniture, and to cook, especially to cook! I was truly little "Suzy-homemaker."

We held endless dinner parties and Sunday lunches for friends and family, and they flocked to our home, knowing I would ensure they went home well-fed. They always asked for my recipes as they left. All of that and taking care of Amy, plus doing most of the gardening, kept me busy morning through night.

I was sometimes tired, but always happy, always cheerful, always ready to help a friend or neighbor, especially any passing "lame duck." I just loved everyone, with the possible exception of my mother-in-law Cassie and her snooty daughter Isabella, although I tried always to be polite to them, but I did love my lovely, cuddly father-in-law Zack. We always made him welcome in our home, as Jay tried to repair the damage done by the past on their relationship. He always seemed such a sad sack that we included him in holiday celebrations with my family too, we wanted to make him feel wanted. He truly was a part of us. We loved having him around and we missed him every day after he died.

Jay's job provided our income, as once Amy was born I became a stay-at-home mother. That was what women still did back then, and it was unremarkable. Such a change from today when women almost have to apologize for being staying at home mothers who care for their *own* children. Jay had worked his way up over the previous decade from being a clerk in the office of an auto parts company to a minor managerial job. Now he looked set to be moved to another branch as a manager in his own right within a couple of years. His promotions meant that we had already moved to two different cities since our marriage, as each was located in a different part of the country. The next promotion would probably mean another move too.

The pay still wasn't wonderful, but that next move up would provide greater compensation, so for the most part, Jay was content. He was happy to return at night to a home-cooked meal and his little loving family, with a minimum of drama, which gave him a greater peace and stability than he had ever known growing up.

Overall, we were satisfied with our lifestyle, despite like most young families, struggling financially. Neither of us had ever lived in a home with much money, but it had taught me thrift, so I was efficient at managing our income. Growing up, under my mother's tuition, I had become a good housekeeper. In my mind, Jay and I were settled, and I expected that our life together and our relationship with each other would remain this way forever.

How *foolish* to be so trusting of life!

How naïve to take it all for granted!

For that is just the point when Fate steps in with a smirk and says, "Nah, not going to happen!" and sends in the "Gods of Chaos" to wreak havoc and destroy everything you hold dear!

Despite our successes though, there had been sorrows too over the past few years. With Jay's father and grandmother both dying so close together, they left issues we were previously unaware of in their wake.

However, in this year of 1980, we were treasuring the fact that after we had traced Jay's paternal family in Canada after Zack's death, but we had built a burgeoning, friendly, long-distance relationship with them. They seemed to be so different from Cassie's dysfunctional relatives in Britain: so normal!

As a result of our growing relationship, after three years of corresponding with Jay's aunt and cousins, this summer we were finally going to Canada to meet them person. We felt we had grown close to them during that time, particularly Sally and Aunt Penny, or as close as letter writing and exchanged taped conversations would allow us to be. We liked them. Now Jay was super excited, and like me looking forward to finally meeting them.

That we felt this warm toward them was not a surprise to me. I had a tendency to like everyone. As a result, I was so sure I would like them all as much in person as I did on paper. Jay laughed. He said I was like a friendly, happy puppy with people, always ready to love them, warming to them, trusting them to like me back, and expecting that they would treat me the way I would treat them. Stupid Stacey! In total trust mode!

The fly in the ointment came early in the year, when I found out I was pregnant right after we had booked our flights to Canada. This pregnancy came hard on the heels of an ectopic pregnancy the year before (another one of our recent sorrows), and an operation to relieve it. My doctor was apprehensive about the new pregnancy. It was too soon, he thought, given my age (I was well over thirty). I had been so sick during my first pregnancy, and he was concerned for my health in the coming months.

Jay was beside himself; my due date meant that I would be beyond the number of months into my pregnancy that airlines allowed women to fly. Plus, Jay said, it would be no fun for me to be pregnant and on vacation (or for him either, I think was in his mind).

Perhaps we could delay our trip for another year, I suggested.

"No, we'd lose money on our plane tickets now, and then we'd have to pay for a baby's fare then too, and it would be even more inconvenient. Likely we'd never get there at all," had been Jay's response, his disappointment evident.

He had a strong ally in my doctor, and between them they convinced me to let this baby go, in the interests of my health and in truth as much to pacify Jay, which the doctor picked up on quickly. He didn't want to see a failed marriage.

"Give your body more time to recover before you try to carry another child. Take the summer to recover, build up your strength, and you will be more ready then," said the doctor.

"We can try for another baby in the autumn when we get back," said Jay, never knowing what was to come, and anyway not enthralled with the idea of another child. "I promise," he added. But, more than once since Amy had been born, he had commented that she was enough for him and he wasn't bothered about having another child. At the time I felt he was kind of relieved, although he wouldn't say so, and in the end it was a promise he was destined not to keep.

So, I gave in, caught up in Jay's excitement and not giving myself time to think about the impact on my physical or mental health. It hurt, but I kept my sense of loss to myself, instead focusing on preparing for the summer trip.

It was all going to be so exciting, meeting these new relatives. It would all be so wonderful!

It was all so incredibly naïve.

Chapter Ten

Canada, 1980. Be Careful What You Wish For

Stacey

If 1980 was truly the last happy summer for me, likely that was also true for Jay, Sally, Lauren, Corinne, Amy, and especially Ted. After the euphoric summer of 1980 and all the promise the future seemed to hold, by the end of the following summer, flickering flames of passion had erupted so unexpectedly that they turned all our lives into the fires of hell, charring our hopes and burning up everything we had treasured. There were some survivors who moved on, callously ignoring their part in the damage that surrounded them, but others could not - helpless victims of circumstances beyond their control.

One tiny life was snuffed out almost before it had even begun, begetting untold, never-ending grief. Later another would depart from life way before his time, as repercussions echoed across the decades, mirroring the past: an ironic counterpoint to the death in 1977 that in effect started the whole saga, ending with the demise of a second Mackenzie generation.

In time, repressed guilt and stress caught up with the instigators who had moved on, disregarding their part in the disaster they helped to create. But Karma is relentlessly awesome to watch in action. After they had abrogated all responsibility, keeping secret their roles as they completely denied any culpability, finally Fate caught up with them too, as the first tragic result of their culpability came back to haunt them.

For decades they had remained doggedly oblivious to anyone else's hurt or pain, exhibiting righteous indignation about how they were taken in by relatives, whilst forgetting that Fate knows the truth and is unforgiving. When it finally caught up with them, the pull of the past and inner guilt diminished their capacity to fight off diseases, snuffing out their lives too soon also, their own actions contributing to their own passage from this world.

A quarter of a century later, almost defiantly, they would publicly claim to have enjoyed years of happy memories, daring contradiction.

If so, then I am glad that Ted made that possible for his children, for his family. He was my love, my soul mate. Why would I not have wanted him, or them, to enjoy a happy life?

I'm glad that Ted found some peace, made life enjoyable for those around him, for it would be too sad to think that even more lives were scarred by those events from the past, that even more sorrow resulted.

But it was naïve of them to assume that his memory had been suppressed completely, that both our feelings had died, or that a conscience can stay unassailed. Memories regurgitate when you least expect them to, and at the end of life, they become something you must deal with as you look back. That Ted's soul sought me out so quickly after his death seems to indicate that after all those years, I was still a part of him that he could not let go.

When faced with undeniable consequences to those actions, the conscience finds ways to remind you. If you turn your back on what your heart desires, a void remains, regardless of the happy experiences that ensuing years hold. A constant sense of loss stays beneath the surface that cannot be explained and is not erased.

Claim, as they might, that there were years of happy memories, beneath that façade for two of their number, guilt for the anguish they caused, bitterness for decisions that were made, regret for their own actions must have surfaced from time to time. They were not monsters, were intrinsically nice people, who like me, made bad choices. Nice people have consciences, and consciences will not be denied when finally faced with consequences.

Subsequently was not that public bravado merely a performance to distract people from the truth? For nearly a decade, the drama played out, leaving bitterness, anger, and guilt that were too deeply ingrained to be easily dismissed, in the end. How bitter a pill to have to face that maybe, for three decades, a lie was being lived, no matter what public face was put on it. A fiction continually proclaimed to the world: we are as we were, everything is good, nothing has changed. When in effect, everything had.

But despite any repercussions in Ted's household, it was Jay and his little family who bore the brunt of this disaster. Caught up in the past's need for revenge, we experienced the most devastating consequences, helplessly watching as our once-rosy future shattered into a million pieces, closely mirroring the events of the past.

Our happy, loving family was gone, wrecked by secrets and deceit, when honesty could have salvaged it. Zack's family continued on their destructive path, which had originated in the 1940s in the mountains of Alberta.

We became the victims of a betrayal we knew nothing about until death opened all doors.

CHAPTER ELEVEN

CANADA, JOURNEY FROM HAPPINESS, 1980

STACEY

On that first visit to Canada, the brightness of the future seemed all sweetness, all promise, and all adventure as Jay, Amy, and I traveled to meet his father's family. We went blindly and trustingly forward, stumbling into the nightmare that our lives would become. Unaware that what would be promised to us would be undeliverable. Stupidly, we based our decisions entirely upon one enjoyable summer in Canada, which bore not even one glimmering, shimmering hint of the reality we would eventually face. Overwhelmed and starry-eyed, we experienced a month filled to abundance with affection and thrills, with discovery and pledges that would eventually be buried underfoot within the shifting sands of time.

The affection and thrills came for Jay, who had found himself a family to whom he could finally feel a real connection. They were his own father's kin and seemed in person to be what they were on paper: a happy, friendly, ordinary family just like our own (well, just like mine, at least). Not once did we question how, if the family had been so close-knit, how had they managed to lose touch with an apparently beloved member? When the question was raised, the blame was cast on Cassie and her mother.

Jay reveled in all the attention being paid to him, all the expressions of affection. It opened up a happy avenue, leading to the belief that he did have relatives he could be proud of, ordinary, friendly people with no odd quirks, no unkindness, no maliciousness. He was welcomed with love, their link to his father giving him the roots he sought and a perspective on his life he had not previously seen. He was overwhelmed by the intensity of that welcome and took it at face value.

We were sublimely unaware of issues simmering below the surface, of the need for vengeance against his mother beating in some breasts. Our whole visit was steeped in the excitement Zack's family expressed in reuniting with the son of their beloved long-lost brother, to whom Jay bore an uncannily close physical resemblance.

The discovery of that month came from finding a country so full of beauty and splendor that it took our breath away, as we toured the two westernmost Canadian provinces. We were completely overawed by the size and diversity of this land: the towering mountains, the wide-open skies, the winding rivers, forests, and plains during the downward drive to the glistening, silvery-blue seas of the Pacific as it kissed the western Canadian coastline. In effect we were seeing Zack's Eden.

We totally fell in love with a country that was full of wealth and variety, ease of living, and abundance of seemingly everything, in effect, a paradise.

The promise? That came from these newly discovered paternal relatives who were so happy to finally have Jay be a part of their family after the decades of ignorance about his existence. Enthralled by his physical likeness to his deceased dad, they urged Jay on, saying that he would have been so much better off if he had been raised in his homeland. He was still young enough, and he could move back to the land of his birth. Why didn't he play catch-up now?

We received endless assurances that they would help us settle, help build a better future for Amy, stressing that Jay would finally be where he belonged, living within the portals of his father's family, who welcomed him so joyously—seeing in him a reincarnation of Zack. What could be wrong with that?

They had loved his father, so they said, had missed him so much when he left, regretted losing touch. All we saw was that they were overjoyed to welcome Zack's son, to hear about Isabella, and wanted to show him the best of his homeland. Aunt Penny, particularly, was very taken with Jay; for her it was if Zack had come back to life, the way he was when she last saw him. Within that image, they also imbued Jay with all his father's personality and attributes, which he simply did not have. Penny, overwhelmed by the outer veneer she saw that first summer, did not perceive that Jay was not his father at all.

In reality Zack and Jay shared few characteristics. Zack had been very mechanically minded, simply educated, and practical, while Jay was an aesthetic who could have gone on to do his A-Levels, and who should have majored in art or literature, and who hated anything practical, hence my home décor talents coming to the fore. He was always a most reluctant do-it-yourselfer, not handy at all, really.

Not seeing this, Penny and Sally filled his head with visions of what his past should have been and what his future could be, with Ted echoing their enthusiasm. They made many promises based on our visit with them, without any thought as to whether that was right for Jay, or for his little family, and whether they could or would fulfill the undertakings they gave so freely.

Jay was no better. Completely swept off his feet by such a warm and openly loving welcome, in sharp contrast to the coldness and rigid formality of Cassie's family, Jay saw only their relaxed lifestyle and easy ways. His envy gene kicked in, and he coveted their nice homes and big cars and trucks. He was wholly taken in as they convinced him that this could have been his way of life too if his mother had not fled back to England. But, they said, it was still within his grasp, if he moved back to Canada now while he was still young enough to get a new start.

He was an easy target for their blandishments. He wanted to have it all, to be a part of it all. More than anything, he desired the chance to learn more about his father and have a relationship with these warm kinfolk that he had just discovered. His roots were calling him, and so he made the reasoning fit.

We would all have that better life by immigrating to be near to these nice people, wouldn't we? It would make up for not being a part of their lives as he had grown up, wouldn't it? He had missed all those opportunities to be a part of a big, happy family, and now he could experience all the things he could have had if he had lived in this land with his father.

Everyone would be happy. Penny would have her brother back in the persona of his son, and he was persuaded that it was all what he really wanted. The way they all laid it out, it sounded so perfect, and I fell for it too. In truth, how could one resist such a warm welcome, such kind words and such enthusiasm? It was contagious.

It would be fine. I so much liked Sally and her daughters. We enjoyed each other's company, and she went out of her way to make us comfortable. I felt not a frisson of apprehension about any of them. I found Ted easy to get along with too taking too little notice of the fact that he spent more time with me than he did with Jay. His wife and mother-in-law were monopolizing Jay's time, wanting so much information about Zack and the previous three decades. It was natural that they should. I'd heard it all before, so in the meantime I was happy to sit and listen to Ted and share details of our lives with him, learn more about Canada. He was friendly, funny, and charming, and seemed so nice. He was, wasn't he? I had no doubt.

My strong liking for the old lady was tinged with pity for her, as I saw her sadness over losing her brother twice: first when he fled to England, and the impact on her now, after learning of his death and knowing she could never see him again. Stacey's "lame-duck" mode on high alert again!

Aunt Penny and Sally had tut-tutted endlessly over tales of Jay and Isabella's youth, which really had been pretty awful. He had cried recounting it to me when we were first together, so I understood how it impacted them. I didn't see at the time that

Aunt Penny et al, seemed much more interested in Jay than Isabella, I knew they had been corresponding with her, but perhaps they had understood her kinship in spirit to her much-despised mother. In any case, their relationship was not quite so warm, until much later in the relationship. Then they visited England, tried to justify their actions to her, and destroyed my name.

But in those first days, they listened sympathetically as Jay shared how he and his family were never able to own their own home and his tales of Zack and Cassie moving from one rental home to another, with he and Isabella in tow. They were genuinely shocked to learn of the vicious fights with Cassie's brother that had made it impossible to share her mother's home for any length of time. It also hit them hard when Jay told them of Zack's challenges as an immigrant, scrabbling for jobs, always short of money. Ironic that the same scenario would play out after they lured Jay to Canada.

"I wish we had known how his life would be when he left," Penny had said in a choking voice, tears in her eyes. "Maybe we should have tried harder to make things work when he came home from the war with Cassie, not isolated her so much. We didn't understand her or take the time to find out what she had been through in London during the war years. We could have been kinder to her. It might have changed things; that's what Chuck said several years later."

But her lips had tightened and she had grimaced as she mentioned her husband's name. So was there something between Chuck and Cassie too? If Penny's husband Chuck had also been enthralled with Cassie, it would explain a lot.

Cassie was really beautiful when she was young and would have made other women jealous, especially plain, unsophisticated countrywomen in a back woods mining town. We had pretty much guessed at her problems with Haley from a couple of hints she had dropped, but she had never even mentioned Chuck until we showed her our vacation snaps. Some comments that Cassie made after we came home showed that she had more than a passing interest in Chuck, so was it only her interaction with Haley that had caused their flight to Edmonton? She had seemed almost sad when she heard that he had died, said it was a shame, and had not asked after anyone else after that.

With barely suppressed anger, Sally and Penny had listened as Jay recounted the way Cassie had pressured Zack to pursue her dream of moving into the more elite circles, where she thought she really belonged. Although they were impressed to learn that Zack at one time had actually been accepted as a Mason, they saw that it put more pressure on him both financially and socially. They recognized what Cassie did not. Zack had been a simple country lad, short on education, and she took him way out of his depth, leading their family to a life of penury as he struggled to meet her demands.

For the Logans and Zienkos, the Mackenzies' comparatively impoverished years in Britain contrasted sharply to their own comfortable way of life. They had their nice homes, their modern vehicles, the plentiful vacations, the fun social life, and the expensive sports they and their daughters were involved in, all in sharp contrast to our daily struggles.

They expressed surprise that a short annual visit to the seaside, a trip or two to the local swimming pool, and occasionally visiting a stately home was about all we could afford. British wages were low by comparison, and the cost of living was much higher. We had very little disposable income left after all the bills were paid, apparently unlike people in Canada.

Ted asked about Jay's involvement in the stock market, which he followed closely, Jay had laughed. They hesitantly asked how much it had cost to come visit them and were shocked, especially when Jay owned up to putting it all on credit cards—live now, pay later, he had grinned in reply.

"Your life would have been so much better if your dad had stayed here with his own people. There was always work, and we all helped each other. I wish we could make it up to you. You're still young, why don't you move here now?" Penny and Sally encouraged.

"The jobs pay well, we have great schools, and there's lots of space—so much better for Amy."

The idea took root over the entire four weeks while we were there and played into Jay's belief that he deserved more out of life than he had got, fostered over the years by Cassie's point of view, and he listened avidly. Coupled with their naïve enticements, it prompted him to want to leave behind his English home, his mother and sister, without giving it any serious thought. Xanadu beckoned, and these kind people would live up to their word, wouldn't they? We did not doubt it.

Without even examining his qualifications, Ted and Sally said that Jay could easily get employment in their part of Alberta. There were lots of jobs for people who wanted to work, and we would fit right in. The whole scenario sounded so tantalizing to Jay, especially after the years of hardship he had endured growing up; he was easy to convince.

With barely a backward glance, he prepared to abandon the managerial position that he had worked so hard to achieve over the past ten years, and made the assumption that I would go along with his new plan. He was so besotted with the idea that he did not take the time to work it out. His British job held as much promise for his future as any proposed job in Canada, and he was already halfway up that ladder.

Within a few short years, he would have been a branch manager, with a much higher pay grade, taking him to the level of income he sought. But he just didn't see that. His progress was moving too slowly for him, and he wanted to be on a par with his wealthier cousins, especially now he had seen how the other half lived. The impact on his life following his parents' decision to leave Canada gave him an understanding of the future he and his father had lost because of Cassie's insistence on returning to postwar London. His anger toward his mother increased, and he coveted the life that should have been his, making an assumption that he could walk straight into the same kind of job immediately he arrived in Canada. We knew nothing of the hierarchy of business or the tenets of seniority that ruled at a certain level.

He swept me along with his enthusiasm, generated by all that he was seeing, so enthralled by his aunt and cousins. It was an exciting idea, and like Jay, it seemed to beckon to me too. Although I did have some reservations, in the end, Jay was my husband. Wherever he went, Amy and I must go too.

My mother's constant mantra of, "You go where your husband goes and are always home to cook him dinner," rang in my ears. It was how I had been raised. Had she had the gift of foresight, she might have rethought dinning that into my head over the years, but she was the one who taught me that women are camp followers. And, after all, I reasoned, airplanes flew back and forth regularly, and it wasn't like this was Australia, was it? It was just an eight-hour trip, once you got to the airport!

As Jay's fixation to live near his new family grew, he gave scant thought to the fact that it meant I would have to give up living close to mine. I really loved my family; our lives revolved around each other, and we spent a lot of time together. I wasn't sure I wanted to leave them, but I also had fallen in love with this beautiful country.

Chapter Twelve

1981 Into the Future

The possibilities, dangled in front of him over the weeks by Penny, Sally, and Mattie, completely blinded Jay to any real practicalities. His focus was on wanting the larger house, the big garage, a couple of vehicles, vacations, money in the bank, stock investments, the whole nine yards.

At the time, neither they, nor we, took the time to make the comparison that they were ten years older than us, and in ten years' time, if we stayed on track in Britain, our lives would likely be as comfortable. Within that future we would have been able to visit on vacations, and we could have avoided the upheaval, and the impending destruction, of our lives.

Although it was not just the improved lifestyle that tempted Jay; he was also partly driven by the feeling that he might get to understand his father better if he learned more about the country where he spent his early years, since they were such a mystery.

But in the end, it was mostly the two women (ably assisted by Ted) who kept up the chant about a better life, urging Jay to return to the land of his birth.

"Join us here. We will help you."

"Come back and enjoy a new future here. This is where you belong."

So flattering to Jay that he was so sought after. So nice for him to be made the center of attention by these warm, encouraging relatives, and it was such a pity that he hadn't grown up with them. He felt a sense of loss he found hard to understand and wanted to catch up.

The future offered was a wonderful fantasy, and might almost have become reality, but for that budding situation with Ted, who was subtly wooing me, so subtly in fact that I didn't even notice. The insinuations completely slipped past me because I was plump, plain, klutzy Stacey with the nice, handsome husband and sweet little girl. I had never been a target of amorous advances, except maybe from a couple of dirty old men at the office, so who would be interested in me? Anyway, I was still focused on the new baby that Jay had promised we would try for when we got home and the need to get stronger.

Hindsight is twenty-twenty, they say. I should have paid more attention to Ted's advances, for it was his reaction to me that meant our lives were doomed to disaster before our plane ever touched back down in England after our vacation ended.

But we had no crystal ball and couldn't see that, didn't know that. Those who knew did not share the information because they were intent on encouraging Jay to leave his home and Cassie, to hurt Cassie. Revenge!

We arrived home in Britain still basking in the love and affection we felt for Jay's new family, and which it seemed they felt for us too. Jay was just so happy to have met them in person, feeling that they more than lived up to expectations. They made him feel a part of something now. He was looking forward to going back to Alberta, settling with his father's kin, and planning a new future for us with them.

We were sublimely unaware of the event that happened on the eve of our departure, creating a complete sea change in Sally and Ted's relationship with irreversible life-altering results for us, bringing chaos and tragedy in their wake.

Jay and I knew nothing of the tensions in their home that grew exponentially during the ensuing year. It was not shared with us as we gaily raced headlong into doom. We did not know that Sally and Ted's focus shifted away from the promises and assurances given to us, making them unable or unwilling to live up to their stated goal of helping us to settle in this new land. Instead a mini-war grew between them as they sought to retrieve their own marriage from the battleground it had become.

Sally, caught up with her own challenges, kept silent, did nothing to forewarn us that their situation had changed, either before we started packing up our home or when Jay arrived. It was the root cause of the wanton destruction of my happy little family forever, leaving ashes, destruction, and death wherein nothing could be salvaged for us.

Cowardly, they took refuge in assigning blame to the newcomers, content to hang the responsibility for their annihilation of our lives elsewhere. Their support vanished into the four winds as they totally abandoned all the promises of support without a backward glance at the mayhem left in their wake. And they cut us off from all the avenues wherein help might have been available. We became totally persona non grata in the tight-knit erstwhile community from Mountain Reaches.

Ironically, their actions reflecting the distant past, wherein lay their original need for revenge that had been gnawing away since the 1940s. It was a primary motive for Aunt Penny. Her bitterness toward her sister-in-law never wavered, as she set in place her goal to separate Jay from his mother in order to hurt Cassie.

There was apparently no acceptance of the impact on innocent people involved. Did she never reflect on the harm done to Zack's beloved little granddaughter? Never feel any regrets that she had not used her many Coal-Branch contacts to seek assistance for Jay (whose father had been known to so many) when he first arrived?

Amy was an innocent child who had done them no harm at all. But she paid the highest price of all, losing her secure childhood and in time the father she had adored, as his inbred penchant for bitterness and spite, inherited from his mother, took him over.

Amy also was a part of the sacrifice made at Ted's altar to save himself and salvage his relationship with his own daughters. The bright futures, happiness, and stability of her cousins' lives were founded on that. Sally's daughters continued on, sheltered in comfort, thriving, getting a good education, living in comfortable homes, and eventually having families of their own.

All those things were denied to Amy due to the perfidy of their father, and the cowardice of Sally, who could have prevented our tragedy if she would have sent just one letter, or made just one phone call, warning Jay not to leave his security in Britain because the timing wasn't right.

In contrast to Ted's daughters, Amy found herself facing one challenge after another; constantly on the move; left with strangers until she was old enough not to need childcare. While all the time I scrabbled to earn a living for us both. Our lives reflected everything that happened in the past: mirroring all that Jay and Isabella had endured when Cassie and Zack had struggled to survive in an inhospitable world. Their future destroyed by the Mackenzie sisters, ours by the Logan daughters.

Amy has been the never-ending victim of Lauren and Corrine's father's duplicity, of their mother's secrecy, of their grandmother's spite, and of her own mother's stupidity and naïvety.

Do Ted's daughters ever wonder what has become of her?

Did it matter to them? Did they care?

Not one whit! Not one jot! Ever! She was just collateral damage in the quest for vengeance, the satiation of spite, and callousness. Perhaps they couldn't help it. Perhaps it was inbred.

It is hard to believe that anyone would consciously intend to cause such harm or wish to set others along such a path to chaos, using them as a tool to take retribution. Looking back, should I have been aware of it? Should Jay? Were there clues we didn't see? Should we have analyzed more closely what Penny said to us?

"We came to England to look for him," Penny had sadly said more than once. "We went to the address we had for him, in North London, and the elderly lady there said she had never heard of him." Jay recognized immediately that it was Maria they had met and reluctantly said so. Penny had looked hard into his face and then added bitterly, "What would it have hurt her to let us know he was alive, to put us in contact with Zack after we had traveled so far? To tell Cassie we were looking for him? We were so near, and yet we never got the chance to see him again after he left Canada."

I recognized after we arrived for our permanent stay the following year that Aunt Penny derived some satisfaction out of tearing Jay away from Cassie, as did her sister Agatha. But did they ever wonder if taking revenge on their sister-in-law was what Zack would have wanted? Did they ever think that their brother's lack of contact with them might have been at his own behest, not because of some Machiavellian actions of his detested spouse and her mother?

The Zack I knew and loved would have been horrified by such actions. He was a kind man, a gentle man, and despite his abysmal, miserable life, he loved his children, albeit Isabelle more than Jay. But he most definitely would not have wanted Jay used as a pawn in some kind of misguided game played by his sisters and their daughters. He would not have wanted such a legacy of betrayal visited on his son, or to see the life of his beloved granddaughter so sadly afflicted.

Did Penny, Sally, or Mattie ever acknowledge their part in the destruction that they had caused? Never to me, and I doubt even to each other. It seems as if toward their ends both Sally and Ted felt pangs of remorse or guilt when they heard of Jay's early demise. Conscience is a weird thing. It can stay suppressed for many years and be reactivated by just one event.

Sally's choice was to take the easy way out: first by her secrecy, and then by playing the blame game, ignoring her own part in events, unable to publicly face the facts of her husband's disloyalty, and unwilling to lose the breadwinner who was providing the roof over her head. She did not want to join the ranks of single women left to raise their children. Marriage, whatever its true status is, maintains respectability, and saves one having to make a living for oneself.

But no, I mean, really! Nice people don't do stuff like that, do they? Really, *do* they? Do they? Really? Nice people? No! Never!

Chapter Thirteen

Summer 1980

SALLY

Sally, as the youngest in the family, always felt she was in Mattie's shadow until she got married to Ted.

Ted was the popular kid in school, the class clown, the athlete, and with his dark, Slavic good looks, no one could believe that he had settled for little Sally Logan. Although she was a lot of fun, popular, and well liked, after the accident, well, they had been friends since high school, and stayed together once high school ended, so really, what choice did he have, since he had been driving?

All the girls liked him, and he liked them right back, sometimes taking it further than he should have, even after he was married. He rationalized it as just sex and no big deal, not quantifying it as being unfaithful. Anyway, he was comfortable with Sally. She was a good wife, and her family filled a gap in his life, especially after his father died.

All Sally knew was that they were together and the other girls envied her. Their first year of marriage had not been easy. Ted's father had died, and it hit him hard. He was very quiet for a time, wouldn't talk about it, and drank a little more than he should. It was years later before he mentioned his fears that he too would face an early death, like his father.

Sally loved him and turned a blind eye to his flirtations as he worked hard for her and his two daughters. They were a couple, and while she understood that he might have a roving eye, what she didn't see, she didn't worry about. Let people drop all the hints they wanted! After all, any small errors he made were always atoned for with a gift of some kind, and she learned what to ask for and usually got it.

She had her two little girls to be concerned with, and they loved him and needed a father. With all his faults as far as being a faithful husband was concerned, Ted was a doting dad, a good provider, and he always came home to her. She and his daughters were his rock, he said, and never referred to his occasional playing away from home.

The summer that the English cousins visited changed all that. She couldn't close her eyes to Ted's philandering any longer when she walked in on him fondling and kissing her cousin in their garage as the door slammed into Mariska's back!

Of course, she should have expected this from Mariska! She was into her second divorce, and given the reputation that Uncle Haley had in the past, according to Mom and Mattie, that apple didn't fall far from the tree. It was a case of like father, like daughter, and Mariska had always been flighty. But *Ted!* That her Ted would carry on with her cousin right under her nose in their own garage, while many members of her family were still all around, appalled her.

She couldn't ignore his infidelity any longer. In twenty years of marriage, never had she had actual proof right in front of her eyes, and it shattered her world. Her initial reaction was hurt and shock, followed by fury, ably assisted the next morning by Mariska complaining that her back hurt to anyone who would listen whilst the final family group photos were being taken. She made a special point of whining about it whenever Sally was near, and then she would cast a smirking glance in her direction.

I should have hit you with a hammer, not with the door, Sally had thought vengefully.

All she wanted to do initially was cry. Tears of frustration and hurt hovered behind her eyes, and sweet Stacey had kept hugging her and saying that they would soon be back. In her naïvety, Stacey thought Sally's emotion was because they were leaving.

Jay and Stacey were totally sold on the idea of moving to Canada, and so excited about returning as soon as they could pack up their home and sell their house in the United Kingdom. She, Ted, and her mom had promised to help them. Sally and Mattie told them it would be such fun having them live nearby after decades of hardly being aware that they had a cousin after Zack lost touch with them all. Sally's excitement was driven by the fact that she and Stacey got on so well and she had hoped Ted and Jay would too. Now she was fearful that Ted would leave and not be in the picture at all to help anyone, including her.

The whole day Sally had kept up the pretense of being excited about the future, but at the airport, she couldn't wait to see them go. She hardly took in her mother's hugs for Jay and Stacey, with urgings to come back "home" as soon as possible. She vaguely remembered hugging them herself and hearing her girls tell their little cousin how much they were looking forward to her coming back to live. And then they were gone.

Sally packed everyone back in the van, her insides torn up and her mood morose. Her family, like Stacey, put down her apparent emotion to her cousins' departure, as they headed for home. Home! Was it going to stay a home after last night? She now had no idea what she would face. Ted had left the house this morning, letting the screen door slam behind him without a backward glance.

By the time she, Penny, and the girls had returned home, Sally was in shock at the betrayal by Ted. She was full of rage that he would so disrespect her by carrying on with another woman at his house, at *her* home, while she was just feet away in her kitchen. Worse, she was humiliated that it was with her own cousin, who was younger and prettier than she was. It made her sick to her stomach. It would shame her within her family if it ever came out, and now she was terrified that Ted was about to abandon her and his daughters to run off with that harlot Mariska who was about to be single again.

She winced, remembering Mariska's smirks earlier in the day. The miserable witch had been laughing at her. Growing up, Mariska had referred to her as "poor little Sally," and her mocking eyes and simpering smiles seemed to say just that this morning.

Fearful thoughts ran through Sally's head. What was she to do now? How would she and the girls live if Ted left? Would she be able to afford their sports on her own? How could she keep this from Mom? If it all came out, she and Agatha would be bound to fall out, and then Mom would have lost her brother and her sister. Sally shuddered.

All Penny had done on the way home from the airport was talk about how much Jay resembled her brother, and how she wanted to help Jay and Stacey once they arrived.

Sally shook her head, no way was she sharing what happened last night with her mother, or worse, Mattie. She couldn't face the humiliation or the pitying looks her sister would give her. Both she and Mom would be horrified by Ted's behavior, especially Mom, who thought the sun shone out of her son-in-law's eyes. Sharing the information would change all their relationships.

From occasional conversations she had overheard between her parents, she had an idea that even her own father might have strayed once, or thought about it. Suddenly that vague thought took form as an overheard conversation, long past, flooded back to her from those far-off days in Mountain Reaches. She could hear her mother saying in a cold and serious voice, "If you ever even think of doing something like that, I'll take the girls and you will never see them again."

In a flash she had her answer. In the last resort, if it came to it, her girls would be her weapon. Ted would have no choice but to stay! In the meantime, she had to find a way to live with this. The last twenty-four hours had shattered her.

Last night after the shock of what she saw, and her furious outburst at Mariska, Sally had retreated to bed. She had curled herself into a ball and cried herself to sleep. At some point Ted had slithered into bed beside her but said nothing, did nothing, and stayed clear of her. There was no way he could defend himself, especially in his inebriated state. Now he had all day at work to mull it over.

Once she arrived back in her own home, her mind continued to race. She had no idea what would happen next, but for sure if Ted said their marriage was over, he'd lose big time. She'd clean him out *and* run off with the girls. She'd go and stay way down south with Mattie and make it as hard as she could for him to see them. They would hate him for breaking up their family; she would see to that! This would be her plan to protect herself, to make him stay, but she dreaded Ted's return from work.

When he walked in shortly afterward, he all but ignored her, his attitude bordering on the surly. He said little to her but chatted quietly to the girls about their day, and about them getting back into training again.

After they had eaten, Sally retreated to her mother's house next door, on the pretext of catching up with her now that the visitors had gone. She was afraid to have the conversation with Ted she knew had to come. She wasn't even sure she could bear to be in the same room with him at the moment. Nor was she confident that she would be able to stay calm around him as she needed to. Could she continue to act normally in front of their daughters. She needed time to calm down and to think before she spoke to Ted, and it took several days before she could trust herself to be civil to him. In the meantime, they went to bed at different times, and slept as far away from each other as their bed would allow.

Then came the evening after the girls had gone to bed when they both headed toward their own bedroom at the same time. More confident, she finally decided to confront Ted. Her face tight and her eyes flashing, she stared up at him. He eyed her defiantly, realizing what was coming. "Well, what have you got to say for yourself?" Sally demanded angrily, dashing her hands across her eyes as tears started.

Trying to keep calm, and be conciliatory, Ted replied quietly, "Sally, you haven't given me a chance to explain what happened with the way you've been avoiding me. I'm sorry, really I am, but it was no big deal. Just a bit of kissing. It only happened because I'd had too much drink, and Mariska about threw herself at me and caught me off guard. She'd made remarks all weekend about how lonely she was now that she's getting divorced yet again. You know what she's like—man crazy," Ted said, still unwilling to accept responsibility for his actions.

"Just a *bit* of kissing!" Sally exploded. "That wasn't just a bit of kissing! Your hands were all over her, *and* you're not supposed to be kissing *anyone* else like that but me! How *could* you do that here, with my own cousin, in our own garage? What would have happened if Aunt Agatha or Mom had seen you? If Stacey or Jay had seen you, how would that have made us look? You could have ruined our whole vacation and their visit with my family! I've ignored all the gossip about you over the years, but this is different! How could you hurt *me* like that! Sorry doesn't cut it!" Sally wailed.

Ted had no defense. He knew he was in the wrong, and he didn't know what he could say other than to apologize, so he tried again.

"Sally, I'm sorry. I know it doesn't change it, but I am sorry. I should have seen what was coming. Jay and Stacey had just gone to bed, and Mariska was the last one there. I didn't have time to think. She just said, 'Give me a good-night hug,' caught me off guard, and then she was all over me!" he answered, moderating his tone.

"*She* was all over *you!*" Sally hissed, her face a mask of fury, wanting to scream at him, but afraid to wake her daughters.

"Caught you off guard! *Your* hands were all over her! It looked like you about had your tongue down her throat, not to mention her hand was in your fly, and you didn't seem to be stopping that!" Sally retaliated.

A sob escaped her, and she had to stop before she completely broke down. She pressed her hands to her mouth to stop herself from sobbing out loud, her shoulders shaking. It was a moment before she regained control, and she looked directly at him, gulping in a deep breath.

"How long has this been going on for?" she added, fighting her hysteria. "Are you in love with her?"

Not giving him time to answer, and looking him straight in the eye, Sally said almost calmly, "Do you want to split up?"

The color drained from Ted's face. He suddenly understood just how bad his situation was, and he immediately shook his head, gasping out a shocked, "No! No, Sally that never even entered my mind. I told you I was caught off guard, and it just happened, and I know it shouldn't have happened."

Sally ignored his gasps, pressing her point. "If I am not enough for you, if you are so desperate to be with other women that you'll even go after my cousin here in our own home, does that mean you want to leave us?"

Up to now, Ted had just been annoyed with himself for getting into this situation. He knew that it had been a bit of a poor decision on his part, but as far as he was concerned, it was just a little petting session. True, it was bad judgment, and he should not have gotten into it so close to home, but he'd had too much to drink, didn't have time to think about it. He definitely did not expect the aftermath would blow up like this. He groaned inwardly. *Why* did women take this stuff so *personally* and make such a drama about nothing?

How had thoughts of ending their marriage entered Sally's head? Why would she face him with this kind of ultimatum over something he regarded as so trivial? His marriage was fine, as far as he was concerned, despite his forays into playing the field. Those quiet little sexual excursions were just to let off steam, nothing more than a little fun to spice his love life up, feed the need he felt sometimes.

He liked flirting, liked women, but it was a game with him, nothing serious. Sally, Lauren, Corinne, and Penny were his *family!* This house was his *home!* He had no wish to leave!

Despite his wanderings, he had always been comfortable with Sally. Their relationship was an established one; it had warmth, if not excitement. Now here she was threatening to tear his world apart? Ted was aghast! He should have paid more attention, but he just thought Sally had been sulking about what had happened. It never occurred to him that she was thinking about ending their marriage! Especially after they had such fun all summer, and he had thought their relationship was real tight, but now? If only he had stayed clear of Mariska after he had kissed Stacey good-bye!

He tried again. "Sally, no!" he said more urgently, moving a step closer and reaching toward her. Sally did not give him the chance to hold her, as she moved away from him, her hands out in front of her, warding him off.

She didn't react at all to what he was saying. Instead she spoke quietly in a flat voice.

"Before you make any decision to abandon your family, you should know that I won't make it easy or cheap for you. You'll lose this house. Remember, it is still in my name. After all, it was *my* family's home long before you came along. Also, I will demand half of everything you have: savings, stocks, everything. More than that, I will move away and take the girls with me, as far as possible, and you'll never see them again! Is the price of your freedom to whore around worth it?"

There was coldness in her voice that Ted had never heard from her. His stomach churning, he finally caught Sally by the shoulders, saying, "Sally, truly this was nothing, meant nothing, definitely not anything that should interfere with our marriage. It was really stupid. I didn't mean to hurt you, not with Mariska, not with anyone, but I never want to leave you or the girls. You are my family. This is my home, where I belong. Leaving all of you never entered my head at all," he added almost desperately.

Sally looked at him, her eyes narrowing, and her brain went into overdrive. She had not expected his complete capitulation, and suddenly she saw how much of a hand Fate had dealt her. He had finally admitted how much life with her and their daughters really meant to him, and she was going to use that.

She was still seething with anger, her mind replaying that moment when she had seen him and Mariska together. It was still too fresh in her mind, the hurt digging deep. She was unable to simply put it to one side, so she shrugged off his hands, turning her back on him. Her voice icy, she spoke again, "Oh, no, it's not going to be that easy, Ted. Saying sorry isn't good enough; this is way past that."

She brushed her hand across her eyes again. "I've forgiven things in the past, ignored stories about some of the things you get up to, at the bar and other places over the years. You've always been a flirt, which is why people gossip, but seeing you with… with…that…bitch, with my *cousin*, in our home, with my own eyes, changes things. There will be consequences if you want this marriage to continue!"

Ted nodded miserably, "What do you want, Sally? Do you want me to leave? It isn't what I want. What can I do to make it right?"

Sally looked at him, vague thoughts running uncertainly through her brain. She didn't want him to leave, but he was going to pay. Finally she sighed and said, "No, I don't want you to leave. Lauren and Corinne would be brokenhearted. But I'm not going to stand for it this time. Right at the moment I don't want you near me. You've spoiled that part of our relationship, and now you are on probation with me. I also need some time to figure out what you will have to do to make it right for me."

Relieved, Ted moved toward her to pull her into his arms, and Sally went rigid with anger. She pushed him away again, raising her hand as if to slap him, but she held back.

"*No!* Have you not heard one word I've said?" she snapped angrily. "You are not going to make this all better with a hug and a kiss, or anything else that you might want to follow up with! You are not screwing me, and then thinking that we have made up so you can carry on like nothing has happened!" Sally snarled.

"I feel physically sick just thinking about you with Mariska. It has threatened my peace of mind, so stay away from me, and sleep on your own side of the bed. *Don't touch me!* If we didn't have the girls and it would raise all kinds of questions with them, I would go over to Mom's to sleep, but I can't for appearances' sake, but you stay away from me in bed. One more thing: not one word of this is to go any further! I don't want our daughters, Mom, or anyone else inside or outside the family to know about it." She stopped, heaving for breath, her stomach in knots, watching Ted's face.

Ted was appalled. He wished he could explain to her that his quick hops into bed with other women were really nothing to do with his feelings for her, his marriage, or his family. It was just sex, to fill a need that somewhere he knew wasn't met, but he was smart enough not to say so. Wives just do not see it like that, but Sally saying that he should not come near her shocked him. She had always been so compliant in bed, unadventurous but warm, willing, responsive within her own barriers, and now she was not even going to…and on top of that she was warning him not to go elsewhere! How would he survive?

It was like an Arctic wind had blown between them. When they eventually got to bed, sleep was far away for both of them, and his side of the bed felt lonely. Ted also had a feeling Sally was going to make all sorts of demands as her price for letting him stay, and it began to irk him. It was just *kissing* for Christ's sake, not anything more! A couple of minutes later and there would have been nothing to see, his sense would have caught up with him.

On her side of the bed, Sally was miserable, filled with anger and hurt, but a burgeoning feeling of victory started growing within her and gave her a small thrill. There was one thing she had always wanted, and now she might finally get it.

The next evening, after the girls went to bed, Sally said coldly to him. "We need for you to mend fences. You've hurt me deeply and ruined what had been a lovely time with Jay and Stacey for me. You need to clean up your act, because the next time I hear of anything you have done with another woman, you will be out of here permanently."

Ted just stared at her, and then he nodded curtly at her, resentment building. Be was beginning to realize what a few kisses was going to cost him and true to form, Sally did not disappoint him.

She continued, "I'm sick of begging for every penny, so once we've caught up after the expense of our trip, you can stop being so miserly with money. The girls need stuff, the house needs things, and although I can work with Frankie and sell some of that restored furniture, it still needs you to open up the purse strings without grumbling."

Sally went on, really beginning to enjoy her newfound power, and Ted scowled at her final demand.

"One more thing: I've always wanted a nice fur coat, but you've been too miserly to buy me one! Now is the time, and I'd like it under the Christmas tree, to show everyone, including Mom and the girls, how much I mean to you. Maybe then we can get back to normal, but for now I don't want you touching me until I'm ready. *And* I meant what I said yesterday. Not one word about this in front of Mom or the girls. If they find out about it, we're done!"

Ted bristled. It didn't sound as if he was going to have much say in all this. Sally had just handed him a list of demands, and that was it. When he started to protest, Sally reiterated her promise from the evening before. "It's your choice, Ted. Make things right, or lose your daughters!" With that, she turned on her heel and headed into their bedroom.

She undressed, got into bed, turned her back toward Ted, and shut off her lamp. She was determined to keep her distance from him, because she just could not feel the same about him anymore. Later Sally wondered if she had gone too far and cut off her nose to spite her face. By cutting off Ted, she had cut off herself also.

Ted was a good lover, and she had enjoyed him, but now their bed seemed to have turned into the frozen tundra north of them, like the rest of their relationship. She missed his touch, but he had built up the wall between them with his behavior, and she was afraid to capitulate too soon. He had to learn his lesson not go back to his old ways. Anyway, she thought, practically, she'd better wait until she got her fur coat; it was nothing less than she deserved.

At that point, Sally didn't realize that the situation with Ted was the least of her troubles. Despite the change in their relationship, she still trusted in him intrinsically, although her faith in him had been shaken. Firstly, she still did not know the whole story, or the real cause of Ted's actions that night. Secondly, she did not stop to ponder on Ted's reactions to Jay and Stacey moving to Canada. She didn't know what thoughts were playing through Ted's mind about Stacey and how her effect on him had led to the scene with Mariska.

Unknowingly, she put her marriage in much worse jeopardy again less than a year later, as her silence and secrecy betrayed Jay's future.

Chapter Fourteen
1980 The Frozen North

Ted

Ted was churned up, and although he seethed at Sally's demands and her ultimate threat to take his daughters away from him, he dreaded what else she might demand. She was making such a big deal about just kissing. He'd blamed it on too much to drink and Mariska targeting him, and apologized. Why couldn't Sally understand that it meant nothing to him. But she didn't see it like that. Women never did!

When Sally mentioned running home to her mother, he felt prickles run down his back. That damned Stacey. This was all her fault. She had him so worked up with that farewell kiss. Then she had blown him off with that brother remark! He was relieved that Sally hadn't noticed his interest in Stacey during the previous month, or linked that to his behavior with Mariska. If only he had not given Stacey that hug and good-bye kiss, none of this would have happened. Just as well that Sally didn't know it was that encounter that had really shaken him up. Stacey had sent tingles all through him, and he hadn't been expecting such a response from himself. He was a middle-aged man, and was at a loss to know what it was about Stacey that had roused him so. It wasn't like she was pretty, and she was a little chunky, forever blurting out what was uppermost in her mind, but she was just so nice, so happy, so much of a girl, so loving with her daughter, so thrilled for Jay. She was all happiness.

He had wondered if it would be possible to make Stacey another notch on his belt during most of the cousins' visit. But for all his charm, he hadn't been able to get to first base with her. She seemed impervious to his charm. She was all about her husband, though obviously nonplussed by the attention Ted had given her. Totally ignoring his flirting, she had remained friendly and happy to sit and talk with him. That had just amused and challenged him, until he had watched her one afternoon sitting with Amy on her lap. She showed her daughter such tenderness that it gave his heartstrings a jolt, rousing something in his deep memory that he could not quite capture, but it changed his focus on her.

On the night they were leaving, he didn't know what maggot got into his head, as he walked her outside to say that final farewell. They had stopped for the customary family hug, but what should have been a brief kiss on the cheek turned into something entirely different. His own reaction had set him back and seemingly embarrassed Stacey, who had naïvely brushed it off with a quick remark about how she was looking forward to coming back and how nice it was going to be to have an extra brother. Then she hurried away into the night, back to Penny's.

Brother! He had been irked! That wasn't the usual reaction he got when he kissed a woman like that. He had not been trying to convey "brotherly" to her at all! Was it his age? He must be losing his touch! Frustrated, he had slammed back into the garage and straight into that vixen Mariska, who was all over him in an instant. Already churned up, he had responded to her as much out of pique as anything else. Here was a girl who had made a play for him the entire weekend, would have known exactly what he wanted had he targeted her, and the way she was kissing him back clearly showed she didn't want any "brotherly" advances from him, and so he just gave in to his baser instincts.

Then Sally walked in and had now made it clear that their relationship was going to change, and she was not only going to keep a tight leash on him, but she was looking for major compensation as the price for allowing him to keep his daughters and stay in his home.

He had never seen her this angry, or so cold toward him before. In the past her anger flared and died. It had never gone on for long, and she had never been so unwilling to let him cajole her back into a better mood.

This time, however, Sally just would not let the incident with Mariska go! To escape her attitude and sour face, he kept himself busy in the garage or yard, going back to his ice hockey as soon as the season started—anything to keep him out of his wife's way.

None of it was helpful to their relationship, driving an even deeper wedge between them as they spent less and less time in each other's company. The barrier between them built, and with both of them nursing resentful thoughts, seemed to be erecting an almost insurmountable obstacle between them. The saving grace was when the girls or Penny were around, and they tried to be normal with each other, easing their relationship, but it was strained at best.

Both were fearful that their marriage would not recover, that their comfortable relationship would not return. Sally was unable to get the image of Mariska out of her head, and Ted was beginning to question everything he thought he could trust in.

He was miserable. He didn't like this at all, and he didn't know how to fix it. His home wasn't contented or welcoming anymore. Sally continued to stay cool toward him. Even worse was that, for whatever reason, he could not get Stacey out of his mind. Her image popped into his head whenever he sought to relieve the sexual tension growing inside him now that he and Sally were not cohabiting and he dared not seek companionship elsewhere.

Fantasy was fine, but he began to wonder what would happen when Jay and Stacey returned and she was here in person. Could he trust himself to stay away from her? At that thought, he started to try to figure out ways to prevent the young cousins from settling too near them. Contrary to the promises they had made to them, he started to put barriers in their way. It was a wrong decision that would lead to a greater disaster than he could have ever imagined.

Ted set his mind to meeting Sally's terms, and as December came and went, he hoped that she would soften her attitude toward him. The treasured fur coat was under the tree, bringing many comments of admiration from her daughters. Although Sally thawed somewhat, there was still an atmosphere between them. His mind was so concentrated on getting his life back to normal that he paid very little attention to assisting Penny's plans to get Jay and Stacey back to Alberta as soon as possible. Deep down he did not want them to return.

The next blow came when his mother-in-law excitedly told him that she and Sally had talked Jay into moving to Canada ahead of Stacey and Amy. It was so he could help Jay get settled before the job market dried up. In shock, Ted voice his opinion that it was a bad move. He wished that Sally had not done this without telling him, but they were still scarcely talking. Jay should wait…the job market was even slower during the winter months.

He argued that Jay should not come alone, that they should all come together in the spring when the economy improved a bit. But the women would have none of it and forged ahead, encouraging Jay's plan, and the die was cast.

Somewhere deep inside Ted, apprehension arose, heralding disaster, and he just did not know why.

SALLY—JUST ONE LETTER

It made no difference what Ted said, his mother-in-law and therefore his wife were both determined that Zack's son should come home, and they had convinced Jay that Edmunston was where he should be.

But in supporting Penny, Sally had to hide the truth of the situation between her and Ted from her mother. The less Penny knew about their current relationship and Ted and Mariska's encounter, the better. But it was hard to keep it from her given that she lived right next door. Over the years she and Mom had developed such a close bond because Mattie lived several hundred miles south of them. Usually her mother didn't miss much, although she never interfered when they had their little spats from time to time, but this time she seemed to have missed all the clues.

So Sally stuck to her guns and did her best be jaunty and upbeat in all the letters and tapes crisscrossing the Atlantic, but in the face of the threat to her marriage, her inner enthusiasm waned as she struggled to keep her family together. She wished there was someone she could talk to, but after demanding Ted's silence, she could hardly go and blurt it out to anyone in town, so she held on to her secret until the fateful moment she blurted it out to Stacey way later than she should have.

Sally was also aware that the success of Jay's transition to Edmunston depended very much on Ted helping to find her cousin a job. The surliness he had shown toward her in the aftermath of her threats to him had led Ted to be unenthusiastic about Jay and Stacey moving to Edmunston. Sally did not know that his uncooperativeness veiled his concern about what might happen if Jay and Stacey moved closer to them.

Sally's turmoil grew as the day for Jay's arrival came closer. She knew that nothing was as it had been a year ago. Her own excitement of their cousins' visit had waned now buried within the battleground of her marriage. A part of her never wanted to see them again as it would remind her forever of the last night of their vacation, and its impact. Deep down she knew she should warn Jay and Stacey that the situation had changed. She could have focused on the worsening employment situation, rather than her situation, but she knew Penny would have none of it. Her Mom was determined to get Jay "home". Penny had confidence that Ted would fix things—he always did she told her daughter when she broached the subject. Sally just groaned inwardly and gritted her teeth.

She knew that Jay would be expecting an inbuilt support system when he arrived based on their promises last summer, but now she wasn't sure how much of that he would get. However, she always came back to her sticking point: in order to warn Jay, she would have to tell them what had happened, and then Mom would have to know, and Mattie, and probably Aunt Agatha, and ultimately Lauren and Corrine. No, she couldn't do it.

Now Jay was on his way, the die was cast, and only Fate knew what was going to happen next.

Chapter Fifteen
1980 Meanwhile in Britain

Stacey

All of a sudden Jay's family in England were paying us some attention. Isabella and Anton made a pit stop at our home, which was halfway between their home and Anton's parent's house, but in the four years we had lived there, they had never once made the detour to see us before, despite being invited.

Next Cassie rounded up squiffy Megs and her car, and they motored up to our house—another first. Additionally, Cassie was never off the telephone, also encouraging Megs and Isabella to go overboard and show Jay some attention, all the while trying to talk Jay out of moving to Canada.

Cassie's motive was clear; she had hated Canada, and she loathed Zack's family. Isabella's angst sprang from resentment that Jay had received the Prodigal Son treatment as he was taken back into the bosom of her father's family, but she was pretty much ignored by them. They found her standoffishness daunting. In contrast, after years of getting the cold shoulder, I was suddenly flavor of the month as they all tried to enlist my support to persuade Jay that we shouldn't emigrate.

For once both our families were in agreement; my family did not want me to go either. But the attention Cassie and Isabella paid to me was too little too late. I had been the redheaded low class stepchild within their family unit for too long. Cassie had made her contempt of me very open over the years, and Isabella was so wrapped up in her job and keeping her unemployed husband going while he tried to start his own business, that she showed little interest in her brother or me, or come to that, Amy.

My own mother was very unhappy about my moving so far away, although to her credit she agreed that as his wife, I would have to go where Jay went, and obviously Amy would come with us. Since Cassie and Isabella's barely concealed tolerance of me for most of the past ten years had been very hurtful, I was disinclined to assist them in any way. In stark contrast, the family in Canada had made me welcome, and they recognized my open adoration for both my husband and his late father. For me, moving to Canada had the added bonus of being as far away as possible from the British Mackenzies and not having to deal with them much anymore! I well knew that if I talked Jay around, I'd get little credit for it, and they would soon cast me back into red-haired mode again.

Jay was amused by their reactions, less so by me expressing some trepidation about leaving my own family. "It's not like it's Australia, Stace—only an eight-hour flight. Just a little longer between family visits, and in any case, Amy and I are your family now," he had argued. There was no answer to that.

Having seen Shangri-la, Jay would not be budged; he could visualize himself with all the accoutrements of a wealthier income. From then on, almost every waking moment was taken up with sorting through our house to decide what we needed to take with us, which came down to personal possessions, including our books, youthful memorabilia, clothes, way too much china, and too many household goods.

Next time I move across an ocean, I am taking photos of the memorabilia, transferring photos and books to electronic versions, and turning everything else into cash to replace them in the new location. The more I move, the more I realize that you don't need stuff. But people often make bad choices initially, and it is only practice that improves those decisions.

Of course, friends and work colleagues thought we were crazy to move too, but Jay was utterly convinced that this would be his Xanadu. He was sure that he was going to amass the riches and wealth that he thought had eluded him in Britain. Ironically, his mother's lifelong mantra about being "misplaced" in society played well into this. Poverty had filled his youthful years, and now at the start of our life together, like others we had been enduring all the financial challenges to build our home. We had met in our late twenties, when so many of our cohorts had married earlier and achieved a greater rate of progress. Once he had seen what his cousins had in Canada, he felt left behind and wanted the same for himself, for Amy, and for me too, if he thought about it.

Upon our return after the vacation, letters and tapes from Sally and Aunt Penny bombarded us. Each expressed how excited they were about us moving to Alberta, and as weeks passed into months, it seemed they were getting impatient for Jay to return. When they warned that the job market was dwindling a little, we didn't heed the implied warning that this might not be a fortuitous time to emigrate. At that time we paid scant attention to the dip in the world economy; it was outside our realm of interest or understanding.

At Christmas we all talked on the telephone and joined in with the excitement in Sally's home over her new fur coat. Jay said, "See what can happen? Once we have moved, you may get a fur coat too!" Then Penny and Sally expressed concern that Jay needed to think about moving sooner rather than later to maximize current job opportunities. Ted said nothing.

What part of "red flag" did we not see? If we had been more aware of the downturn in the economy, not only in the United States but also Canada, would it have made a difference? Would we have put that decision on hold and saved ourselves so much agony and pain? At that point in time, I don't think it would have. Jay was so set on his course, and he was not going to deviate from it.

That Christmas call motivated Jay to move things along. He sat down with me and asked how I would feel if he went out ahead of Amy and me? He felt we had broken the back of the logistics of the move. But he asked if I could cope? It would mean that I would have to wait until we found a buyer for the house, oversee the sale, deal with the movers and pack the house up; then move Amy, me and the cats. Fortunately, we had been able to re-home Candy our little whippet but no one would take the cats and I balked at having them put down. For all my confidence, I was nervous. It seemed like a lot of work and responsibility, and I wasn't sure I could handle it all alone.

But Jay was persuasive. "You are so capable, and it will make it easier, because while you are packing up and seeing to things here, I can get somewhere ready for us when you both arrive.

It will make the transition easier, as you'll just move from one home to another," he said earnestly.

Oh, right! Dumb, trusting Stacey relying on Mr. Practicality, who barely knew where to put the dishes when they were dried, and ran over the power cord for the mower nine times out of ten! I finally agreed, but wasn't thrilled with the idea of Amy and I being left alone to cope with everything. "Your parents will help," he said. "They are always willing to lend a hand."

So, in mid-January, we called Canada again to talk to both Aunt Penny and Sally, who were delighted that Jay was leaving soon. They would make sure he got a job and a place for us to live, and they would make sure it was ready for Amy and me when we arrived, they said enthusiastically. They reassured both Jay and me that he, and if need be we, could stay with Aunt Penny until we found a home, and that Ted was working on a job for Jay.

So easy to make that promise on the telephone, not so easy when it came down to the nitty-gritty, or to keep to it when their interest in first Jay, and then me, waned.

JAY—1981—WARWICKSHIRE

Jay took one last look around the house that had been his home for the past four years. It was clean, comfortable, and always smelled fresh. Stacey was a good housekeeper, and he thought back to the first time she had cooked him a meal in her tiny bedsitter next to Ladbroke Grove station.

She had made a delicious meal of chicken livers in a creamed wine sauce over angel-hair pasta, followed by zabaglione. He was amazed at how cozy she had made the little room, and how she had managed to make such a wonderful meal with just a hotplate.

As she began clearing away the plates, he had looked at her trim body, her long brown hair, big, soft brown eyes, and wide smile and thought that she would make someone a wonderful wife. Another thought quickly followed, "Why not me?"

And that had been how it started. Each time they moved, Stacey had managed to make them a comfy home setting in short order. She fed him well, knitted and sewed for him, and provided the sort of home he had always dreamed of as he had grown up. She was the kind of mother he wished he had, and years later he would wonder why he was ever so stupid as to give that up.

Stacey was a loving mother to Amy, and she worked hard at making Jay happy. Their friends all envied him her talents in the kitchen and her natural homemaker skills, although at times she showed just a touch too much independence for a wife, but…there was still that "*but*" as he was a little less excited by her now. She was turning into a middle-aged housewife, with not a lot of care for how she looked (that she did not have either the money or the time to do more for herself bypassed him completely), plus she had put on a lot of weight, but she was so good…there was that *but* again…until Stacey, he had always had a passion for tiny blondes.

He sighed, turned to close the front door on this chapter of his life, and headed for the car. Stacey and Amy were already sitting there, allowing him a few pensive final thoughts in his home. He looked at them in the car. What would his next car be? What would his next home be like? What would the next few months bring for him? He didn't spare any thoughts on his wife. He had no concerns about Stacey. She was so very capable; she would cope with anything. She always did.

Chapter Sixteen

1981 Gatwick Airport

The previous couple of days had been spent in London at Stacey's parents' flat, like so many over the previous years. They had also crossed London to visit Cassie. Isabella, Anton, Megs, and Cassie had all gathered, and they spent a couple of hours in the nearby London park, talking and laughing at Amy as she ran excitedly around the children's playground. Isabella had been her usual self: all softness on the surface, hard as nails underneath, and all about herself. Nothing had changed. She told Jay how much she was going to miss him, when he could count on the fingers of one hand the number of times she and Anton had put themselves out to come visit his home.

His mother kept making oblique statements about the wisdom, or lack of it, of departing to Canada. It had been such an unhappy experience for her, and left issues for him, from whence all his angst about his homeland had originated. But for once she kept her bitterness in check, and overall it had been a pleasant farewell.

Now he, Stacey, and Amy were at the gate, awaiting the call for him to get on the plane. In these early 1980s there was scant security at the airport, and family could come right to the gate, see you get on your plane, and watch it take off. His feelings were very mixed: apprehension at leaving Stacey and Amy, yet excitement about starting a new phase in his life. He is concern was for Amy, knowing that his daughter was unhappy about his departure.

"Daddy, do you really have to go?" said Amy, tears starting in her eyes.

"Yes, I do. I have to get a job and find a home for Mummy and you. Then you'll get to see me and everyone else in a few months. You want to see Lauren and Corinne again, don't you?" Jay responded, feeling a lump welling up in his throat. Now that it was time to leave, it was harder than he thought it would be to say good-bye.

"I will send you tapes as often as I can. You will hear from me all the time," he said reassuringly to her. "And you can tell me what you are doing, and I'll share your tapes with your cousins."

Stacey watched them. Swallowing hard, she said to Jay, "You will keep in touch, let me know when you get there?"

She didn't want to break down in front of Amy, and it wouldn't take much to set her off wailing again, as she had done the night before.

Jay looked at her, raised his eyebrows, and smiled. "Of course. You just have to get this house sorted out, see to the packing, and then you can bring the money when you join me, so we can get started. It will be fine."

Stacey said anxiously, "You will find somewhere for us to live? Have something ready when we get there?"

She was remembering the moves to Scotland and then to Warwickshire, when people at the office had pointed them in the right direction for their new homes, after she and Jay had been stuck in hotels for too long. She hoped that Sally and Aunt Penny would help him find something suitable…

Deep inside was the fear that she knew he just was not that practical!

Jay replied, smiling, unwittingly mirroring her thoughts. "Of course! Aunty Penny and Sally will help. They promised. Ted will help me find a job…they said he would. We will be fine."

He raised his eyebrows as he looked at her, thinking again that she had put on way too much weight and really should slim down, but all he said was, "Don't worry."

Why wouldn't she worry? An unbidden thought drifted into Stacey's head. Hmm, that translates into, "They will find me somewhere, and you will make the place cozy like you always do once you get there." But that was Jay, and she loved him.

The call came over the tannoy for passengers to board, and all of a sudden the moment of final parting was imminent. Jay had bags to pick up, and then they were all hugging, whispering soft words of love and encouragement, and kissing each other good-bye.

Just as Jay reached the gate, he turned back and caught Stacey in his arms and gave her one last, long kiss. "See you soon," he said hoarsely. "We'll soon be together again."

Then he turned and walked through the doors to get on the plane.

From his seat he could see the plate glass windows of the gate area, and Stacey standing with Amy beside her, holding her hand. They were waving at the plane, even though he was sure they couldn't actually pick him out, and suddenly they looked so lonely standing there.

His heart started to pound as the plane taxied down the runway, and as it took off, Jay looked down at the countryside below getting smaller and smaller, saying softly to himself, "Good-bye, Britain. Canada, here I come. Time to start my new life."

And a still, small voice inside him whispered, "What have I done?"

Chapter Seventeen

1981 Canada

New Beginnings—Sad Realities

Jay

After nearly three months spent fruitlessly job-hunting, resulting solely in a temporary job washing dishes at a local diner, Jay finally applied for a stock control job with the Alberta Department of Natural Resources.

It wasn't in Edmundston, and Stacey had been less than thrilled when she heard that his job was going to be two hundred miles way from Sally and Aunt Penny. For himself, he wasn't unhappy about it. On closer inspection, his family didn't really pass muster, but he would not share that with Stacey. At least, not until she got here. Wouldn't do to put her off and have her balk about the move, especially now they seemed to have a genuine offer on the house.

After living with his aunt for a few weeks, he found that when there were no visitors around, she was a bit of a slob, and he saw her native heritage as an influence on her. After his mother's fastidiousness, and Stacey's good housekeeping, he was a little taken aback. He was also really disappointed with Sally and Ted. Sally was friendly enough, but Ted hardly put himself out at all, and it was clear that they really had little in common, which made it difficult to relate to each other. It was the middle of the hockey and curling season, and Ted seemed never to be home. Once he took Jay with him to watch, but he barely bothered to introduce Jay to his teammates, or point out Jay's roots in the area, and it seemed like he had taken Jay with him on sufferance.

Jay also picked up on the tension between Sally and Ted that hadn't been there last year, and he wondered what had happened. He got a better idea weeks later when he was working at the diner and heard some local gossip about Ted's proclivity for extramarital exercises. He figured Sally had caught him out.

Then Jay's natural lack of tact had led to him putting his foot in it with Aunt Penny. They had been discussing his parents' move from Mountain Reaches, and he asked if they had left anything behind that he and Stacey might be able to use. Maybe something tucked away in the little house at the end of their yard? It had been their original mountain home and was packed with furniture and other items, which Penny had proudly showed him one afternoon.

There had been an awkward pause, and Aunt Penny had been distinctly frosty. He backtracked immediately, but could see she thought he was being impertinent and also that "helping" was not going to translate into "sharing."

Fortunately, that same week the news came through that it seemed Stacey had accepted an offer for the house. Likely in six weeks or so, she would be able to fly out with Amy to join him. That week he also had confirmation of his new job in Rougeville.

"That's good," said Aunt Penny. "It will give you time to find a place and get ready for Stacey's arrival." She looked relieved, unaware of Jay's lack of forethought, which he lived up to.

Once Jay arrived in Rougeville and started looking for homes and apartments, he balked at the cost of renting a place for a family while he was on his own, and settled for a tiny basement apartment in a larger house.

"After all," he told Aunt Penny, "no point in paying for something I am not going to use, and in any case, I think Stacey wants to settle here in Edmunston, so I expect eventually I will need to get a job here."

Penny had raised her eyebrows. It seemed he was in no hurry to reunite with his wife. While Penny was not averse to having Stacey and Amy stay with her once they first arrive in Canada, memories stirred of the problems they encountered when they had set up a home for Zack and Cassie. She knew that Jay would likely need several weeks to get a place prepared for his family and felt he had made a bad decision. But she forbore to say anything. She liked Stacey and did not foresee the same kind of issues they had with Cassie.

SALLY

Sally's woes were growing. She felt guilty that Jay's arrival had not been more fortuitous. He had been unable to find work in Edmundston, and clearly felt let down when he had to take a restaurant job, but now he had found something two hundred miles away in Rougeville. Stacey still had not arrived, and Jay seemed to be making no preparations for her doing so. He didn't seem much perturbed about that and had shocked Penny by making it clear that he objected to spending extra money on larger accommodation until Stacey arrived. On the plus side, it meant that Sally might be able to spend a little time with Stacey. Last year they got on real well, perhaps they could become real friends. Maybe eventually she could open up about what happened with Ted and Mariska, because it was still tearing her apart, and she needed a friend to talk to. Stacey had been really easy to talk to, maybe she could trust her...maybe.

Coupled with her uneasiness about Jay's situation was Sally's growing trepidation about the commitment they had made for the girls to return to the skating camp this year. Last year, when everything had been so happy, they had signed up and paid the deposit to return this summer. Now the tension inside her grew until she was nearly frantic, wondering how she could get out of going to British Columbia with her daughters. She didn't trust Ted now, and she certainly did not want to leave him alone and "unsupervised" for a month. How could she be absent for that long and trust him to be faithful? They hadn't discussed it; nor had they talked about him coming out to join them as he had last year. Neither of them could see how they would be comfortable in such close quarters again.

By contrast, Lauren and Corrine were excited about their trip, and Sally couldn't see how she could back out without a very good reason. That reason didn't include telling them that she was afraid to leave their father on his own for four weeks or that she was fearful about what might happen while she was gone.

Images of him fondling Mariska flooded back every time she thought about last summer. Her imagination worked overtime and took her to wondering just what he had been up to before Jay and Stacey arrived last year. She reviewed all their female friends and acquaintances, considering if one of them had a summer fling with Ted. Were people laughing at her behind her back? It gnawed away at her and did nothing to diminish the coolness between her and Ted that was making him surlier every day. Their situation was more miserable than it had ever been before.

She wondered if she could get Mom to act as a watchdog while she was away. But she shook that idea off straight away; she would look such a fool, and Mom might say something to Aunt Agatha, or worse Mattie, then she would have Mattie looking pityingly at her, and saying kind things! Ugh!

So when they heard that Stacey had sold the house and Jay expected her to arrive in late May, the timing could not have been better. She encouraged her mother to let Jay know that she should come straight to Edmunston until they could get settled and their things arrived from Britain. Stacey wanted to settle in Edmunston, not Rougeville, and a plan formed with Sally's mind working overtime. First she worked on her mother, suggesting that it would be nice for her if Stacey could stay in Edmunston while she and the girls were in British Columbia.

"Mom, they will be company for you, and it will help get Stacey acclimatized to life here, and you really like her," she said. Her mother just looked at her and agreed it would be helpful, so Sally just left the idea to sit with her.

Then she worked on Jay, saying that maybe it might be an idea for Stacey to stay with Mom rather than be thrust straight into homemaking right away. In any case, didn't they have to wait for all their things from the United Kingdom to arrive?

By the time Stacey and Amy arrived, Sally had both her mother and Jay convinced. She said little to Ted about it; after all, he would see straight through her idea, but she knew he had caught the drift of what was happening.

She didn't forewarn him, but Sally knew he had got it when she spoke to Stacey just before they left for their trip. She had been a little short with Stacey, who had asked if she and Amy could go with them like they had the year before. Sally said that it was not possible, as there just wouldn't be room for them, and it would not be comfortable, as they all started the day at the crack of dawn. Seeing Stacey's disappointment, she softened her attitude by pointing out that Stacey needed to catch her breath before she started on settling in. Casually, she suggested to Stacey that as she was going to be staying in Edmunston for several weeks while Sally was gone, Stacey might like to use Sally's more modern washer and dryer, instead of her mom's antiquated set up.

Encouragingly Sally also suggested that they could use her house during the day when Penny was sleeping before going to her night shift at the hospital, where she still worked, so that Stacey would not have to worry about keeping Amy quiet.

Stacey had been hesitant initially, and asked several times if Sally was sure about it, and if it was OK with Ted. Sally had reassured her that Ted wouldn't mind, and Stacey was so touched by Sally's generosity that she offered to vacuum and dust while she was gone. Sally, shrugging of feelings of guilt, had laughed off the offer, but said she appreciated it.

Good, thought Sally smugly, I have put a watchdog on Ted, and she doesn't even know it!

Ted might suspect, but there was nothing he could do about it without looking churlish.

Chapter Eighteen

1981 Edmunston

Ted

Ted was shocked by the lurch his heart had given, and the warmth he felt, when he saw Stacey again. It brought back memories of that final night of their visit last year. Really, why would that be? She was hardly much to look at, but she had such beautiful skin, and those eyes...then he had thrust those ideas out of his head. It wouldn't do. After this past awful year, it just wouldn't do.

Everyone was pleased to see her and Amy, and there had been some family things going on over the next few weeks, before school was out. They had all gone together to the big Mackenzie family reunion in Edmonton. Stacey had been fascinated by the huge family tree and meeting the members of all its branches. Relatives who had known Zack had gasped at his son's likeness to him, which by now Jay was getting used to.

Ted noted that Jay didn't seem to be in too much of a hurry to reunite with his wife and daughter and thought that Stacey seemed a little quieter than before. She and Amy had been over to Rougeville a couple of times looking for accommodation, but were unsuccessful. Ted knew that it would have been far better if he had helped Jay find work in Edmunston, and he felt a tinge of guilt.

But he was more focused on Sally and his girls leaving for the summer, and suddenly the day of departure arrived. Ted was inwardly relieved, as the tension between he and Sally had not fully abated. Apart from knowing that he would miss his daughters, he was not going to be sorry to have a break from Sally's attitude.

When he heard Sally telling Stacey to use their house like a second home while she was gone, he saw right through her ploy. At first he was furious, and then his heart sank, Fate for sure was working against him.

The irony of Ted's unhelpfulness to Jay when he had first arrived had rebounded in a way Ted could never have predicted. If he had been as helpful as he had promised, Jay would be settled in Edmunston, and by now the two of them would have their own home in town somewhere. Instead, Jay was in Rougeville all week, Sally would be in British Columbia, and he and Stacey would be almost alone…temptation walking right in his path. Could he resist it?

Chapter Nineteen
1988 Aftermath in Edmunston: The Last Encounter

Stacey

Nearly a year ago, Ted had accosted me outside Marta's, and afterward I had to accept that he would continue tormenting my soul for as long as I stayed in Edmunston. He could not let me be, but would not leave what he had to be with me. He could not say that he loved me, but would not say that he did not.

What was worse, he could not and would not ignore me, especially after our up-close and personal encounter at the hockey tournament and banquet. The air had crackled again between us, and later I realized that we both felt that slam in our hearts that first moment he had come into the arena, shock emblazoned in his eyes. At the time I had thought it was rage that I dared intrude into his world, his family had me so intimidated.

Later, during our brief conversation that evening, I had made it clear that he was the reason for me staying in Edmunston, and unable to deal with it, he had reverted to cruelty once more.

It appeared that what I said had resonated with him, because that whole year, all of a sudden, he was driving past my office. Unexpectedly turning up at places where I was, watching but never acknowledging me, back to the same behavior I saw when he had first fled from my store after saying he could not lose his daughters. He was my own personal stalker.

Now I understood that there would never be anyone else in my life as long as I stayed in town. I was not even sure if there would be if I left, but if I stayed, I knew that however much I might try to get on an even keel, thrust him away, he would come back again and again to disturb my equilibrium. Apparently he couldn't ignore me, even though he would not openly acknowledge me. Now I think that somewhere inside he needed to keep reassuring himself that I still cared about him. His half of the magnet needed that comfort, but it was truly selfish, and cruel, and innately unfair to both Sally and me.

In the intervening years, I had put on a big front, concealing the untold damage done to my emotions, to my broken heart, clearly fooling those around me. Even Ted had thought so, saying so callously, "Well, you're doing all right now!" during that final bitter telephone conversation, when I had tried to explain all the pain he had wrought in my life. I had come so close to telling him about his lost child, but that would have been in retaliation, and I wasn't doing that. But I told him clearly that whatever his assessment, I was not doing OK. Then at last it seemed he understood. Even then he still could not face it, because it raised such guilty feelings in him, that he still could not deal with. If I had told him about his child, I think that guilt would have finally destroyed him, and I could not do that.

I had been so successful at fooling those around me during that whole ordeal that many years later one old friend would say, horrified, "We never knew you were going through so much; you never let on!" And there was I thinking the entire town knew. That everyone thought that I was a pariah of immense proportions. But despite the positive attitude I tried to exude, the pain and grief stayed inside me, creating so much damage to my emotions and my soul that it never went away, despite all my efforts to make happier memories for me and for Amy.

But how could real happiness ever return? Our erstwhile happy life was destroyed, the lives of my husband and my child, all reduced to ashes. There was no way back to the cheerful, carefree, loving wife that I used to be. I could have no happy relationship with another person. All had been swept away.

My now ex-husband, disillusioned with his newfound family, his new life worse than anything in his childhood, blamed everything on me. He deliberately relinquished almost all ties with Amy, telling her that he was using her as a weapon against me. How cruel.

In truth, our relationship was destroyed even as he boarded his flight away from Amy and me and walked into the battleground that his cousin's marriage had become during the eight months since our first meeting with them.

During the intervening seven years, I had lost my marriage, my spouse, my home, and my own family through being so far away from them. I had lost my most-longed-for baby and been parted from my daughter. I had nothing during the first half of that time until I was able to retrieve Amy and take care of her again.

If only Sally would have been honest with us and prevented our doomed move to Canada, but she was so embedded in the shibboleths of that inward-looking mountain society that she had not the courage to take that step.

The aftermath had ruined our child's life. It scarred me irrevocably and condemned me to a lifetime of inner loneliness. Try as I might in later years to move on, rejection after rejection when I dared to trust another revived that pain, destroyed my hopes. I learned too late that Ted's shadow would lay across the rest of my years.

I tried so hard to rebuild my life during those intervening seven years in Edmunston. The challenge made more difficult, initially, because I was the stranger in a town that thrived on gossip and innuendo. The community was chock-full of old families, with strong ties, who stuck together like glue, excluding outsiders and isolating incomers. But by perseverance and sheer bloody-mindedness, I had been successful to the extent that I had overcome some of those barriers and built a new image.

Once people got to know me, found out that I was intrinsically nice and honest. I found a respectable job in a school. I had finally managed to buy a small house for Amy and me. On the surface; as Ted had said, "I was all right now." But it was just a façade. It was survival at best. I knew it, and Amy knew it, as we both held our breath, waiting for the other shoe to drop.

Then came the day when Ted approached me outside Marta's. Decades too late, I understood that I should not have fled from him. If I gone into his house, if we had been face-to-face, and listened to each other, I think it would have been a turning point in our history.

Instead, in fear of the pain he could cause me, and through lack of trust that he could have anything good to say, I had fled. Our ensuing telephone conversation seemed to confirm my fears; it had deteriorated into a bitter trading of hurts, and then Ted finally broke my heart.

So many decades later I realized likely he had broken his own heart too, as he recognized that he had left everything until way too late and created way too much damage and mistrust between us. Had I not I fled, had I been face-to-face with him, I might have seen how deeply he cared and what the past few years had done to him too. He might have realized what a challenge he left me with and understood a little more.

Instead I telephoned him. It was totally the wrong way to deal with a man who had so much trouble articulating his emotional feelings. I now see that he was dealing with so much guilt and shame over his own earlier actions. In a room, facing him, I would have seen that; on the phone, I could not hear it in his voice. All I heard was his callousness and cruelty. The agony of my decision and its impact will haunt me to my dying day.

But that stoic little boy, who lost his momma when he was so young, had never been able to overcome his childhood fears as he matured into a man. He hid what he felt behind a cold attitude toward that which hurt him, while he continued playing the clown to his friends.

By the time he approached me, he wasted another year agonizing over the impact of seeing me unexpectedly, had on him.

The moment when our eyes met had shaken me to the core, but I had thought it was my own reaction to him. It did not occur to me that it was his reaction to me that caused the impact in my heart. His behavior toward me later in the evening did nothing but reinforce that my feelings for him would never change, and it reinforced my belief that he would continue to hurt me as long as I remained in Edmunston.

So focused on the fear of my own pain returning, I didn't recognize what a huge step Ted was taking by inviting me into his home again. After all we had endured during the previous five years, he must have been aware of all the potential repercussions. How I did not see that at the time, I do not know.

But his destructiveness in our conversation a year earlier, and his sudden appearance, so filled me with fear that it put me into flight-not-fight mode. In response, I fled, and buried everything deep inside, not daring to think of it, because it would have destroyed me right there.

It was not until two decades later when his aura materialized in my house after his death with such force, and walked me through our whole interaction again, it finally dawned on me that I had rejected the one opportunity I had to turn our lives in a whole new direction.

We were soul mates. He knew it; I knew it. We should have been together. His spirit invading my life and my home for so many months after his death seems indicative of his need to find me before his spirit left this world completely. It is also clear that it was Ted at the time of his death whose ghostly spirit I saw in my bedroom, who also finally understood what he lost, not my vision of the younger man, or his of my younger self.

The younger Ted never was able to say, "You mean nothing to me. Go away." At some stage should he not have said so? Never once during any conversation did he say to me, "I love Sally. You are making us unhappy." Other men in similar situations rush to hide behind their love for their wives, are quick to say the relationship is over, that they want you out of their lives.

My response to Ted, lashing out at him, retaliating in fury as pain engulfed me once again, aghast at his callousness and not seeing the agony that lay beyond his words, must have hurt him too. But even with my harsh words, even as he retaliated in kind, he never, ever once said to me, "I don't love you." In seven years, he never once said, "Go away. I don't want you."

Poor Ted, poor Sally, poor me.

Chapter Twenty

1988 Good-bye Forever

Stacey

I came face-to-face with Ted outside a store a few days before we left Canada. I hadn't spoken to him or seen him alone since our last terrible phone conversation followed by my angry and bitter call to Sally. My heart started pounding.

"You're leaving?" He asked abruptly.

"Yes."

"For how long?"

"Forever," I had answered, a glimmer of hope still in my heart, adding, "Why? Are you finally going to ask me to stay?"

Ted looked at me. He was now just into his fifties. "Too late to start over now," he had said. His response was what it always had been. "I can't. It's too late." And there was a break in his voice.

"Then I'm going forever," I told him, and I turned to go into the store.

"Stacey…" his voice seemed to crack. I looked at him. I turned, still hopeful, but he just shook his head, and once again those unshed tears glistened in his eyes.

"You're the only woman who has ever made me cry since my mother died," he said sadly. Then he turned and walked away.

"How lucky for your mother that she died," I murmured under my breath. "I still have to live…"

Yes, I did have to live. No matter that life held no appeal for me then or now. Whatever else, like him, I was a parent and had a child to consider, who needed me much, much more now than his daughters had ever needed him. So I had to live.

Faced with a shocking discovery about Amy, I had to make a new start for my daughter away from those who had harmed her, hurt her. She was struggling and getting weaker each day both mentally and physically. Hard as it was going to be, I had to do it. I had to suppress it all: the past, my feelings for Ted, and my grief for our lost baby. I had to thrust it all into the deep recesses of my brain. I would not look back. I could *not* look back. I *dared* not look back! It was buried, gone. Amy needed me, and I had to get her to safety.

Destiny laughed!

Chapter Twenty-One

1988 – Edmonton, Alberta

Jay

"What do you mean you are leaving?" Jay had demanded. He was in high dudgeon, and deep down just a little scared. This past couple of years, even though he now lived with Lucy and was a hands-on goat farmer, among other things, little tinges of something he couldn't identify bothered him.

At times he found himself longing for his little house in Warwickshire, trying to remember what it felt like to come home from work, with Stacey's good hot meals waiting for him, Amy cuddling up to him, friends all around them, bitterly aware that he would never see those days again. If he had stayed, he would have climbed the ladder at work, had his own branch, and they would have been comfortably off by now. Then his lips would tighten—all Stacey's fault, unfaithful bitch!

In those moments, his enmity toward Stacey would reignite uncontrolled wrath aimed at her and the snake-in-the-grass husband of his cousin. His cousin! There was another person who let him down, her and her mother. All their promises and inducements enticing him to come back to his "homeland," a place he had no memory of, all the stories of the past and then telling him how wonderful his life would be. Sally and Aunt Penny had been constantly urging him to rush over, to leave Stacey and Amy.

But then, when he arrived—nothing! They pretty much left him to fend for himself apart from letting him stay with his aunt.

No wonder his mother had been so against him moving to Canada, she *knew* firsthand what his father's sisters were like! He felt the bile rising to his mouth. He should have listened to her. But he couldn't tell her, lose face, let her know that she had been right. He would never have lived it down. He couldn't tell Stacey either, look a fool, so he had kept quiet.

They totally failed to fulfill their promises to him, and he stupidly had not just turned around and gone straight back home, which is what he should have done. "Mr. Wonderful" Ted had signally failed to show that he had any influence in getting Jay a job, just another blowhard. Then Jay heard stories that Ted was a womanizer to boot, and he wondered if that was the cause of the friction he had noted between Sally and Ted.

Guiltily, he recognized that he had been less than welcoming when Stacey and Amy had arrived, certainly toward Stacey, although he tried to spend time with Amy.

In his new job he had a social life he was beginning to enjoy, liked the freedom of his temporary bachelor-style life, and frankly had been shocked at how little feeling he had for his wife when she joined him.

He saw her through others' eyes, saw them look at him, still good-looking and trim, and then when he overheard the perceptions of his new friends, it shook him. She chattered too much, and since Amy had been born, she had let her weight take over. He had never liked fat women, wife or not. He had seen the bewilderment in Stacey's eyes when he rushed away from her after each weekend and constantly put barriers in the way of her and Amy joining him in Rougeville.

Then came the debacle with Ted, Sally, et al. Infuriated that his fat, plain wife had been the one to wander, he leapt on the chance to blame Stacey for everything. The irony was that his total rejection of her and all the stress had taken their toll on Stacey. She'd slimmed way down, looked more like the wife he had married, and for a brief while, her attraction for him reignited. For a while he built up her hopes about their future, took her on vacation with him and Amy, let it seem like things were getting back to normal between them.

He let her think they were having a reconciliation weekend by inviting her to spend a couple of nights at an Edmonton hotel with him. When she asked about moving back in with him, he fended off the question.

Then the Jay who was his mother's son took over, and he had gotten great satisfaction from filing divorce papers on her when she least expected it. He thought she would cave, but she rebutted his first attempt and left him infuriated that she had outsmarted him, and he waited for her response.

She hadn't retaliated at all. She went quietly away, just keeping in touch with him about Amy. Once he relinquished care of Amy to Stacey, she kept him at arms length, except for asking him to help her with money for Amy. Stacey always wanted money; she had everything they had worked for and still wanted more. Later he understood that by comparison with other ex-wives, her demands were very reasonable; all she asked for was a small contribution to his daughter's care. But then, why should he have to pay for a child that didn't live with him? Not his responsibility! The courts saw it differently, and he added that to the "reasons I hate Stacey" list.

He went through a string of girlfriends. He lived with a girl named Nancy and her small daughters—not his bag at all, but he tried to look as if he cared for them. It had been a relief when it broke up, and he moved on. Finally he found Lucy. Like Stacey, Lucy was older than him, but by more years than Stacey, and he stayed with her. Lucy was short and blond. Until Stacey came along, all his girlfriends had been small and blond, so clearly Stacey had been a mistake. Plump, plain Stacey—what had he been thinking?

Lucy, a landowner, who had more than enough room for him to live with her, listened sympathetically to his sad story of betrayal by a faithless wife who had wasted all his money. Then she met his daughter and ironically paid the same attention to Amy as he had to Nancy's daughters. Amy didn't like her, and the feeling was mutual. In the end, the visits between them ended when Stacey went back to Britain, taking Amy with her. Unlike Zack, Jay's care for his daughter didn't extend to following her.

Lucy was very happy. She retained a coworker for her farm, which had been getting too much for her to handle alone. Jay had come along at just the right time. He was so biddable, so dependent, and she was quite prepared to play on his weaknesses. Together with inviting a foreign exchange student to come for a "working" holiday, the three of them could easily maintain the work with the animals; she wouldn't need to pay anyone.

Jay saw himself as the victim of his faithless wife and the way she had dissipated his wealth, and Lucy fed into his view. It was all Stacey's fault, she would coo as she assisted in separating him from his daughter too. Slyly she would hint that Amy did not bother with her father, and wasn't she just cast in the same mold as her mother, always wanting money? Lucy conveniently forgetting how much she supported her own children whose hands were always held out to her.

But, Jay thought, Lucy was his friend, his lover. She cared for him; she would think for him, plan for him, so he wouldn't need to worry about a thing. They could work together with the goats; it should be perfect. But it wasn't.

He gnashed his teeth in frustration and irrationally longed to be able to turn the clock back.

Chapter Twenty-Two

1988 and Beyond
Edmunston

Ted

Ted had watched Stacey as she had left Hans and Marta's house for the last time, unbelieving that after all these years she really was leaving Edmunston. Sally muttered something under her breath, and he realized she was watching him, so he moved away from the window and picked up a beer from the fridge.

He sat in the living room and put the game on, his mind numb. He wanted to go out, go anywhere, but he forced himself to focus on the game on TV, although he had no idea who was playing. It was just figures moving. Who cared who won?

Next morning he got up and headed for work, taking time to drive past Stacey's house. It was deserted, drapes gone, empty boxes on the steps. She really had gone. At Ted's morning tryst with chums for coffee, now there was no Gino either; he had gone home to seek a wife now that he had given up on Stacey, so there was no one to ask about her.

For a couple of days, Ted went around in a daze as that last encounter at the store played over in his mind. "Forever," she had whispered, but her eyes said, "I love you still."

Once again she had asked if he was finally going to ask her stay. He'd almost said yes, and then he'd panicked, and fell back on his usual answer, "I can't," this time adding his main fear, "it's too late," but not adding, "I'm too old to start over."

What was wrong with him? He was still in love with her, despite her dropping him into the shit again last year, still unable to put her out of his mind. The same old arguments raged inside him. If he had not been afraid that it wouldn't last, not listened to gossip about her, taken a chance with her at the very beginning, she would have been with him all these years. He didn't doubt that now. She was still single, and none of her relationships seemed to last long, if there was anyone at all now. Last year she had pretty much told him why.

But where would they have lived? Would he have been able to cope with such a devastating life change? He'd known no other home but his with Sally for nearly three decades, and he had invested so much time and effort in it. He was now over fifty. How did a man start over at that age, albeit with this woman who turned out to be the love of his life, his soul mate? There, he had finally admitted it to himself! But Stacey was gone, and it hurt.

His girls were out in the world and didn't need their dad much any more, but there was his relationship with Sally. Even though the gulf between them was enormous, would she ever have let him go peacefully? Could he ever have been free of Sally or Penny?

He knew Sally would be unable to cope on her own. If she had thought that she could fend for herself, she would not have put up with all his philandering over the years; she would have thrown him out. She had no training and wouldn't be able to find herself much of a job. He was her meal ticket, and she knew it. For sure Stacey would have thrown him out if he had cheated on her, he thought ruefully, but then he would never have strayed from Stacey. Even though she was not his wife, he hadn't been interested in anyone else all the years she had been here. He still flirted in public to show others how much he didn't care about her, but his heart wasn't in it. What was he, a child still?

His thoughts turned to Lauren, who had been the major barrier to him leaving. She was now married, out of his home, and it felt so empty, even with Corinne still there during her breaks from college. For that brief moment, he had thought he could see a way forward with Stacey, and then came his gauche approach to her, the destructive conversation and its aftermath with Sally.

But that last little murmured phrase that he thought he had heard Stacey mutter as he walked away from her earlier that week kept nagging at him. "I still have to live." It set fear up in his heart as he recalled that awful night at the hospital when they thought she might die. Guilt began building up in him, disgust and anger at his bad decisions, hurting Stacey, hurting Penny and his girls, and setting Sally on the path to bitterness he saw stretching out ahead. He should have manned up when he saw the cracks in his marriage turning into a crevasse after the incident with Mariska. Instead, he had harbored resentment for a year, then he and Stacey…Pain gripped him, and linked with the sorrow at what he had given up, his health began to suffer.

For a while he had tried to convince himself that he really hated Stacey, tried to hate her as much as he hated the disruption she had caused. He thought it had worked, and then had come that unexpected meeting at the hockey tournament. It regurgitated all his feelings for her again, shocking him with their intensity, and now, the final realization that she would not return pulled him up with a jolt.

He could feel that drum beating deep inside, knew that she would always be a part of him now, but he had to bury that. He had to let it go, he had to...

It was way past time to move on, close his mind to the past, mend fences, and keep busy, very, very busy. He would move on with his life, get back to partying with his pals, drink, shut her out of his mind completely, drink...fill that void that still never seemed to close inside him.

Destiny laughed and kept pricking him when he least expected it for years and years, even unto his death.

Chapter Twenty-Three

1988 Edmunston

Sally

Sally all but did a little dance around the house when she heard the news. Stacey was going home to England, and she noticed the grim smile on Penny's face when she shared the news with her. "Good," was all she said.

The past few months had been very uncomfortable after the telephone confrontation with Stacey coming out of the blue, just when she had been so happy again. Stacey, clearly upset, had emphasized that Ted had approached *her* and went on to say that was the way it had always been from the beginning! She, Stacey, had reacted to what Ted had initiated, and it was those reactions that drew all the fire down on her head. She had been beyond bitter about the way all the blame had been heaped on her head.

She had sounded close to tears as she said how everyone had abandoned her, how they had all hounded her!

Sally had smiled grimly to herself. At the time, Stacey and Ted had played right into her hands, with a little help from Jay and from Mariska too, which she never knew about.

Alone and lonely, Stacey had started being seen around town, visiting the bars with her new acquaintances. It had been easy to poison Ted's mind against her. He was so stupid. He had been taken in by another English floozy. Stacey unwittingly had played right into Sally's hands, as no self-respecting Canadian woman went to a bar alone. Stacey didn't realize this for all she was seeking was solace and company. Sally made sure Ted heard all about Stacey's encounters with other men, actual or just gossip, ridiculing him for thinking that Stacey cared for him, emphasizing that she was cast in the same mold as her flirty mother-in-law had been.

In the meantime, Jay was poisoning Stacey's mind, calling her a fool for falling for Ted's usage of her, and making it into something it wasn't.

The two of them were complete idiots who had never worked out how much they were manipulated. How fortunate that Ted had set up that barrier and would not talk to Stacey. If they had ever compared notes…

Sally thought that she had been successful in destroying Ted's feelings where Stacey was concerned, until those remarks last year in the newspaper after the hockey tournament dance. Even though he had denied it being true, she had wondered if his feelings for Stacey lingered, or even if they were as strong as ever. She wondered why Stacey couldn't see it too. She really was "Stupid Stacey," especially asking *her* why she did not let Ted go! That would *never* happen, and if it did, it would cost him dearly. She had put up with his antics all these years. He was hers, her meal ticket, and she wasn't handing him over to anyone else, especially Stacey! There was one thing she was determined about, she would outlive Ted just to make sure that he never ended up with Stacey.

It was so easy to blame Stacey, even as she forced herself to swallow the bitter pill that Ted was still besotted with her. Why else would he have gone after her again? Despite his many lies about it, she was *not* going the divorce route, and she had to stop the outside world from knowing what was really happening in their house.

Now, again Stacey was playing into her hands, had finally given up on Ted, and once she was gone, they could all forget about her.

Ted, trying to curry favor with Sally, now had said they would have a summer break with their friends, the Carsons. Lauren and Nicole had been at school together, close friends. Nicole was horse mad, but now she was engaged to a teacher at the school where Stacey had worked; everywhere she went, she seemed to overlap into their lives. Ted and Sally were looking forward to getting to know Barry; it would be a bit different now that the girls were older. It was all planned. They were taking the holiday trailer down to one of the lakes in British Columbia. Lots of fun. Life could get back to the way it had been before Jay and Stacey had come along, ruining everything.

She convinced herself that none of this had anything to do with her; none it was in any way her fault. She kept up that mantra, stayed in denial about her own culpability for destroying everything that they had, with her silence. Sally pushed the guilt she felt into the background and focused on her home, her daughters, and soon her grandchildren. She deliberately forgot about Jay too, until two decades later when Karma took a hand.

All she focused on was that Stacey was going, and they need never think of her or Jay again. Stacey was in the past. Jay was in the past. They would never think of them again, never think of *her* again…never, never…never…

Part Two
Moving On

Chapter Twenty-Four

1988 Patterns – London and Beyond

Stacey

We were leaving Canada for good. Ted was over, Jay was over, and I was going to brush their dust off my feet, start anew, and put the past behind me! I was going home, back to normality, where I belonged. That is what I told myself, and what I said so cheerfully to anyone who would listen. But I hid the real reason for our final departure from Edmunston from everyone, including my family.

After Amy's revelation that she had been molested, I was in shock. This was the final straw after all we had faced in Edmunston, particularly coming so close on the heels of my last confrontation with Ted. It all seemed to be one. Jay's hostility, Amy's fragile health, and my inability to break free from the threads that Ted had so wantonly woven around me for nearly ten years. It seemed insurmountable and finally overwhelmed me.

Needless to say, Jay would continue to turn the knife in his daughter's heart, sending cold letters that preached to her and constantly bemoaned his financial status. This was always laid at our doorstep because he had to make court-ordered support payments for her. "I don't know how we make ends meet," he moaned!

How sad is it that two hundred dollars a month child support is seen as the root cause for a man's failure to meet his own goals? How sad is the father who constantly lays responsibility for his failure on his own child? How pathetic is the father who doesn't ask about his child's welfare or understand that all she needs from that father whom she so adores is just a kind word of love, not a lecture?

For me, I nursed that final accidental meeting with Ted in my mind, and it had thrust me deep into depression again. What had he hoped to achieve, telling me that I caused him as much pain as his mother's death, especially given his cruel words during our last telephone call? It achieved nothing, and without knowing it, he reawakened my sense of grief over our lost baby, the boy I was so sure had been growing inside me. Now just a sad memory, like everything else in my life.

Once I was gone, he would forget all about me, about the destruction he had caused. I made the assumption that I was water under his bridge, out of sight, out of mind. That was reinforced by my friends from whom I heard he was seemingly safely back in his fold with Sally now that the cuckoo had been banished forever from their nest.

When I heard that, I firmly told myself that I would not look back either. My focus now had to be on trying to repair

Amy's life and injured soul. We had to start over, unwittingly following partway in Cassie's footsteps. In retrospect I see the pattern that life seemed to have set for us, hindsight is twenty-twenty.

In panic over Amy's deteriorating health, I had not fully analyzed our situation. I did not see that, yet again, we would be leaving a cozy home, where we were becoming more secure, a place where we were gaining good friends, and instead headed back to what we thought would be safety and security for Amy and peace of mind for me.

The reality was that in fact we were going back to square one. We would be trying to fit in with a world that had also moved on, trying to make friends, struggling to find work, all the while putting on a front for the outside world that the past was over.

Destiny laughed again at my naïvety, knowing my new reality would be that real happiness was gone forever. The softness, tenderness, and caring of my innocent personality from the past lay shattered in the mountains of Alberta. Try as I might to ignore it, to submerge it inside me, it never really let me go.

Two and half decades later, when Ted died and grief overwhelmed me, I realized it had all been for naught. Not a moment had been forgotten; neither had I really recovered from the pain caused. I had just buried it. All those memories were still lurking, ready to strike, for Ted had tied silken bonds around my emotions, and nothing would ever sever them. They are destined to be a part of my life forever.

It is fortunate that we do not have a crystal ball to see our future, and lucky that I had a whole boatload of challenges to face on my return to my homeland, or I would have disintegrated completely.

But for the moment, I was determined that I would forget Canada! Move on!

I put on my happy face. "So glad to be back here," I gushed to friends and family. But just like Cassie before me, the refuge of the home of my childhood existed only in my imagination. People had aged, and moved on, and death had taken its toll on family dynamics, had altered them. And so even here, where my roots were, I found that I didn't belong.

The euphoria from our visit of the Christmas before, when we experienced the welcome of prodigals returning, dissipated almost as soon as the plane landed for our permanent return.

What kind of an idiot was I? Why did I not realize that you couldn't leave everything you have for a future based on a happy vacation, even if it had been in your old home, with your own family? I truly was terminally stupid! Dumb Stacey on a roll again!

This was no Eden and would be far from the sanctuary that I envisaged. Life continued underscoring that everything I had loved, apart from Amy, was truly gone, forever. I had come home wounded, looking for reassurance, for comfort, but as my new life unfurled, it was clear that this was history repeating itself, and no comfort existed for me.

I had done exactly what Cassie had done four decades earlier, fled home because I thought it would be safer, and it was likely to bring the same results! What on earth made me think I would have any different an experience? I had been stampeded by panic and fear for Amy. Had I bothered to compare and analyze our situations, I would have seen that.

But this was *my* family; we all loved each other, cared about each other, didn't we, didn't we? I could rely on them, couldn't I? Couldn't I?

Destiny tittered.

Chapter Twenty-Five
1988 Reality with a Vengeance

Stacey

Once more we flew into a new life, this time an early English summer, to the apparent thrill of my parents, especially my mother, her sisters, and relief from my brother, who felt that finally someone else could shoulder the yoke of responsibility and take care of our seniors.

After all, I was the girl in the family, the eldest, and it really should have been my job all along to care for them. I had abrogated my filial responsibility by moving so far away with my husband. What a selfish person I was!

Where else should I have been? He had heard the same mantra from our mother as I had as we had been growing up. "It is a wife's duty to help her husband, be there to see to his meals, and if his job takes him away, then as his wife, you have to follow."

And that was what I had done, left to be at my husband's side, but apparently once my husband was no longer in the picture, I should have rushed back to shoulder my duties as a daughter. Instead I stayed overseas, living the high life! How little he knew, and he continued to make those same misguided assumptions about me for our entire lives.

My mother hugged me, her face wreathed in smiles. "I have got my Stacey back again!" she said, near to tears, and I hugged her back.

Not for me to tell her that actually her Stacey laid broken back in Alberta, her heart shattered into a zillion pieces, her soul destroyed. All that had returned was a shell. I was empty inside, damaged beyond repair, and try as I might, each time I saw hope, ensuing rejections distanced me farther and farther from the warmth that had once made up my entire personality, isolating me inside.

"Yes, Mum," I had answered, putting on a bright smile and trying to stop my voice from shaking. "I am here, right where I started, where I belong."

After nearly fifteen years, I was back in my old bedroom again, and Amy was tucked into my brother's tinier bedroom next to me, as we crammed our luggage and ourselves into these two spare rooms in my parents' flat.

It was all utterly alien to both of us, unrecognizable. So much had changed, having been absent for so long. The noise was astronomic after the peacefulness of our little house. Apartment neighbors were noisy. The traffic streaming past the windows was incessant, and outside on the street, you had to raise your voice to be heard above its roar.

The first night back, I sat up in bed hugging my knees, tears running down my cheeks, looking at the sad relics I had left of my life: three suitcases sitting dismally in the corner.

It was not even my cozy bedroom of old, with its blue ceiling (which Mum hated), mauve walls, and pretty ice-pink satin bedcover and curtains. They too were long gone. Now it was a room refurbished in my parents' taste. Drab, cheerless, all brown and cream, paisley wallpaper, cream ceiling, net liners, and beige curtains: a reflection of my world for years to come.

Had I but known it, drabness and drudgery would be my soul mates now. It was fortunate I did not know it on that first night home, for I am sure I could not have survived. However, a little part of optimistic Stacey still lurked inside me. As ever, hope sprang eternal.

I told myself I had two choices: sit, whine, and mope, or try to move forward. I was stubborn too; it was what had gotten me through the previous decade, so I shook myself, sat up straight, and moved forward.

As was to be expected, at first we experienced the usual honeymoon period following our return, as do all prodigals, lifting my spirits and Amy's. We made the rounds of friends and family, all were so welcoming and seemed so excited to see us home. It provided an oasis of fun for a short while, but once those first contacts and visits had been exhausted, everyone moved back into their own lives again. Little room there for Stacey and Amy, leaving us to our own devices, with loneliness and homesickness our companions as we tried to make our way into our new future.

Once again I was the sole provider for Amy and myself. I needed to get a job and then get us our own accommodation, and there was a new school to find too. As I started to work my way through these issues, I finally understood the daunting task ahead of me. I wasn't in a small town now, where I knew a lot of people. I was back in a big city, anonymous, where apart from my family, no one knew me now. In a big city, no one cares about anyone else.

I fought back against the depression as my self-esteem sank lower and lower. I thought about the two men I had cared for the most in my life and how I clearly hadn't measured up for them. First Jay had made it obvious that he did not need or want me as a wife, then Ted had…no, I still could not even think of Ted. The lesson they had taught me was, that no matter what I did for them, no matter how much I loved them, it had not been enough. They had both made me feel that I was unlovable, unwanted, unnecessary to their happiness; that my only attraction lay in being useful to them, and another part of me withered away.

There was no point in dwelling, it wasn't helping, and so I forced myself to bury the overwhelming sense of loss that was threatening to overcome me. Resolutely I pushed it all to the back of my mind, refusing to examine it, or think of it. So I took Amy out to rediscover London. We found something fun to do that would spur us forward again, and bring a smile back to Amy's face. I told myself, I was home here with my own family supporting me; I could do this. I had to, as no one else would do it for me.

In the end, I was fooling myself about the support. My mother, in the very early stages of dementia, worn down after caring for my father through his recent bout with cancer and keeping herself going, did not understand and was struggling with all the changes his illness had brought to her life.

My brother, well, we'd never been that close, although I was very fond of his wife. However, there were never any opportunities to be on my own with her, to confide in her. I thought she might have been sympathetic, but then again, maybe not. In the end I never remade the same kind of friendships that I left behind after first Ted, then Amy's molester chased me from the home I had finally made and the possibility of a better future.

People were always too wrapped up in their own lives and made wrong assumptions about mine. So I started building a barrier again to hide my true broken self, would let no one see behind it, for what was the point? No one really cared. It became a way of life: to hide the hurt, bury the pain. If I could not open up to them, then there was no one, no real friend, and that has proven to be the case ever since.

What I had to do was develop a sunny façade with a bright smile and cheerful outlook and hide the real me behind it. Over the years I developed that outward show by becoming a bit of a comedian with a lot of quick quips, and in the end, I almost believed it was the real me. But in quieter moments, I heard Destiny's mocking laughter…

Edmunston, much as I liked it, was a small town, where gossip and rumor ran rife. It had not been wise to share the shock and horror of learning that Amy had been molested by a person I had so foolishly trusted. I at last had realized that one didn't share information like that in the community, or it would tarnish the victim more than the perpetrator. They would also judge me for not being aware, for not protecting my daughter, so we had kept silent.

Perhaps if I had shared it with some of those closest to us, it would have explained Amy's erratic behavior at times, which people had been wont to criticize. Heaped on top of her constant displacement during our early days in Canada, and her father's cold behavior toward her, it had all taken a terrible toll on her. At thirteen she weighed less than one hundred pounds, her cheeks hollow, her eyes sunken in her face—couldn't my family see how frail she was? Didn't they care? Seemingly not, and at times they all joined the "she is very difficult" chant.

I had been so frantic about Amy's health and psychological well-being, not knowing what to do for the best, that I had listened to the mental-health counselor who advised me to take her as far away as possible. Coupled with my own anguish after that final encounter with Ted, it seemed that we had no option but to abandon the home in which we had invested so much time and effort to make it ours, cozy and comfortable. It had seemed that if we were to have any peace, we had to move away, which I had done, and so here we were, starting all over again.

In hindsight, we should have gone to Naomi, in British Columbia, spent the summer with her. She was the most understanding and kindly of my friends; she would have understood. We might even have made a life near her and her family. Coupled with that, she had nothing but contempt for Ted and Sally, and had told me more than once to stay away from them, as they made me feel bad about myself. One day she even told me that she thought their encouraging us to move to be near them and then abandoning us was cruel. She was the only one to see that the rot had set in before I ever even landed to join Jay. She understood Sally and Penny's betrayal long before I ever did.

What chance did poor Amy ever have? She was blessed with "Stupid" for a mother and "Cold-heart" for a father, and the witches from Hamlet for her family. It was so unfair to her, the total innocent in the center of all this mayhem, which had originated in Mountain Reaches with her grandfather's kin long before she was born. With the actions of the next generation continued forty years later, it destroyed our little happy family.

I had to stop this! I knew that it would not do to dwell.

For Amy's sake, I *had* to put the past behind me, behind us. I *had* to forget, to stop thinking about it, focus on being somewhere new, spend time putting happy thoughts into my daughter's mind. We *must* move on!

Chapter Twenty-Six
1988 – 90 London: City of Fun

Stacey and Amy

Amy was enjoying getting reacquainted with her cousins, uncles, and aunts, seeing all the sights of the big city, and visiting parks and zoos. It was fleeting, but it was helping. London was full of big, exciting stores, and everything was within walking distance or a just short bus or train ride away. Throughout those early days of summer, we took time to have some fun together, taking the Tube into central London, seeing the sights, acting like tourists, and being friends, as I watched over her anxiously, not knowing what to do for the best to heal her.

Amy was always an avid nature lover, so she reveled in the chance to feed the birds in various royal parks, laughing as she was getting her picture taken with all the birds fluttering around her. She loved the London Zoo, and we spent happy hours there making faces through the glass at the monkeys, laughing at the antics of the penguins, and shying away from an open-air opportunity to make friends with a tarantula—not even for my daughter would that happen. I had been in a cage with a tiger, and had petted a cheetah up close and personal, but anything with more than four legs—absolutely not on my agenda!

We did the round of the rest of London's tourist sights—Buckingham Palace, Whitehall, and getting more pictures taken with Lifeguards doing their utmost not to smile back at her as she stood beside them pulling faces.

London fed Amy's magpie instincts. She loved exploring the wealth of street markets, browsing the boutiques and booths at the revamped Covent Garden market, taking in the city smells and voices, finding something pretty, buying trinkets and clothes that she simply had to have. She too was filling the void inside her, left by the sadness, loneliness, and disappointment of the past years—the anguish caused by her father and others.

We never discussed it, and probably that was a mistake, because all the things we did overall were really distractions, keeping our thoughts away from our old life, so that we did not have to talk through what had happened.

Both of us pretended that this new life was good, and that we were not missing our friends. We ignored the challenge of living with my father, who was reinforcing her belief that men were unkind, selfish, and uncaring. We never said that this move was yet another mistake in her short life.

Chapter Twenty-Seven

Life with Father, or Not

Stacey

Life with my father had always been difficult for my brother and me as we grew up. His nerves had never fully recovered from a breakdown during World War II after being assigned to working on London's ack-ack guns.

That was a time when the military's treatment for shell shock was, "Pull yourself together, man!" Dad had been unable to do that, and so was eventually invalided out of the service for health reasons, well before the end of the war, the damage to his psyche permanent.

As children we had learned to live with Dad's erratic temper, with all of his obsessive-compulsive behavior, and nervous irritation. Cruelly, sometimes we had scoffed at it, but overall we accepted that it was the way he was. We had no knowledge back then of posttraumatic stress disorder, which the military is now more sympathetic toward, or so they would have us believe.

In the aftermath of his recent cancer scare, Dad had regressed, his recent brush with death, including the ensuing cancer treatments, regenerating his nervous disposition. He followed Mum around like a Siamese twin, never more than two paces behind her, driving her crazy and probably assisting in her early descent into dementia.

He became querulous, quibbling with everyone over the slightest thing, and was wholly self-absorbed, but he saved the worst of his behavior for his granddaughter. He tut-tutted at everything Amy did, and he made it clear that she was an intrusion into his home that he didn't want. He had little in common with her, besides, she took attention away from him, which didn't sit well with him at all.

Her uncle, likewise, took scant interest in her. It wasn't that he was intentionally unkind; he had a busy job and he just did not understand that she needed a kind, gentle man in her life. No matter what the reasons were, it all contributed to her self-esteem sinking even lower.

It added to the aftermath of the molestation she had endured at the hands of the teamster and exacerbated her father's calculated callousness toward her, doing nothing to ease her pain. The disappointment in the rest of the men in her family pushed her sense of her own value even lower, making her even more vulnerable to disappointment.

We talked with the new family doctor, a pert thirty-year-old, who had replaced my own dear doctor. But she proved unsympathetic, as both of us were reluctant to be too specific, and so my fears were dismissed. "She'll grow out of it. She's at an awkward age," was the response.

If my father and her uncle showed less than warmth to her, there was no refuge in distance from her own father's ability to hurt her. Amy bore the brunt of her father's attitude toward us as Jay continued to turn the knife in his daughter's heart. His monthly letters to her, enclosing his support check, were full of cold messages as he preached at her and incessantly bemoaned his own impecuniousness. He consistently cited the court-ordered child-support mandate as the root cause of his poverty and struggles. He claimed the pitiful monthly encumbrance was standing in the way of all he wanted to achieve. It made one wonder how he would have coped with the full-time expense of a child's needs.

I wondered why he didn't take advantage of his freedom now that he was not living with us, to pursue the university degree he had wanted. So often he said that we had held him back because he had no time to study once he had a family. But it could have helped his earning potential. However, it seemed that he was more intent on proving that my actions and Amy's monthly stipend was the root cause of all his penury and every bad thing that happened in his life.

He never understood that all Amy really needed from him were kind and loving words from the father she had so adored. When I once tried to get him to understand this, I was coldly told that his relationship with his daughter was not my concern, so each month she continued to be hurt by his behavior toward her, each letter stealing another piece of her innocence.

How sad for Jay that he didn't better spend his time getting to know his daughter, asking after her interests, encouraging her.

More than anything, he would have been able to feel the pride in having a smart and wonderful daughter.

We had a telephone, so Jay could have called Amy now and again, but he never did, even when we moved to America and were on the same continent as him. How unjust that in later years Amy was blamed for not taking an interest in her father prior to his death. His longtime paramour used e-mail to announce his death to Amy. Her prior e-mails about her father's illness had gone astray. Her motive we realized was a concern that Jay's gold-digger daughter would come running for her inheritance.

Amy said that since he had not chosen to give her anything while he lived, she didn't want anything from him after his passing. So sad that Lucy never gave herself or Amy's father the opportunity to understand the truly good person she is.

Fortunately for her that Amy did at least have love and care from her step-father, who proved to be more of a real father to her than her natural parent.

UNEASE

Out of necessity I was focused on my job search, but I was still uneasy about Amy. She really wasn't getting as much attention as she should, but things would improve for her when she went to school, wouldn't they? Shouldn't they?

There seemed to be a ray of light when Amy made friends with a girl about her own age who lived in the same apartments as us. She went to the same school that Amy would start at the end of the summer, and they would be able to walk there together. Once she started school, she found two classmates who liked her, and they all clicked, so she became firm friends with them too.

It helped her feel better about herself, or so I thought. But Amy too was hiding her feelings, her focus being on not burdening her mother with her woes.

The friendship with Rosie brought a brief respite of pleasure into our lives. As a result of Amy meeting Rosie, I met her mother. We had very little in common other than being solo mothers, but she was a kind and fun person, and we formed a new friendship. It was a start, a new step forward, not necessarily what I was looking for, but it was something new, something different, a relationship with no ties to the past that I needed to escape.

Our friendship gave respite from my thoughts, which were still a challenge. It was proving hard to smother those ghosts, as my stubborn heart refused to dismiss the longing for someone to care about me again, for Ted. I needed someone who would kiss away my tears, reassure me about my fears, hug me, love me, and say everything would be fine. But I could see no way that would happen or how to fill the void inside me.

I gave myself a mental shake and told myself I *had* to move forward, all of that was gone forever, stolen by the cruelty and deceit of those I had trusted and those I had loved.

I was not going to think about Canada again, and I started to cut myself off from our old friends. I wasn't going to think of our home there again. I wasn't going to think about Ted again, feel that pain that never diminished. I wasn't going to mourn my lost babies any longer, think about any of it any longer.

I wasn't, I wouldn't, I shouldn't, I couldn't! I *won't!*

Move on! Destiny smirked...

Chapter Twenty-Eight
1988 Accommodation, Lack Thereof:

Stacey

After all that I had survived during the previous seven years, I thought I was up to anything but the challenges of trying to find our own accommodation in this new London did defeat me.

I ought to have been eligible for an apartment through the local council, but the staff people were condescending and judgmental. Our conversations got more and more intense:

"Well, yes, you *are* eligible, but we have a very long waiting list, and there are lots of immigrants like you."

"But I am not an immigrant. I was *born* here. I went to school here, worked here, my daughter was born here, I have paid taxes here, I am British!"

"Well, that's as maybe, but then you *did* make yourself homeless."

"How did I make myself homeless? My husband did that to us when he abandoned us in a foreign country. What else should I have done then, if not come home?"

"Well, yes, but then there is only you and your daughter, and you do *have* somewhere to stay at present."

"It's temporary accommodation with my parents. I don't think they want us here forever."

"Well, yes…well…um…well, we might find you somewhere in a few months, but you will have to start with a trial period on the Broadworth Estate. We need to be sure that you will be a good tenant before we put you somewhere more permanent!"

"The *Broadworth* Estate? Are you kidding me? I lived in this borough for nearly thirty years, I *know* what its reputation is, and I have a young daughter. That's just not acceptable!"

This was a troubled estate. It was renowned for rampant criminal activity, not to mention intimidation of other tenants by the core gang that ran it! How was that suitable for a middle-aged woman and a teenaged girl? I was enraged!

"Well, that's all we have to offer at present, or for some time to come." And that was that.

In disgust, I turned to the private market.

Grr! Those folks were even more patronizing and dismissive than the council!

An underdressed, over painted seeming, sixteen-year-old began by looking down her nose at me from the first moment we met, saying straight-out that they would find it hard to place a "single mum."

Indignantly, I pointed out, "I *am* not a single mother. I am divorced and there is a *big* difference!"

Apparently, according to the sixteen-year-old, it made not an iota of difference in the private landlord market. One woman plus child/children is a single mother—unsupported, untrustworthy. So much for working for the wedding ring, I thought!

As such, I was prejudged, particularly since I had never rented in my own name or owned my own house, other than jointly with Jay.

"There is no credit history to check on, really, and we don't know that you are a reliable tenant, especially since you have been living abroad!" she responded. As she examined the chipped polish on one of her nails, and then reached into a drawer for a bottle to touch it up, I thought there was a real interest exhibited here in helping a client!

I about smacked this tightly skirted, narrow-hipped, bouffant-hair-styled little witch! She was not in the least apologetic, and acted the whole time as if she was doing me a favor just by talking to me. I hoped she would find herself in the same position one day and meet with a similar response.

Pretty sure Karma dealt with her later. She seemed just the type to marry the jeans without checking into the genes! The judgmental attitude of the private sector landlords appalled me, but once again it was an indicator of my ever-changing London.

After Miss Miniskirt, I tried a couple of other agencies, mostly with similar results, or suggestions that I try sections of Leyton or Walthamstow, where landlords might not be so picky. They mentioned a couple of neighborhoods that I *knew* I didn't want my daughter living in, any more than on the Broadworth Estate!

With virtually no other choice left, we settled in uneasily with my parents for the long haul, while I searched for jobs to prove my stability, build my credit rating, and expand my bank account.

I felt like a stranger in my own city.

Just as Cassie's London had so disappointed her when she returned home in the 1940s after fleeing from Mountain Reaches, my London likewise had changed. It was no longer the city that I remembered and loved for its free-spiritedness of the 1960s and 1970s.

How ironic that the one person who might have understood our plight did not want to have any contact with us. Well, most certainly not with me! Cassie had jumped at the opportunity to cast me into the mode of "scarlet woman." What else was to be expected from that girl from East London who had impoverished her son, and abandoned him at the first opportunity, and was now likely playing darts somewhere in an East End pub. Actually, that did come later, but at least she never heard about it!

Clearly Jay had told his story well, ignoring the parts he didn't like about it, understandably unwilling to lose face with his mother and sister and expose his own lack of judgment. I made an easy scapegoat to save him having to admit to Cassie that she was right about his move to Canada and he was wrong. How could he have told her that his father's family had turned out to be idols with feet of clay and that their promised help to him had never been forthcoming, almost from day one? That, instead of retreating to Britain at once, when he might have salvaged his job and our lives, he balked, and then found it so much easier to blame me for all the ills that followed him. It enabled him to also roll the antipathy of Zack's family into his whole story, so he was not faced with her inevitable "I told you so!"

How could he have acknowledged that we hadn't researched the situation well enough before abandoning our life in Britain? How could he tell her that he should have turned right around and come home to reclaim his old job that was still open? Jay had not given any thought to the impact his straightened circumstances would have on Amy and me. As luck would have it, the situation that developed between Ted and me gave him all the excuse he needed to abrogate all responsibility for dragging us away from our secure life in Britain on his whim.

In part, too, Jay was still convinced that he could grasp the golden ball that he trusted existed and was his due. Raised with the belief that he was entitled to more than life had so far rewarded him with, he stayed, and we all became victims of that decision. He made himself a prisoner of that belief, so how could he return to what he saw as his previously humdrum life and predictable future.

I suspect that Cassie would have gotten more satisfaction out of knowing that Penny's plan to separate her from her son had been thwarted than gloating over him being taken in by them. Had she been in possession of all the facts, she might also have seen how Sally's silence doomed us all, that one letter warning us to reconsider our move could have saved all our futures.

But that hadn't happened. Sally's pride hadn't allowed it, so now after all that we had been through, here were Amy and I, starting over once more in London with Jay and Cassie maintaining a long-distance relationship. Once she learned that I was back in London with Amy, Cassie expressed a wish to see her granddaughter, and being Cassie, instead of being straightforward and contacting me directly about it, she told Jay to tell Amy, who was living with one grandmother, that she should telephone the other and go visit her.

Oh, really? When Jay's directive arrived, I was disgusted with Cassie. Your granddaughter doesn't know you, you've hardly ever written to her, now she's a teenager, and you are demanding that she dance attendance on you! I just wanted to scream at her, "What makes you think that she even wants to phone you, much less see you?" But to keep the peace, and keep Jay off Amy's back, I stepped in, and before additional pressure arrived from Jay in his monthly diatribe to Amy, we did make contact with Cassie, and made arrangements for Amy to go to see her.

Amy was none too happy about. "I don't want to see her. I heard her say such mean things about you on her tapes to Dad. Anyway, I hardly know her, and she almost never wrote to me." But finally she agreed to go to please me, and stop the harassment from her father.

Cassie was still her grandmother, and I was tired of being cast in the role of demon. I wasn't going to give her any more ammunition and be blamed for being a barrier to her seeing her granddaughter on top of everything else.

So on one Saturday afternoon in late summer, we took the Tube across to Notting Hill Gate, where Cassie lived. As I walked with Amy around to her grandmother's flat, her trepidation grew, not least because I wasn't going in with her. First, I hadn't been invited, and second, I couldn't see how my being there would do anything other than raise the tension and make it more uncomfortable for my daughter. Cassie had never accepted me prior to leaving for Canada; now I was evil personified.

Or course, I did have reservations about leaving her alone with her grandmother, but I felt that Cassie wouldn't be mean to a little girl. She wouldn't, would she? I kissed Amy at the street corner, watched her walk up the steps to her grandmother's flat, and made sure she got inside safely before I turned away.

For the next two hours, I wandered up and down Portobello Road, to check out the market again. It was near to the little flat that had been the first home for Jay and me. It seemed so long ago. It hadn't changed much—just a different balance of ethnic faces, but it was still full of fascinating antiques at one end, and multitudes of food at the other.

Later, as agreed, I went back to fetch Amy. I waited her on the corner until she finally came down the steps and headed toward me without looking back. She didn't seem upset, so hopefully all had gone well. Amy hardly discussed the visit; she just said that Cassie had not asked after me at all, and that Cassie had pressed some English pounds into her hand as she left, which pleased her. Bribery always works with children.

That she had not asked after me didn't worry me. Frankly, the less I had to do with her, the better. Cassie had never been my friend; it was Zack that I had adored, not her. But clearly she had no idea how to talk to a young teenager, which did not auger well for the future. In the end, Cassie's behavior made it almost impossible for Amy to have any kind of relationship with her grandmother; neither did she want one, but at least it was her decision.

Now that she had distanced herself from her grandmother, the ever-snooty and patronizing Isabella made no effort to get in touch with Amy, either, or even introduce Amy to her son. To this day, Amy has never met Isabella's son; doubtless we are relegated to the black-sheep branch of the family. But it is sad that the only two remnants of Zack and Cassie's poor benighted family will never get to know each other now, nor apparently, want to.

It was to be expected from such a dysfunctional family that they never gave a thought to how lonely Amy might feel moving back to Britain, nor how much a little kindness to her might have made her feel a part of a family, any family. They didn't ask if she might miss the father that she loved so much but who continued with his coldness toward her, even from across the Atlantic.

A pity, but another indicator that on both sides of the Atlantic, Jay's family lacked something intrinsic in their relationships with each other, which the word *dysfunctional* didn't even begin to cover!

It also put poor Cassie back to the hamster and the wheel thing again. Once more driving her family away from her, once more justifying her hatred for the world that was always working against her. Complaining was so much easier than taking the time to build a relationship with a granddaughter she might have come to really love, and who might have come to love her too. Sadly, it left Amy with a very one-dimensional view of her forebears; the only people she really knew were my family, and even they were proving to be disappointing too.

Ironically, we came across Cassie on one more occasion, several years later, after I had remarried. Amy and I were at Selfridges in London, looking along a row of scarves, when I came face-to-face with Cassie. Not completely sure that it was her, after so many years, I swallowed hard, "Are you Cassie?" I asked tentatively to the aging, gray-haired, pinched-faced woman opposite me.

There was a second's pause, and then she looked like a rabbit caught in car headlights as she stuttered, "Oh, no. People are always mistaking me for her. Sorry, no, I'm not her!" And she bustled off, not even looking at Amy. Really? No, *really!* How pathetic!

I was absolutely stunned, unless Cassie had a twin or a sister that I knew nothing about, who spoke in the same way, had the same voice, and who could possibly have been mistaken for her, Amy and I had just been blanked!

But no! Really? People don't do stuff like that, do they? They don't walk away from their only granddaughter, do they?

Well, really, I should have known by now that if they were a part of the Mackenzie family, particularly if they were Cassie, they could, and they did. They were capable of any unkindness, any cruelty, any lie, even to a child—all of them!

So much for the Mackenzies, then!

Chapter Twenty-Nine

1988 Job Search

Stacey

Along with accommodation, finding employment was not so easy, either, and I really had to work at it. In Edmunston, I'd pretty much walked from job to job, the latter two positions being offered solely on my reputation for hard work and integrity. It had been the same when I had lived in London before and had been poached from one firm to another. Back then it was fine to keep changing jobs; in fact it was almost expected, especially if you sought any kind of promotion. But then, I was much younger. The world is a friendlier place when you are young and thin, with long, red-brown hair, and big, dark eyes. You could get away with almost anything. However, if you were tiny and *blond*, you could get away with absolutely everything!

Now I was older, plumper, plainer Stacey, with the sad, unhappy eyes. In my new reality, people would not take work experience gained in another country on face value. I was relegated back to single mother, returning to the job market after fifteen years, with no skills. No skills? When I pointed out the experience on my resume, I was met with eyebrows raised, and challenged with cynical questions. "Really, and where was this? Canada? Rural Canada? Well, it's not quite the same as a big city like London, is it?"

I felt like an immigrant in my own country, just as the council lady had described me, and ultimately, interviews were conducted by the same type of little smarty-pants as I had encountered in the accommodation agency, although in the end, that proved advantageous!

"You should really try to ease back into the job market at your age."

(At *my* age—what was I? Methuselah?)

"Get a job as a waitress, get back into employment that way," one of the insolent teenagers had said. I'd swear she was related to the girl in the private landlord agency—but by that time all those sixteen-year-olds looked the same to me. (Well, she may have been twenty, but the attitude was mid-teens.)

I applied for job after job, went for round after round of fruitless interviews until I finally used my brain and fell back on my last resort—a temporary staffing agency, which really should have been my first resort. I don't know why I didn't do this sooner, as it had served me extremely well when I was younger.

In the 1960s, there had been loads of temporary agencies, all staffed by the same kind of little bimbos who still seemed to run them twenty years later. Switching agencies to gain experience in a certain job or gain a particular skill was how I had become proficient enough if a career change took my fancy.

Inevitably I landed with an employer who offered me a full-time job, much to the chagrin of the temp agency staff, who would warn me that they wouldn't employ me again. Um, well, actually that's OK, as I have a full-time job now, and can parlay that into another one when I'm ready!

This technique led me through several different careers when I first entered the job market at sixteen. On-the-job training was so much more profitable than taking a whole bunch of college classes that I had to pay for, then still having to take an entry-level position after all that.

I had learned *in situ*, and was paid to do so. Lucky for me, I had always been a quick learner and had a high IQ. The first couple of employers lost out a bit during my learning process, but by the third employer, I'd be golden, and by the fourth, I would be on their permanent staff list!

Fifteen years later, though, it was not quite that easy, now I was bracketed into the "middle-aged mum" category, which I found patronizing and irksome. So it was very fortunate that the same types of girls still ran these agencies. Overall, they were pretty much not too smart, just very presentable, but they *thought* they were smart.

After a couple of forays into the nearest agencies, I figured I could still manage to fool them into employing me. It was any port in the storm that was now gathering into tempest proportions. I'd pretty much run out of money, and I wasn't going to go and claim welfare money; I could have, but wouldn't. In any case, I was white and could type; I'd be laughed out of the welfare office when they were dealing with so many non-English-speaking immigrants with no skills at all.

My typing was never fast or accurate during tests, but back in my youth I got particularly good at faking a typing proficiency test, helped considerably by the naïve teenagers. I mean, how dumb is it to leave a kitchen timer beside someone, set it for ten minutes, and then go off to make phone calls while waiting for the "ding" to tell you the test was over? How did they not catch on to how easy it was to add another five minutes to the timer while they were distracted? I got such praise for my speed and accuracy. I could not believe they were still falling for that old trick as I told my Mum later!

"You didn't!" gasped my mother, stunned at my audacity, while Dad looked at me like I was a creature from another planet. Mum giggled. "I don't know where you get all that sauce from," she said.

"Well, it's not like I can't type fast or accurately, in the right circumstances, but they test you on such crappy machines that I have to do something to set the balance in my favor," I had answered. The reality was that I did have good typing speeds, just not on tests, and anyway, I was only using typing as a way in!

Really, no! People don't do stuff like that really, do they?

Well, if they are desperate for a job, and have a teenaged daughter to support, and they really need the work…they just might!

Once I was back in employment, I started bouncing back and forth between a number of small companies and smaller agencies. I got used to hearing "very nice, but not quite suitable" at the end of the first week. Frankly, I didn't have time to spare; nor was I going to put any effort into a job that was going nowhere. No way was I going to work for a moron whose job I could have done better myself, or for someone so condescending to me that it made me want to cringe, but it seemed there was a dearth of those kind of employers in this new London. It was Thatcher's London, all stockmarket spivs and dodgy entrepreneurs!

However, with some perseverance and a couple of changes of temporary agency, eventually it all came together when I was assigned to a small independent company run by a local couple, Stacie and Biff.

Stacie and Biff were just full of themselves, and fell into the "dodgy entrepreneur" category! They ran a legal typing agency among their many other ventures. They had rolled a travel agency and a small catering firm into the mix, plus sold insurance on the side and called themselves "nouveau capitalists"—how funny! Big deal! They skated by, but they were pretty naff at nearly all their ventures, and if it hadn't been for Stacie's government gained office expertise, it would all have gone belly up!

Most of their typing work was for City of London-based legal companies that specialized in the new laws of the European Union. I learned much more than I ever wanted to know about the intricacies and failings of the European Union's legislation (backed so hastily by the British government) as I typed document after document.

One of their clients, who reminded me a bit of Winston Churchill, would boom at me down the telephone as he asked for corrections to his manuscripts. "Hasty legislation, Stacey, hasty legislation. It will take decades to unravel, and in the meantime we lawyers will make a fortune!"

By virtue of my "make sure you are useful" philosophy, I got on well with most of their clientele, particularly "Winston," which made Biff and Stacie uncomfortable at times. They were concerned I might get hired directly by one of their clients, instead of doing the work via their typing service.

But life with them suited me better at the time. It was close to home; I could actually walk there. The work was not too demanding, and as I had learned how to charm people over the years, an absolute must when you are thrust into a hostile environment with no one to support you, they took to me.

Despite their little irritations, Biff and Stacie were interesting, although it drove Biff crazy to have "Stacey" and "Stacie" in the same room! Through conversation, we figured out that Stacie and I had shared some old acquaintances via our involvement with politics in the late 1960s and early 1970s. Stacie had worked in the UK government during the Profumo affair and knew one of my old friends who had also worked for a prominent politician a little later.

For anyone who ever saw *Scandal,* the movie about Christine Keeler, well, Stacie had been one of those willing, nubile secretaries who headed off to naughty weekends at the country homes of top-level Tory leaders. Of course, Stacie denied that she ever participated in the naughty bits, but I knew whom she had worked for, so I was not convinced! I think her denial was as much for Biff's benefit as mine. "Oh, no," she said in shocked tones. "I *never* went on one of those weekends!" Yeah, right!

As it happened, in the next job, I worked with the son of a well-known British actor who had played a key part in that same movie. He was fascinated to learn that I had met one of the actual players it was based on. We glossed over the fact that his own father's "left hand down a bit" sexual reputation had rivaled anything in the movie and his marriage break-up had been headline news! Small worlds that I observed from a distance!

Back in the sixties, like most of the rest of my life, I was caught up on the outside looking in, often a part of an outer circle that saw what was going on, but never a part of it. So although I knew about the more outrageous behavior at that time, and knew a lot of the same people that Stacie did, I was never offered the chance to say yay or nay to the experiences that could be had.

But I did have some stories to share with her about a particularly overfriendly, somewhat extroverted Member of Parliament and his sloppy kisses. *Yuck!* But Stacie was much more interested in learning what I knew of his secretary, whose own husband had just been elected to the House of Commons. In latter years, he too became embroiled in a political scandal, and so the wheel turns! All the gossip helped to add a little excitement to what was otherwise a mind-numbing job, but satisfactory for the time being.

Until, that is, Biff and Stacie's marital difficulties spilled over into the office. I pretty soon tired of being the buffer between them, having both of them bend my ear about the inadequacies of the other, and also with the pinches on the butt and innuendoes from the errant husband. So after working for them for nearly six months, I moved on. It was time.

Chapter Thirty
1989 Intrepid Reporter Once More

Stacey

Faced once again with unemployment, and stuck for choice, an ad that looked promising caught my eye. After some fast-talking, I ended up taking a job with a small weekly newspaper as I morphed my reporting experience into something recognizable in the UK. The job was supposedly for copywriting, which I could do, but in effect turned out to be mostly a sales job, which I couldn't. I couldn't even sell Mary Kay to my friends. I am totally useless as a sales person!

But I stuck it out for a while, as it came with a company car, a useful asset to Amy and me for weekend adventures. Nirvana!

The car was a cute little Peugeot, stick shift, which did umpteen miles to the gallon. It was a challenge, since it had been years since I had driven a stick shift, and the crunching of the gears for the first couple of weeks drew shivers from all who heard me driving around!

Monday to Friday was a challenge, and far from enjoyable, as I tried to wheedle ads from unwilling clients. Although I quite enjoyed helping to design them, but when the end of Friday rolled around, the opportunities to hit the road at weekends broadened our experiences.

We got to see old friends from further away in Warwickshire where we used to live, had more visits to parks and zoos surrounding London, and even found a theme park where we spent an enjoyable day with my oldest friend and her children.

But it was inevitable that the sales part, which was the grander portion of my income, was going to be far from successful. It petered out too when "Stacey's six-month rule" struck and ended the misery of both my stressed employer and myself.

I responded to an advertisement for a position with a private Arab bank in the West End of London.

Now this looked much more promising!

Chapter Thirty-One
1989 Up West! And Bugger the Trains!

Stacey

In my younger days, working in the West End of London used to be the epitome of 'made it'."

When I first saw the Arab bank's offices, I subscribed to that theory. They were lush to the point of opulence, plus there were lots of staff perks (which sadly did not include accompanying the bank owner's wives on their shopping trips to Harrods… Oh, well…). Additionally, they had a well-stocked canteen, plus luncheon vouchers. They was all very civilized, everyone seemed very professional, and they were all incredibly polite. Best of all, this position was actually very well-paid, and the luncheon vouchers eked out my salary, saving on lunch costs.

The personnel manager, who reminded me of an oversized Ronnie Corbett, offered me the job on the spot and wished me a long and happy stay at the company as he congratulated me on my appointment.

Long stay? Oh, dear, not likely to happen! And inwardly I rolled my eyes.

This was six-month Stacey he was talking to. In all honesty, he had questioned this during our interview. However, he was quite content when I told him I had just returned from overseas and had to take some temporary jobs prior to finding a permanent position. Stop laughing; it was true, even though I still wasn't sure if "secretary" was where I wanted to end up. But as the breadwinner, I had to go where Fate led me in order to provide for Amy.

In the event, I did actually spend a very pleasant nine months there—progress—and I also learned a lot about the Arab international banking system, which is really neat, although I'm not really a banking kind of person.

I was working with an old Etonian type, and from him I learned that the bank bought and sold debts. Well, sort of. If they had a client in one country who wanted to buy something in another, they would fund the client in his country of origin, and get their contacts in the country where the purchase was being made to make the loan. I am sure it was more involved than that, and we constantly seemed to be talking to banks about currencies, and entering panic mode when they dropped against each other. Frantic phone calls as the exchanges closed for the day were the norm. However, while I might learn quickly, the international banking world decidedly would not be long-term. There was no way I could be promoted into this male-dominated environment (not a girly thing, apparently), so I stuck to the typing and filing for my socially elite public-school type and tried not to draw attention to myself.

Eventually, the erratic nature of the London Tube trains, coupled with the effort to actually be at the office on time every day, proved to be too taxing. I did love the bustle of that part of London, but with an hour's travel on either end, it made for a long day, especially with the never-ending delays on the Central Line.

Amy fretted that I was getting home so late that she hardly saw me, stressing both me and my mother, who was hard put to keep the peace between the two children in the house—Amy and Dad.

But I did tolerate it until I had saved enough to buy my own small car. When I spotted a promising ad for a job closer to home, I told the personnel manager I was quitting.

He was apoplectic, his little Ronnie Corbett face scrunched up, and he could be heard berating me all over the building.

"What do you mean, you are leaving? I thought you planned to stay with us for several years!" he said testily. "I thought that was made clear when you started that we wanted someone to stay longer than a year!"

I smiled apologetically and said, "So sorry…family pressures." While thinking, "Good luck with that! Six months is my usual length of employment. Be grateful I've stayed this long!"

Then I merrily went on my way with nary a backward glance, not knowing I was leaping from the frying pan into the proverbial fire, and that the job I had found, with a private addictions-clinic-come-nursing-home, was somewhat more than flaky, bordering on criminal. Who knew!

Chapter Thirty-Two

1989 The Essex Mad House!

Stacey

Goodings Manor was an expensive private nursing home, which catered for those suffering from a variety of addictions, and mental conditions, and those whose families just couldn't be bothered with them or their afflictions.

My interview for the new position was conducted by a charming older man, who introduced himself as Philip. He had a polished plum accent and wore a custom-tailored, three-piece suit, and had twinkling blue eyes. He had been very impressive. I was very taken with him as much because I later found out that he had worked with my beloved aunt in a major London merchant bank prior to becoming the chief administrator at the nursing home.

This should, of course, have raised a red flag. Who leaves a highly paid job in a merchant bank to run a nursing home? He had not long left the bank, and the job I interviewed for was as his aide and marketing assistant. That would have been just fine with me. We hit it off really well. I thought he was absolutely charming and smart, such a change from most of the other people I had been working with up to then.

Oh, dear Stacey! Kiss of death! Surely we know by now that I am a *terrible* judge of men's characters!

But the clinic seemed on the up-and-up. Set in the grounds of a former private estate, it dealt with things like anorexia, the occasional alcoholic rehabilitation, short-term mental health commitment issues, and also cared for Alzheimer's patients, while charging this private clientele the earth. I came to like the patients, but I realized in short order that the owners of the facility and the doctors were an insalubrious lot.

I arrived with high hopes on the day I started, and immediately the fly in the ointment became apparent. As I arrived, I was greeted by the owner's daughter, (who I subsequently dubbed "Miss Horse and Hounds"), instead of the charming Philip. She tartly informed me that during the short time between my job interview and actual start date, "Mr. Prince Charming" had been whisked off to jail and was not expected back for two years, if then. Oh, shock, horror, not an auspicious start at all, and it set the tone for the next six months!

Later in the day, I asked my aunt about Philip, and she told me the whole story. It seemed that as a result of an embezzlement scam when Philip was a director at the high-class merchant bank, he had now ended up in the pokey. If I had bothered reading the newspapers, I would have known this. She thought it was a shame, and she suspected that he had been made the scapegoat. He had always been nice to work with, seemed on the up-and-up, and she had been very surprised to hear he had been sent to prison.

No matter the rights and wrongs of *his* situation. now he was in jail for the foreseeable future. So now I had to deal with what I soon discovered were the bosses from hell. Stacey's gremlin had struck again! (Destiny leaned against the wall, screaming with hysterical laughter!)

Instead of working for a nice, charming man, with impeccable manners, now I was stuck with dealing directly with the clinic owners. They were the complete antithesis of the poor man who was now pacing a jail cell, not an ounce of charm among them.

The entire management was made up of members of one family who had diverse ideas about how the home should be run. They also had vastly differing competency levels. Ernest, the father, was mostly on the absentee list; William, the son, was a real contender for the "Mr. Chinless Wonder" award. And then there was Ernest's daughter, Jocelyn (Miss H & H), who was far and away the most efficient of the three, but lacked both in charm and timeliness.

There was also a legally required accredited doctor on the board, who appeared on their headed notepaper, but for the most part, he was there in name only. In theory he was the head of the medical unit, and could be relied upon to prescribe medications at any hour of the day or night, whether he was at the home or not.

Jocelyn, who took the reins after the demise of poor Philip, was by far the worst to work with, and had an uncertain temper. All three family members also shared a common trait, and had clearly been taught at the same school of learning as Jay. They totally subscribed to Jay's theory that if something went wrong, it was always someone else's fault, and they were not culpable at all! Unease set in. If I had been working with Philip, the job might have worked out, but with characters from "happy families"—no chance. It all went downhill from there.

Their communications system consisted of yelling something over their shoulders to each other as they left the room, or dumping a pile of papers on my desk with no instructions. In short, their management skills were abysmal.

Ernest, recognizing Jocelyn's superior intellect, tacitly acknowledged that she was in charge, which, naturally, William resented. Cast into a relatively minor role in the company apparently abrogated him from any kind of consistency in his attendance at the office. Not surprisingly, he was rarely up-to-date with his work. Jocelyn's superior attitude, coupled with her spiteful nature, meant her appearance in the office rapidly led to me immediately find something I had to do in the main building, or go into town for.

Ernest, Jocelyn, and William each complained to me about the competency of the others, while the hapless doctor threw up his hands in frustration in his dealings with them. When he did turn up, I actually got on with him, but I've often wondered if the popular TV show *The Office* was based on the office practices of the clinic, as their management style would have fit right in.

Despite the drawback of such challenging managers, the rest of the work was enjoyable. The others on the staff were friendly, and the working conditions were ideal.

The clinic was situated in a former stately home, which had been converted to suit their needs. My office was on the ground floor of the former lodge—all old wood and leaded windows. It was set in beautifully landscaped grounds, with lots of tall trees, rhododendrons, hydrangeas, and immaculately kept flowerbeds. There was a covered walkway to the main clinic building where I could eat for free in the staff restaurant. Apart from the total lack of organization anywhere in the system, it was all rather nice, as long as you ignored all the crazy people—both patients and on staff.

Its picturesque setting, looking wonderfully tranquil and serene, came across in all their brochures, and I am sure was the major draw for their clientele. The drive through the winding Essex lanes each day was enjoyable and relaxing and so much better than fighting the London Tube and the uncertainties of the Central Line into the West End.

Many of the patients were really sweet, and I built a good relationship with one particular Alzheimer's patient who always mistook me for one of her old friends. But, the nursing staff was constantly changing. Another failure of a management focused on selling dear to the clients and buying the staff cheap. The more responsible among them voiced concerns that they were not meeting the regulations on staffing levels. Many nights they were not even close to the legal requirements, and there was tension about what would happen in an emergency. This set the nurses and nursing assistants against each other adding to the tensions.

But by far the biggest bone of contention for just about everyone was the cavalier approach to payday by Jocelyn. Since this was rooted in the casual attitude to handling the clinic's finances in general, it was probably the major reason for them trying to install a banker to run the administration. Each time payday rolled around, Jocelyn and William spent most of their time blaming each other for the tardiness and inaccuracies of time cards and record-keeping, and the staff resented it.

In turn, Jocelyn would blame staff for submitting late time cards, not withstanding that often the delay was caused by a sloppy credit-control process collecting revenues that led to less than the required amount being deposited into the bank in time to meet the anticipated salary costs.

As the sole provider for my two-person family, clearly this was not acceptable for me. I could definitely see the writing on the wall with regard to my long-term commitment to the job almost from day one, pretty scenery or not.

Once again it was going to be Stacey on the move!

I began looking around for my next placement right away, but even so, I somehow managed to endure the situation for, yes, the requisite six months. But it was precarious at best.

By now I had been back in Britain for nearly two years, floundering around from company to company. It was time to get serious about a proper job!

One October morning, I thought it was too good to be true when I received a formal offer for a job in the neighboring borough council's further education department, after what I thought had seemed a less-than-successful interview. But I congratulated myself that I had successfully parlayed my community-school-coordinator role in Canada into something comprehensible to a British employer.

Later I learned that my first impression of the interview was more accurate than I understood, but I was aided by the complex "points hiring system" implemented as a part of the borough's agreement with their union workers. It forced the interview team to evaluate prospective employees fairly and indiscriminately. Fortunately, my past experience meant that I kept coming up with maximum points, which qualified me for the post.

Stupid Stacey didn't know a thing about this until months later, when one of the interviewing team told me that they had not really wanted to hire me but they had no choice! Thanks for that! A real morale booster!

Finally, Fate was on my side, and *hooray* for the unions, with their little book of rules! I was in, and that union remained my friend as once again I fought the challenges that would come my way, not knowing how much our lives were about to change again.

Chapter Thirty-Three

1988-9 England

Amy

Amy was excited to be back in England again at first. The visit last Christmas had a good effect on her, and she felt loved again, especially by her grandmother. It had been fun to meet up with her cousins and her mom's best friend's children, who she vaguely remembered, and she had loved their dog!

Now, the stay was permanent, more than just a visit, and she was not so thrilled. She felt a lot less pressure at being away from all the bad stuff that had been around her in Canada more recently, but living with her grandparents was not as nice as she thought it would be. Of course, she adored her grandmother. What was not to like? She was kind, baked great cakes, and was always giving Amy little hugs, even though as a teenager, she was really past all that...well, almost. But it did make her feel good.

But Granddad was a miserable, mean old man. Mom and Grandma made excuses for him because he was getting over cancer, but, Amy thought, he was not very nice to her and clearly didn't really want her in his home, taking Grandma's attention away from him. Men seemed to be like that.

She and Mom had sort of settled down and were getting things organized. Once again, though, she had ended up in a new place, at the beginning of school holidays knowing no one. She hoped she would be able to spend some time with her two cousins or it would be really lonely through the summer.

They had managed to get a school sorted out for her to start after the vacation. It was the local "secondary modern," whatever that was. It was not like a regular high school in Canada, but she guessed it would do. The teachers had been unsure which grade level to put her in because apparently her Canadian learning was behind the English standard. As a result, suddenly she found she would be one of the oldest children in the class as she needed to redo a year. Oh, well. How bad could that be? She might get better marks.

Mom and she had a nice summer after all, traveling around London to see the sights and parks, until Mom got a job. It was a bit lonely for Amy, but then she had met Rosie, who went to the same school and things would improve even more once school began.

It was a bit of a walk down to the school, but they were nice, quiet streets. As well as Rosie, there were other kids too along the route, all in their school uniforms. That was a shock, too—a uniform for school! No more wearing what she wanted each day. No jeans, but skirts! Everyone wore the same stuff and high fashion it was not! But at least she had Rosie who lived in the same block of flats as her grandparents. Rosie's mom, Jennie, was on her own too, and Mom had made a friend as well.

To her surprise, Amy did quite well at school and it boosted her confidence a little. The school was a bit of a change from the one in Canada, where she had not felt comfortable that past year, with her self-esteem at such a low ebb.

Her father, whom she had so adored as a young child, didn't seem to see her as anything but an expensive encumbrance and was constantly lecturing her. And there had been the other reason too, and finally she told Mom about it. She had been so shocked, but had sought help from a counselor, who had been kind. It was the counselor who encouraged them to return to the United Kingdom. She told Amy she was trying to cope with too much, and might be better with a complete change of scene—somewhere where she wasn't likely to run into her predator, and where her father's meanness to her would not be so close at hand. Her mom decided to go home at last, but it wouldn't be to their old home near Coventry, but to London and Grandma.

Now she was at a new school and it was a pleasant surprise. Initially she was the center of attention, being the new girl. For a while, she was a bit of a novelty because she spoke "American," and eventually she stopped pointing out that it was actually Canadian. The local kids apparently didn't know the difference, eh!

The teachers were like anywhere—some nice, some not so nice, and some who really took an interest, particularly when she showed a flair for writing. Math she could take or leave, but she did enjoy some of the other subjects, which had an artistic bent. Although she balked when Mom encouraged her to join the acting group, but it really wasn't her, so she stopped going.

Amy liked weekends. She and Mom would go around London a lot. They walked around the big parks, and she loved all the birds and pretty flowers in them, and the street markets.

It was better when Mom got her own little car, then they went to other places too: down to the coast, to a place that her mom used to go to a lot when she lived in London in the past. They went to a big adventure park with some friends of Mom's, but of course it wasn't up to Disneyworld standards, where Mom had taken her several years ago.

One weekend, they went back to the Warwickshire town where they used to live and met up with old friends there. But still, something was missing and she worried because Mom still looked so sad sometimes. Neither of them was really happy.

However, on the plus side, it was kind of nice having a sort of family again. She enjoyed spending time with her own cousins and going down the road to her grandma's cousin, who had twin sons that were nice to her too. She like going over to see her grandma's two sisters, who were always very kind and welcoming, but it was good to be in school with people her own age, too.

She missed Dad, even if he had been mean to her, she missed her cat and her dog, but most of all, she missed their own little home and her friends in Canada.

Chapter Thirty-Four
1989 and Beyond— Canada

Jay

Amy and Stacey were back in Britain. He got letters from his mother asking why he didn't come back too, and he wrote that he was happy with Lucy, had a good job, even though the pay was pretty poor, and what was the point in uprooting again?

He wrote to Amy, sending a letter each time his court-ordered support was due. He need not have sent it, and how would Stacey have dealt with that? But paradoxically, when Lucy had suggested that he ceased sending money for Amy, he had become extremely pompous with her, saying it was his duty, and he did not shirk his duty.

However, in his letters to his daughter, he did not miss an opportunity to constantly carp about his financial situation, hoping to prod Stacey's conscience and losing no opportunity to tell Amy how hard his life was. Coupled with his tendency to lecture her, Jay was rarely encouraging, and he lost any closeness he had ever had with Amy. He would pontificate about the benefits of working hard and tell her that she would only appreciate things that she had worked for. All Amy wanted to hear from him was that he loved her and missed her.

From Stacey he heard nothing. He had made his decision about her, and she abided by it and refused to let him talk down to her or bully her again. She had sold her house, packed up her things, and returned to Britain. Then, a couple of years later, she had remarried.

For some reason, that made him lose heart more than anything else. Deep inside, he knew he had been berating her, picking at her, in the hope that she would retaliate, give him some point of contact again, but she didn't. When she remarried, he knew that phase of his life was even more at an end than it had been when their divorce papers had come through.

He and Lucy had talked about marriage before Amy and Stacey had gone home. Amy could be their flower girl, Lucy had said. (Amy, in her first year as a teenager, had pulled a face and said indignantly to her mother, "How old do they think I am, five?" and stomped off.)

In the end, they had not married. Jay shied away from it, saying he'd tried it once and that was enough. Lucy let it go because the acreage was hers. If they married, it changed the whole ball game, and she preferred remaining in control. She also knew that marriage would give Jay, and likely at his demise, Amy, an interest in her property. She said they were fine as they were. "Who needs marriage? We've made our commitment to each other." And so that was where they left it.

Jay tacitly agreed, after all, Lucy was his closest friend. She took care of him, thought for him, planned for him, and he needn't worry about a thing. It was all taken care of—they had their land, their goats, and a new puppy to add to their other dogs, and it was perfect, wasn't it?

Chapter Thirty-Five
1990 London—Homesick, Heartsick

Stacey

The need for permanent employment, moving from job to job, and home hunting had taken the better part of two years. During that time I had tried to keep in touch with my closest Canadian friends with letters flowing back and forth. I always kept up a cheerful commentary, not sharing how lost and alone I felt or how much I missed everyone. I couldn't see my way to going back, so what was the point of dwelling on it?

The loneliness that had encompassed me in Canada, despite the kindness of people there, had deepened, not decreased after I returned home. I missed everyone. I missed seeing Ted, and deep inside, I still mourned for my baby.

I jumped on every crumb of information about what was happening in Ted's household from different people. I heard mostly, "Ted is keeping busy" with a new project every week, seemingly.

The family was always into something. Ted incessantly keeping active, always so busy. In my ignorance, I didn't see that he had to keep occupied while he too tried to bury the past, and nobody mentioned the increase in his drinking. I heard about that many years later. All I heard at the time was that he was busy with his family. It seemed he had forgotten me completely.

My heart constricted when I heard that he had to spend some time in the hospital with stomach problems—easy to see how that happened, brought on no doubt by his internalization of his unhappiness and guilt over the years. He'd told me before I left that he had to take blood pressure medicine, but hurt and angry at his callous comments to me, it had not really registered. I had been smarting over his assertion that I only ever thought of myself. Well, when you are all alone, when everyone has abandoned you, you have to think about yourself, no one else will. And in any case, Amy was primarily my concern by then; she had to be.

I also heard about Sally's run in with cancer. Sympathetic as I felt toward her, inside I wondered what I would do if she died. Would I, could I go back. See how Ted would feel then. In the event she survived, I guessed determined to outlive her errant husband.

After my last phone call to Sally, then all the issues with Amy erupting, I had begun to see that my presence in Edmunston was going to be a continual source of unhappiness for both Ted and me.

It couldn't go on. I knew that at some point in the future, he would head my way again, or I would try again with him. That bond between us seemed unbreakable. For all the heartache it caused us the link was still there. It was unfinished business.

At our age, once engaged, our feelings had been so deep they were impossible to discard, despite our efforts to walk away from each other. Talking it through at the start might have made a difference, but Ted never would talk about it, and I never could tell him everything, so the barriers remained.

Now, my new job seemed to have real potential, so it was time to be done with it. I had been home for two years. Canada was the past. Couldn't hurt me any more. Couldn't, shouldn't, wouldn't, won't!

So I shut it in, burying that deep feeling of loss that would not abate as I pined for my Canadian friends. As hard as life had been at times, I felt I really belonged there. Back in London I so much felt like the odd one out, the spare wheel. Old friends from the past had moved on, had new friends of their own, families had lives of their own, and we did not fit in with any of them.

The one little ray of hope was that finally we had our growing relationship with Amy's friend Rosie, and Rosie's mother, Jenny, to build on. It provided a new direction and some respite for us. They were members of a local social club, and both great darts players. Just the kind of people that Cassie looked down on, and if I had been honest, it really was not my scene. But they were kind and tried to include us on their outings, and Amy had a friend her own age and they had fun. So why refuse?

We gravitated toward Jenny and Rosie and joined them when they went away on weekends with their club team to darts tournaments. There were always men around who were friendly, but none of them interested me. Not one among them could start that spark, or repair the immense hole in my soul.

But I had to put it behind me. *Had* to.

Chapter Thirty-Six

1990 Walthamstow — A Government Job!

Stacey

This new job in local government was a boon! I wished I had known before how easy it was to earn money! Those words echoed in my head, as my father had voiced a similar sentiment when he went to work for the post office after a lifetime as a barber.

Talk about a lucky break for me! The job had been tailored for a friend of the head of the department; unfortunately the friend had then decided to work elsewhere. This left an open vacancy for a position they didn't really need, or really want to fill. However, having created the post, the head of the section was honor-bound to hire someone, having worked so hard to create the position and not wanting to draw attention to the fact that she had really just manufactured the need.

Really lucky break for Stacey, and it worked to my advantage in so many ways.

As the department head had lost interest in the position, other staff members had few guidelines, and had not worked out exactly what the job should encompass. In effect, a level of management they didn't really need had been created to provide a job for a friend. They had totally shot themselves in the foot, because now they had to justify and fill it. Bureaucracy is like that.

The position was union-approved, so it would also be almost impossible to get rid of the post now. Yes, definitely a lucky break for Stacey, (and about bloody time) or, maybe not.

The department head, Edna, was a throwback to the 1930s. A more unpersonable person it would be hard to meet, and she could not have been a more homely woman if she'd tried. She looked like a school teacher out of a Billy Bunter story!

Tallish, thin, and rangy, Edna was totally devoid of any clothes sense. Her bob-cut hair style, and bottle-lens glasses sitting atop her thin nose, gave her the plainest face I have ever seen. Coupled with shapeless tweed suits, thick lisle stockings, and flat brogue shoes, her feminine allure was totally lacking. There were also rumors about the little cadre of women she kept around her, but back in the early 1990s, one didn't ask, or comment.

Her staffing preference was for academically qualified blue stockings, so she did not like girlie girl Stacey one bit.

The cohorts in her faction were all a part of her inner circle and complete boot-lickers. I later learned that the woman whose job I fell into had apparently been her "closest confidante" in need of a job, so Edna had made shifts to provide one at the council's expense. Sadly, it seemed that the "sisterly" love hadn't prospered, and said friend had evaporated into the distance, leaving poor Edna with the vacancy to fill, both in the office and in her social circle.

Ouch, that bullet in your foot hurting, Edna?

Notwithstanding Edna, and one or two of her managerial pals, I liked most everyone else, and I found that others on staff liked me because I was just me. I didn't try to pretend I was something I wasn't, and was very much prepared to ask the staff I was responsible for to explain things and help me out. In return, I stood up for them if things went awry; that was my job.

The department looked after the administrative needs of further education and youth, encompassed educational opportunities for the disabled, and dealt with oversight of a cluster of small units of further education and youth centers within a borough of well over one hundred thousand people.

In my new role, I had two teams to look after overseeing youth activities and adult education. On the youth center team, there was Alumba, of West Indian descent, who was the cleverest person I ever met at looking tremendously busy while achieving absolutely nothing. He was the world's expert in blinding you with science, scattering reams of paperwork over his desk, and generally looking under pressure, when in fact he had none.

Alumba was blessed with an assistant too. Kirsty, a totally sweet girl, who should have written the book on *"How I managed to stay employed while taking an average of two weeks sick leave each month."* She also could have written a sequel called, *"One hundred and one excuses for being late."*

The two of them were a nightmare to supervise, they were both very personable and likeable, but they utilized every part of the union rulebook to avoid disciplinary action. They knew just when to pull back and toe the line and when they could blatantly ignore it. Each time they reached the point where a written warning was the next stage, miraculously they became model employees, and stayed so just long enough to put the whole discipline process back to step one. Amazing! If only they would have applied their skills for avoiding work to actually doing it!

The further education centers team, however, was the complete opposite. The staff was pretty contemptuous of their colleagues across the room. Weiwei was an Asian from Guyana, exceedingly smart, and unbelievably in this day and age, tied into an arranged marriage with a pig of a husband. She was efficient, well organized, and a joy to work with. Her sidekick was a nice, quiet young man, Fred, who worked hard and had a wry sense of humor. This team's workload was higher and they had a third staff member. Valerie was a cheerful, friendly Jamaican. She was open and honest, with a huge smile, and a really hard worker. I liked them all; they never ever gave me a moment's worry, and we shared a mutual respect.

Presiding over all of them was challenging and interesting, not least because I had not a clue what my job was, or how to do it! Edna had somewhat washed her hands of me, and handed me over to her two underlings, Cherry and Vonda, both of whom made it clear I was there on sufferance. So much for enlarging my social circle and being upwardly mobile!

However, I had an impressive title: I was now an Administrative Officer, and I had my own little office where I could hide while I tried to figure out what the heck I was supposed to be doing. Fortunately, I was now covered by the union's little book of rules! Hey folks—look at me! Stacey protected!

One by one, I identified the roles I seemed to have. These included acting as secretary to a high-level committee of pleasant tutors and academics, all very highly qualified, with not an ounce of common sense among the lot of them! They were exceptional at theoretical discussions, but attained no practical outcomes during the whole time I worked with them, other than compiling endless reports in time to meet successive deadlines with recommendations that never came to fruition!

Vonda, all short-cropped hair and ill-fitting trouser suits took me to the first meeting of the committee. She had thawed slightly, and actually was quite nice on her own, much more likeable than personality-minus Edna. Keen to set the ground rules, Vonda had impressed upon me before we arrived, "You are here to take the minutes *only!* You do not participate in discussion, you do not speak at all unless directly spoken to, and you do not comment."

Destiny roared with laughter at her naïvety! We all know dumb old Stacey, and her excellent blurting capacity! Do not comment? In your dreams!

After three meetings, at which I did behave impeccably, Vonda felt safe in leaving me unsupervised with the group. Oops, whata mistaka to maka!

At first, I interceded gently with little comments like, "Did you want me to repeat back what you said in the last meeting's minutes? I think it differs from what you are saying now…" When they were clearly in a muddle. Until the time when I eventually started focusing them by asking, "Shall I put this all together into a draft proposal for you, so you can look it over at the next meeting?"

They adored me—it was hilarious. However, I still never quite managed to get them completely on track, even though in effect I was running their meetings for them. The chair was happy to defer to my practicality, which eluded her, and also relieved her of doing much else other than turning up to each meeting.

When I finally left after working with them for over six years (Yay! I finally broke Stacey's six-month barrier! Yippee!), they asked me if there was something I thought they hadn't managed to achieve.

I told them, "Yes, you still haven't addressed the transportation issue."

There was a stunned silence before one of the male professors nodded his head, rubbed his chin, and said, "Yes, I hadn't realized it had been so long. I see that we really must do something about that."

I gave up!

Chapter Thirty-Seven
1990—Enter American, Stage Left

STACEY

My life was now work and home, which consisted of taking care of Amy and trying to keep the peace between her and my father. And I began recognizing that I was living the life of a nun.

I hadn't been on so much as a one-drink date since I arrived; I hadn't even wanted to. However, I knew that this was not good, either for me or for Amy; she needed a happy mother. I also didn't want to turn into one of those divorcées who can't let go of her kids because she has no life of her own.

But I really was not interested or motivated to make any changes, and that's when Fate gave me another kick in the pants.

One day, a loud voice drifted into my office as the owner of said voice was busy berating Alumba. The accent was pure North American, and the thought ran through my head, "Oh, that sounds so much like home…" and pangs of homesickness started up. (How did I not get that Edmunston was my heart's home and that I should return there?)

Intrigued, and a little irritated, I stepped out to see what Alumba had done to incur such wrath. (Alumba was a soul man, always totally chilled, an altercation was never in his arena) I saw a pleasant-looking middle-aged man who was waving his arms around, telling Alumba that he'd better double-check his facts or there would be trouble! Uh-oh!

Alumba saw me, and as I walked forward, I asked what the problem was. Alumba spoke up at once, saying there was not a problem, really a bit of a misunderstanding; it was just Damon's way of talking. Hmm, that needed to change, I thought! But then he introduced me to his protagonist, who turned out to be Damon Morris Jr., one of the youth center managers whom I had not yet met. Well, that was a shock. I had heard the name and assumed he was one of the black center managers, with such a foreign-sounding name. Not so.

Damon's eyes lit up, and his whole demeanor changed, as he realized that I was the new person in charge of the contingency fund for the youth centers. Money was his God! The fund was dubbed "the slush fund" by the center leaders, as it topped up their budgets when unexpected costs occurred. Damon, it seemed, was all about money, and later I learned not just with regard to his youth club (shades of Jay; I do pick 'em).

Damon shook my hand and then pushed his way into my office. He sat himself down and asked to discuss the fund with me. I was not inclined to do so until I'd had a further chat with

Alumba, but I did ask him what part of Canada he was from, as I had lived there.

He looked nonplussed. "I'm not Canadian, I'm American. But as it happens, I just came back from visiting relatives in Canada. Where in Canada did you live?"

That led to a brief conversation about my time in Canada and more of his recent trip to Ontario after his wife had died the previous summer. Warning bells should have clanged in my head! Uh-oh! "Lame duck" seemed to murmur softly in the background.

Later, in discussions with Cherry, when his name was mentioned, she looked horrified. "Oh, be so careful how you deal with Damon! He's newly widowed. He is a total pest. If he finds out you are single, you'll never get rid of him, especially if you are nice to him. He is an absolute menace," she added unkindly.

Oh, dear, so entirely the wrong thing to say to lonely, plain, plump, and "entirely stupid when it comes to men" Stacey! Disaster train number three heading down the tracks! Would I never learn?

Chapter Thirty-Eight

1990 London—Lame Ducks Encore

Stacey

I had survived my three months probation period, broken no rules, and so had been reclassified to permanent status. Edna still wasn't sure what my role was, but that also meant no one could say I wasn't doing my job! *Yay*, for stupid managers, who set up criteria for hiring staff, with no "get-out" clause!

Luckily, I was enjoying the job and mostly still liked the people. Now that I was permanent employee, I thought that Amy and I had some security at long last. A place to be safe now, maybe we could find a home of our own and have a real future. But no, I hadn't reckoned on the bitch fest that was the upper management in my department.

Edna was determined to be rid of me, and her dirty-tricks campaign started, asking me for reports that had not been requested, getting others to tell her about my time-keeping and how often I was out talking with staff from another section. I definitely needed help against these women.

As it happened, Damon came to my rescue during one of his forays into my office when he was looking for some extra money after his center had a burglary. I was feeling a bit intimidated after a conversation with Cherry, and told him about it, in some angst. He grinned and recommended that I speak to one of his staff members, Roy, who was a senior union shop steward, and he suggested I find an excuse to visit his center.

Roy, a bluff, burly man who hailed from Tyneside, took me under his wing, listened to my story, grinned even more than Damon had, and said as he pushed a form across his desk, "Oh-ho, we'll fix them. Here's what you do...!"

Hey presto! In a blink I had joined the union, Roy, seeing an opportunity to extend his bailiwick, and also insulate me further from the "all girls together" cadre. Then he suggested that I became the shop steward for our building, which at that point didn't have one. In an environment where unions still ruled, it was a masterstroke! Shudders went through the upper management, and Edna decidedly flinched. For once Stupid Stacey had made the right choice and all Edna's spiteful actions had achieved was a fully operating union shop in her building! She also learned that I am better as a friend than as an enemy!

Hands off me, bitches! *Now* I have protection! Edna gnashed her teeth!

As it happened, I thrived in the union environment, because it fed my lame-duck-rescue persona. My new role meant I was always helping out someone who had fallen foul of management, who, apart from Edna, came to respect that all I sought was fairness in their treatment of employees. The constant exposure led to me eventually moving on up to be the shop convener for the whole section of our department.

The coup de grace for Edna, came when I won a battle for the typing-pool women who had been wrongly classified a couple of years earlier to a grade lower than they should have been. Eventually, with the help of the leader of the union, the matter went before an administrative hearing that ruled in favor of the typing pool! Yay for Stacey, and a big bunch of flowers from the girls and bonuses all around for them!

Edna was incandescent! It totally threw her budget, and in the process, I had learned that my role not only gave me more cover, it also allowed me infinite time away from my desk during work hours to represent other colleagues, courtesy of the union/employer agreement. I loved it!

Due my apparent grasp of the union/employer relationship, I was asked to join the "Staff Side" committee comprised of staff, higher echelon managers, and council members, which made me totally fireproof. It was close to impossible to get rid of me now, and it seemed finally that Fate was on my side!

The freedom that union officials had in Britain at that time was amazing. Union duties were all considered a part of employment and could be undertaken within working hours. This meant that I could leave my desk, or even the building, with prior notification, to deal with a union or staff issue. It was all considered "work time" and there was nothing my management could do about it. It was all entirely permissible under the union/employer agreement. I also found that any evening meetings I attended had to be compensated by time off in lieu! Lucky for Edna that power doesn't go to my head!

I could've taken advantage, but I didn't because it wasn't my way. But I did play games with the Edna set at times, because it amused me and gave me immense satisfaction that the bitch-fest group had no way to push me out of my job. They were an unbelievably spiteful set, though, and Edna tried all sorts of things to undermine me. I also kept notes. Useful for the memoirs!

Poor woman, she didn't know who she was dealing with! I had survived starvation, abandonment, and almost total isolation for years and regarded her as an amateur in the arena of hateful behavior. In addition, a couple of close escapes when planes had almost crashed, and being up close and personal with a tiger and a leopard had really toughened me up. I had also endured the worst that my ex-husband's family could throw at me in a foreign country all alone! Edna's Evil Gang was a doddle compare to that!

In the meantime, while I had been concentrating on firming up my position in the union and learning more about my job, Damon "the menace" had come up missing. I realized I hadn't seen him in the office or had any begging phone calls for slush funds. I asked Alumba why Damon was so quiet and where he had disappeared to, when he'd been pestering me for extra money for his youth center for weeks and then suddenly nothing.

Alumba looked perplexed. "Didn't you know?" he asked.

"Know what?" I replied.

"Oh, he was injured in an accident at his youth center and has been at home on sick leave for the last three weeks."

I was stunned.

"No, I didn't. Why didn't someone ask me to sign the get-well card?" I asked (stuff like that was always running around the department when the girls were ill).

Alumba had the grace to look embarrassed. "There hasn't been one. I guess that is really his line supervisor's job to handle that kind of thing, and Yasmina hasn't done anything about it."

Well, really, I thought! We're all in the business of caring for people, getting them better education, better opportunities, and yet we don't take care of our own? I called personnel and asked for Damon's home address, and sent him a card myself, after telling Yasmina what I thought of her. She too looked ashamed and finally moved herself to make sure that at least he heard from his own center's staff. That was Yasmina, always flitting around and looking pretty, but very self-absorbed and not wonderful at her job either.

Two weeks later, I got a phone call. "Hi, it's Damon. Did you send me a get-well card?"

"Yep, I did," I responded.

"Ah, I've been racking my brains, wondering who Stacey was, and I finally thought of you," he said. I wasn't sure whether to be amused or offended, as clearly I had not made much of an impression on him, despite my management of the slush fund! Too plump, too plain, and too utterly Stacey, and so forgettable!

We chatted for a few minutes about his accident, and I told him that I had forwarded the accident report that Alumba finally handed to me. He mentioned that he had been confined to bed, and I asked how he was getting along, knowing his widowed status. He said a friend had been helping him out, but that he was dying of boredom on his own and did I want to come over one weekend afternoon? He could show me his Canadian photos, which he had promised to do some weeks before. His plea for company and his accent brought reminiscences of "home" flooding through me. I felt sorry for him, so I agreed.

Here we go again! This was a lame duck just begging for "Stacey care," and I fell straight into the pond again.

Chapter Thirty-Nine
1990 Walthamstow— A Fresh Start?

Stacey

The next Saturday I pulled up in front of Damon's semidetached, which was a couple of miles or so away from my parents. The house had seen better days and was in need of a paint job, but then I wasn't there to critique the decorating, so I rang the bell.

I could hear Damon slowly coming down the hallway, and he grimaced as he opened the door.

"Hi," I said. "Still in pain?"

"Yes," he answered, and led me into the front room, which held a multitude of books, bric-a-brac, an ancient saggy-looking sofa, and a couple of armchairs. It too could have used a lick of paint, but no matter.

His photo albums were out on the little coffee table in front of the sofa, and we shuffled past it to sit down. Almost immediately a huge black-and-white cat jumped up and began walking across toward me. Damon tried to shove it away, but I stopped him, saying, "It's OK. I like cats. What's its name?"

"Rupert," he answered, and the cat started purring his head off as I found that spot on his head that cats love to be scratched.

I handed Damon a couple of paperbacks I had brought for him. Westerns that seemed pretty masculine, as I was not sure what he might like. "To help pass the time," I said.

"Oh, thanks," he answered, "but I am not a reader!"

Note to self, tact not one of his attributes, should be a part of your learning curve, Stacey! (I also did not discover for several that he suffered from a form of dyslexia so reading – no!)

But I just passed it off, saying, "Not to worry, just thought you might be interested." Then we got into thumbing through the photo albums filled with memories of his recent visit to Canada.

Most were pictures of Niagara Falls, but there were also some of Michigan, where his parents lived. I found it interesting, as I had not seen Eastern Canada, or been to that part of America. Although I found it a little awkward being in his home, he was amusing, and it was a long time since I had laughed.

Cherry had been right about his tenacity, as, before I left, he made me promise to come back. I wasn't sure that I wanted to, but he seemed so lonely, and apparently a nice person, so I could not refuse.

After all the long, lonely years, it was a change to find someone who made me laugh and was showing an interest. It was nice too that I didn't feel intimidated by him like I had with other men in Edmunston who had been interested in me. So I followed up when he asked me to come over again.

One visit led to another, and before I knew it, I was spending a fair bit of time with him, as he recuperated from his back injury. I should have been more wary, as he moved things along real fast within a few visits. We barely knew each other when he started asking where the relationship was leading.

What relationship? I hadn't progressed to that stage, but he had his own agenda to some extent, which became apparent later. Even so, it started me thinking. We seemed to get along; he was certainly funny and nonthreatening. It was time to live up to my promise to myself and shut the door on the past, and an opportunity to move forward was presenting itself. Why shouldn't I give myself a chance at another shot at happiness? Damon certainly seemed to need it, as his brief references to his life before his wife died sounded pretty grim. Maybe he was ready for some fun times too.

We never dated conventionally; in fact we didn't ever go out anywhere. But all of a sudden, we seemed to be spending most of our free time together. In hindsight, that was probably a mistake. I put our lack of outside activity down to Damon still being in recuperation. But even when his back progressed and he started getting better we still always met at his house. I was grateful for the companionship, so I didn't realize until much later that the main reason we didn't go anywhere was because he hated spending money. He was always looking for a bargain, something for nothing, or with a coupon, and raising his eyebrows at the cost of things. Sadly it seems to me that pretty much sums up most men, since Jay, my father, and even Ted were much the same. Stinginess seems to be a major male trait.

My dad had always been on the parsimonious side, Jay was all about money, and in the event, Ted's possessions as much as his daughters were more valuable to him than the lure of the happiness he wanted with me. But then that's probably why we have wars, which are all started by men, and at the root of which usually lies with men wanting another country's assets.

However, at the time, I had lulled myself into the idea that Damon was very amusing, had lots of tales to tell, and after a while we seemed to be making enough of a relationship for him to ask me to bring Amy over to meet him.

I was nervous about that, not sure how she would react, but Amy found him kind, not a bit intimidating, and she seemed to like him. More to the point, she appeared to trust him. Of course that was to be expected of a man who worked full-time with young people and had the knack for dealing with them. She had lacked his sort of kindness from an adult male for so long that it was a refreshing change for her to find one who liked her company and just wanted to be her friend, and made her laugh too.

Naturally, a few weeks later, Damon's real agenda surfaced. He was set to go on a prearranged pilgrimage to Lourdes, France, with the Catholic church group that his late wife had belonged to. He needed someone to look out for his pets while he was away. He asked if Amy and I would stay at his house to take care of the cats (Rupert was not alone), while he was gone.

I asked Amy what she thought, and she leapt at the chance to have animals around her again. She had taken a real shine to Rupert on her visit. By this stage too, it was anything to have a little break from the undercurrent between her and my father, so we said yes.

In his absence, Amy and I took one look at the sad, neglected state of his home, and decided to spend some time tidying and cleaning, because it was pretty clear that housework was not Damon's forte, and he obviously needed help.

By the time he got back from France, the house smelled clean and looked bright. Damon was a little shocked by our work, and a bit defensive about its previous state, but overall very appreciative. As he admired our work, he said, "Would you and Amy like to stay here with me on a permanent basis?"

I talked to Amy about it, and by now she liked Damon enough to feel safe with him.

It seemed like a no-brainer. We got on well, and it was a move forward, maybe to a better life. It also was a release from the pressure of living with my father. So we packed our bags again, told my mother we were only going to be a couple of miles away, and headed out on the next chapter in our lives.

Chapter Forty

1990 Walthamstow — Same Tune, Different Words!

Stacey

Damon's house wasn't in the best area of London, parking was a nightmare, but we did like the closeness to the huge street market nearby, and the absence of the disapproval on a daily basis we endured through life with my father. This was a welcome boon for Amy and me.

On the negative side, it was several miles away from Amy's school, so it would mean transporting her back and forth. But that was OK, and it was only for a couple of weeks, as it was nearly the end of term.

Amy and Damon got on even better than I had hoped, and I seemed to be finding a way to develop a low-key relationship with him, which was making some progress. It was making me feel more settled, and I was determined to make it work. It was unfortunate that Amy was now not so near to Rosie, but as they had begun to grow apart, it did not faze her much. She was in her last year at the school and would be starting at the nearby sixth form college soon, so the move would not interfere with her education.

The house was much closer to my office, too. A "quick" (roll eyes—this is London traffic) drive across the borough, making for less stressful travel, especially once I learned to take the back roads.

Damon, although his back still giving trouble, was still employed and his flexible work hours coincides with Amy's school schedule. Now he and Amy always seemed to be out shopping in the local market, or doing other things together before I got home. He was kind to her, made me laugh most of the time, and all in all, it seemed as if all the past pain was finally receding.

We were moving forward, and we all seemed to be benefitting from this new relationship. The sadder memories ebbed, thrust even deeper inside me. I resolutely would not think about Ted. I also gained some satisfaction from writing to Jay to advise him of our new address. I told him just enough to stir him up, but not more…Karma assists in all sorts of ways!

Our life was companionable. We played chess in the evenings, walked down to the local market each Saturday, ran Amy to her social events, took my parents shopping, and had occasional sex. At last there was a kind of stability, finally a home life as close to normal as we could manage, with all the inside burdens we each carried.

I began to let down my barriers, and risked developing deeper feelings for Damon. Maybe this was my chance to find real happiness again, for me and for Amy. Once more Destiny giggled.

In my naïvety, it did not occur to me that Damon was still carrying a lot of baggage from his own past. He had been married twice before. Firstly to the wife from hell, who had made his life miserable and separated him from his own daughter, a separation that never really healed. His second marriage was to a permanent invalid, who constantly berated him; and more to the point, for most of the previous ten years, their relationship had been purely platonic.

Trying to take him down a different path, encouraging him to feel passion eventually proved to be a barrier he was unable to overcome in his attempts to start a new life with me. That reluctance was exacerbated because we lived in the house where he had nursed his previous wife and where she had died. A strong impression of her remained.

I tried so hard to draw him out of himself, to enjoy the passion that I missed so much, and that he had lacked previously. It proved to be untenable.

Each time we seemed to move forward, he would pull back, reactivating the deep feelings of rejection that had left me so bereft after Jay's and Ted's actions toward me. Those memories came back to haunt me again and again. Damon's lack of trust in his feelings hurt. It was like a knife going through me, so the only way forward was to suppress that side of myself. Stick to being the busy working wife, focus on our affection and companionship, be a busy homemaker and mother, and forget that I had ever had a more passionate relationship. I understood that was gone forever, nevertheless we developed a close bond.

I also did not grasp that Damon never once asked about our life in Canada, or showed any interest in what had come before I met him. Years later, when I asked him why, his response was, "It was not my business." But he did not extend those same criteria to his own life before me, sharing endless tales of woe about his past. If you really love someone, it *is* your business to learn everything you can about the one you love. It should be something that you want to know.

Looking back, I think his lack of curiosity stemmed from the fact that his focus was solely on what he wanted for his future. He didn't want to be alone, and in Amy and me, he had found the ready-made family that *he* sought. To his credit, he did put a lot of effort into making Amy happy, and so he was not interested in what came before, as far as I was concerned.

By contrast, I had learned all about his previous marriages, his family, and his trials and tribulations through all those years exiled in the United Kingdom. The dramas of his first marriage and the pain it inflicted on him tore at my heartstrings. Lameduck mode kicked in again, and my focus became making a safe and happy life for both he and Amy.

Moving in with Damon changed our plans in lots of ways. Over the months, I had been exchanging letters and the occasional phone call to Lane and Shelley about taking a trip out to see all our old friends, and Amy had been looking forward to it. After we moved in with Damon, those plans were shot down, and I was faced with calling Shelley to tell her that now we would not be traveling back to Canada for a visit the next summer. In retrospect, that decision might have changed the course of our future once more, but it was not to be.

Instead, within weeks, we had become engaged. Damon had finally taken me out, for my birthday, to a local hotel dining room (complete with the requisite discount coupon, of course). There he proposed, catching me completely off guard. For once I was lost for words until I stuttered "Yes", and so we began.

Damon's focus was now to take me to America to meet his parents instead of my planned visit to Alberta. When I told him about our plans to go to Canada that year, Damon said, "No, come to Michigan instead to meet my parents; we can always go to Canada next year."

Next year? Dumb Stacey, where had I heard that before? What lesson had I not learned?

"We can have a baby next year," said Jay, and though I nearly did, it wasn't his. If he had followed through with his promise, we might have still been together. Now I was putting my plans on hold again for someone else, hearing, "We can go to Canada next year," from Damon—it never happened. Next year never came until Ted's spirit lured me back, and I went alone.

So instead we went to Michigan for two weeks, while Amy stayed at home with her grandparents and a promise that we could go back to Edmundston another time.

Amy was the only one who ended up going back to Canada. The following year, for her eighteenth birthday present, we bought her tickets so she could go and take her new boyfriend with her to see her friends and her father. Needless to say, Jay didn't provide one cent toward the trip, even when she went to stay with him.

Damon never, ever kept that promise to return with me to the home I missed so badly, where my heart lived. If we had, maybe loose ends could have been tied up. Perhaps I might have had a chance to really close the door on that life; as it was, I was left with unfinished business. If I had returned as a happy newlywed, seen my friends, had them excited about my new life, it might have given me closure. It might have shown both Jay and Ted that I finally had someone who cared for me, as they did not. But we never did go back, and the reality was that yet again I had tied myself to someone who cared more for himself than for me. Poor, dumb, stupid Stacey.

More recently, I wondered what impact at trip back the following year might have had on us. It was the year when much changed for Ted too. That year Lauren presented Ted with his first grandchild, moving his life into a different phase, where there would have been no room for Stacey, whatever he felt. Perhaps he might have found the courage to talk to me, or not, what if…maybe…maybe…?

We had mutual friends, so perhaps there would have been an opportunity to find some time to talk. But we will never know. That step was never taken, and for the following twenty years, I pushed all that had been soft, kind, and good in me into the background, together with the memories that had changed me as I struggled with sadness and drudgery.

Our lives moved on, and I suppressed all feelings I had about the past. I would never see Ted again. "Forever" was what I had said. It was not what I meant, but it is what happened. Nothing can change that now.

Chapter Forty-One

1992 and on Canada

Ted

Ted thought about Stacey, and his chest clamped again. When he heard she had remarried, was happy with someone else, he had been overwhelmed with jealousy, anger, and pain. She *had* finally betrayed him, he thought irrationally, just like his mother. His mother's last words to him, just before she died had been, "Don't worry. I will always love you and will never leave you." And those words came back to haunt him. Within days, she had been gone, buried in the cold earth of the little town's cemetery, "Forever Remembered" carved into the tiny stone that marked her grave. Her last words had cut through him, a sad little boy, left with a huge sense of betrayal and loss. Momma had said she would never leave, but she did, and never came back.

Now, decades later, when the news around town was that three years after she had left Edmunston Stacey had remarried, he was aghast. Those same feelings of betrayal from his childhood washed over him again. "I will always love you." He could still hear Stacey's soft voice saying. Ted had blamed Stacey so many times in the past for betraying him, ratting him out to Sally, after he walked away from her. Then he was beside himself with jealousy for a time when her name had been linked with almost every barfly in town.

The years he had spent tearing himself apart inside, watching her with Gino every morning, until he realized there was nothing between them. She was still his, even though he wouldn't claim her. Then he stomped on her feelings every chance he got, but he still felt that *she* had betrayed *him*. He well understood that she had stayed because she knew how he felt about her, and was waiting for him. But when she finally left, irrationally he waited for her to come back again, like she had before.

Like his mother, Stacey words meant nothing. Always? Liar! Liar! Now she had married another man, repeated his mother's betrayal of him, despite telling him all those years how much she loved him! He hated her, all that disruption to his life, and none of it meant anything to her, now she had blithely gone on her way.

Logically Ted understood that he had driven her away, let her go when…but it was no use rerunning that scene; it only brought on feelings he wanted to avoid. When those childhood feelings of betrayal had returned after so many decades, it appalled him. He should be past that. But he had been the one who forged the link in his mind between Stacey and his mother. It was what had initially drawn him to her, and the two were linked in his psyche, eternally. Now he understood that his indecisiveness and cruel attitude had brought it all on himself. Try as he might to deny it, the magnet in his chest was still there, and pain shot through him like a knife.

Now it was truly over, and it was way past time to put it all behind him. Time to concentrate on his family and his baby grandson fast becoming a toddler. In truth, his family had no knowledge of the battle that raged inside him for so many years; he had kept it well hidden. But up until now nothing he had tried had worked. Stacey was a part of him; she still lingered in the back of his mind. And yet she *must* be gone. He *must* bury the past. To do that, he would have to keep busy.

He looked at his house and made a decision. "Right," he said to Sally. "I'm going to expand the basement and extend the rest of the house. Time to do what we've always talked about."

Sally had been shocked. "That is so much work, Ted."

He nodded. To Sally he said, "Well, we need to do something about the layout of the house, especially if we are going to have grandchildren coming to stay with us."

Ted thought, I'm going to do this; I will erase every association with Stacey that this house holds. She has no place here; she never should have. He would exhaust himself so that he would be too tired to even think of her. He was right, as he became frenzied about eradicating the past, ostensibly remodeling his home for his grandchildren, he pushed Stacey out of his mind. That was where she stayed for nearly twenty years, until the year when it all came back to haunt him once more, and eventually led him to his death.

But for now he was determined. The future was going to be all about fun, fun, fun all the way with his own family. He would make happy memories with them, with Lauren and Randy, and Sally. He would be the life and soul of the get-togethers with his friends. Fun and parties, the old him, back again. Maybe he would even dally with a new woman—that would help eradicate Stacey from his mind, from his soul. He would eradicate her forever…hockey, curling, golf, partying, and fun, fun, fun!

Sally eyed Ted. He seemed focused on the rebuilding, but she had known him since high school. She too had heard about Stacey's new marriage to some American she met in London, and Sally saw that look in Ted's eyes again, and her heart sank. Was she *never* going to be out of their lives, and out of Ted's heart?

On the bright side, Stacey had remarried. She wasn't coming back, so yes, she was going to be out of their lives for good…forever! Stacey, Jay, and Amy consigned to the past, swept from the family tree, erased, forgotten, forever!

Chapter Forty-Two
1992 London—In Sickness and Health

Stacey

Damon and I married in March. We had a large wedding at the local YMCA surrounded by work friends, old friends, and family. Life had progressed in the eighteen months since we met. We had survived a lot, but more was to come.

I began returning to my natural nurturing role. While trying to reinstall my optimistic spirit, I was helping Damon rebuild the estranged relationship he had with his own daughter, Adele. That bond had been scarred, both by her unbalanced mother, and her clinging grandmother. Sound familiar? I was well versed in dealing with that scenario. The clinging granny had died when his daughter had barely left school. She had faced who knows what horrors while taking care of her ailing grandmother, alone.

We were also battling the undeclared war between our two daughters, who had taken an instant dislike to each other. The one was unhappy that a newcomer appeared to have usurped her place as Damon's daughter, while at the same time declaring herself "too old" to need a father; the other was angered by the patronizing attitude and muted jealousy of the other. Over time those initial reactions muted, but it was never a comfortable relationship. Damon made his preference for his adopted daughter too obvious.

We had also faced the stress of the wedding that had been enhanced as usual by plump, plain, entirely stupid and way-too-softhearted Stacey, who was trying to be kind. I really should have learned by now to be a tad more selfish before I invited imminent disaster to be a guest!

One evening I naïvely said to Damon, "Let's ask your sister to come over for the wedding. She was so keen about it, having missed your last two. Let's see if she wants to come." Oh, Stacey! Mistake, huge, *huge* mistake!

When we had made our visit to Michigan the previous summer to meet Damon's parents, his sister had really clung to us. She told us how much she wished she had been present at his previous two weddings. She had just split with her husband and was a sad case. She had never been to Britain, so we thought it would be nice trip for her.

The lesson learned by trying to include Cassie at Amy's birth had clearly passed me by; I had forgotten that the road to hell is paved with good intentions. When I made that suggestion, I still didn't understand that a kindness offered always blows up in your face. I truly wish my mother had raised me to *never, ever* help anyone!

Like Topsy, the invitation for the *one* sister to attend our nuptials, grew spiraling out of control until it finally morphed into the addition of Damon's brother, sister-in-law, niece, niece's baby, and nephew! Oh, no!

There was no way our small semidetached home could house all of them. We had only one extra bedroom. Where would they stay? Trying to rein them back, especially as the sister was the only one to whom we had actually extended the invitation, proved impossible. Three days before the wedding, in they all flew. The ramifications of this were horrendous so close to the actual event.

They had all jumped on the plane, ignoring our concerns, and arrived expecting us to house and feed them. While my prospective brother-in-law and his wife could well afford a hotel, there were none close by, but his sister and her vagabond children were poor as church mice, so we were stuck with them.

Nightmare does not even begin to cover it. It was like a swarm of locusts had descended on us. They were everywhere, ate us out of house and home, poked through everything, and expected to be treated like tourists while we were getting ready for our wedding. Inevitably both teens were bored and unhappy with the lack of entertainment provided for them. Neither did they want to lend a hand with the catering and all work we had to do preparing the wedding feast.

"We're on vacation!" the niece said insolently.

With some help from my family, we did at least off-load two of them on a nearby cousin. We also managed to get everything sorted out, so that, in the event, the actual day went off well. There were lots of my relatives there, plus old friends, new work colleagues, Damon's work colleagues, Amy's school friends, old Uncle Tom Cobley, and all.

From the photographs it looked like we were having a whale of a time, and it was so nice to see all the friends and most of the family gathered together. The food went down well, Damon managed a comical speech, and my dad, being now an old hand at speeches for his daughter's marriage, showed amazing sang-froid! Our multinational work colleagues managed to be amused rather than insulted when an elderly aunt remarked in shocked tones to her hapless husband, "There are black people here, dear!" She didn't get out much!

All in all, it was not a disaster. Fortunately, Damon's first wife did not live up to her threat to turn up for whatever crazy reason ran through her demented head, but didn't, and everyone apparently got on famously.

The following few days (no honeymoon), were spent just trawling around London with the visiting family. It went fairly quickly, even though it included an emergency room visit for the baby, and people in sleeping bags all over the living-room floor!

Finally we got shot of all of them, and I heaved a sigh of relief, thankful that they all lived in America and I would not have to deal with them much in the future.

Uh-oh, there goes Stacey tempting Fate again. I should *so* not have had that thought!

Destiny sat on the sidelines, once more rocking with laughter, tears running down her face!

Chapter Forty-Three

1992 London— Destiny Rides Again

Three weeks after our wedding, just as we were settling into what hopefully would be a normal life, Damon collapsed and was rushed into the London Chest Hospital for major heart surgery.

It is hard to explain how I felt during that time. Three weeks married, I felt alone and lost while I tried to take on the enormous impact of the surgery and its far-from-certain outcomes. There was also the issue of dealing with Damon's daughter, who had a complete antipathy toward hospitals and resisted visiting until honor bound she had to. Her hospital phobia manifested itself soon after she arrived, when she nearly fainted, overcome by hospital aromas, and had to have the nurse bring *her* a cup of tea to restore her. Poor Damon was ignored!

Then there was concern about Amy, who was genuinely fond of Damon and fearful about his illness. With these stressful events heaped on top of working full-time before driving back and forth to the hospital, and endless challenges of parking in the city, I was shattered!

I had been stretched and stressed and was about to collapse myself, until one of my friendly union colleagues pointed out the provisions for caring for ailing spouses included in the borough employment manual!

Oh, happy day!

The handy little manual revealed that I was entitled to "ten days paid leave" to cope while Damon was in hospital, plus at least "two weeks of care" after he returned home to act as his nurse. At the end of those two weeks, a visit to see my wonderful doctor brought about another bonus. She took one look at me and signed me off from work for a couple more weeks. She said I was suffering from exhaustion—no shit! I truly was by then. The grinding of teeth as more grist was added to Edna's Gang's dislike of me could be heard all over the building! They were beset by more problems too, another colleague they had promoted over my head had already started a two-month sickness leave, which I saw as their just deserts. For me, that recovery period was very necessary. Bite me!

Borough policy covered me, the terms were union negotiated, plus I was on the staff-side committee, and the union rules! *Yay!*

Weeks of care followed as Damon recovered from his surgery, complaining all the time about why I had let them operate on him. "To save your life, duh!" During that time I discovered that yet another "hero" had feet of clay. No more the bold, brave former Marine able to withstand anything, with stories about his leadership skills in the military and brushes with death. Nope, now I found a Damon who did not do well with any kind of pain and eventually turned into much the same kind of lifelong hypochondriac that my father was. Oh, dear! Is it something about those born under the sign of Leo?

However, despite my irritation, Damon's saving grace was that he was so good and kind to Amy. If he didn't make me as happy as I thought he might, he did still make me laugh at times, and could always bring a smile to Amy's face. Once he recovered from the surgery, I also occasionally lured him away from home for short away trips into the country. I felt a little hopeful; maybe after his brush with death, things might improve, and we could all have a good life together. Maybe he would understand that we both needed to have some fun.

Ever-optimistic Stacey: destined once again to be disappointed!

Fortunately, as Damon was now retired, he was able to rest at home while I went back to tackling the finer administrative details of further education, and fighting a rearguard action with Edna, et al.

Amy caught up with her schoolwork, found a boyfriend, and landed a part-time job. She seemed a lot happier and was spreading her wings.

In the aftermath of the stress of the wedding, the drama of the heart surgery, and the challenge of the recovery, we did finally manage a little relaxation time to break up the challenges of my job that summer. We took trips away to parks, and animal sanctuaries, and Damon seemed to be settling down to his enforced retirement and concentrated on family matters

We were trying to build bridges with his daughter Adele. Their relationship had always been strained, and in true Stacey mode, I was determined to heal the breach. Oh, poor Stacey, so slow to catch on to the fact that you should leave well alone. However, things seemed to be progressing, and once or twice we joined her and her partner, on weekend trips to Holland and Belgium. It seemed as if we might drifting toward being a happy family all leading normal lives. I started to breathe again, unless Adele was in the same room as Amy, at which time tension set in: one afraid that her new father was going to abandon her, and one jealous that the father she had rejected appeared to have found a more amenable substitute.

We also still had to deal with the monthly letter from Jay, enclosing his child-support check. It always brought tension because of the never-ending diatribe about how his monthly payments to her were crippling him financially and how she should work hard so she could support herself. Each month she hoped for more from him, but his mantra was set. Each month he disappointed her yet again, and made her wonder why she was not good enough for him.

This continued until her eighteenth birthday, when the payments immediately ceased, and he never sent her another penny. Once he had no monthly deadline to meet, his letters became scarcer. When they did appear, inevitably they still contained lectures on how she should be living her life. He also kept up the never-ending complaints about his impecunious state and the poverty he lived in, still with the implication that she and I were to blame for that! Really! What a sad case he was. It was nearly a decade since we parted. How pathetic!

It was so sad for Amy. All she wanted were kind words from him, for him to ask how she was doing and say that he missed her. Jay just never grasped that and instead sent her maudlin poetry.

Each time a letter arrived from Jay, casting Amy into gloom again, Damon stepped in to cheer her up by taking her down to the local street market after school. They would trawl the stalls, and occasionally he would buy her little trinkets to satisfy her magpie instincts and show her that he at least cared about her. After that they inevitably would stop into the nearby McDonalds, grab a burger, and by the time I got home, they didn't need supper, as they had already eaten.

Um, you couldn't bring me one? Nope, apparently not!

However, life was tolerable overall. We seemed to be moving forward; the future had real possibilities for us all. We started to think about maybe moving further out into the country when Amy completed her sixth form college. She was doing well and seemed to be heading toward going to university.

I thought we were settled. Tensions with Adele had finally calmed down, and she appeared to have started to like her father. I started to relax. But then it all changed.

America called.

Destiny tittered, and then burst out laughing!

Chapter Forty-Four

1993 America: Land of the Free, the Brave, and No Health Insurance!

Stacey

The Americans had called.

Damon's mother was in the hospital, having had emergency major back surgery that would leave her in a wheelchair for the rest of her life. Damon got on a plane and headed west.

Then the helter-skelter that seemed to follow us everywhere, started, as once again life spiraled out of control. The family had a powwow. Well, Damon's family did; British in-laws were not included. It was decided that the senior's current home was not going to be big enough to accommodate a wheelchair-bound resident. The consensus was that they either had to get a larger home, or poor, frail granny would have to go into a nursing home.

The entire family balked at the nursing home scenario, as the old lady made it clear she would not stand for it. She had a horror of nursing homes since Damon's grandmother had been starved to death in one, she claimed. They pleaded with Damon. He was needed to assist with alternatives. They said he was retired and should come home to help. Before he left, they had also gained a commitment from him to help finance the new home.

What an irony! It was just like Jay all over again! After a lifetime of absence, Damon's homeland and family roots called him, and he ran toward them, heedless of the impact on himself and his new family. A bare six months after his own heart surgery, Damon had left for his parent's home in Michigan, leaving me behind, and our boat rocked precariously again.

I was not forewarned that a planned, stable, happy future would once more slip from my grasp, and Amy's too, as Destiny wreaked havoc on us for years and years with the decisions made during that visit. All made regardless of how they would impact us.

Within weeks of arriving back in the United States on his mercy mission, Damon added to his massive debts in London with a commitment to his parents in America to install a new modular home on their property, replacing their too-small mobile home and enabling them to stay there.

More debt? What had he taken on? *Why* was it *our* responsibility? I seethed, but Damon's brother and father had guilted him into it. He was the one who had abandoned his home and duty for so long, and I had to go along with the program.

Really? The family that he had spent nearly twenty-five years apart from suddenly could not manage without him? Could not get along without our money, just as he was finally settling into a newer, happier life. Now stupid Stacey was apparently committed to *dumb* Damon!

Life seemed to be leading us back on the same merry-go-round that we got on when we left for Canada all those years before.

How do we spell fool? Yes, you have it, S-T-A-C-E-Y!

My heart sank because we had just reached the point where we were getting Damon's debts (incurred by his spendthrift, deceased previous wife plus one other reason it took me years to discover) under control. His credit card set up had been a fiasco. Before I came along, he only ever paid the minimum installment, then when it started getting out of control, opened another card and just transferred the balance, without actually ever diminishing it. With my additional income and cooler financial head, instead of just paying the minimum each month, now we were making inroads into principal, and I had hopes that we could get them mostly down to zero within the year. We could at last now see the light at the end of the tunnel, and then we could tackle the home equity loan. That would eventually leave us just with the outstanding mortgage, which was much more manageable. My steady government job had assisted Damon's retirement pension with making those inroads. We still didn't have quite enough to consider ourselves comfortable, and certainly not enough for largess to be distributed willy-nilly to my new in-laws!

I had thought we had enough left in the kitty to be able to do a little traveling, have a little fun, enjoy life more, but seemingly that was not Fate's intention for any of us. I also think maybe Damon had hidden his actual financial situation to his family, not wishing to appear a failure.

His agreement to the demands of his parents meant that we were now committed to our share of a long-term mortgage on their new home. We were going to be buried in debt once again for people I didn't like, with a property we didn't want or need, and which we would never live in.

Never live in? Oh, don't even have that thought, Stacey…you should know by now there is no *never* in your life!

Two months after he left, Damon returned, sharing the details of the situation in Michigan. Then he broached the big question he had held on to until he came home, a question sent our lives in a totally new direction, heralding more upheavals and a desperate situation for Amy, if we had but known it.

Damon said that he (that meant we) needed to move to Michigan so that he (that would mean we) could take care of his parents! Are you *serious?* What had they ever done for him, or for me? They had never come to visit him in England once in twenty-five years, or sent him money to help him out when he was struggling.

On *my* first trip out there to meet them, I'd barely unpacked my suitcase before his father had handed me a chainsaw! Later I saw that they were users and moochers and had been all their lives, according to an aunt of Damon's.

I felt like I had been hit with a shovel. *No!* What about Amy? What about *his* own daughter too? We were just rebuilding that relationship. What about our life here that we had begun to plan out together? Didn't that have a place in *his* life?

Stupid, dumb, trusting Stacey—there would be no deviation. This was a fait accompli set up by his brother and father, and more especially his sweet-as-apple-pie, butter-would-not-melt-in-her-mouth mother!

I tried to say "No," but I had just got married, and fear of being alone again, plus a lack of belief in my attraction for anyone else, held me back. Once again I was swept up in my partner's plans for his future, with the assumption that I would follow blindly on behind. I could see what choice I had…none!

It seemed Fate had decided that it was my lot in life to take care of everyone else, and if I could have seen into the future, I would have seen that it was going to be all drabness and drudgery from now on.

While I had sort of liked the area where his parent's home was, I had in no way viewed it as a place to live in the near future, especially so soon after getting married and with Amy still at school.

She was now at a sixth form college, and her grades were so promising that her teachers had suggested she apply to an Oxford college once she left. Now was not the time to disrupt our lives. She had a boyfriend too, a nice if somewhat nerdy boy, but they seemed happy. Would she want to leave? Could I ask her to disrupt her education again at this point?

All my questions and concerns were brushed to one side. Damon's focus had changed, and now his parents' needs superseded ours to the exclusion of all other considerations. All gratitude for caring for him through his surgery, for bringing some semblance of normality into his life, was swept away. Looking back I wondered if he regretted our marriage, had he remained single there would have been no barriers to overcome. Now he was looking at an encumbrance that forced him to make decisions. All his life he hated having to make decisions which is why he fitted in so well in the military, and with his previous two wives. They usually prescribed his actions for him and his parents had always been controlling as he grew up.

To this day, it seems to me that the elder Morris was doing fine on his own, but just decided he didn't want to take care of a wheelchair-ridden wife and all that came with it. But both were arch manipulators and had been since the early days of their marriage. They always importuned relatives to run around after them, imploring those with more assets to rescue them and save their bacon in one way or another. The aunt who warned me about this shortly after we arrived in the country hit the nail right on the head about them.

Prior to Damon's reentry into the family fold, his brother had been the one chiefly held to ransom by them over the years. That was changing, as now he was moving further away and would have less easy access to his parents. That coupled with working much longer hours in the new job mad assistance to his seniors untenable. It was not longer possible to provide the back-up that the seniors claimed was needed.

Damon's sister (mother of the locust children) was more than hopeless still, in the midst of overcoming a nasty divorce and not much able to help herself, much less her parents. Although it did later become sadly obvious that she was already showing the effects of early-onset Alzheimer's, which claimed her life a few years later, when she was only in her middle fifties. So sad.

Now the family, mostly Damon's mother, had decided it was all down to Damon to come home and take up the slack to care for them. Their reasoning was that he was retired and therefore was free to do so, and better yet, he had another younger, fitter wife. They disregarded his new marital responsibilities, his blended family, and his improved relationship with his own daughter. None of it mattered to them.

There was much family discussion about it. Amy did not want to accompany us right then, and Damon's own daughter just clammed up. She was obviously hurt at being abandoned by her father again. Amy wanted to stay and complete her college year. She was capable of staying in the house on her own, she said. She was happy with her boyfriend, his family, and her friends. We had also become friends with the boyfriend's parents; they were kind people, and her grandparents were close by. They would all keep an eye on her. After all, she was nearly nineteen, and in other circumstances would be at university by now, if she hadn't been held back that first year we moved back home.

I was between a rock and a hard place. Six months or so earlier, I had begun what I thought would be a normal married life again, despite the brush with death that Damon had right after the ceremony. What was I to do? Say no and be left alone again? Or say yes and have to leave Amy on her own? Neither seemed a happy choice.

Earnestly and optimistically, Damon said that we could work it out—perhaps just go for six months. It sounded feasible, the way he put it. Courtesy of the amazing union deals for family-care time, I could get a year sabbatical from my job for close-family care. We could see how it would work, and given ongoing pressures at work from the bitch-fest group, it sounded like the lesser of two evils.

With hindsight, I should have said no, and stuck to it, but I felt completely helpless.

Also, I was still laboring under the mantle of guilt laid on me by Jay, Ted, Sally, et al. Still lost in the belief that all the disasters in Canada had been my fault, I wondered if this was Fate's payback. Due to my still ongoing feelings of insecurity and low self-esteem, ably fostered by Jay and his family's attitude toward me, I did not more closely examine the past. It was still too painful. They had convinced me that the disasters that befell us were entirely my fault. I didn't say no to Ted, and I spent all Jay's money on *my* business venture and *my* mobile home. This had been ingrained in me that I alone was responsible for wrecking our chances of success in Canada, and even ten years later, I did not question it. I could not think clearly about it even then.

It took twenty more years before I realized I was not alone in the blame, and in retrospect, more the victim than anyone else, except for Amy, who once again was going to pay for her mother's stupidity, heaping more grief on her fragile shoulders as she spent four more years in limbo as a result.

It was a bitter irony to eventually understand that my life, Jay's, and Amy's would have been so different if only Sally would have had the courage, and the integrity, to send just one letter warning us not to leave our safe, secure life in Warwickshire. Sweet, innocent, wronged Sally – not!

Again Amy and I would face more challenges as the fickle finger of Fate rewrote our script, stealing another happy and secure future away from us as we headed into what was later aptly described to me as "The Twilight Zone"!

CHAPTER FORTY-FIVE

1993 AMERICA THE BRAVE? NOPE, AMERICA THE LONELY!

STACEY

There are no words adequate to describe the loneliness of living in American society. In the end it about killed my inner self, so the only thing keeping me going was the need to care for Amy and love for Amy.

Don't get me wrong. America the country is beautiful. But the lifestyle, the politics, and the unadulterated greed of its culture make living in America ugly and isolating for foreigners.

A totally self-absorbed, predominantly judgmental attitude pervades, and makes it so alien to anything in Europe, or Canada. It renders America a harsh place to survive. The glitter and the glitz of their international image is illusionary. It exists only for those who can afford the cost of high living, for everyone else nothing is left but penury and hopelessness.

I do love all the scenery—the beautiful lakes, the lovely coastlines, the wildlife, even the weather—but the insular outlook of America's humanity turns it into an entirely hostile and cold environment for any newcomer, or for that matter any one else who they deem 'does not fit in'.

As with all generalizations, there are individuals who buck the trend, where some with compassion and care manage to survive, but incipient tribalism draws most into closed groups. Those groups are accepting only of those who are mirror images of themselves, who live the same kind of lives. Contrarily Americans love and are hospitable to visitors, but there is a dislike of permanent immigrants and an incredible parochialism, fostered by centuries of isolation from the rest of the world.

Any newcomer finds it almost impossible to get more than a grudging acceptance by the community, especially if one does not belong to their church, their social club, or have kids who compete in their school's sports.

Money is the measure of acceptance. Strike one—we had no money, so the acceptance level was considerably diminished. Strike two— we lived on a side of town not only away from the wealthier subdivisions, but within the 'black' area. Over the course of twenty years, Damon's parents had never made any move to become a part of their local community, and we pretty much should have realized that we would have to work extremely hard to be accepted in a town of less than ten thousand people.

Damon's inbuilt penny-pinching left him with a complete lack of understanding for the need to speculate (i.e. join clubs and pay their dues) in order to accumulate social status, and for a frugal-natured person, those challenges would keep us always on the outside, no matter what we did. We have never belonged.

There were a few people included us within their tribes. One very kind soul who invited us to join the evening coffee group at the local restaurant, and made sure we were always guests at his table on high days and holidays. But that welcome vanished the day he died. His relatives did not share his kindliness and compassion, and clearly had never wanted to include us in their circle in the first place.

Friendship, as I had understood it in London, in Warwickshire, and in Canada, would appear to be an alien concept in this rural American society. We did not fit the tribal profile; too old, no profession, no kids, no hobbies and not churchgoers. There was no place of contact that made us accessible, so after we were briefly investigated for background, once the gossips had drained us of information, they lost interest. After a while I truly understood why I had viewed the visiting vagabond relatives as locusts.

Locusts descend on a new area, or flock around new people, gobble up everything they want, strip the landscape, suck out the lifeblood, and then fade away once they are sated. I could see the parallels in my new world all around me.

Once the discoveries were made as to whether there was any intrinsic value in accepting us, into their circle, and after clarifying whether or not we might pose a threat by being the possessor of superior knowledge, then barriers would go up. The tentative hand of friendship was surreptitiously withdrawn and the locals withdrew into their clans.

So here I was, stuck with it. No matter, it was back to using my ability to make myself useful, and my experience in trying to fit in. Aided by my willingness to help others, I have survived, or at least a part of me has.

With hindsight, I wonder if Fate had been telling me that I should have fled back to Edmunston the minute my feet touched American soil. I could have returned to the only real friends I ever had, and learned to live with being close to what I wanted but could never have. I will never know what the outcome of that might have been.

Back in North America, I craved a visit back to my heart's home. But in the meantime, Damon substituted constant home-care and promised that we would go to visit my friends not this summer, but maybe the next, every year thereafter it became "we'll go next year," or the next, or the next…

In the end, it was yet another promise he made but never kept. Damon never recognized all the sacrifices I made for him, or the help I willingly gave him to take care of his family, and to take care of him too. Seemingly my sacrifices were not enough to have my feelings or needs recognized or rewarded.

As a result I have learned to accept loneliness as a lifestyle, for nothing now will ever change, neither do I care any more.

Chapter Forty-Six

1993 to 2003 America— The Perfect Slave

Stacey

Once our feet had hit American soil, thirty-five years of Damon's independence from his parents had dissipated.

He reverted to being their obedient son, their controlled creature. Everything we did, and every action we took, was ruled by them. Damon would not make a decision that they did not approve of.

My father-in-law had spent a lifetime controlling those around him by bullying and irascibility, and lived out his life by rote. He got up at 5:30 in the morning, because he always had done so. He went out to his shed to fiddle with whatever gadget he was trying to fix, or work on one of his crazy quilts, because that was what he always did.

At noon he made lunch for him and his wife, and then he spent the next five hours laying on his couch, watching one John Wayne movie after another (my mother-in-law could recite the screenplays verbatim). Then he would make the couple's evening meal of instant oatmeal and occasionally a slice of toast, and at 6:30 p.m. he went to bed, regardless of anyone else's wishes or timetable.

This took care of Monday through Friday. Once Damon and I arrived, then Saturday and Sunday were reserved for one or both of us to come over to do whatever heavy jobs needed to be done outside, or to clean the house inside.

It was like being a slave. Fix a door, cut wood, chop down a tree, mow the grass, tar the driveway. Inside it was wash the laundry, catch up with the dishes, vacuum, and dust, with barely a word of thanks.

Santa's helpers had nothing on us! The sheer arrogance of the expectation that we would do everything they wished and have no life of our own, plus the total lack of appreciation, made me even more depressed. It wasn't what I signed on for, but it was what I was stuck with.

Whenever the in-laws had a problem, we were expected to drop everything and rush over to them, regardless of the hour of the day or night. "You'd better come over right now! I've pooped the bed!" became a battle cry from sweet, little old Mom.

While the elder Morris ruled with bullying, by contrast Damon's mother controlled with sweet, sugary, but determinedly insistent demands. Everyone who knew her found her charming. "Such a sweet old lady," said one old friend of theirs.

It completely escaped them that she did nothing for herself, just waited for everyone else to run around and do it for her. Her logic being that she was in a wheelchair and therefore did not need to do anything for herself because someone else would always do it for her. Had I but realized it, her attitude set up Damon to become cast in her image as the one demanding constant attention when she finally passed away. He then thought it was his due to not have to do anything that he did not feel like doing, "because he didn't feel good"!

On the home-front things intensified once the true situation with regard to Damon's sister became apparent. She had gone through a harrowing divorce, and been left almost penniless by a bastard of a husband who acquired nearly all the joint funds they had. She had worked for a while and was a good cook, but all of a sudden she became a permanent houseguest at her parents, and it became apparent that she had some kind of mental issue. Now Damon's family's favorite imported hausfrau became responsible for her too, with her children washing their hands of all care of her or interest in her. Until, that is, any mention of her money or belongings came up!

Needless to say, I was completely underwhelmed with having to care for her, clean her, and accept the odd little brown tokens she would deposit on her bedside table overnight, the reason for having a bathroom next door to her room completely escaping her failing mind.

Adding to the stress was the difficulties were facing as we tried to bring Amy to join us. She had completed her schooling and the boyfriend relationship had ended and she wanted to join us. We had run foul of the infamous American immigration service who fed us a wealth of misinformation, denials and outright lies about events during our efforts to complete the process for our daughter's visa. This was principally, we later learned, because periodically they destroy embassy records when there was a staff turnover. It turned into a two-year nightmare!

Poor Amy, her romance had floundered, and we were the only close relatives who cared about her so it made sense for her to come to live with us.

Suffice it to say, after all the unhappiness they caused Amy, if I were standing outside an INS office and it was on fire and if I had a cup of water, I would drink it. Then I would throw the cup on the fire to help the burning process with the addition of any nearby gasoline.

Believe everything bad you have ever heard about the American immigration service; it is all absolutely true!

It is sad that Americans are *so* badly let down by their gatekeepers, who lack compassion, understanding, and any kind of charm. It's no wonder that the members of my British family have found that one last visit to the United States was more than enough. Vacations were always spoiled by the intransigence and sheer nastiness of the immigration service, and latterly the TSA, not to mention the cavalier way in which their luggage was treated, even though they had followed all the instructions issued by those same services.

None of this behavior says, "Welcome to America," so I don't blame any of my relatives for staying away now.

Chapter Forty-Seven

2002 America, Ten Years On…

Stacey

We had survived our first ten years in America somehow.

Damon, returned to aspiring salesman mode as he was never one for a nine-to-five lifestyle and he tried to carve out a career in real estate. However, from whatever cause, he never quite settled with one company. Initially he went back to sales with the mobile home company that had provided his parents' new abode. Sadly, the company selling mobile homes turned out to be a little suspect in their dealings with the public, and after a year or so, Damon parted company with them.

There followed a scary few weeks while he looked around for another job, although he spent his time in conversation with the supervisory governmental agencies that eventually closed down the mobile home company for their lack of compliance and some shady financial dealings.

Damon just grinned. They didn't know whom they were dealing with!

Next he tried full-time real estate sales, but sadly not with the family friend who had her own real estate business and expected him to work with her, thereby offending her and further reducing our friendship circle. Again he wasn't too successful, and as I struggled to put all my experience to good use, a chance remark at a local public meeting moved him into a new career when he was elected to a post in local government.

Lucky break! Local government was something we both knew. His years of working for a London borough council provided good background experience in the inherent bureaucracy of his new post. He knew how to manipulate the system, and his new role gave him an opportunity to find me an opening too, as his deputy.

This was good news, as I had become quite despondent at this stage. I had tried a couple of part-time jobs, but upon arrival in America, I had become adjudicated as head cook and bottle washer, plus driver, cleaner, and general dogsbody for half my new in-laws, which didn't really leave a lot of time to devote to employment outside the home.

There was care for the seniors, followed by a stint as rehab nurse for a sister-in-law I hardly knew after she had surgery. What an eye-opener that was!

Her husband was a pip! He let me pay my own bus fare to their home a hundred miles away. Then had me cook and clean for him and his wife for two weeks, in addition to the nursing duties, and with hardly a thank you. Neither was anything in the way of a gift or compensation offered for my time. So like father like son it seemed – moochers and users.

Truly a charmer outside the house, his charisma did not extend once he entered his own home—truly street angel, house devil. He had dropped his hapless wife off at the entrance of the hospital on the day of her surgery, saying, "You can get up to the ward on your own, can't you? See you later."

Then he had just taken off. Her retrieval from the hospital was left to me. I had to drive to the hospital in a strange city, in a strange vehicle and then try to bundle her bulk and heavily bandaged leg into said vehicle. Oh, the total charmless-ness of them just took my breath away, almost as much as the sheer assumption that I was the resident slave.

After that magnificent sojourn I returned to my regular "duties". The ongoing care of the seniors, not only took up a lot of my time, but also took up most of Damon's spare time too, except for the few hours a month he found to volunteer for the local sheriff's department. He was such a wannabe, and the appeal to be a law officer never left him. Unfortunately, his face didn't fit, and he always ended up on the periphery of events.

It now appeared that we existed solely for the benefit of his parents, then later his dementia-afflicted sister. Those first ten years contained a life of pure drudgery, caring for two people that I hardly knew and did not particularly like. The drudgery and lack of appreciation ate away at my relationship with Damon too.

I kept waiting for a break, waiting for my promised trip to Canada. After all, Damon had said that we would go the next autumn after we were married, but that was before he had rushed home to take care of his parents' needs.

More and more it became apparent that this would never be on Damon's agenda. He had no interest in visiting Canada and if I became upset about it, his response was always "You can go, I am not stopping you." That was not the point, I wanted to do something with *my* husband, but I should have known by now that men rarely keep promises, unless of course it is something that *they* want to do.

Just like Jay's broken promise to me when I gave up our baby to make that first ill-fated trip to meet his father's family, now Damon's promise that we would make the trip to Canada for me to see *my* friends (and maybe Ted) never materialized.

Broken promises, broken dreams, broken hearts, and broken lives, all compounding the damage done so many years before by the thoughtless, selfish actions of Jay's family and my own stupidity falling for and trusting a serial philanderer.

Despite all my efforts to start my life over with Damon, to suppress the past, build the partnership we could have had, real happiness had vanished. In my desperation to make it happen, to start anew with Damon, I had overlooked Damon's past and his inability to fill my desire for passion and his complete lack of interest in my needs at all.

Damon had lived nearly twenty years in a mostly platonic marriage. Exacerbated by his continued poor health, he had little desire for a full married life. True, he wanted a companion, but added to a lifetime's attitude of parsimony always wanting something for nothing it turned out to be a poor foundation for us to form the close or passionate relationship I was hoping for.

But I did try. I really, really tried, but each rejection, each disappointment wore away at my soul, driving me deeper into depression. The only way to survive was to do what I later realized Ted did: bury myself in keeping busy. Initially, "busy" became all the work that was imposed on me by Damon's family of locusts. Later, in the world of politics, I was always much too busy to think about or examine the past, until that night when Ted's ghost came back to haunt me and put the final nail in the coffin that holds my soul.

Chapter Forty-Eight

2003 America— Another New Direction

Eventually, despite the utterly awful INS, we did overcome the barriers, and Amy was finally able to move and be with us. It was wonderful to have her around again, but she had not been left unscarred by these latest experiences, not to mention that her further education opportunities had been blown out of the water. So she had not gone to Oxford, and felt pretty much done with education at that point.

However, I was hoping to be able to spend more mother/daughter time with her now that she had arrived, despite my career duties for the elders. But that never materialized either, as a crisis developed with Damon's family, so after a short while, Amy found a job. A local bank about fell on her neck when they found someone so well educated. (She could spell, write her own name, learn, and was willing to work for the pittance they offered.)

Unfortunately, the association with some of her new colleagues led to a local boyfriend. Honestly this child had no luck except for bad luck.

Loser doesn't even begin to describe the young man destined to bring us drama for the next few years. But like many losers, he managed to hide his true personality with his charm until he had inveigled his way into Amy's life. Her soft heart led her to follow after the example her entirely stupid mother's lame-duck philosophy had set for her.

At this point in time, social services advised us to move my paraplegic mother-in-law into the same nursing care facility where my father-in-law had recently been incarcerated after breaking a hip. It was also where the dementia-ridden daughter had died shortly after Amy's arrival. Oh, they sure could pick their timing.

On the plus side, I was finally relieved of the extra care duties, and stupidly I thought things might start to look up. Amy was finally with us, and seemed to be doing OK, but I soon learned that I still had daily care duties, as we were expected to make daily visits to the nursing home. But at least it was only visiting, not general dogsbody work.

I broached the subject of a summer trip to Canada for us all.

Amy balked— "I have a job now. I can't take the time off, because I don't have any vacation time yet."

Damon said. "We can't leave Mom and Dad, and anyway, we can't afford it." So shot down in flames once again.

Eventually Fate intervened with regard to patient visiting and in the space of two years, first one in-law, and then the other passed through heaven's gate to join their departed daughter.

How do you spell relief? D.E.A.T.H. I foolishly thought we would finally have greater freedom, and that now maybe I would get my vacation in Canada, and maybe Amy could come with us!

With the carer pressure off, I was hoping to spend more time with her. I was beginning to enjoy having her close again. But Amy was hiding secrets. The new "charming" boyfriend was an alcoholic, lazy bum and out of work more than he was in it. He also had a small child for whom he had to pay child support. He took us all for a very expensive and unhappy ride, dragging Amy's self-esteem almost down to zero before she finally rebelled and kicked him out. He is on Karma's list. I know, because I put him there!

It was a classic example of moving down-market to find a partner. In Amy's case, her already low self-esteem caused her to endure the relationship longer than she should have. Not wishing to worry us, she kept quiet for several years about her true situation, and put up with endless misery. But once again, her fragile hold on herself had been badly fractured, and her father's continued lack of interest in her, despite the fact that she was now a mere phone call away, hurt her deeply.

His parents' death had channeled Damon into full retirement mode, and in true parsimonious form had found a cheap way for us to get a vacation through offers of free trips to various retirement communities in the south, He was determined to check them out, regardless of my wishes. Free or cheaper was his family motto!

This man, who in the past decried leaving home for the time it would take to travel to Edmunston, now set up a nearly three-week tour of Florida. The main attraction was that it would mean expending little finance except for gas or meals—Nirvana for him. He proudly offered me a free vacation!

I wasn't keen on going, I didn't like the heat, but he was insistent, so we went. "We'll go to Canada next year!" (Hollow laugh from now not quite so stupid Stacey.)

My trepidation about the "free and cheaper" tour was not unfounded. We stayed in some very odd places, some still in the process of being built, some stuck out in the wilds. We had a few days of some fun experiences, but the endless heat bothered me, and the whole trip was made momentous when I contracted what eventually would turn out to be West Nile Virus.

Within a week of our return I was deathly sick. Our medical insurance plan, tailored for the individual, barely paid for my mediocre treatment, the norm in the rural United States. It meant that my illness went undiagnosed, until eventually I ended up partially paralyzed, with all sorts of uncomfortable happenings all over my body. There followed months of misdiagnosis, when I was told I had everything from Lupus to rheumatoid arthritis, not one of those being correct. In the meantime, I drank through a straw, wore an eye patch over the one that wouldn't close, and kept dropping things with my right hand.

Oh, the joys of living in an America with no National Health Service!

The aftereffects went on well into the following year, leading once more to the proposed trip back to Canada being put on the back burner. "Next year," said Damon.

Destiny rolled her eyes and chuckled again.

Chapter Forty-Nine
2002-3 America— Campaign Manager

Stacey

Naturally, "next year" didn't come, as yet another life-course change beckoned, and Canada was going to be outside my grasp for the next decade.

A family acquaintance decided to run for state government. Damon shared with him that I had a strong background in politics over the years, and he roped me in to help. Hey, presto! Stacey, campaign manager, appeared, swiftly followed, after a victorious election, by Stacey, political aide! Oh, this was more like it! An escape from my dire surroundings!

I must admit that during the campaign I thrived! It was hard work, but I always had a flair for organization, and my experience as a journalist and on the different boards I had joined in our local area just strengthened my abilities.

Once the hullaballoo of the election had settled down, I found myself with the offer of a job that had a regular income and, wonder of wonders, excellent health insurance! It was way too good to turn down, especially with Damon's constant poor health, and his eyes lit up at the thought of "free" insurance.

There was one slight drawback: it was in the state capital, ninety-plus miles away. Damon wasn't too keen on losing his housekeeper and gardener, but the lure of the regular and more substantial income held back any real opposition from him. I could go during the week and come home for weekends, to do the housekeeper and gardener jobs.

That year our income had been at a particularly low ebb, and with Damon's ever-mounting health-care costs, bankruptcy seemed to loom and was definitely taking a bite out of my aunt's legacy. Despite his ongoing supervisor role, with its minimal income, Damon had struggled to find a good-paying job, and my own savings plus good housekeeping skills just kept us solvent. An offer like this was manna from heaven, and neither of us could refuse.

Damon and I talked about him moving to the state capital with me, but during the entire twelve years I worked there, as with the trip to Canada, there was always an excuse as to why it was not plausible, until shortly before his death. His dreams of public office fading along with his health he could see the logic of having in home care if he didn't want to take care of himself.

Over the years his reasoning had gone from: we couldn't abandon Amy, to he couldn't leave his cat; from he wanted to stand for another local office, or he just might have a possibility for a job he had always wanted. Either way, like Jay before him, his wife's wishes were secondary to his own for twelve years.

Somewhere, someone was playing "It seems to me I've heard this song before."

In the end I became a commuter wife during the week, coming home at weekends, and I became the major breadwinner. Any other woman would have left him, I did not. My loyalty ran deep.

Life in the Capitol was everything I expected, and then again nothing like I had expected.

I had thought that being in the state's capital city would be a new opportunity to make real friends, that I could become a part of a real social circle. It was the state capital; there *had* to be a social life! How naïve was that thought! There are *no* friends in politics. As in any enclosed society, the judgmental attitudes of society are honed to a fine point, because the categorization of your beliefs and character are based on a person's political affiliation.

Age played a role too. Now I was too old to join in with the young scene (Americans are terrible ageists), and those in my own age group already had their own circle, so once again I didn't fit in. Not to mention that the long hours and having to do two jobs due to the incompetence and laziness of Lacy, my young, thin, blond, hedonistic bimbo colleague left me little time for a social life anyway.

My boss, was somewhat smitten with Lacy and loathe to dispense with the office eye candy. He dismissed my workload with a continual extolling of my workaholic focus. "You just breathe this stuff, Stacey. You are like the Energizer Bunny!"

This, of course, abrogated him from all responsibility for his lack of action with regard to a girl who constantly sent him to the wrong place for appointments, or left them off the schedule altogether. Not helpful when he was electronically challenged and needed help setting up his voice mail, although strangely, Lacy did teach him to text, eventually!

Looking back, I sometimes wonder if, by some fluke of nature, she was related to sweet little Kristy from my days with the London borough. If not related, for sure they had read the same books on how to avoid as much work as possible without being fired.

But despite the pressure of keeping the office running efficiently, I did manage to hook myself into the gossip loop. It added a little spice to the daily grind. One of my informants was a mine of information! I learned who was sleeping with whom, and who was breaking the rules. I had the scoop on almost everyone, in fact!

I heard about the aide who was fired because she wouldn't lie to her boss's wife about his whereabouts while he carried on an affair with another colleague. Later, that wife and girlfriend had a screaming match, which could be heard all around the echoing chambers of the Capitol, amid snickers and shocked looks. That building had marvelous acoustics. As to be expected, that marriage disintegrated, and the term-limited offender crawled back into the woodwork from whence he had emerged.

There was one advantage to being older, and friendly. People talked to me, especially some of the younger girls, who clued me in to a really nasty piece of work. This charming example of humanity (state representative) had brought a sweet, young staffer to tears, sexually harassing her, even on the House floor with other representatives around. He became renowned for sticking his hand up the skirts of the more innocent, timid girls. But he was never reprimanded for his predatory behavior, and in fact seemed to acquire the admiration of his peers. Incredibly he went on to become a state senator. Some voters will elect just anybody into office.

But there was good stuff, too, opportunities to work on ground breaking legislation, which quickened my heart. It also led to more whispers when I learned of the shocking behavior of a leading lobbyist, so full of his own self-importance that he attempted to coerce a governor.

Clearly the obnoxious toad should have been flung out on his ear, particularly as he was breaking the law. It is highly illegal to try to use coercing or threats to get or to fail legislation, which said governor should have known.

But Mr. Toad's own supporters heard about that and suddenly dropped their opposition to the legislation while walking rapidly in the opposite directions, not wishing to be tarred with the same brush.

Really this was just the tip of the iceberg, and frankly very disillusioning. The halls of power are paved with inflated egos, self-aggrandizement, and in some cases blatant corruption. Trust your government at your peril and the larger the government, the greater the corruption!

Tales from Peyton Place paled by comparison, and I started to keep lots of notes to use in my memoirs when it comes time to retire. The power struggles and the bullying were sad to see, particularly when those who had let their own sense of power go to their heads then used it to intimidate younger and more inexperienced workers.

I almost fell foul of one such person who stands above all others in terms of believing one's own publicity to completely mesmerize the Capitol patch. I'm pretty darned sure that she must have been the model for Meryl Streep's interpretation of Miranda Priestly in *The Devil Wears Prada,* or Glenn Close's evil version of Cruella De Vil in *101 Dalmatians!* Just perfect for either part.

However, I survived the onslaught, because she didn't really know who Stacey was. Stacey had fought off the entire coal-branch cadre, been in a cage with a tiger, spent the day with a cheetah; Stacey had been a block away when an IRA bomb exploded, had another near-death experience with several moose, and survived several car crashes. The list was endless. By comparison I saw her as a lion that meowed, rather than roared!

A collective sigh of relief went up when Ms. Nasty was involved in a plot that nearly brought the state house to its knees, and came so close to a huge court case that the door barely missed her ass when she scurried out to protect it.

Ultimately, the real lesson I learned best was that in politics there was no such thing as a friend and to never trust anyone. All interaction was based on expediency and usefulness, as well as party designation. Party affiliation categorized people, and assumptions were made with regard to political views, regardless of whether those assumptions were accurate. Thus individuals were categorized, and for the most part isolated from interaction with others. It was not unusual to be asked with in an apologetic tone, "Most of the people are from the other party. Is that OK? You won't feel uncomfortable?"

No, I hadn't been feeling uncomfortable that was until you kept making inane remarks like, "She works for the other side, but she's more like us, really," to your cohorts!

So if you want a friend when you move to a state capital or a country's capital, take a dog along with you or get a cat or even a budgerigar! But not a canary—they sing!

There was a plus side, it was a great learning curve and gave me an opportunity to do what I liked to do best: help people, particularly help people who were fighting the bureaucracy and the arrogance of those paid from the public purse. Whatever the drawbacks, the job brought a regular wage. It also brought a pittance of a pension and some ever-reducing health insurance, which likely will vanish altogether in the not-to-distant future.

Thankfully I will be out of that world by then. In fact, with any luck, I will be out of the world entirely, for I am done with it and now just want to lie in the cemetery beside my soul mate, for eternity.

Chapter Fifty
2007 Onwards—Edmunston

Ted

It was the summer of 2007, and Ted was almost content with his life…almost…

At seventy, retired for five years, Ted's days were full, and he seemed to have accomplished the most that a man could wish for despite a massive glitch along the way.

He had finally got his life back on track after Stacey left, and in the following years had completely renovated his house. Now his home had a fireplace in the bedroom, a new bathroom, a new bigger basement, a new deck, a totally renovated interior, and finally a new roof. All traces and memories of Stacey in his home were eradicated forever, and he and Sally didn't fight any more. Their relationship would never be the same, but they managed, and to the outside world, they put on a united front.

He now had two grandchildren from Lauren, of whom he was extremely proud. Both were great at sports, especially his granddaughter Melanie who was great at field sports and loved golf every bit as much as he did. Soon there would be another grandbaby, as Corinne had finally settled down and was expecting her first child soon. He winced as he reflected on the irony of Corinne's relationship, then shook himself, he wasn't going to dwell on that. Never again would he let his mind go to that place, but his subconscious had a will of its own.

He thought that his life could not be much better, and maybe he should have been uneasy. Should he have realized it was all too perfect? Later, looking back, he knew that this was the summer when his life took its final downward spiral. That year that the ghosts of the past, banished for so long, came back to haunt him and all of them once more as Destiny took a hand again.

At the height of that midsummer, Ted's longtime buddy Brody died, in his early fifties. Brody, who was like a younger brother to him. Ted had been a substitute father to Brody, who never got along with his own dad. One day, when they were joking about, Brody had said, "You shouldn't be called Ted. You're more like Fred Flintstone." Ted, laughing, had retorted, "Then you are Barney Rubble, or should that be Barney Rubbish? Yabba dabba doo!" and walked off chuckling. The "Barney" stuck, the "Fred" did not, too much like Ted…

Now Brody was gone, and even in an oil-and-gas town, where early deaths from cancer proliferated after all the contact with dangerous toxins over the years, Brody's death had come as a real shock to Ted. It shattered his belief in his own mortality – reinforcing the knowledge that he was not going to live forever either.

Ironically, on that same day that Brody died, Corinne's baby girl, Brenda, had arrived. Ted mused how tragedy and happiness always seemed to come along together. The sad emotions mingled with joy at Brody's funeral, when Corinne had wheeled her newborn daughter into the service in her tiny baby buggy. Sadness and joy always seemed to have been partners in Ted's life, and Stacey's memory fluttered across the back of his mind. Sadness and joy were always partners: sadness that Stacey had left, and joy when his first grandchild was born shortly afterward.

Despite his mixed emotions at the funeral, Ted had done Barney proud, making a heartfelt eulogy for his closest friend, who had died far too young, leaving another hole in his soul, bringing with it a sense of foreboding for his future.

GHOSTS HOVER

Later that summer, Sally and Ted had to finally face up to the challenges of Penny's deteriorating health. Mattie and Sally had finally decided her care at home was too much for them to tackle. Penny needed twenty-four-hour care, and to get it she would have to be moved to a nursing home, something she had always been opposed to. Despite her wandering mind, Penny had fought them every step of the way. In truth, with Mattie's nursing background, and Sally to help her, Penny's two daughters should have been able to cope. But neither was willing to continue to put in the time, and each sister had the feeling that the other would off-load most of the responsibility on to her as the old lady got worse.

They took Penny to the senior's home, and what she saw as their betrayal took the heart right out of her. Ted, seeing her reaction, suspected from her deteriorating demeanor that she would not be with them much longer. Another funeral coming, he thought, his heart sinking. Just before Christmas, his predictions came true when Penny finally left them.

As they planned Penny's funeral, bickering started about the wording of Penny's obituary. Sally didn't want any mention of Zack and his family, but Mattie insisted that Penny would have wanted her brother's life recognized. "How can we include Aunt Agatha and not Uncle Zack?" Mattie had reasonably intoned.

But the discussion about Zack brought back memories of the reasons for Jay and Stacey being ostracized, and on that point they agreed. Neither of the girls wanted them recognized in the obituary, so in the end they had compromised. They included Zack's name and his military rank, but the rest of Zack's family was consigned to obscurity at Sally's insistence.

Whatever hopes he may have had that his wife had allowed the past to stay in the past receded when Ted saw that Sally's enmity toward her cousins was still much in evidence. They never spoke about them, and he had worked hard at banishing Stacey from his mind over the past two decades. On occasion Stacey had commented on stories in the local paper, and seeing her name in print caught him off guard each time. He always felt disbelief as the hammer smacked his chest once more, and all his feelings would flood back to the surface. For days afterward, his dreams would be of her again, his feelings mingled still with sorrow, rage, and shame, and the urge to keep busy came on him again.

He should have understood at that time the depth of his feelings. He had been a mature man, not an untried boy, when he had fallen in love with Stacey. It was not a young man's infatuation, but an older man's passion, ingrained deep within his soul.

His ardor for Stacey ran deeper than anything he had ever experienced before, and he resented her for it, wished they had never met. After Sally had delivered her ultimatum, he had cut all ties with Stacey, or tried to, knowing that he could not leave his girls, expecting her to be out of his life forever.

But Stacey stayed in the town, seemed to become more a part of his life every day. Aghast, he found that his passion for her built up over the ensuing years, try as he might to ignore her, but she had been there each morning. Hating himself for not helping her while she struggled, and trying to hate her instead, in the end he had been forced to admire how she coped and was able to recover. Belatedly he understood that he should not have let her go; as time passed, he had found no way to remove her from his heart, and by the time they had their final confrontation, she was an obsession with him.

Stacey had once said they were soul mates, and it seemed that there was a bond between them that would not be broken. However hard he tried to bury her into the depths of his mind, he knew she still lurked in his heart.

At first, after she had blurted out everything to Sally in the hospital, he did think he hated her, as the layers of his life unraveled in full public view, embarrassing him beyond belief. The contempt of his wife and mother-in-law, the shock and disappointment of his daughters, had nearly taken him to the edge as he tried to salvage his relationship with his girls. Having to contend with the glances and sniggers from some of his workmates had not enhanced his feelings. His emotions were in turmoil when Sally had insisted that he go to see Stacey and, as she put it, "sort it out" with Stacey. What Sally had really meant was for him to make it clear any relationship was over, that he was not ending his marriage to be with her. That meeting had been the last thing he had wanted to do; previously the last time he had seen Stacey had been when they had rushed her to hospital. Then his life had spiraled out of control. Torn between his fear of losing his daughters and his home, and the knowledge that he was in love with Stacey, he had known that he had to stay away from her to salvage what was left of his sanity. He could not control his heart, but he had to control his actions.

Reluctantly Ted had complied with Sally's request because she held all the cards. He had been shocked that when he saw Stacey again the spark of passion that lay between them ignited once more. It had taken all his self-control not to tell her how he really felt about her, but Sally's threat to take his daughters was like a sword dangling over his head. He had to admit to Stacey what he had known since the previous summer, that Sally would take his girls from him if he left her. Then he had fled into the night, Stacey's pleas ringing in his ears. Yet, despite Sally's warning, he was unable to tell Stacey that he did not love her or that say he didn't want her. Not only was that not true, but he knew Stacey would not believe him.

After that confrontation, his wife and mother-in-law had expected Stacey to close up her store and flee back to Jay, but she stayed put. The family's bewilderment at her continued presence in town led to some very ugly scenes in his house. Sally's anger toward Stacey had reached extreme proportions, exacerbated by her own realization that if she had prevented Jay from coming to Edmunston in the first place, the whole ensuing debacle would not have happened. She should not have been so secretive in the beginning about Ted's encounter with Mariska; it just made everything ten times worse.

Stacey had done her best to stay out of their way, initially, and ran her store on her own. At first Jay still appeared in town with Amy each weekend. Then they came less and less, until it became clear that their marriage was likely over. Ted didn't see her for several months except when he could not stop himself trying to catch a glimpse of her as she left her store after work.

Things settled down a little, as a peace offering to Sally, he took the whole family on an expensive trip to Hawaii for spring break. It seemed Karma did not approve. It had rained incessantly during their entire stay on the islands, which did nothing for his temper. But the break had restored him somewhat in his daughters' eyes, bringing him a measure of peace again. Sally also calmed down, realizing that if she made his life too uncomfortable, Ted might be drawn back to Stacey. But Ted had vowed to himself to put Stacey completely behind him. After all, he loved his girls, loved his mother-in-law, did love his wife, but he just was not in love with her any longer, and he loved his home. He wanted to stay, so he decided he would not go seeking Stacey any more.

Those good intentions had lasted just two weeks after the family's return, when they were unexpectedly torpedoed. One morning, as he met up with his workmates for their early morning coffee before heading out the their gas plant, Stacey had walked into the café to have coffee with Gino, the owner. Ted had been appalled and completely unnerved for a moment, then full of rage and jealousy, mistakenly assuming that Gino was Stacey's new lover and she was there to rub it in his face.

Three years of torture had followed, as almost every morning Stacey continued to come in for coffee, refusing to allow his presence to deter her. Intimidated by Sally's anger, Ted completely ignored her. Equally Stacey, learning fast, never acknowledged him, just chatted happily with Gino. He concentrated on his pals, but it caused more trouble with Sally, who demanded that he find a different place to have coffee. He had told her *no*, he was not going to change his whole routine or make himself look like a fool in front of his friends. It was a small town, and there was no avoiding being at the same place at the same time on occasion. Luckily, for his peace of mind, he got used to her presence, and since he saw her only once a day, and then not every day, he was able to come to terms with her being there. Still feeling threatened, Sally started to show an interest in going places with him. With his girls moved toward graduation and college, he found plenty to occupy him and keep his feelings for Stacey at bay.

He never let on for a moment that each morning, as unmoved as he appeared to be by Stacey being in the same room with him, it took a toll on him. Surprisingly, in the end, it was almost a comfort to see her each day until her store failed. Then she closed it up and disappeared. Suddenly there was no more Stacey at breakfast each day, and he was bereft.

His own reaction had bemused him. He had become accustomed to seeing her, had enjoyed seeing her blossom, as jealous of Gino as he might be. When she left town, he thought she might have finally made up with Jay. He was stunned when he discovered that she had left with someone he had never heard of. One morning as Ted left the restaurant, Gino, taking pity on him, had quietly told him where she had gone, adding, "Don't worry, she'll be back. Treat her better next time."

Ted found out that she had actually moved to the next town, so he found excuses to drive there, and had haunted the supermarket parking lots, hoping to see Stacey, but equally hoping she wouldn't notice him. She had, but ignored his presence, putting it down to coincidence, not even considering that he might have been trying to see her. After all, for three years he had stolidly ignored her; surely that told its own story.

But Gino had been right. It was not too long before Stacey was back in Edmunston, this time with Amy in tow. Her return boded ill for his household comfort again, and Sally's rage and pursed lips had put their reviving relationship back a notch or two.

Sally's temper got worse when they found out that Stacey's new best friends were Hans and Marta, their next-door neighbors! Ted's heart sank and from then onward, until she and Amy finally left Edmunston, Stacey never seemed to be away from the place. Sally never forgave Marta for befriending Stacey.

While his home now seemed under attack at least the early morning breakfast routine wasn't reinstated. Stacey's new job was working at an out-of-town gas plant and she had to leave very early to get there.

It was eighteen months before Stacey quit that job, almost immediately was back to dropping in to sit with Gino early in the morning again. Ted's heart gave a lurch the first time she had walked in. It was luck for him, he had issues at home to concentrate on. Lauren's college graduation and soon Corinne's leaving for college, and he didn't have time to wonder what Stacey was up to

That shock came straight out of left field when they saw Stacey's name emblazoned across a column in the new local newspaper. It was like a smack in the face for his whole family.

"How does she do it?" Sally had exploded. "Anyone with any sense of shame would clear out of town for good." Once again the telephone lines between the coal-branch cronies buzzed. Not for the first time, Sally tried to recruit her friends to isolate Stacey, but it was a losing battle. She just charmed people, and there were many in town now who didn't know her history. When he had realized what Sally was doing angrily Ted forbade her to spread their story around and shame him again. They could ignore Stacey, he said; they didn't have to have anything to do with her. Stoically he stuck to that plan, but two months later, Fate dealt him a blow that left him reeling.

Chapter Fifty-One

1986 Edmundston—Banquets

Ted

The day of the old-timers hockey tournament dawned like any other tournament day, and he had no intimation that this would be any different, or that the ensuing banquet would be the catalyst for him when he finally had to face up to his real feelings for Stacey.

He had trudged into the locker room area that morning, his hockey gear slung over his shoulder, preparing to get ready for some rip-roaring games. In the doorway, he had stopped short in shock as his gaze fell on Stacey talking to Ray, the team captain. Their eyes had met, and for him, it was like an explosion in his heart and his head, and he knew he was still in love with her. But Stacey, inured by years of him ignoring her, looked straight through him and not by so much as a glance acknowledged him.

After all, that was what he had told her he wanted, wasn't it? It hurt, and that it hurt shocked him too.

That whole day long, he could not get his brain around the fact that Stacey was close-by, chatting to all his hockey pals, with them teasing her and laughing at her teetering across the ice for a shot of the opening puck drop. All day she was in the stands with his teammates, or the referee's wife, or other team wives, and they all seemed to like her. He could *not* keep his mind on the ice or focus on the games, and he had garnered some harsh comments from team members about his ability to recognize a puck when he saw one. He was numb. This could not be happening again! It was *over!*

In the evening, he had arrived at the postgame banquet and was stunned to see Stacey sitting there too, happily chatting to Don Merkle, Leroy Long, and others. Challenged by her ignoring him all day, he sauntered over to the table where she sat, ostensibly to sit with his friends, but in reality to be close to her again. Then he had excelled himself in crass behavior.

He acted like he didn't know her when Don Merkle had introduced her to him. He taunted her by running his foot up and down her leg while she tried to ignore him. Then, left on his own with her for a few minutes, his confused feelings led to him being hurtful, ignorant, and terse. Later, he had been ashamed of himself, and his behavior. He had gone off and acted out with other women at the banquet like an immature schoolboy. Glancing across at Stacey, he saw the pain in her face.

And yet, and yet…tears lurking behind her eyes, just before he had walked away from her, she had said softly to him, "I still love you," The bewilderment in her eyes had left him torn apart inside, unable to come to terms with what he now knew he wanted and, what he now could see no way to get.

He thought of his folly in how he had handled things in the beginning, not found a way to talk to her and ask her to wait until his girls left home, what would she have said? But instead he thought only of himself. Hiding behind lies he had cruelly walked away, refused to talk to her and left her to struggle. He was not even honest with himself and now he recognized that he was in love with her, and still wanted her.

The evening had repercussions in his home again. Deeply hurt once more by his churlish behavior, Stacey had retaliated in fury with the only weapon she felt she had—publicity! The comments in her column had set Sally off again and he had gnashed his teeth.

But what he didn't know, and what would spell ruination for him a year later, was that this time Stacey had decided there and then he was never getting the opportunity to hurt her like that again.

Ted would be fifty next year—he was afraid time was running out, he was almost too old to start again, now. If he were going to make a change, it would have to be soon. But once more he dithered. He still needed a little more time until both girls were gone from home, and he had to organize an exit strategy.

He spent the next year trying to figure out how to ask Stacey if she would still have him, and how he could leave his marriage and salvage as much as he could from it without leaving Sally with nothing. But the damage he did at the banquet, after so many years of his cold behavior toward Stacey, was his undoing.

It caused her to distance herself from him, even cutting down on her visits to Marta.

In sheer desperation, after one of her rare visits to Marta, on an evening when Sally, the girls, and Penny were for once all away together in Edmonton, he raced out to accost Stacey as she got into her car.

In his haste and panic to grasp the opportunity of Sally's absence and Stacey's sudden appearance, all the pretty speeches he had made up in his head dissipated. His mind blank, the best he had been able to muster was a terse, "Want to come inside?" At Stacey's raised eyebrows and questioning, "What about Sally?" He had compounded that with his magnificent rejoinder, "It's OK. Sally's gone for the weekend!"

He had watched the initial spark of joy in her eyes, chased away by shock, then fear, which flitted across her face as she heard his second remark.

Turning away from him, she had said, "No!"

Her refusal stunned him.

"Why not?" he had asked, still not comprehending the emotions that his invitation had set off in her again. She used Marta as an excuse. "Marta will see."

Her response bewildered him. What had Marta to do with it? This was about the two of them and their future. He desperately tried to convince her that Marta didn't need to know. Stacey could drive around the block and then pull into his front yard. Marta wouldn't be able see who was in his driveway. But Stacey seemed really spooked, and she had been adamant. "She's my only friend. She won't understand. No!"

Then she had fled in her car, leaving him feeling like a fool.

Ted had stormed back inside, slamming the door behind him, and hurling a chair to the floor. Pain flooded through him. He reached for a bottle of alcohol, and with each drink, his resentment toward her grew. What had he been thinking? He had been about to lay his soul bare to her, and she was more concerned with the neighbors and walked away. All the memories came flooding back and he relived the hurt of the time when he had been forced to tell Lauren and Corinne about her.

What followed after Stacey fled away set the final seal on his relationship with her. It ended their contact with each other, but still resolving nothing nor severing the bond that lay between them. When Stacey got home instead of ignoring him, as she knew she should, she had telephoned Ted. There followed such an awful, heartrending conversation that if it didn't break her heart, it surely came close to breaking his.

Overwhelmed with shame and disgust at himself for his past behavior, as Stacey revealed the excruciating impact of it on her and Amy, he resorted to denial again. On the defensive, he made things ten times worse by belittling the difficulties she had faced. He had heard her gasp in disbelief when she had stopped talking about her struggles, he coldly said, "Well, you're doing all right now!"

It was like he had opened a weir. Stacey ripped into him, and her anguish poured out. He cringed at the pain in her voice as she relived the horror of being left entirely alone in a strange country. "*You* watched me *starve,* and didn't lift a finger to help me. You left me writhing in pain, without a home, without friends. God help me, I am still in love with you, but I can't let you hurt me again, I have to take care of Amy!"

He had hated the picture she painted of him. That was not *him*! *He* was not the hateful person she was talking about. So he lashed again out at Stacey, saying hurtful things instead of telling her that all he wanted was to have her in front of him and be able to hold in his arms forever. Unable to gather his thoughts together coherently, he was faced with her bitter annihilation of his character.

"You are a user, devoid of compassion, an actor, a philanderer, selfish, and self-absorbed." Her words burned into his soul. He poured himself another drink to dull the pain as he had hung up on her. He had been on a binge of drinking that lasted until just before Sally returned, and by the time he was pulling himself together, Stacey dealt her final blow.

She telephoned Sally, after she returned from her trip with Penny and Lauren. His conversation with Sally that followed, was burned into his memory as one of the worst days in his life.

In self-preservation mode, despite the pain Stacey's call had caused her, Sally did not share all of her conversation with Stacey. All he had heard as he walked through the door was Sally saying, "Don't worry, Stacey. He won't bother you again!" Then she had turned to face him

The disbelief in Sally's eyes as she realized his complete betrayal of her, his duplicity from the beginning, and how he had continued his interest in Stacey over most of the last decade, set their revived relationship back ten years.

She had flown at him in fury and grief. "Are you still wanting to leave me for her?" Sally had yelled at him. Then she continued on. "The same rules still apply."

Angrily, Ted had shot back, "You can't use the girls against me now! They're spreading their wings, moving on with their lives." And, he thought to himself, just like I want to do with Stacey.

Sally retorted spitefully, "So, you never want to have anything to do with the grandchildren coming along, then?"

Right there Ted knew he had lost, and that nothing had changed. Sally could still turn his girls against him. She pretty much had in the beginning, until she realized that she might be driving him into Stacey's arms. Now his daughters were all about their mother, first and foremost. He would lose them.

Sally would never let him live happily with anyone else, and he understood the confidence in Sally's remark to Stacey. He would not ever bother Stacey again. He now knew he could not. It was a battle he couldn't win. Inwardly he shrugged. He was pragmatic if nothing else, so once more Ted took refuge in throwing Stacey under the bus.

He responded sulkily to Sally, "Anyway, I don't even know why she phoned you, or what she said. Was it to do with me being in the yard the other evening when she came out of Marta's? She approached me, and I turned her down. I guess she's made up some cock-and-bull story. Why would I have anything to do with her after all the trouble she's caused in the past? It's just another one of her tricks."

He was enraged with both of them.

Stacey had ratted him out again!. Also telling Sally that he should leave her alone. His fury at this new disruption in his life was aimed at Stacey, exacerbated by the fact he knew he had instigated it. He had left it way too late to ever be with Stacey.

That was clear. His only option was to retrieve what he could and so he set about trying to shore up what remained of his relationship with Sally.

In self-protection mode, he had directed his anger toward Stacey, determined that he would hate her. But that was as bad as loving her, because he was still thinking about her. She was too deeply embedded in his soul and he knew that bond would never be broken.

Within a few short months, Stacey's house was up for sale, and she had finally fled back to England with Amy, her last words to him being that she was going forever. He did not believe that she would never return, that he would never see her again. Gino's conversation with him years earlier played in his head: she would always return. But he had ignored Gino's advice and had not treated her better. Now it had come back to bite him.

Stacey's departure seemed to Ted to have left an immense void inside him, and he needed to keep it at bay. The only way he found to do that was to throw himself into one project after another, constantly live life at the run, and be the life and soul of every party, while his lonely soul wailed inside him.

Finally, almost burned out, he ended up in the hospital with stomach problems. He knew they were caused by the constant stress of all that had happened with Stacey over the past ten years, and all that he had buried inside instead of sharing his thoughts with the only person he could, the only person he should have.

Chapter Fifty-Two

Moving On

Ted

Three years later, after had Ted had pushed Stacey into the recesses of his mind, his feelings suffered a jolt. Rumors swirled that Stacey was planning to come back for a visit with Amy. He started to feel a little smug. Gino had been correct; she couldn't stay away! Ted smirked.

In the end, Stacey hadn't come back that summer, or any other summer. Stacey did not return, ever.

But the following year, Amy returned with her boyfriend in tow, bringing news about Stacey that hurt him beyond anything he had envisaged.

Amy didn't make any contact with her family, neither did she visit Marta, but she did meet up with her own friends, including Lola Long. Happily she shared with Lola, and thus half of Edmunston, that Stacey had gotten married again early in the spring. Amy had raved about what a wonderful wedding it had been. How her new relatives flew in from America. How Stacey's new husband was a former American marine, and Ted pictured a muscular John Wayne type in his head. Her mom was very happy, Amy said, and for herself, she said she liked her new stepfather very much.

Lola, a naturally gifted gossip, shared every last detail of the news with her parents. Next morning Leroy Long couldn't wait to relay the information to Ted at breakfast. Ted had managed a nonchalant shrug and answered, "Oh, is that right? Doesn't matter to me or anyone in my family," and turned back to his coffee.

For days afterward, inside, his stomach clenched, as jealousy, rage, and grief had engulfed him. The depth of his anguish shocked him and brought home to him the true nature of his feelings for Stacey. He became enraged that Stacey still had this hold over his feelings, felt fury that she had betrayed him by marrying someone else.

Stacey's message was clear. She had finally moved on, was married to someone else, loved someone else. She was truly lost to him forever. She could be nothing to him ever. Wasn't that just what he had let her think from the start?

Be careful what you wish for, he pondered wryly, for when you get it, it tastes like ashes and destroys you inside.

In order to suppress thoughts he could not bear, he looked around for something to distract himself. He looked at his house and then threw himself into a major project to renovate everything in it that still reminded him of what had happened there a decade ago. When he had finished, there would be nothing left to remind him of the past, and his home would be even more comfortable

Fortunately there was a new grandbaby on the way to join his feisty little grandson, who was renewing warmth in his heart. To ensure that he had no time to sit and brood, he had thrown himself into more community involvement in social clubs, more sports, and campouts with friends. To Sally's chagrin, he even tried to return to his old philandering ways to prove that he still had it, could still enjoy a fling, and for a few years became a permanent fixture at a bar in town. He was going to prove to himself that his life was back on track. Stacey was just another woman, meant nothing. Destiny laughed at him.

Really, old man, not going to be long now before you will be past all that playing around with other women!

Then age had caught up with him, reminding him that everyone is mortal. He faced a couple of spells in the hospital for operations to deal with a lifetime of tough sports putting pressure on his knees and hips. That defeated his extracurricular libido, and he finally retreated to Sally's side. She heaved a sigh of relief that she didn't have to hear whispers about his exploits any more.

Even so, in Sally's mind there was still a question mark over Stacey. Noting a look in Ted's eyes sometimes, she wondered what would happen if Stacey ever came back. The feeling it roused made Sally doggedly determined that he was never going to have the chance to go to Stacey. She made a promise to herself to outlive Ted. Stacey would never have him. No matter how much they tried to make a new life with their daughters and grandchildren, Stacey had cast a long shadow over all of them.

Life moved on. Lauren's children grew. Then finally, Corinne came home to tell them that she was moving in with her boyfriend, Pierre, and that she was pregnant. They'd known about Pierre for some time and been concerned that although separated, he had waited until his father died before officially leaving his wife and openly living with Corinne. Even so, there would be no divorce. His wife's strict Catholic commitment would not allow it, but the couple shrugged it off. It was enough to be together.

Whatever Ted and Sally felt about the arrangement, they were adults and it was their choice. For Ted, given his own history, he was in no position to comment. But uncomfortable thoughts assailed him as he watched the two of them

The irony of his daughter's relationship was not lost on him (as Karma snickered in the background). Pierre was the same age that Ted had been when Stacey had come into his life, and Corrine was the same age as Stacey had been then. But, unlike Ted, Pierre had not been prepared to remain in an unhappy marriage. He had determinedly put his faith in the woman who had stolen his heart, had trusted her to love him back, and stay beside him, despite their age gap. It rankled, revived memories he did not want, feelings he thought he had consigned to the depths of memory.

Corinne's pregnancy set Ted thinking. They had all been surprised when they heard the news about the baby, as they thought that in her mid-thirties she was too old to have a child.

Ted began to wonder what might have happened if Stacey had become pregnant during their encounter. That would have been a game changer.

He did not want to remember that terrible time, but one thought kept niggling at the back of his mind, disturbing his dreams. One night he had woken up with a start. *Stacey!* Had she been pregnant? During their time together, he had never given a thought to birth control, was so caught up in the passion between them. Their sexual encounters had been unprotected on his part. Why would he even consider it? Sally was way past the age of conception, and subconsciously he had made the same assumption about Stacey too. But she had been the same age as Corrine!

Now the desperation in her attitude after he had…after they had…after…took on a new perspective. There had been a feeling he couldn't shake whenever she tried to talk to him that there was something else she was trying to tell him. He never gave her the chance—but *pregnant?* Had she been carrying his child? What if her breakdown had come as a result of losing a child? After all, she had shown no signs of a pregnancy thereafter. But what if she had lost his child because of his cruelty toward her?

It was too terrible a thought. It left him aghast, and he pushed it away. What did it matter now? It was water under the bridge. It had all happened so long ago, he could not raise all that again, could not broach it with Sally, and there was no way to ask Stacey about it. But once more the taste of ashes seemed to linger in his mouth.

Although he tried to shake it off, it seemed like a premonition of ill things to come hovered.

No, he was *not* going down that road again! He was not! His family was all that mattered now, and he forced his focus back to his girls, his grandchildren, and Corinne's happiness. His life was still tinged with his sadness that Brody was so sick, and he was afraid for him. Death and life always linked.

Time to get busy again, plan a new project. The house needed a new roof, and he started planning how he would do it next year. They would make it a family affair, get the kids and grandkids involved, gather his family close around him, to prove to himself that he had made the right decision. The relationship between him and Stacey could not have ended in the same way as that of his youngest daughter and her beau, but the hammering in his chest started again.

He wished with all his heart that he had not hurt his family so much or Jay's little family, but as he tried to suppress the past once more, Karma started to wake, deciding that payment was now coming due.

This year his past actions began to haunt him, and to weigh on Sally too. It began with Brody's death, then Penny's death cast another shadow. Add then finally, one fateful day the following summer, Ted shepherded Melanie to a tournament, leading to a chance encounter with a forgotten face that shattered his peace of mind for the last time.

Chapter Fifty-Three

2008 Edmundston— Chill Winds

Ted

The hands of Fate were finally moving, blowing a chill breeze, as another death came stirring up memories of the past.

Penny, in her nineties, had finally succumbed to old age and infirmity, her life ending in a nursing home. She had fought so hard over the years to stay out of that home, and had been bewildered when Mattie, self-centered as ever, had persuaded her sister that it was too much to look after their mother themselves any longer.

No matter that Mattie had years of training as a nurse, and could give Penny better care than she could ever get in an institution. She and Sally disregarded all the help that Penny had given them over the years. Against the old lady's wishes, they practically bundled Penny out of her home, placating her by saying it was just for a short time, to give them a rest.

Penny knew better, and that betrayal of trust by her daughters shocked her; she could not believe that Sally and Mattie would abandon her after all the years she had spent telling them that she did not want to end up in a nursing home.

Bleakly, she had pleaded with friends who came to visit her or other seniors in the nursing home. "I hate it here!" she would cry. "Can you ask Sally and Mattie to take me home? I want to go back to my own home." Her daughters remained unmoved. And although they visited her, they did not take her home.

Penny's thoughts wandered through the past, thinking of her brother and sister, and their children, and she speculated about her nephew and his wife. She thought of Stacey and wondered if things had worked out differently, might Stacey have taken care of her, where her daughters would not? Would Stacey have let her end up in a nursing home?

She had really been a kindly girl, if only she would have kept out of her son-in-law's bed...poor Sally, poor Jay. They should never have encouraged Jay to come here, and she whispered those words aloud to her daughter as her mind wandered. "What did we do to him?" With only the memories of the past to keep her company, Penny lost interest in her surroundings, and in less than six months, she had relinquished her fragile hold on life.

"Poor old lady," said a neighbor, shocked that her daughters would abandon Penny to an institution, when they were capable of looking after her. But Karma smiled, noting that there was some justice in her end for her actions in the past.

Penny's demise and its aftermath brought about a kind of retribution on Mattie, who busied herself in anticipation of moving permanently into her mother's pretty house. Although Penny's home belonged jointly to the two sisters, they agreed that Mattie and Otto should reside there. Sally felt some trepidation, since Mattie seemed to be assuming the mantle of family matriarch toward her younger sibling. Things might have been fine but for Mattie's inability to gain control of her tongue, or her critical nature.

Ted, his emotions already riled up by all the rigmarole that surrounded his mother-in-law's funeral, found his sensibilities further exacerbated when he was tasked with upgrading Penny's house. His decoration of the room where he had spent so much time with Stacey stirred up those ghosts of her once more. Despite his determination not to think about her, he found could hardly bear to be in the room where he had spent so much time with her. It made him angry, and having to keep a tight rein on his temper did nothing to enhance his disposition.

Mattie's constant carping exacerbated the situation and was aggravating him, but he kept his cool until the day his sister-in-law went too far for his nerves to tolerate. Her comments about the color of the paint in the kitchen, its texture, and the way it was being applied migrated to a dispute that blew up out of all proportion.

"Really, Ted," she had said, "I am not sure about the color, and it doesn't look as if that wall is covered evenly."

Ted, his patience exhausted, was in no mood for Mattie's criticism, and the conversation had not ended well.

"I don't care whether you like the paint or not, or the way I am doing it. I'm done with this!" he had roared as he slammed out of Penny's house, heading across the driveway to his own home.

"That's it!" he stormed as he stalked back into his own kitchen, startling Sally, by slamming that door behind him too.

"Sally, I am done with kowtowing to you and your family! Tell your sister we will buy her share of the house from her. I am done dealing with her, Sally. I am done with all of it. Either we sell the house or we have to buy out her share of the house. That's my final word."

Aghast, Sally looked at him. "What did she do now?" She sighed.

"Criticized once too often. She has always been a domineering busybody, but enough is enough! I do *not* want her living just across the driveway from us. She'd be interfering and remarking on everything we do. Either we buy the house from her, or I *will* leave! I will *not* live next door to her!"

Horror struck. Sally gaped at him. She couldn't lose him now, not after all they had been through. Not after having to endure for so many years the knowledge that he had loved and still loved another woman! No! She turned on her heel, headed for the door, and had one of the most unpleasant encounters with her sister that she had ever had.

Sally was taken aback by Ted's rage, as for the most part, he outwardly retained his stoic attitude, and her conversation with Mattie was tinged with despair. In the end Mattie had no choice. She and Otto did not have enough money to purchase Sally's share in the home; neither was Otto strong enough to do the necessary work, and so Ted and Sally made Mattie an offer she could not refuse.

When the sale was completed, Sally breathed a sigh of relief. All along Ted had expressed his concern about Mattie living permanently alongside of them. She had reveled in his discomfort all those years before and always looked at him in a condescending manner. Now he was done with her and could relax.

But his optimism was short-lived. Mattie found out that a house a couple of doors down from Penny's house was on the market, and now she had the money to buy it, so she and Otto moved in there. Although the house was somewhat run down, Ted said, "She will have to work it out herself. It is up to her and Otto to fix it. Not my business, and I am never doing any repair work for her ever again!"

Sally, torn between loyalty to her husband and love for her sister despite everything, retreated even further into herself, and was barely seen outside her home. Her relationship with her sister had taken a blow, and although they visited with each other still, the visits were short and generally just between the two of them.

As the summer started, they found some tenants for Penny's house. It was a relief for Ted that they were young and fit, so they gave the younger couple a break on the rent, provided they helped complete the upgrades and painting to bring the house up to date.

Life now seemed brighter for Ted and he looked forward to finally enjoying his retirement without any family upheavals. He and Sally had put a little distance between themselves and Mattie, they were free of the onus of taking care of Penny and now they had a rental property bringing in a nice income to add to his retirement money. They could enjoy the coming summer.

Destiny laughed at his naïvety! Now she had awakened, was working her way toward him, taking him where he would be unable to escape either his history or his future. Ironically, Melanie, in innocence, would put him in Destiny's pathway, from which this time, there would be no escape.

Chapter Fifty-Four

Summer 2008— Destiny Rides In

Ted

It was turning in to a lovely summer, and despite the challenge of his new granddaughter's health problems, they were all doing well. Ted, free from the responsibility of taking care of someone else's life, someone else's home, could spend time in his own garden and in his workshop. He was also free to step in if needed to take Melanie to golf tournaments when no one else was available. He had no presentiment that this would open the doorway to the specters rising from the past coming to haunt him once more.

On a lovely summer's day, bright sun filling the beautiful wide Alberta sky, but not too hot yet, thankfully, Ted chatted happily with Melanie as he drove her to her tournament, his mind focused on the upcoming afternoon. Their conversation was all about her game, how well she was doing, and how proud he was of her. Who did she think her competition was? Ted had paid scant attention to the others in her age group until this summer. He knew the families of some of the girl players, but not much about the boys. She had mentioned the leading contender among the boys, Andreas, and he had an idea she might have a crush on him. But she didn't mention his last name, so Ted was unprepared for what followed.

After he and Melanie pulled into the parking lot, she rushed off with an excited, "Oh, there is Andreas," and he watched her greeting a boy standing with an older man, who had his back to him and who he assumed was the boy's father. Ted strolled over to join them, but as the older man turned toward Melanie, his blood ran cold as their eyes met.

Andreas's father was Gino! Long-since dubbed "Gino Casino" by the town as he now owned half the property in town. The self-same Gino who had run the restaurant where Ted and his workmates had gathered each morning for coffee so many years ago. Now Gino was staring back at Ted.

Ted's mind went blank. All that came into his mind was that it had been Gino whom Stacey had sat and chattered to every morning, creating so much jealousy within Ted for so long, eating into his soul as he had oscillated between love and hate toward Stacey.

Stacey's migration back to her home in Britain had coincided with Gino going back to his European roots too, and Ted had wondered about the motive for his departure. After a while, Gino had returned with a bride from his homeland and Ted understood. Whatever his intentions to Stacey nothing had ever come of it, and so Gino was back with a pretty, pregnant wife. Shortly after his marriage, he relinquished the restaurant with its unsociable hours to dedicate his time to his wife and baby daughter. If Ted had but known it, the birth of his daughter had filled Gino with the same emotions Ted had felt when Lauren was born. For the past sixteen years, their paths had rarely crossed, as Gino built his real estate empire, and devoted to his family, moved in completely different circles from Ted.

Melanie, ever mindful of her manners, introduced first Gino's son, and then Gino himself to Ted. As Ted nodded in greeting, and before he could say anything, Gino replied with a grin, his eyes sparkling, in his still thick accent, "Oh, sure, Melanie, I know your grandfather from a long time ago!" A ready quip on his lips about their past encounters and their mutual relationship to Stacey died on his lips as he caught the look of distress in Ted's eyes.

Gino was shocked. Still? Still Ted remembers her? Still she can hurt him, after all these years? Gino thought, and he felt pity for Ted as he glimpsed the agony in his eyes. Ruefully Gino grinned inwardly, laughing at himself. Why are you surprised about that? She was the first thing you thought of when you saw Ted! Stacey, always so naïve about how pretty she was, or how desirable, or of her attraction, had stirred Gino deeply too at the time, but she had that fatal flaw: her devotion to Ted.

Ted was struggled to appear normal in front of their children as they exchanged greetings, his color draining under his tan. Gino, always a kind man, immediately felt compassion for him. He saw that Melanie was about to ask an awkward question about how they knew each other, and quickly distracted her, joking with her that she and his son were the stars of the game this season.

His remarks headed her off as he wished her luck with her game that day.

As she and Andreas moved away, discussing their game plans and talking about the upcoming match, Gino mused over the expression he had seen in Ted's eyes. He gave him time to calm himself, and then said in a matter-of-fact voice how nice it was to have two such talented kids who were doing so well. He kept the conversation in that vein for a while, saying how proud he was of his son, giving Ted time to organize his thoughts as they flashed back uncontrollably into the past.

Gino previously had not realized who Melanie's grandfather was, but had immediately recognized him, and like Ted felt that jerk back to when Stacey has been in both their hearts. He had not really been in love with her. He knew she was too old to bear the children that he craved, and he learned over the years that she would never care for anyone but Ted. But she had been fun and bright and good company each morning. He had admired how she overcame all her struggles and kept her dignity, despite having been so badly hurt by both her husband and this man.

Glancing surreptitiously at Ted, he saw that the man's eyes held that same haunted expression he had glimpsed two decades ago as he had watched Stacey each morning at the restaurant, when he thought no one else was looking. Poor guy. Gino sighed to himself, I won't tease him; I should give him a break. Thereafter, he resisted any further temptation to remind him about Stacey, but it gave him an understanding greater than he had before.

His reading of the situation back then had been wrong. Stacey had been right with her continued insistence to him that Ted was in love with her. Ted would not be reacting this way now if Stacey had meant nothing to him then, but Gino was truly amazed to think that those emotions still affected Ted at his age.

How sad, thought Gino, an inveterate romantic. What a pity for them both, and he made sure to steer their conversations into neutral territory. He realized how lucky he had been to find his Lila, and to have his three wonderful children. They were his world, and his world was very, very happy with them in it.

For the rest of the summer, he and Ted shepherded their children around from one match to another. Although they exchanged comments to each other about the kids' games, there was never any reference to early morning coffee or Stacey. They never referred to those mornings at the restaurant, with Ted determinedly ignoring Gino's occasional raised eyebrows and questioning looks.

That chance meeting with Gino, naturally, brought the past to the forefront of Ted's memory once more. And was followed by an exchange with Brody's sister not long after.

Brody's nephew and his mother were playing in an adult-and-child event along with Ted and Melanie. Brody's nephew hit a ball into a bush, and as he went to look for it, he heard Brody's sister, Maggie, say, "It's over there, in that thicket," using the English terminology.

A "Stacey" word, thought Ted. He said quietly to Maggie, "Such a long time since I've heard that word," and raised his eyebrows quizzically at her. Maggie was perplexed. The only English person they both knew had been Stacey, who had been a good friend to Maggie and her daughter. In all the years she had known Ted he had never made any reference to Stacey. Could it be what Ted was referring to? Was he talking about Stacey? Was he asking about her?

She was about to ask him when her son yelled that he found his ball, and the moment passed. Ted breathed again. He had so nearly asked her if she ever heard from Stacey, and that wouldn't do. His family and Brody's were still close and it would get back to Sally.

The two encounters first with Gino, and then with Maggie had brought about the re-emergence of the hammer in his chest and his disturbed dreams. Images of Stacey chattering and laughing each morning with Gino, while Ted had to observe without making any sign that it was affecting him flooded his mind.

Once more he raged at himself about how ridiculous it was; it had been over for so long, and he was an old man now. But his feelings were not those of an old man. Each time he thought of her, it still felt like it was yesterday. His sleep was filled with memories of how it felt to hold Stacey, her perfume, her smile, and his own anguish when he had told her he couldn't leave. Then he thought of all the times that he had hated her for disturbing his life and ratting him out to Sally. But even so, eventually his mind would return to the knowledge that no matter what, he had fallen in love with her, should have gone with her, and he still grieved for the loss of her.

Those memories sparked others that he would as soon forget too. The scene burned so deep in his brain when Jay had shown him and Sally absolute contempt as he stalked out of their kitchen, leaving Ted feeling like the worst kind of heel. Ted had suppressed the guilt about reneging on their promises to help Jay; it had been so long ago…Now he began to wonder what had become of Jay.

Except for the time around Penny's funeral, no one in the family had mentioned him or Stacey for years. Neither had they heard anything about him, after Jay's final visit to Penny. Then he had told her exactly what he thought about his father's family and how he now understood why Zack had cut off ties with such people. After that, Penny said she never wanted to talk about him or Stacey again. And they hadn't.

To their surprise, just before Penny had died, she had mentioned Jay and her sadness at how things had worked out. Later as they all discussed her obituary, Jay's name had come up again. Now the emergence of past memories made Ted wonder what Jay had been doing all these years. Those thoughts lingered in the recesses of Ted's mind during the entire summer. Jay and Stacey had never got back together. How had Jay fared when Stacey and Amy had gone home to Britain? Unlike his father, he did not return with them. Why wouldn't he have followed in Zack's footsteps and followed his child home? Did he find someone else? Had he remarried too? Did he have another family now?

Ted angrily told himself to put Jay out of his mind it was in the past. Not his problem now, not his business, but those musings still hovered in Ted's mind and shivers ran through him, as if someone walked over his grave. He felt an overwhelming premonition as if something he could not control was heading toward him.

BAD NEWS

In late September, the irony of Ted's focus on Jay and Stacey all summer was not lost on him. He returned home one evening to find Sally looking agitated. His immediate concern was that something had happened to Brenda. Struggling with health issues since her birth, she was due to go to the children's hospital again very soon.

"Sally, what is it? Is it Brenda?" Ted asked anxiously.

Sally shook her head and looked at him, a slight trembling in her speech. "No, nothing like that. I just had a call from Patsy. Jay has died. It shook me up!"

Ted went cold. "Jay? Jay is dead? But he is years younger than us! How can that be? What happened to him?"

"Cancer, I guess," Sally said. "It was pretty sudden. It happened back in July, just before your birthday. Patsy said she had heard about it from Angela, who Stacey still keeps in touch with. Stacey told her that she and Amy didn't know about it until very recently. Seems like Jay and Amy hardly kept in touch, probably Stacey's fault, and his girlfriend didn't bother to notify them. I guess Isabella flew over, but apart from that, he died pretty much alone. I don't understand why Isabella would not have let Amy know. Stacey apparently was really angry that they had not let Amy know at the time and hardly made any effort to get in touch with her until nearly three months later."

"It doesn't seem like there was an obituary in the *Edmonton Journal*, or I'm sure that Mattie would noticed it. Stacey told Angela they didn't have any kind of service for him, just had him cremated, and the ashes had been scattered somewhere, but they did not know where. She said Amy was very upset, all fine and well, because it is yet another thing that Stacey is responsible for!" Sally added bitterly.

Ted's mind whirled. All during these past months, when Ted's mind had kept coming back to Jay, he was already dead. What a strange thing! It had to be just a coincidence. His chest tightened, and old feelings bubbled to the surface again. Jay could barely have been sixty. How awful to die so young, and be almost alone in such circumstances. It struck Ted how different it all should have been for Jay and would have been if not for his own pursuit of Stacey. It was also uncanny that the circumstances of his death almost mirrored Zack's own lonely end. It had been the primary reason why Penny had gone to such lengths to persuade Jay and Stacey to come here. What an awful mess!

He said quietly, "Sally, be fair. It wasn't just Stacey. We all encouraged them to come here, and in the end we let him down too because we were fighting before Stacey even arrived and didn't help as much as we promised. You know that, and even Penny said much the same thing a little while before she died. But I can hardly believe it! He was so much younger than us, and to die so soon! What a terrible thing for him and for Amy."

Sally looked back at him sharply. "That is the first time I have ever heard you defend Stacey." Spitefully she added, "What happened? An attack of conscience at last?"

Ted didn't reply. He could see she was upset, and an upset Sally was usually spiteful. Sally's bitterness toward Stacey had never diminished, just as her mother's antipathy toward Cassie had never waned. That was the Logan way—like mother, like daughter, he thought.

Not only had Sally never forgiven Stacey, but she still harbored a grudge against Marta, who had befriended Stacey at the time.

Sally's antipathy toward their neighbor had remained intact all these years. There was little forgiveness in her Logan nature. No matter what outsiders thought of her, house devil, street angel did not only apply to men, he pondered.

Now Ted was desperate for information. All sorts of thoughts ran through his mind throughout the evening, and he wondered if Hans and Marta had heard anything from Stacey. Hans, garrulous as ever, had mentioned a few times over the years that they still heard from Stacey at Christmas, but Ted had never commented to him, or shown any sign of interest. If Hans knew about Jay's death, surely he would have mentioned it when they had been chatting earlier in the week?

Ted's mind kept coming back to the lonely manner of Jay's death. With his own family all around him, Ted could not comprehend the isolation of dying alone, with no loving family nearby. Even though Sally thought that Isabella might have been there, it was not enough. Amy should have been there too, and for the first time, he started to wonder about the impact of that terrible time on Amy. It sounded as if she had pretty much grown up with little contact with her father. Was that why Jay's girlfriend and Jay's sister had not bothered to contact her? Was that Stacey's fault, as Sally said? But in his heart he knew that Stacey was not vindictive. She reacted badly to being hurt, but wasn't spiteful, that he had ever heard. When she had lived in Edmundston with Amy, he knew that Jay had seen his daughter often. They had even been out on the golf course together one day when he had almost walked into them.

Sleep would not come that night, and each time he tried to close his eyes, it seemed Jay's face appeared, staring at him, wearing the same look of contempt that he had on his face as he had stalked from Ted's kitchen after condemning the Zienkos to the devil.

The next morning Ted was in the yard when Hans walked out of his house. He wandered casually over to greet him. "Hans," he blurted out, unable to hold back. "Just wondering, do you ever hear from Stacey? We heard a rumor that Jay had died and wondered if she had mentioned it. Sally doesn't know much about it."

Hans shook his head sadly. "No, we hardly hear from her except a card at Christmas, and occasionally a photograph of Amy."

Ted shrugged. "No problem. Just heard a rumor, that's all, and we wondered." And he walked back to his vegetables.

Hans looked at him. In all the conversations they had over the years, Ted had never made mention of Stacey to him, nor Jay either. Sighing, he wandered off to look at his vegetables, tut-tutting under his breath and thinking how sad it was that Amy had lost her father so young. He would tell Marta later. Then he continued with his hoeing.

Chapter Fifty-Five

2009 Edmunston— Toward the End of Days

TED

It seemed to Ted that the news of Jay's death was the catalyst for stirring up all the phantoms of the past that they had tried so hard to obliterate over the years and brought consequences.

Life seemed to be spiraling out of control. Brody's death barely a year ago, followed by Penny's death a few months later, opened the doorway to memories and feelings returned that he would as soon forget. They were also affecting Sally, he noticed. Now more echoes from the past reverberated around them, renewing feelings of guilt from decades before, and Sally's attitude told him that she was remembering that time too.

Jay's death brought home to him the serious consequences that his actions had. It made him examine the impact of how he let Jay down for his own selfish reasons. Not content with disillusioning their younger cousin, he compounded that by using his charms to target Stacey. With hindsight, he could see how wrong that had been. His whole focus had been on the impact on his own family, but now he could see the devastating long-term consequences of those actions on Jay and Amy. And then he had abandoned Stacey too.

Sally meanwhile was fighting her own demons, and she was glad her mother was not still alive to hear about the nature of Jay's death. It brought back to her the role she had played in the debacle when her cousin moved to Alberta. As much as she tried to lay all the blame on Stacey, she knew deep down that she should have warned Jay how circumstances had changed. Instead she kept quiet and had thrust Stacey into Ted's path. The misery of that time washed over her once more.

Sensing Ted's unrest too, finally she blurted out, "Ted, it wasn't our fault that Jay died so young, was it? I keep thinking about Uncle Zack when he died in England and Mom's reaction to it. She had been horrified. He died before his time in a foreign country, cut off from his family, and we all blamed Cassie for that. We didn't do the same thing to Jay too, did we? There are so many similarities with their deaths."

Ted couldn't answer her. He knew his own role in coveting Stacey and other details that Sally had never known. He had told Stacey, and always wondered why she had not shared it with Sally. It would have gotten him into so much more trouble. Even now there was no way he would share that information with Sally.

He just shrugged, saying tersely, "How was it our fault? Jay was a grown man and made the decision to move here. It was up to him to make a success of it. If he didn't like it here when he first arrived, he could always have gone back home before Stacey arrived. It was his decision." Sally must never know about his designs on Stacey from that summer before. Now it would destroy her.

Sally jumped at his reasoning, willing to abrogate her part in the disaster that Jay's move had become and nodded quickly in agreement, "Yes, you are right. He didn't have to stay. It wasn't up to us to babysit him," she replied. So much easier to dispose of the fact that they had all urged Jay to move to Alberta, promised him help, and then when it turned out he wasn't who they thought he was, callously dumped him. No, she reassured herself, they were not responsible for Jay dying so young; it was just the way it worked out. It was Jay's decision to move. It had been Stacey's decision to be unfaithful to her husband with Ted… nothing to do with her, Sally kept telling herself.

But conscience, once awakened, is difficult to still. Both Ted and Sally found it hard to thrust Jay from their minds, or to deny the guilt they felt for their roles in the disaster that his life became. That guilt gnawed away at them, little by little, day by day. But they did not discuss it further. Each kept their own secrets to themselves. Nevertheless, however much they consciously tried to forget or deny it, each was forced to inwardly accept that they had contributed greatly to Jay's sad, lonely end.

Ted, the deeper thinker, felt his conscience prick at him. His angst about the effects on his own family and his sense of loss over Stacey still lingering in his heart affected him greatly. But, as in the past, he kept his thoughts inside him, and once more the stress built, undermining his health and making him more vulnerable to disease.

Sally, noticed how morose he became. She worried about him, inevitably affecting her own immune system and her remission from her earlier brush with cancer.

One by one, Karma took advantage of their vulnerabilites, finding a good breeding ground to work her magic. Now the time had come, The piper must be paid.

Chapter Fifty-Six
2012—Welcome Says Karma

Ted

Ted was back in the hospital, just for a couple of days, they said; just to check on the effectiveness of the new treatment, nothing to worry about. He had been in remission for a while, and thought they had the cancer in his blood beaten. But this time, almost overnight, he had contracted pneumonia, and now he saw worried eyes all around him.

He drifted in and out of sleep. He was oh, so tired. He had been in and out of hospital for nearly three years, and he was so ready to end all this, especially now that it seemed the treatment was losing the battle.

During the previous month, he'd realized the end might be coming, and since the anniversary celebrations in town last year, the heart had completely gone out of him.

Through these final days of winter, he had been working on a little gate to put in the fence between his and Hans's gardens, to give Hans easier access to their mailbox. Hans would walk up to the block mailbox each day and pick up Ted and Sally's mail while they were away at the hospital in Edmonton. It was a long walk around to his own driveway for the elderly man after dropping Ted's mail into their box outside their kitchen door. Now he would have a shortcut, be able to move across the yard and through the fence, making it easier for him, not so hard on his aging legs.

Ted would not ask Sally's sister Mattie, who still lived two doors down from them, to collect their mail. Not only did he not want her knowing his business, but also he was still rattled over Mattie's attitude toward his mother-in-law before she died and the ensuing unpleasantness over Penny's house.

So he had made a little opening in the fence that separated their yard from Hans and Marta's, and he built the gate. As he toiled over it in his garage workshop, he began to feel things inside he hadn't notice before. He was getting more and more tired, and wondered if maybe the end was near.

Working in the garage, sudden thoughts of Stacey had caught him off guard again. It revived that memory of being caught with Mariska in this very spot, and unbelievably he found he could still taste the sweetness of Stacey's first kiss. The memories swept over him, reopening that unhealed wound. Echoes of her naïve remark, "Oh, it will be so nice to have a new brother," swirled around him. He recalled his chagrin at that remark, followed by such a monumental error of judgment that changed all their lives. And then Jay was back in his thoughts once more. For decades he had never given him a thought, but after Jay's death four years ago and now through these final days of his illness, memories of Jay filtered into his mind. Inevitably, other memories surfaced too, bringing the echo of voices, whispers and those last words...

"How long are you going for?"

"Forever."

Stacey had meant it. She had left, then married someone else and never come back. Yes, truly gone forever.

There was no point in staying now. He'd known that since the town's Centennial Celebrations last year. His dreams and desires of seeing Stacey once more, had crashed and burned. He had pinned all his hopes on her coming back again for the town's revels. He didn't know what it would achieve; he was dying, and they were both old. Even so, it was a hope that had lingered.

Surely Stacey would come he reasoned. She had been so much a part of the celebrations twenty-five years earlier. He heard from town chatter, that she had sent her photos from the 1980s via Facebook whatever that was, to be shared. She was obviously still interested in Edmunston. How could these celebrations pass without her returning? The chatter that she was intending to come continued, but in the end she did not.

Maggie had been the one that he had overheard saying to her daughter, "Oh, that's a pity. I was so looking forward to seeing her again."

Family issues Stacey had said, according to Maggie's daughter. They were Facebook friends, he wondered if he could see her on Facebook, but knew the computer was something he could not get to grips with.

That was when he realized the depths of his anticipation. Disappointment flooded through him. He pined to see her again, just once more. He had missed her so and finally admitted it to himself.

The sledgehammer tapped softly in his chest again. His memories of how wonderful that month with Stacey had been, before everything exploded into disaster. That month had shown him what life could have been like as he fell in love with her. His confused thoughts as the medications took hold circled around each other.

She had stayed close for nearly a decade, while he dithered about his feelings for her, hating her one minute then wanting her the next. Ignoring her in public, and stalking her in private. Wanting to be with her, but afraid to lose his daughters' love. Crushing her feelings each time he had an opportunity to try to resolve things with her. Never able to openly tell her that he loved her, and never able to tell her he did not. He had cringed and despised himself when he finally accepted how badly he had treated her. It was no wonder she never returned, and now was happy with someone else.

That one month that could have changed the rest his life instead had led him to so many bad and cruel decisions. It still made him ashamed. Try as he might, Ted was unable to shake himself free of his dreams as his life passed before his eyes. His fear had come from that awful time in his childhood after his mother had died. He was overlooked and thought he had lost everything. The desolation he faced made him afraid to put himself in that position again. He had been so afraid of losing his girls, which, in the end, he so nearly did anyway.

But he had stayed, lived through the nightmare, and kept his daughters' love, then their children's love too. It left a bitter taste when the realization had come upon him that his own actions had ended by thrusting Stacey, Jay, and Amy into that same nightmare. Alone, with nothing and robbing them of their future together.

From nowhere he heard Stacey's voice when he had churlishly snarled down at the phone at her, "Don't you think about anyone but yourself?" He heard once more her intake of breath, and the unsteadiness in her voice when she had asked him, "Why wouldn't I? I had to struggle on *all alone* while *you* watched me nearly starve and didn't lift a finger to help me! Where were you when I needed you? Safely tucked up at home with Sally, denying all responsibility, and heaping coals of fire on my head!"

"Stacey, I am sorry," he tried to say.

He had known it was the truth; it exacerbated his guilt over how much he had hurt his girls, Penny, and Sally too. For years it left him hating himself. He couldn't talk about it to anyone, although Brody had tried a couple of times to root out what was wrong with him, but he had resisted and suppressed his thoughts. Instead burying himself in his job, working in the yard, going to the bar, and wallowing in beer.

The two years following Jay's death had sped by, bringing retribution in their wake. The shock they had faced with the diagnosis of Ted's cancer, just as they thought life was settled for a good retirement. Then came all the treatments to try to destroy it. For a time it seemed like they had succeeded, although he was rail thin and seemed to have aged twenty years, leaving Ted more tired than he had ever felt in his life.

He had managed to rally for the party the girls put together to celebrate their parents' fifty years together. Ted found it hard to get his head around the idea that he had been married to Sally for half a century!

Their big day dawned. Everyone was dressed in their best clothes. The party was to be held at their beloved golf club and theirs was the first group to be using the newly renovated banqueting rooms. The upgrade brought the golf course up to country club standards with its new curling rinks too. The landscaping with beautiful trees, and a fountain as the center piece, made the perfect backdrop for pictures before the guests arrived. Ted swelled with pride. Who would have imagined such an event for Sally and himself? Who would have thought they would have over come all the hurdles and survived fifty years together?

Without bidding the past came flooding back into Ted's mind. His first years with Sally; their girls' births, their father's deaths, one reflection led to another, then inescapably Stacey's memory was once more in his mind.

The camera caught him just as she had flashed through his mind, and his expression was caught forever in time, sadness in his eyes and a smile at his mouth, as mixed feelings about her once again overtook him.

In his speech, given his extramarital exploits that had been well-noted throughout the town, it seemed hypocritical to dwell too much an ecstatic married life. Too many of their guest knew differently, but he gave recognition to Sally for her loyalty in sticking by him all these years. But he focused on his love for his grandchildren and especially on the welcome addition of little Brenda. For all that it had been a pleasant day, it had seemed that ghosts hovered in empty chairs. Jay, Stacey, and Penny all there in spirit if not in reality, and regret lingered.

Was that why he had put all his hopes on Stacey returning later that summer? Would he have had the nerve or the opportunity to tell her how much he regretted his actions, and seek her forgiveness, as he had now done with Sally? Oh, Sally, poor Sally.

Saddest of all, he recognized that Sally knew the truth of his feelings for Stacey. It subscribed to her bitter attitude, no matter how she tried to hide it, or for all his attempts to make it up to her. In truth their relationship had never really recovered, but tacitly, for the sake of their family, they agreed that they would show unity to the outside world, and their children. But no matter how they tried, Stacey's shadow always fell between them.

He never revealed his disappointment that Stacey, despite all the rumors, had not returned for the town's one-hundred-year celebration. The town's centennial came and went, but Stacey did not appear. He knew then he would never see her again.

It was when he gave up. Much as he loved his daughters and his little granddaughter, much as he loved seeing his older granddaughter become so successful, they didn't need him now. There was no point in staying and fighting this agony in his body and his spirit. He was done.

These reminiscences had run through his head as he worked in his garage, completing a gate he was going to put into their joint fence for Hans. By the time it was finished, he was sure that he was not going to make it through much longer. He set the gate in place, laughing as he said to Hans, "Well, that's my part of the job done, it's all up to you now."

Hans looked sharply at him. The old man despite his physical challenges, still had all his wits about him. He started to ask if Ted was OK, but Ted was already heading back to the house, Hans's words of thanks and good wishes echoing in his ears.

Now, listening to the muffled sounds around him in the hospital, with the little glimpses of his life flitting through his semi-comatose state, the little sledgehammer was tapping softly inside him.

Now Ted's thoughts of Stacey were all about her sweetness, her softness, her brown velvet eyes, and her big, happy smile. Burying her sadness and anger, instead remembering a time when he had finally experienced how tender and satisfying love could really be. He had yearned for it never to end, was in love with her before Sally came back, and then he had run from it.

How he wished he had done things differently, not hurt Stacey, not hurt Sally or Jay; not hurt himself or destroyed so much with his lies and denials. It could all have been so different but for that one fatal moment.

Stacey! So warm in his arms, so loving, whispering sweet words to him about how wonderful he was, soft lips seeking his, and he moaned in misery at what he had lost back then. He never intended for that to happen. It caused so much destruction around him, but he could not stop loving her, no matter what he tried. He had not understood how deeply it went with him until he heard Stacey had remarried. The agony of that day came right back, and he moaned again. The nurse, standing close by, thought his illness was giving him pain and gave him another shot of morphine.

He briefly roused a little while later, and for an instant thought he saw Stacey there in front of him. Her eyes so inviting…then fading to holding so much grief when she looked at him. He again saw her gazing expectantly, hopefully, at him as she asked one final time, "Are you going to ask me to stay?" Then sadness filled her eyes once more and he could hear himself once more denying her, denying his feelings for her, as he had turned his back on her for a final time.

His thoughts were spiraling quickly now: his wedding day, his father's sudden death, Penny's disdain, and Jay death! Gino smiling mockingly at him, his grandchildren, little Brenda skipping by his side as they went to the mailbox. He loved her so. Suddenly, Brody was in front of him beckoning to him. It puzzled him when he heard his mother's soft voice calling him, and because of the link his mind had made with her, back finally to his over-riding passion...Stacey.

As weak as he was, that faint hammer started up again tapping in his chest, bringing that rush of need, and his last conscious thought was of wanting Stacey, needing to see her one more time...he *had* to see her one more time...had to before he died...

Chapter Fifty-Seven

2012 Transition

Ted

There was a haze around him. Ted was trying to wake up, but he couldn't work out where he was. He was floating. Why was he floating? That made no sense. How was it even possible? He couldn't even walk, so why was he up here, looking down at himself? Sally! What was wrong with Sally? Why were his daughters sobbing, holding each other, clinging to Sally?

"I'm up here! Look up at me," he tried to say, but they didn't seem to hear him, Why? Then he knew! He was beyond them. Finally he was at the threshold that led into the next world.

No! In horror, he tried to cry out. No, that couldn't happen! He wasn't done yet! He didn't want to leave them yet. He had things to do…Stacey! He *had* to see her again, had to see her. How could he leave his life without seeing Stacey just one more time!

"Please, God, let me see Stacey again, and make my peace with her," he asked. "Just one more time…" as he felt himself fade into the mist…

Chapter Fifty-Eight

2012 – An Aura is Born

Ted

Awareness returned, and the mists cleared. Ted was in a white room, still floating above everything. Where was this? It looked like a hospital surgery. Did he dream what happened earlier? Perhaps he was really still alive?

He was puzzled. There was a man standing alone. Then he bent over…bent over what? Shocked, he saw that the man was leaning over a body. *His* body! The body was him! But then he understood. It wasn't him; it was the shell that had held his soul during life. The man was his oldest friend, Ray.

The elderly undertaker, true to his word, was doing what Ted had said he would. A few months earlier, Ray had walked into his hospital room while Ted was trying to pacify some of his nurses as they hovered anxiously around him, so concerned for him.

"I'll be fine," he had said and laughed. "I have my old friend Ray over there," he said as Ray had walked through the door. "Don't worry, he will take good care of me. Won't you, Ray?" Smiling, Ray had nodded in agreement. Then he had laughed too. "Oh, I always take good care of all my friends!"

Now at this moment, Ray was doing just that. He was taking care of Ted's body as tears ran down his face. Ted felt a warm glow toward this man who had been one of his oldest friends, and whispered, "Thanks, Ray."

Ray shivered suddenly and looked up, a puzzled look on his face. For a moment he thought he had…no, not possible. Then he shook himself and continued his work. That must have just been a draft coming in from somewhere But just for a moment, he thought he heard Ted's voice saying with a laugh in it, "Thanks, Ray." But no, that wasn't likely! How many years had he been doing this? It was all in his head. Had to be, didn't it?

The mist closed around Ted again. He seemed to be drifting toward a hazy light in the distance. He struggled against it! *No!* He wasn't ready yet. No, please…no, please…he tried to say… panic overtaking him.

He saw a light in the distance, but the path suddenly veered away from the light. He felt a hand pushing him away, and a soft voice said, "Go! Go see your Stacey. I will give you time. Your soul won't rest while you have unfinished business." Then Ted floated away from the light.

Chapter Fifty-Nine

2012 America—Souls

Time and space didn't seem to exist anymore. He wasn't sure if it were seconds or hours later when Ted found himself in a strange house, in an unfamiliar bedroom.

The room was welcoming, very feminine, and very girly. White lace and pink roses swathed around it, soft pink on the walls, and smelling of what…? Smelling of Stacey's perfume!

In the bed a sleeping woman lay alone, turning restlessly, dried rivulets of tears staining her face. As she moved, the moonlight caught her face. Stacey! It was Stacey. Older, plumper, but still Stacey!

Ted was puzzled. Why was she alone? She was married. Where was her husband? In that same instant, Stacey seemed to sense his presence, opened her eyes, and looked straight at him. There was no shock in her face, just recognition and her gentle smile, as half-awake she pulled back the bed sheet, stretching out a hand toward him, calling softly, "Ted?"

He was shocked. She could see him! He wanted to move toward her, but he had no form, and instead he changed into shimmering wisps of white dancing dust. But he heard her as she lay back down, starting to cry again and whispering his name softly. "Ted, why did you die before I saw you again? Oh, Ted, you broke my heart."

Then even more softly, those words so familiar from their last encounter, "*You* are dead now, gone forever, but I *still* have to live."

Rage burned inside this new form he had. Rage for having no faith in her, pain for all that he had given up, and now seeing all the hurt he had caused, still torturing Stacey's heart all this time later. He knew that he could not leave yet until he had unraveled the mystery. There had to be a way to understand what happened to Stacey. He needed to know.

The kinetic power forming inside his half-being, his unquiet soul, exploded as he sought ways through the next few days to get Stacey's attention. The disruption he engendered found its freedom through light bulbs, electronics, and clocks, hoping that Stacey would see the clocks stop and understand that it was the past calling to her, and that he was calling to her. He had to communicate with her, and he would need to delve back into the past and find a way to explain that deep down all he had wanted to do was shelter her and love her, as he had from that first night.

Yes, his soul cried out, "Yes, Stacey, you do have to live. You have to know, and then you can pass through that barrier and join me forever."

PART THREE
THE PILGRIMAGE

Chapter Sixty
2013 – The Circle Completes

Stacey

Against the protests of my family, I had insisted on traveling alone.

This was *my* pilgrimage, *my* farewell, and in truth I was in part irked because of all the past refusals to make this trip with me at times when it had been possible. Those refusals had hurt me deeply, especially given all that I had sacrificed to be the supportive wife in my second marriage. But now I was determined; this was *my* good-bye. They were *my* sorrows waiting to be buried once and for all. I did not need or want any other company.

So, one fine day in May, armed with my Garmin, suitcases full of clothes, and the inevitable credit cards, I started the drive north and west.

Paradoxically, in the year or so since Ted died, my attitude toward life had changed. I discarded the frumpy, aging, old woman I was becoming and had uncovered my former girly self again. I had not realized how deeply I had papered over the real me during all the drudgery and soullessness of the previous two decades.

I had cheerfully clambered back into clotheshorse mode once more. I lost weight, poured myself into skinny jeans, helping the overall effect with a China-doll painted face. The real me was determined to emerge after being suppressed for oh, so long.

Inexplicably, I wanted to look good for Ted, show him what he'd missed. But how stupid was that? How would he know? He was dead. Idiotic, really, but it all tied into my regurgitated grief over my lost love, my lost baby, my broken heart, my lost life.

I had been stunned when Ted's apparition appeared in my bedroom two days after he died. It was the last thing I expected. Ghosts? Spirits? Ted's spirit? Why would he come? In life he had done his utmost to show me how little he cared for me, and after all, it was so long ago, he surely had forgotten me by now. But then again, I had never forgotten him, try as I might to make a new life without him. Was that why his ghost had sought me out?

The night I had heard of his death, I had finally given way to tears, which erupted as I went to bed. The sense of loss inside me grew so intense, so unbearable, and it shocked me that I felt so much pain after so many years, and I sobbed until finally I fell asleep.

I had been awakened by the feeling that someone was in my room. I distinctly saw a figure standing by my bed! Instinctively I knew it was Ted as I reached out toward him, inviting him to join me. But the image had disappeared, dissipating into wisps of shimmering light. Still half asleep, I thought I had imagined it, and tears flowed again before I finally rested.

Next day, I was in misery. I knew I had to shake it off and it was ridiculous being this upset over a man who had abandoned me decades before. This man who had been content to watch me starve, shunned me in public, and yet pursued me in private. The turmoil inside me grew as the pull toward him, which I thought was long buried, reared up in my chest again.

The following evening, as I lay in bed trying to sleep, determined to get a grip on myself, once again came the strong feeling of another presence in the room with me. It was not a bit threatening, nothing to scare me, just there, questioning.

I felt an almost imperceptible indentation in the mattress near me, experienced a feeling of someone close by, not quite touching me. The practical Stacey snorted! No, this is not possible! This is nonsense, pure imagination!

Angrily I gave myself a mental shake, issuing my brain with a command to pull myself together. It had no effect; neither did it chase away the feelings I was trying to ignore. Once again I ended up crying myself to sleep.

The next evening, again the sense that I was not alone lingered as I sat in my living room. Despite the heat running, I could feel coolness all around me. But it was only where I was sitting. When I moved to another part of the house, the coldness followed.

Now, I may be Stupid Stacey, and as a rule I am not given to flights of fancy. The harshness and challenges of my life have made me immensely practical, with no time for folly or foolish thoughts. You don't have time for that nonsense when you are fighting to survive, as I so often had been. But now it seemed that I was being beset by something outside of my control, I was trying to deny that it was happening, but it became clearer and clearer that it was *not* my imagination.

For the next few nights, no matter how I tried to shut it out, the impression that I was not alone in the house remained. Moreover, I kept getting a strong feeling of Ted being close by. The magnet that had hibernated inside me for so many years was reactivated, and the only thing that had ever caused that had been Ted's presence. It was so real that I could almost feel him touching me. I had a sense that all I had to do was turn around to see him. My deep feelings of need that I had suppressed for so long, came bubbling to the surface, leaving me shaken and bemused.

I thought I was going crazy. I alternated between unbelievable feelings of loss and grief, and irrational feelings of joy that once more he was near me.

As with any sensible person, I found it hard to accept. For days I kept resisting the idea that this was real, despite all the evidence building around me. To speak these events out loud sounded like the ravings of the unhinged, even so there was no denying what was happening.

It was nothing I was contributing to. There was no logical way to explain the erratic behavior of electronics switching themselves on and off without any help from me. There was no way that I could make a light bulb blow when I turned a switch on or walked past it. But most convincing in the end was that crackle of electricity around me imitating what had happened whenever Ted and I were near each other in the past.

It brought such an aura of Ted, of his presence, that it was impossible to ignore. I could sense him, feel him, and even taste his kiss. In the end, in the end, there was no doubt at all, that Ted's ghost had invaded my home; as impossible as that might seem, he was there.

His presence became so intense, and it seemed natural to feel as if he were lying beside me, holding me. In a strange way it brought me comfort, despite the heartbreak I felt. And after a while, it transmuted into a protective shell all around me, and an insistent, "I'm sorry, so sorry," hanging in the air.

As I struggled with this totally unexpected phenomenon, I tried to dismiss it as just the imaginings of a woman in despair. A long time later after Ted's aura had all but disappeared, I told myself that it had all been in my imagination. However, the reality is that if it had been imagination, then I should be able to recreate those feelings and impressions whenever I wanted, and I cannot. Now I find that either he is hovering, letting me know by small signs that he has returned, or there is silence: the kind of silence you get when you talk into a phone and the line is dead because the other party has hung up on you.

My thoughts and memories brought me to a very low ebb wishing I could stop thinking about it. Then, in one of those unexplained coincidences, another voice from the past contacted me. This time it was an old boyfriend who suddenly decided he just had to unburden himself to me. Men!

Forty years before, I had quite liked him, but he had been torn between Stacey and Stacy. He shared with me that he didn't know why he picked her over me; he wished he had followed his heart, and he'd thought about me often, both then and since. He went on to unfold details about his life since then. He told me of his affairs (lucky escape for Silly Stacey who'd held a torch for him for a while) as his marriage had not lived up to expectations. Then he shared how he'd hit the big time when he started his own consultancy. From then on it had been all champagne and cruises, but he reiterated how he so much wished he had chosen me, because I'd figured in his fantasies ever since. I was so much more woman than his wife!

"Oh, how nice," I said politely in my response to him. "What a pity. Poor you!"

His amorous advances left me cold! How does any man have this kind of logic? Did he think that I'd be flattered? I thought of all my struggles, the time when I had almost starved, always having to scrimp and scrape, and here he was telling me that his wonderful life could have been mine if he had gone with his heart four decades earlier. Really! Really?

With tremendous self-control I held back from telling him that I knew exactly why he had chosen Stacy over Stacey. He'd gone to the rich boys school, while I had gone to a technical school lower than a grammar school! His parents had expectations for his future after his expensive education.

Those expectations did not include marrying the Stacey from a council housing estate who had gone to a technical school and left at sixteen! They much preferred the Stacy whose father was in the diplomatic service, and was now a highly thought of government official. Definitely their kind of person, and so Peter had caved in and married Stacy, and changed both our destinies!

No! Really! People don't do stuff like that: tell you what kind of a life you might have had if they would have showed some courage! Really? Yep, they do!

I was torn between amusement at his sheer effrontery, and despair that once again forces outside my control had consumed what my future might have been.

In the end, it pushed me back once more into despair over Ted's death and the seeming silence from him now.

Then things changed. A week or so after Ted's funeral, when the strongest impression of him dissipated, and I thought he had left, grief began to overcome me once more. As if in response Ted's aura returned and really made his presence felt.

A kinetic force seemed to explode from the walls of my house. Clocks and watches stopped, almost in concert at similar times. Lights blew in every room, sometimes even as I turned on the switch or walked beneath them. Initially unnerved I checked all the fuses and the wiring I could see, but could find nothing wrong. Then the TV turned itself on and off, even though I was across the room from the remote, and that was really spooky. Electronic gadgets of every kind seemed to have developed a mind of their own. By far the favorite trick was to play with the garage door remote (I wondered whether he had ever had one of his own). Whatever, it seemed to be his way of saying, "Hey, I'm back!" I would shut it down, and he would push it back up again—just the kind of teasing he was famed for.

Given all the havoc he was creating, he was hard to ignore now. It all got my attention. His aura now appeared to have mutated to a cool breeze that settle around me each time I sat on the couch, and even sometimes in other places. It was even witnessed by a work colleague who swore there was no cool breeze in our office until she came and stood next to me. She was not happy; it had not been there before. More and more incidences happened around me, until I finally had to accept that some part of Ted was still close, and that he had a mission.

My thoughts were drawn back to that awful time when my world fell apart forever, a myriad thoughts chased each other around in my head. I tried to make sense of the past but could find no logical explanation for the unexplainable. My bewilderment grew at the strength of Ted's spirit in my home until I felt a sudden urge to put some of those thoughts down on paper.

It was like someone cheered, "Hoorah, she's got it!" and my writing became our communication doorway. Ted had found a way to communicate with me, and I had understood his intention.

As I began to put my thoughts and memories down on paper, Ted's spirit hovered all around me. I began to think logically through all that had happened, it seemed at times, with Ted guiding my hand. It forced me to remember what I had tried to bury all those long decades ago, but with a clearer perspective. Now, that which had been unclear in the past became clear in the present. Unexplained reasons for that lack of clarity at the time, provided a clear pathway through the misty veils of recollections from the past.

It was like connecting the dots as I started to make links between first one action or event and then another. At the time those connections should have been obvious, but writing gave me an insight I had not had before, making sense of that whole destructive episode in our lives.

I got angry at times, as I had shouldered the majority of the blame for many things that were in no way my fault. On my part, those missteps had been caused only by my naivety. Ted and Sally's secrecy held far more culpability. That brought me even more pain, as I realized the traps I fell into, had no escape. But the worst thing for me was when I understood a couple of major mistakes I had made simply because all trust in Ted had been broken. That one event could have changed my entire future, if I had not been so intimidated by Sally and Penny's connections in the community, and their ability to damage me once more.

My revelations on paper one day even caught Ted's spirit off guard as I wrote of my agony at the loss of his child. Then I sensed real anguish from him. I was perplexed. How could he not have known? I always thought he had or that Sally had told him. Sally had known, or at least I was pretty sure she had put two and two together after my blurting out about it. Seemingly, she had not shared it with Ted, ever. His aura recoiled and went almost into a frenzy as it swirled and rampaged around the house for hours and then disappeared for a day or so.

As I wrote, I got to some realizations about his character and motivations, which on one occasion my ever-present ghost didn't like at all. He exhibited his power to me then as a whole paragraph deleted itself then he went on another kinetic rampage. I have never been able to recall what that paragraph said apparently he blocked it from my mind too. It was likely a bit too close to the truth, even for him. He always wanted to be seen as the good guy. Really? Hmmm…still under consideration!

While all of this ghostly interaction should have been weird and scary, as an otherworldly spirit shared my house with me, in the oddest way, it was strangely comforting to have Ted near, finally with me, with no barriers or distractions.

It seemed like it was rough justice. Sally, through her actions, had tied him to her all her life and his life in this world. But she didn't need him now. So had he chosen to finally escape? Was he now following the path after death that had been his heart's desire during the latter half of his life?

I wondered how long he would stay. I could not imagine that this sojourn was infinite, or that it could go on endlessly. But it seemed Ted's soul was really trying to make a connection with me, was reaching out, grasping for my half of the magnet that had drawn us to each other so cataclysmically.

In a way we bonded through the writing process. His spirit showed that it was full of grief and loss, sadness and anger, as he careened through my house. At times the certainty that he was close by me, almost breathing on my neck sometimes, was like an ethereal hug. He was not tangible now, or touchable, but feeling his close presence brought me solace.

Ted pushed me onward to investigate, to think back and then to put our story together and comprehend many actions I had not understood at the time. It must also have clarified actions of mine that he could not come to terms with too. There was much that others would not have been aware of either, but it led me to my own personal pilgrimage.

Now, in my little car, I was following the path he laid out for me as I made the trek back to Edmunston. So many things had fallen into place to make this trip possible; it was as if a greater hand than mine guided me.

During my journey, I felt his spirit in the car several times, felt him reach out and more than once salvage me from what could have been a disastrous moment as I was driving. But once I reached Edmunston, that spirit seemed to slip into the background, only once lingering near me, calling to me as I left the cemetery for the last time, leaving me with the impression that I still had not reached the goal he had set for me.

It took several more months for me to understand why.

Chapter Sixty-One

2013 Journey's End

Stacey

For the apparent improvement over the years to become totally practical Stacey, the early part of my drive was done in typical Stupid Stacey mode.

I had prepared a plan for how far I expected to drive each day, but I had no real conception of accommodation available en route, because very little was shown on Google. With good reason, the lodgings are few and far between on the long drive through Michigan's Upper Peninsula. Once again, Fate (assisted by Ted's aura, I am convinced) stepped in to save me from myself. Thus the first night found me sheltered at a soon-to-be-closing mom-and-pop motel, almost in the middle of nowhere. Lucky for me, in this sparsely habited berg, there was a restaurant across the street, or I would have been in trouble, having just nibbled on pistachios, jerky, and bananas all day.

I woke up on the second day, excited that Canada might be within reach. I had not reckoned on a challenging drive through an incredibly foggy Duluth, or weather that would have truly tested Noah. But finally after driving the whole day, I crossed into Canada at the smallest border crossing I had ever encountered. That had not part of my plan either. Apparently the Garmin and I had parted company from the original route, and so unheralded, via a quiet country road, I quietly slipped back to my heart's homeland.

The Canadian immigration official had eyed me suspiciously—who was this aging hippy, draped in scarves, and dangly jewelry, traveling alone down a country back road? He asked me numerous times if I was carrying drugs, guns, or booze, at which I tried very hard not to laugh. I had never been a lawbreaker, far too cowardly, but it amused me, as I thought of how my state office colleagues would giggle at the idea that I would carry contraband! But after a while, when he could not find anything wrong with my responses, or anything bad on my passport check, he finally waved me through the border, taking me one step closer to Edmunston, to home.

A dwindling gas tank now made me nervous. I wasn't sure I could make Winnipeg on the contents. Fortunately, a few miles down the road, I found a tiny store sporting an old-fashioned gas pump outside and thought I had totally stepped back in time. I had barely braked when a nice young lad in a baseball cap came hurrying out of the door to fill up my car. Just as well, really, as I would have been hard put to remember how to use such an antiquated pump with no credit card box on top of it.

He was sweetness itself, and so polite, and my heart did little somersaults of joy to hear his broad Canadian accent. I had forgotten how it sounded, so much warmer than the harsh, nasal

American twang I had become so used to, especially with the quaint "eh" at the end of every sentence.

For the next two days, I trailed my way along Highway 16, through Manitoba and into Saskatchewan, battling storms and traffic, mostly through miles of open fields, or forests, scarcely any industry other than agriculture, before finally crossing into Alberta. Most of the driving had been through small towns, apart from Winnipeg and the nightmare of Saskatoon. (Never drive through Saskatoon. In fact, never *stay* in Saskatoon; it is totally charmless!)

During those long stretches, darker thoughts of the past had returned, as memories flooded back. At times the car seemed to echo with the tinkle of my heart's shattered pieces as that familiar, returning, overwhelming sense of loss was accompanied by a haze of tears. It was good that I was traveling alone at times. To keep my mind occupied, and to stop from brooding, I listened to half a dozen talking books, mostly mysteries by my favorite authors.

I was hoping to make it into Alberta on that third day, and I pushed myself hard. In then end, I found a very comfortable room with great food at one of the dozens of small casinos that seemed to have cropped up in the previous twenty or so years.

The next day, I was up and out early, in a frenzy to make it to Edmunston before evening. Once I crossed the border into Alberta, my excitement about being so close to my goal knew no bounds, especially when I saw the sign for Rougeville.

Rougeville held awful memories. It was the small town where Amy had lived with Jay, and not me, for those agonizingly long three years, and I knew I had to stop. I found that I could not bring myself to explore the town, but I did stop to take pictures of the awesome Pysanka, a nationally renowned sculpted version of a Ukrainian decorated Easter egg. It is an awesome sight, thirty-one feet long, over three stories high, and smothered in a myriad of kaleidoscope colors. It was the little town's sole claim to fame and reflective of the Ukrainian heritage of its citizens.

It towers over the neglected park in which it sits, just off the Yellowhead Highway, and little of the small, grimy town was visible from the park, except for a few down-at-heel houses across the street. It seemed not to have improved at all in the past thirty years.

Once my pictures were taken, I shook off its dust as fast as possible. The sun might be shining, but the darkness of my past there threatened to overwhelm me again. I hated Rougeville… always!

An hour later, I found a bright oasis in Edmonton, where I caught up with one of Gino's children, Valeria. We had become Facebook friends and were looking forward to meeting each other in person. It was a perfectly delightful sojourn. Valeria proved to be a sweet and lovely person, and we chattered nonstop. She, full of questions about my book and her father during the time I had known him, me wanting to hear all about Gino now and her mother, whom I had never met. I felt like I was a part of their family already, and the years fell away. She was also very apologetic, as her brother, who I had hoped to meet, was leaving in a couple of days for a holiday back home, and so had not been able to be in Edmonton with her to meet me. Oh, well. It was a joy to meet his sister, and Andreas would have to wait until another time. I was a little sad, as it was finding Andreas on Facebook that had led me to renewing my links to his father and building a friendship with Valeria. I also would have liked to meet Melanie's friend.

After hugs, and a quick selfie, I drove away to conclude the final sector of my journey: the 120 miles out of Edmonton to Edmunston. I was finally on the road that would take me back to my heart's home, but a town without Ted, as now there was only a lonely grave to visit.

This road that I had travelled so many times, so long ago, was now almost unrecognizable. Over the past twenty-five years, road construction had exploded along that corridor; old landmarks had been relegated into the annals of history by a new divided highway.

Sadly I saw that there was no cozy little roadside restaurant nestling among the trees where Jay, Amy, and I had stopped on the very first day of our initial visit to Canada. All that remained were the memories of how Jay and I had rolled our eyes at Mattie's nonstop narrative, and where I had fallen in love with Canada over fried liver and onions.

Gone also was the roadside country store, whose parking lot had been a welcome refuge one day in dense fog, as I moved out of the path of an aggressive semi-driver highway hog who had been following me. He was apparently unmoved by zero visibility or interested in a more cautious speed. Moments later,, after I fell in behind him, he had slammed on his brakes as we were both brought almost to a halt by a massive bull moose. It was standing unyielding on the yellow line in the middle of the road. Watching interestedly as cars and trucks sidled slowly by him, he showed no inclination to move at all.

Nothing looked as I remembered it until I reached the long sweep of the highway where a bridge crosses the Mackenzie

River, and I started to see familiar sights. I recognized the road that turned off to the golf course, memories of my own futile attempts to become a golfer flooding back, and painfully, the night of the old-timers hockey banquet. Then at last I reached the gentle curve as the highway dropped down into the edge of Edmunston before it diverged through the town.

My first thought was to find Gino's restaurant, but the building that stood in the same place now had a different name. His black, low-slung sports car no longer sitting proudly in the parking lot. The memories of all those early morning coffees with Gino, as Ted had stoically looked on, filtered through my mind.

Across the road, though, Happy's, the pancake house, was still in situ on the little point of land between the eastbound and westbound highways, reminding me of the evenings when half the town had congregated to chatter and gossip over desserts and coffee, those memories of some happier times.

As I traveled slowly through the little town, seeing the new buildings that had sprung up, I watched for the site of my former ceramic store. And there it was! Almost the same, and although it had newer, smarter double doors, the glass block wall beside it still stood in place, maintaining the slightly shabby effect it had always had. Unbelievably, Fred's Travel Company was still right next door too, crowding my mind with memories of running around to see Fred in the dead of winter, only to be berated by him for not wearing a coat. The thought made me smile. He had been horrified, but was always so kind. It didn't hurt that he was drop-dead gorgeous, to boot.

Sadly, the once incredibly smart pub next door, the Magic Lantern, had deteriorated into a neglected and shabbier building, looking very down-at-heel. It was not at all inviting, although it was still sporting a hotel notice in the window. Ugh, not for me!

Through the joys of Google street-level maps, I knew there was still only the one set of traffic lights going west, at Main Street. It was matched two streets down by another set on the highway going east. I could see places where an extra set might have come in useful, but things move slowly in rural Canada.

I glimpsed ahead the pointed roof of the steak house meant to resemble a mountain. Only now a larger roof had been added, making it almost resemble twin peaks. It still bore the same sign, more modern with an outside patio, and trumpeted Chinese food in addition to pizza and steak. My mouth watered, thinking of the meals I had eaten there.

I felt like Alice might have done after coming through the Looking Glass, when everything looked the same, but the dimensions had changed and everything seemed off-kilter. Irrationally, I waited for some member of the coal-branch mafia to jump out, shouting, "Off with her head!" as they recognized me. A white rabbit running across the street would not have seemed entirely out of place.

At long last, I saw the sign for my hotel. What had been there before? I tried to think, but in truth all I could really feel was that I would have a bed for the night and a temporary home for the next ten days.

And now, at last I felt I was home.

Home, where my heart had wanted to be for so long, in the place I should never have left.

Home, but where nothing of my past was left, my only task during my sojourn to say a final heartbreaking farewell at a headstone. This time there would be no quiet urging to visit his home, nor seeing his car drive by me. As predicted so many years before, "forever" now truly was forever.

Almost on cue, I seemed to hear shattered heart pieces tinkling again, crushed once more by sorrow.

Chapter Sixty-Two

2013 Edmunston— For Whom Doth the Bell Toll?

Stacey

I looked around the room that would be my home for the next ten days, and as I unpacked, I realized that I had not packed a couple of vital things. Forgetful Stacey mode had apparently taken over before I left.

I grabbed my purse and hotel key and headed out of the hotel across the street, but the pharmacy there did not have what I needed, even though I recognized the pharmacist behind his counter. So it was back to the car as I headed along the highway again toward the end of town where I knew a Walmart lurked. Those Google map street scenes were proving invaluable for me to avoid looking like a tourist!

I sauntered around the store, trying to get my bearings. As I rounded yet another display, a young man with a familiar face walked past me. I did a double take. Andreas! Wow, what a coincidence!

Poor Andreas, all of a sudden this complete stranger was clutching his arm, saying, "You are Andreas, aren't you?" and burbling on about spending the afternoon with his sister.

At first perplexed, his face suddenly lit up as the dots connected, and he said with a grin, "You're the book lady!"

"Yes," I replied, "and your Facebook friend, and your dad's old friend!"

We chatted for a few minutes, and he warned me that his parents were away and not back until a couple of days later. I wished him a safe trip for his vacation, and we parted company.

I pondered on the chances of such a coincidence and wondered who's hand had guided it. How cool was that to run into him so soon after seeing his sister? It was only one in a series of similar encounters that week, as first one old friend and then another recognized me or was told of my arrival in town. It reiterated that deep-held conviction that I should never have left.

The early summer return to my heart's home, however, old friends or not, was no cure for the deep void inside me. My focus prior to the trip had me thinking that going home would make me feel closer to him and bring some closure, but that didn't happen. Instead, the reverse happened, as I cast about me to feel Ted's presence again. Even though I had felt his aura hovering in and around my car during my journey, once I reached Edmundston, Ted seemed to have vanished into thin air. *Or* did he?

Perhaps I was so caught up with meeting old friends. I saw Gino and his lovely wife, revisited my old house, went to see Marta and Hans, my heart lurching to be so near to Ted's home next door. I was so focused on reviving old friendships and catching up with past events in their lives, that I was not paying such close attention to any presence lurking in the background. Only on two occasions, when moments of despair overtook me, was there any evidence of his manifestation, both short-lived and both shortly before I left to return back to my life in Michigan.

Meeting old friends after such a long absence was heartwarming as I learned how much they had regretted my departure. As I shared some of the reasons for leaving, many people expressed sadness that they had not known, and said if they had, they would have been willing to help us.

Those who knew the entirety of my relationship with Ted and his family seemed to fall into two camps. Some going out of their way to tell me stories about Ted and his family, while others completely avoided talking about him at all, claiming to have had no contact with him. With my journalist's instinct for reading between the lines, both attitudes gave me more information that they would have realized.

Uncannily, so much confirmed my own observations that I had expressed in my book, as well as the thoughts that Ted's spirit had pushed me to reveal.

The day after I arrived, I made my first trek to Ted's grave. To see the stark, black headstone, with its terse information, struck me to the core. I had taken red roses to lay at his tomb, and for a while I sat on the ground, talking to him. I visited every day, sometimes with more flowers, and once I even read excerpts from my writings aloud to the empty cemetery, but the link I had felt to him in my home was not there. Or maybe it was, but my mind was so scattered by all I was seeing.

In effect I was talking to thin air, a strange feeling in a graveyard where I was surrounded by the names from the past. Thankfully there was no one around to hear me, or I would have sounded like a complete nutter, the crazy lady that in many ways I felt I had become.

Finally, as the day for my departure drew closer, I had wept at his graveside, asking, "Where have you gone? Why did you come to me after you died? *What* more do you want of me? Why did you bring me here now?" But deep down I knew the answer. During his early appearance, his apparition had communicated more than once that he wanted me to join him. To finally be with him, in his other world, but I could not, much as I might have wanted to.

I had a daughter who now had finally escaped the umbrella of depression that had lain over her for so many years and was embarking on a new positive future. She needed me to help her complete her journey, and whatever Ted's wishes, nothing was going to deter me, not even the lure of combining the two halves of our magnet again.

On that day, it seemed that Ted relented, and there was a pressure in my mind, a thought that would not go away. "Go to see Ray; he has answers." Now I knew what to do next.

Ray was one of Ted's oldest friends, and had tended his body prior to his burial. I had been in contact with Ray, as a while before Ted's death I had sought Ray's advice about maybe placing a memorial at the Mountain Reaches cemetery to commemorate

Jay's and Zack's lives. They were remembered nowhere else, and it seemed appropriate, but it had come to nothing once I found out that the keepers of the little mountain cemetery were Ted's wife and sister-in-law, Mattie. No point in asking. We'd been removed from the family tree, and there was no chance that either would have given permission.

After Ted's death, I contacted Ray once again when I was first faced with Ted's initial emanation into my life. I had been thinking that a funeral director would know better than anyone about otherworldly spirits, and I asked for his views. I expected him to pooh-pooh the idea of a ghost. But I was surprised when to the contrary, Ray had been most kind and sympathetic. He had confirmed that he himself had several experiences with the spirits of the deceased, including his own mother. He had not thought me crazy at all. After all, if a funeral director believes in these things, who am I to doubt them?

At the time I wondered if he had connected me with his old friend's troubles from decades ago, pretty sure he was aware of the circumstances. Had he connected the dots? If he had, he never let on; although later I realized that Ray did know exactly who I was. His compassion toward me seemed to indicate that he did, and that he was kind toward me also told me more about his knowledge of Ted's history and knew things I did not.

Ray had been the captain of the old-timers hockey team that fateful day when Ted had played such a useless game and then done his best to destroy me emotionally once again. Ray and Dan Merkle been the kind players who had helped totally clueless reporter Stacey follow what was happening during that hockey tournament so many years ago.

After my epiphany at the cemetery, I kicked myself. It should have occurred to me earlier to go to see him, but I was still, thirty years later, unsure of the reception I would receive from any of the Mountain Reaches mafia. But Ray really was the obvious person to talk to, if only to thank him for his kindness earlier in the year, so the next afternoon I visited his funeral home.

Ray still looked amazing for a man well into his seventies. His hair, now a snowy white, still lay in thick waves on his head, his twinkling eyes alert, friendly, his step lively and youthful. It was clear he lived for his clients, was still dedicated to his profession, and that he brought joy to his work for those visiting the funeral home in times of sorrow.

He greeted me kindly and said he remembered my e-mail to him. I also reminded him about my time as a reporter, when we had been at a career day at the junior high school, and the laughter that ensued at the time from the questions that students put to him about his job.

If he had not been sure before, that shared memory made him well aware of who I was, and I got the impression that there was a lot he wanted to say. But many years as an undertaker had bred tact and diplomacy, or maybe he thought it was better left unsaid. I think he was also grateful that I did not quiz him too much about the Zienko family, but I did admit to him that Ted's had been the spirit that had entered my life.

I expected him to be surprised, disbelieving, or even amused that I would think Ted cared so much about me that his ghost sought me out at his death, but he wasn't. He was kind and gentle as he shared some memories of Ted with me, so maybe he knew more than he would admit. Perhaps back then, Ted had told Ray what he would never tell me during his lifetime. Maybe Ray understood that it took death for Ted's barriers to drop.

The one piece of information he did share with me was that Sally was in the local hospital, and not expected to live much longer. He said that her sister had been in to see him earlier in the week to discuss funeral arrangements. Clearly still being a busybody, since that would be a job for Sally's daughters.

Ultimately, with his loyalty to the Zienko family and to Ted, Ray seemed to want to make sure that I would not approach Sally. After a while, I thanked him politely again for his assistance, and his prior help about the spirit world, and as I did not want to wear out my welcome, I left.

Afterward his remarks about Sally hit me. Was this anticipation of Sally joining him in the ground the reason for Ted's absence? Did he fear her joining him, not wanting to antagonize her once more and have her berate him throughout eternity?

Later, in the evening, Sally's name cropped up again as I ate supper with a friend and shared my day with her. She looked a little uncomfortable and then said that when she had been at the hospital earlier that week visiting someone we both knew, she had seen Sally in the next room and stopped in to speak to one of her visitors. The next day Sally had been moved to another wing, so had she forewarned them that I might visit too—was Sally relocated to ensure that we didn't meet inadvertently?

But *no!* I mean, really? People don't do stuff like that, do they? Well, that close-knit former community from Mountain Reaches just might!

I was wounded. What on earth did they think I would do? Did they think I would harass someone who was sick and someone of whom I had been so fond at one time? Did they imagine that I would be so crass as to swing by and say, "Gee, Sally, so sorry to see that you're dying. Did you read my book?"

But then what other opinion would her cadre of acquaintances have of me, after all the poison she had poured into their ears three decades ago? Sally, who could have saved Jay, Amy, and me from migrating to our nightmare, and who never accepted any responsibility for that decision, ever!

In talking with people, I learned that the outset of both Ted's and Sally's illnesses seemed to originate so closely on the heels of Jay's death. Did his early demise trigger guilt in both of them, bothering them so much that it lowered their resistance to disease? Knowing full well that without their intervention, Jay might have still been living happily in the United Kingdom, hale and hearty. Like them, we might have had a happily married daughter with grandchildren of our own instead of Jay's ashes being spread anonymously in a far-off land after he had died almost alone, his little family scattered.

It had to have crossed both their minds, and likely it was Ted who had grown the conscience, who felt more guilty for all that transpired, for Sally and her mother were ruled by revenge. Maybe that is what made him unable to fight his illness.

Perhaps Karma had caught up with them, been working on our behalf. Even so, I left Ray's building feeling that I had missed something, still not understood a point that Ted was trying to make. It took six months and another nudge from Ted's spirit before I finally understood.

There was still one more time that I felt Ted's presence in Edmunston, on my very last visit to his grave. I left a final bouquet of red roses, and a card with just one kiss on it. I caught my fingers on the thorns of the flowers, and little spots of blood dropped to the ground. The irony was not lost on me. Now a part of me would share the ground where Ted lay. What more was there to do? Tears rolling down my cheeks, I said softy to the cold, forbidding granite headstone and unkempt pile of earth in front of me, "This is the last time I will be here. This time I am really going forever," and stumbled to my car.

As I wiped my eyes, and turned the ignition key, setting the car in motion, I nearly jumped out of my skin, as I thought I heard a voice cry out, "Nooo-oo-oo!"

Shocked, my head shot up just in time to glimpse a wisp of...of what, smoke? Mist? Whatever, it was there, and it shimmered in the rearview mirror as I drove down the narrow path toward the cemetery gates before it disappeared altogether. But the echo of the sound lingered on in my head for days.

I shook myself. Really, I was totally losing it, and I had to get myself under control. I came to make my peace. This was over now. Ted was dead. His body was gone and now his spirit was gone. I would never see him again. I would no longer feel his presence in my home. It was over.

Even so, the wish to be with him lingered, and I was determined we should be reunited eventually. Once I was home, I extracted a promise from Amy that no matter what, when I died, she would take my ashes back to Edmunston and surreptitiously scatter them over Ted's grave. I didn't want anything else, but just to be sure my ashes would be near him.

Chapter Sixty-Three
2013 Michigan— The Final Act

Stacey

The house was quiet. Since my visit home to Edmunston at the beginning of the summer, I had seen no sign of Ted's spirit. I felt nothing except a void inside me I could not fill. Then my ghostly lodger briefly returned.

My first intimation that Ted was back came earlier in the day, as yet another light bulb popped. It was the third one that week, so for sure Ted's aura was back. It started when the same kitchen bulb I had replaced barely a few months earlier blew yet again. Apparently full of mischief, Mr. Spirit then hit at a stairwell bulb, and that same afternoon the bedroom light bulb had blown as I entered the room. We were back in kinetic mode again. This time Ted was able to hit on appliances to attract my attention as first the coffee grinder died, then my little shoulder massager quit, and finally, yet another watch stopped. It was all ahead of their shelf lives, and then the clincher, the IPad shut down for no good reason and played dead for a full minute.

"Weird" was back in spades, but why? I was perplexed. What more was there? I understood the whole story now, and the book was published. I had returned to Edmunston and had said my final good-bye at Ted's graveside. What else was he trying to say? What more did he want?

Were these latest incidents just imagination? But I knew better. If it were imagination, why could I not just conjure up his spirit, sense him near, whenever I wanted feel him close by again? But I can't do that. It just doesn't seem to happen. Trying to unite with Ted is like holding a telephone receiver, with the line stubbornly refusing to connect, leaving one unfulfilled, until such time as he is ready for the connection.

However, tonight there is no doubt about whether this is imagination or the essence of another surrounding me. As I settled in my living room after supper, I knew Ted's spirit has returned, renewing that infinite grief I have been unable to shake off since he died. Tonight its misery overwhelmed me once more, worsening the unbelievable pain that has throbbed through every vein, creating an excruciating sadness deep inside me that seems to have no end.

It was the middle of the night and I awoke with a start again! What had woken me?

I lay very still, and from out of nowhere came the thought, "Why are you going to spread your ashes on my grave? Why will you not be buried in the cemetery near me?" I gasped.

Could that be why I had the feeling that I was missing something as I had left the funeral home in Edmunston? Had that been the message that Ted had been trying to communicate to me, to tell me after I had left Ray's funeral home? Was that where that constant feeling that he wished me to join him, came from?

The need to still be a part of him had hovered around me as I had prepared to leave Edmundston, and on my last visit to Ted's grave, as I laid my final bunch of rflowers on his grave, I had pricked my finger on the roses. Droplets of blood had seeped into the ground. A thought had strayed into my mind, "at least some of me will lie with you finally; I am a part of the ground you are buried in."

I pushed these thoughts aside. It was all nonsense, had to be, but as I tossed and turned this night, the image of his gravestone ran through my half-awake brain. I pined to see him one more time, be beside him, and maybe in death my ashes could hover near him. Perhaps our spirits would bond in the next world.

The thoughts from that night would not leave me. For two more ensuing nights, the voice inside my head whispered, repeated the question, until I finally gave in. Why not be buried in that graveyard, in Edmunston?

It was as if a light bulb went on in my head for a change, instead of exploding above me. Why not find out about a burial plot in the same graveyard? There was no other place in the world that I wanted my remains to be. There could be no harm in asking. Although it probably would be way too expensive for me, I could ask at least.

My old home in Britain held no allure for me; neither did being buried in America with Damon's family, with whom I have never felt any real connection.

Edmunston is my heart's home; it is the place I should never have left. Why should it not be my final resting place?

Chapter Sixty-Four

2013 Edmunston— Karma Smiles, Destiny Grins

Stacey

The urge to follow this plan grew stronger, and the household electronics started their promptings again. It seemed like Ted's ghost was doing the happy dance.

After mulling it over, and asking Amy what she thought, I eventually called the cemetery office in Edmunston, to ask about the cost of a burial plot, expecting it to be way outside my resources. I spoke to a very nice lady, Janey, who went through all the options for plots or crematoria places. I said I thought I would prefer a burial plot and asked how much they were.

I was pleasantly surprised to find that the burial plots were unbelievably affordable, so I opted for one of those. Janey looked through her charts and gave me details of the next available plot in the part of the cemetery recently opened up. It sounded as if it was in the general area where Ted's grave was, close enough, I thought. I told Janey that I would take it.

We arranged for payment to be made, I gave her details about where the deed should be sent, and after exchanging all our information I hung up the phone and just sat. I would be near him again. Not the end I had hoped for, but completion of the circle, of a sort.

I pulled out my laptop, Janey had told me how to find the cemetery layout on the computer, and I pulled up the diagram of the graveyard on the site that she had directed me to. I scanned over it, trying to understand the key to the plan. Finally I found the row and plot number that Janey had given me. My heart stopped.

Confused, I rechecked and then double-checked the details Janey had shared with me. My newly acquired burial plot was the grave immediately beside Ted's!

How could that be?

From whatever cause, eighteen months after his death, the plot was still vacant. It was as if he had been saving it for me. It made sense of his recent nightly repetition. Apparently Ted's spirit was also determined that at some point, finally we would lie together, side by side.

So not Janey's or my choice at all! Once again Ted's choice, as his hand, reached out to me, determining where my final resting place would be. The words he had spoken to me that first night, that first moment when he had reached for me, swirled in my brain, and I could hear him softly saying once more, "If it is meant to be!"

My heart muscles clenched. There was no denying this. All paths had led me in this direction. There seemed no doubt that a hand greater than mine had been guiding this.

That night, for the first time since Ted created such havoc in my home after he had died, it seemed as if he was finally at peace. It felt like he had heaved a sigh of relief that we had finally found each other. And throughout my house, all was peaceful at last, and all I heard, was silence.

Soul mates, as I had always told him, in life and now in death. Whatever barriers thrown in the way in life, in death soul mates can finally be united and stay side-by-side throughout all eternity.

But no! Really! Stuff like that doesn't happen, does it? Really? Well, now Karma and Destiny had combined forces and so it seemed it might.

Chapter Sixty-Five

2014 Edmunston— In Memoriam

Stacey

There are still arrangements to make, but at the end of the day, when I leave this mortal coil, my ashes will be interred in that burial plot. With Ray's help, I even found and had my own headstone installed. In contrast to Ted's stark dark stone, mine is a girlie but tasteful pink, and is now set awaiting its inhabitant, with my name engraved on it. It also seemed fitting to add two other names to the stone.

In memoriam for Jay and Zack, I added their details to that stone. Now they are etched in everlasting letters, both having a tangible recognition for their lives in the place where they belonged. No longer anonymous, no longer forgotten, but with a tribute to their existences for all to see.

Once my time to be placed there comes, there will be no pain or hurt, or heartache for all the loss, the death, and the tragedy that the entwining of all our lives brought. That will all melt away; our souls can rest peacefully together.

These two tombstones, in that cemetery at the foot of the Rocky Mountains, commemorating so many members of this family, will be memorialized and united side-by-side forever. At peace in death, something they could never accomplish in life.

Destiny is doing the happy dance.

EPILOGUE—THE LAST THREAD IS TIED

STACEY

History repeats itself.

An e-mail message arrived, alerting me to another Zienko death: this time Sally's.

Her demise fulfilled the prediction made by Mattie's husband to me on my last day in Edmunston that past summer.

I saw him as I left Marta's and he was walking back from the communal mailboxes. I could not help myself. I had pulled up beside him and asked how Sally was doing. With the bluntness of an ancient, and without asking who I was, he commented, that she was not long for this world. His prediction proved accurate. Three months later, Sally succumbed to the illness that had manifested itself so quickly after Ted's death. Ironically, it also fulfilled Ted's prediction to me all those years ago, in mitigation for being unable to follow his heart. He had said that Sally would not be able to survive on her own without him. She could not know that remark had proved more than prophetic. How sad for her daughters.

However, try as I might, I cannot feel sorry for Sally, particularly now that I understand how much responsibility she bore for the annihilation of my little family. Her silence and secrecy, to protect herself from the ignominy of having to openly acknowledge the faithlessness of her husband, so discontent in his marriage at that time, destroyed all that Jay and I had held dear.

We had been so happy together before their interference. His father's family, with their soft words and false promises, proved to be worse than his mother's family with their rigidity of shuttered minds. By abrogating their responsibilities, Sally and Ted put Amy in jeopardy and caused her untold misery too. They had all watched our world fall apart, turning their backs on the cousin they had said they cared so much about, and so we lost everything.

But Sally's death and the manner of her disposal, with so little pomp, surprised me. The obituary told of a quick cremation, no services, and a quiet graveside burial at a later date.

This was in such stark contrast to Ted's departure from life, which was accompanied by all the traditional accouterments of death. He had been laid out in his coffin for all to see. He was the focal point of a very public funeral in the town's largest hall, followed by interment at the cemetery afterward. It marked the death of a man who had gained respect from his community, and maybe at the end he felt he had nothing to hide from.

It was in complete contrast to the way that Sally seemingly scuttled out of the world with so little ceremony. I wondered why such a beloved mother would have been so summarily disposed of by her loving daughters. But the real irony was the similarity between Sally and Jay's departure from this life.

Like the cousin who had betrayed him, there were no funeral services for Jay: just a cremation and his ashes scattered who knows where. Amy did not know of it until months later. She had been ignored in life by her father, and then too even during his fatal illness, another in the long line of tragic bequests from her father's family.

With no word of his illness shared with his daughter, Jay had died almost alone, with only his sister and his live-in partner by his side, the only family that was left to him by the Logan/Zienko betrayals and Jay's own bitterness at the way his life had turned out.

Ted, despite what it cost him, in contrast, protected his daughters, shared in their lives, and gave them one more advantage over Amy in that they know exactly where their father's remains are buried, and their mother's ashes too. They have a tomb to grieve at.

But now Destiny will return a protagonist to the site where sad battles were fought, bringing us all full circle, when my ashes are buried. Truly Destiny did haunt the Logan family in death as in life, so sad for them, and so tragic for those who have loved them.

I too expect a quiet exit from this earth, for there really is no one in this harsh cold country, apart from Amy, who will truly care. I have lived too long among a people who have no real interest in anything but themselves, who do not readily accept or like strangers in their midst, whatever they may profess aloud.

Edmunston was my true home. I should have stayed there.

I had not realized how Ted's death would affect me, or how when he was alive, even if I watched from a distance, the link between us stayed alive, echoing between us. At his death, I died inside. Whatever unrealistic hopes I may have had in the past, for my future, gone forever.

This voyage of discovery, which began for me after Ted's death, gave me answers to questions never resolved. His spirit gave me the responses that I needed to know why my life had been destroyed, and why I had to endure such misery. Then I learned that I was not the only one who felt that pain, that although he hid it, Ted felt it too throughout his life and seemingly into death.

My journey has shown me why during all those years I still felt linked to him, no matter where I went, who I lived with, and what else happened in my life. At Ted's death, I felt as close to him for a while as I had felt during our magical sojourn. Unexpectedly I found that while we were both alive, that bond between us was tangible and real. Over the years since he died, that responding echo from him is fading. I can imagine it, but it is no longer real. In the hereafter he is finally drifting away from me. Those golden ties that bound us seeming to now swing restlessly with no place to reattach, no place they want to bond again.

I hope that when I reach the next life, he will still be waiting for me. But maybe that is why he expressed such urgency for me in the beginning, because at some level he understood that the longer you are in that next world, the fainter the pull from this reality becomes. I hope he has found and, maybe I will even discover, the soul of our poor lost baby so that we may gather him in together.

It matters not. Amy is the only person alive now for whom I truly care.

I am the only survivor of our tragedy. Karma has efficiently dealt with those who harmed us, who left us to struggle alone. Amy has now become a Phoenix arising from the ashes of her past, and will do great things. I am ready to leave, and at least Amy *will* know where her mother lies. My ashes will be dispatched to my heart's home, in Edmunston. There they will lie in that same cold Alberta ground alongside Ted and Sally, while the ghosts of Zack and Jay drift over us, a fitting tribute for us all.

Where else should Zack, Jay, Sally, Ted, and I be remembered, except intertwined together forever in death, as we were intertwined in life, in that place where it all began?

Held for a moment, loved for a lifetime, and finally side-by-side for eternity.

The End

Made in the USA
Charleston, SC
14 October 2015